No Place Like Home

AUTHOR OF THE SUN SERPENT SAGA

GENEVA MONROE

No Place Like Home: Dark Oz Book 3 by Geneva Monroe

Copyright © 2024 by Geneva Monroe

Paperback ISBN: 978-1-960352-20-0

Published by Purple Phoenix Press LLC

Published by Purple Phoenix Press

Book Cover by Stella Nova, Geneva Monroe

Illustrations by Geneva Monroe

Author Portrait Photography by C.D. Redman

S C A N   M E
TO LISTEN
WHILE YOU READ

This playlist is made of music
that either inspired scenes in the book,
was used to choreograph action sequences,
or played on repeat while the story
was being writen.
Some of these songs are an entire mood.
Enjoy.

PLAYLIST

IMPOSTER - HENRI WERNER

WHITE FLAG - BISHOP BRIGGS

BRAVE - DANGER TWINS

CONVERSATIONS IN THE DARK -
JOHN LEGEND, LINDSEY STIRLING

I'LL BE THERE - WALK OFF THE EARTH

LITTLE LION MAN -TONIGHT ALIVE, DAVID PETROVIC

GOLDEN DANDELIONS - BARNS COURTNEY

VILLAIN - BELLA POARCH

GHOST LIGHT - THEFATRAT, EVERGLOW

LOVE IS A WAR - JEREMY RENNER

NO ANGELS - STELLAR

THUNDERSTRUCK - 2CELLOS

MONSTERS (ACOUSTIC VERSION) - RUELLE

WATCH ME BURN - MICHELE MORRONE

DANDELIONS - RUTH B.

DRIP OFF - AUSTIN GIORGIO

AFTERGLOW - ED SHEERAN

FEELING GOOD - MICHAEL BUBLÉ

WICKED ONES - DOROTHY

GOOD DAY TO DIE YOUNG - ADAM JENSEN

EYES CLOSED - IMAGINE DRAGONS

QUIT TALKIN' - DYLN

LIGHTS OUT - BLUDNYMPH

OTHERSIDE - LIVINGSTON

THE FEELS - LABRINTH

BETTER WATCH YOUR BACK - FJORA

RUN - ONE REPUBLIC

CONTENT WARNING

No Place Like Home is an adult, dark, why choose retelling, where the main character has multiple partners. **It is not intended for minors.**

Trigger Warnings (provided in pure chaos order): human trafficking, abuse, discussion of rape and assault, on page assault, public shaming and degradation, torture, death of a main character/s, rampant blood lust, hunting, drowning, beheading, PTSD, animal attack, electrocution, gaslighting, bondage, heights, bombs, extremely graphic violence and gore, forced drug use, grief, loss of a parent, explicit sexual content, sexual content with multiple partners, explicit language, bullying... and murder, there's lots of murder.

Your mental health matters.

HOTLINE NUMBERS

The main character of this novel has a history with human trafficking. There are several characters in the book who have been trafficked. While it is a major component of this story, and Dark Oz is a work of fiction, human trafficking is not.

If you or someone you know is a victim of human trafficking please call the number below. Every call is confidential and they are available 24/7.

National Human Trafficking Hotline
1-888-373-7888

No one should ever struggle alone. Your mental health matters. You matter.

National Sexual Abuse Hotline
800.656.HOPE (4673)

National Domestic Violence Hotline
800.799.SAFE

This book is for anyone waiting for their moment ...

Stop waiting. Your time is now.

THE ITALIAN LINES

In L. Frank Baum's Oz, before the Tin Woodsman was made of tin, his name was Nick Chopper, short for Niccolo. Thus, Nick and his entire family are Italian. Crowe also dabbles in the language, having grown up among the Ciopriani family. Most of what Nick says is in English, but when he feels particularly angry or vulnerable, the Italian tends to find its way out... You may be surprised on a certain other someone who happens to be fluent and drops the odd line in Italian to taunt Nick.

As a tip: There are footnotes with the English translation at the bottom of each page. There is also a list of all Italian phrases and their translations at the back of the book.

Happy reading.

THEA

Clang.

Clang ... Clang.

I gripped the windowsill with both hands. The sounds of metal on metal drew me to the view like a siren on the rocks. Straining on my tiptoes, I peered through the bars to the dusty grounds far below.

A large cart wheeled over the dirt, squeaking with each revolution of the tires. It wasn't the cart that raised the hairs on my arms or the sound that felt like nails being driven into my spine. It was the antiquated death machine sitting on its bed.

Beneath the rattling blade, the metal lock of the stockade beat a steady rhythm against the frame of the guillotine.

Clang. Clang.

"Whatever happened to a good, old-fashioned lethal injection?" I murmured, knowing the guard outside my cell door would never answer me. "This is barbaric. It isn't enough she's framing me for treason, she needs to resort to an archaic means of execution, too? Fucking Gigi."

Behind me, the guard's shoes scuffed over the cement, followed by the rattle of keys. I slunk to the ground, not bothering to look at the viperous woman gloating at my gate. I knew it was her the moment she entered my space. The noxious rose perfume she wore always overpowered the stale air of my cell. I was sure she'd paid a small fortune to have it imported into Ozmandria, probably paying for it with the money she'd seized from *my* estate.

Clang. Clang.

1

I involuntarily flinched at the noise outside. I knew she'd be back soon. It had been days since her last visit. When I first arrived, Gigi stopped by to chat every day. At first, it was updates on Ozmandria. Newsreels rolled over the tablet screen with footage of the capital being rebuilt or her crowning ceremony.

When I didn't give her the satisfaction of a reaction, Gigi upped her game.

At first, I refused to believe the surveillance photos. She handed me dozens of photos of The Villa being rebuilt. Brick after brick, a new YBR headquarters was created, and new crew was hired. I threw the photos back in her face. My guys would never abandon me to my fate. Never.

But then, she switched to live footage and a kernel of doubt started to take seed. A screen was placed outside the bars of my cell. At odd times of the day and night, a feed from a drone would fly over the property. The camera zoomed into the windows, showing me what looked like a very normal life: Nick cooking and laying meals for the family, Danny managing YBR's accounts, even Toto moved about the property like she'd settled into a very average life. There were no battle strategies, no palace blueprints or security feeds from inside my tower, and no signs of them mobilizing a rescue effort.

Most unsettling of all, there was no Crowe. Not one sign of him.

When I finally broke down and asked, Gigi refused to confirm or deny if he'd survived the shot to his chest. Each time I searched the feeds for him and came back with nothing, I heard the echo of my screams at Nick to save him and Gigi telling me that she didn't like his chances.

One week turned into two ... which turned into three ... until I stopped counting.

Gigi knew she'd gotten under my skin. I could see her reveling in it every time my heart cracked further. When that wasn't enough, she would show me updates of how Oz was welcoming their new, *benevolent* queen.

What a joke.

"The only joke here is how one girl can get so dirty while doing *nothing*."

"Did I say that aloud?" I shrugged, resting my head against the stone wall. "Fuck, sorry. I usually try to keep my insults behind your back."

Gigi snapped her fingers, and a tray was carried into the room. The guard sat it on the ground beside me. I sneered at the candied carrots smothered in butter and chives. The rack of lamb beside them looked tender and smelled positively divine, especially after the gruel they'd been serving me.

The worst part of Gigi's lie was that everyone believed her. The maids who cleaned my cell spit on me, the cooks made my food over-salted and bitter, the guards never hesitated to try and take a piece of me. Though they started giving me space after I kicked one of them hard enough to rupture a testicle.

Gigi had done such a perfect job of painting me the traitor that I was beginning to believe the lie. Or at least, I was considering very traitorous things at the moment. Picking up the butter knife, I spun it between my fingers. The silver of the blade was polished enough that for the first time in … Fuck, I didn't even know how long it'd been since I'd seen my reflection. The sallow rings around my eyes and the blanched color of my skin hardly resembled the girl I remembered.

"What's this? Some kind of last meal for the condemned?"

Outside, there was a huge booming thud. The concussive echo was strong enough to cause small bits of dust to rain down from the ceiling. No doubt the guillotine had been dropped into its spot at the middle of the execution grounds. I drew my legs up to my chest, not wanting Gigi to see the tremor growing in my limbs.

"Something like that."

I finally looked up. She didn't deserve my attention, but I couldn't help it. Gigi motioned for the guard to bring in his chair from the hallway. Gracefully crossing her legs as she sat, she continued, "If you don't like it, you don't have to eat it. I thought since this is our last chat, it would be nice to share a meal together."

Fuck her. Gigi preened like an actress taking center stage. Everything about this woman, from the neatly pressed pant suit to the string of pearls collaring her neck, was perfectly in place. Her entire world was one big performance.

"It's not exactly sharing if you're not eating, too." I took a giant bite out of a biscuit and groaned. I no longer gave a fuck if she saw that the flaky goodness brought me joy. In a couple of hours, I wouldn't have a head, so I might as well seize what little I had left available to me. The tender lamb chop separated effortlessly, and the meat practically melted on my tongue.

"I would but ..." Gigi scanned the dusty cell. Her lip curled when she looked down at my dirty hands. "It isn't exactly hygienic."

I studied the way her make up shimmered in a slightly unnatural glow. Could I get a good right hook into that rosy-hued cheekbone? Maybe I could tear a bit of her chignon loose and upset her curated visage right before her big moment. What was she going to do, execute me? At least I'd be headed to hell knowing she had to address the nation with a bruise marring her perfect complexion.

... but first, lamb.

Closing my eyes, I savored the flavor exploding along my taste buds. A bit of juice dribbled down my chin. I wiped at it with the back of my hand, then licked the residue from my skin.

Gigi made a disgusted sound in the back of her throat and tossed a black velvet box at my feet.

"Presents? But, Gigi, it's not my birthday!" An entirely inappropriate giggle bubbled in my throat. "No, it's my *deathday*." I clapped my hand over my mouth, hysterical laughter fighting its way free. Tears leaked from the corners of my eyes. "Get it, deathday?

Gigi blinked in confusion, making me laugh harder.

It wasn't funny. It *wasn't*. The truth was so horrific I couldn't do anything but laugh. If I allowed myself to feel anything more than that, I might never stop screaming.

I sucked down a deep breath. "Sorry ... *Your Majesty*." The end of the honorific broke with more laughter. "I'm sorry. I can't."

"When you're done acting like a child, feel free to actually open the damn box," she spat. I smiled at the tiny chip in her carefully calculated exterior.

Wiping my hands on my pant legs, I reached for the box. The velvet almost purred beneath my touch. It was the type of box that belonged in a vault. I pushed the lid open and drew in a breath. An antique locket sat nestled in a bed of satin. At the center of the silver, a rich blue gemstone sparkled like it was filled with fire.

The flash of a memory, faint enough I couldn't be sure it wasn't a dream, flitted through my mind: My mother leaning in to kiss my brow, and a locket swinging before my eyes. This locket. "What is this?"

"When I moved into the palace. I uncovered quite a bit. These facilities hadn't been used in almost twenty years, not since the fall of the Premiership."

"You mean not since my aunt and the Witchers killed my parents."

"Yes ... I do apologize for that. Unfortunately, sacrifice is inevitable with change." Gigi gestured for the men to exit. Silently, they left the room, leaving us alone. "I've been playing this game for a long time, Dorothea. Much longer than I think anyone realizes."

"So, I'm just a pawn?"

She nodded gravely. "The last."

-2-
THEA

"Don't look at me like that. I'm not a bad person. My intention has only ever been the betterment of Oz." Gigi leaned forward, caressing my cheek in a way that was nearly maternal.

"Are you kidding me right now?" I slapped her hand away. "You're seriously going to try and sell that you're what, The Good Witch of the North? Fuck off. If I'm going to die, spare me your propaganda."

"I'm not a witch." Gigi took the box from me, pulling the delicate chain free. "I'm a queen, holding the hearts of Ozmandria in the palm of my hand." She reached around me, hooking it around my neck. "This was found among a trunk in storage. It held several things of your mother's, but this seemed particularly sentimental. I can't remember her going anywhere without it."

"My mother?" The weight of the locket sat heavy against my sternum. For a second, Gigi's noxious rose perfume didn't smell like roses at all, but like lilacs and soap. It was so warm and comforting that an ache deep in my chest squeezed.

I opened the locket, staring back at me was a small photograph: A woman and a man, their joined hands cradling a red-haired baby. This very necklace was looped around the column of the woman's delicate throat.

A fat tear splashed against the silver lid. I swiped it away before it could mar the photo. The couple in this picture loved that baby. Their tender smiles stared back at me, a memory playing in my mind like a silent film. The metal warmed in my palm.

"I thought you might like to wear it today."

The word *"today"* rang out in the still room like the sounding of a gong, a reminder that these moments were my last. I cast my eyes over the empty room. No guards. No cameras.

I snatched the knife from the platter and, with both hands, threw the tray of food at her. Gigi's pale pink blouse coated in gravy and carrots, the metal of the tray clanging loudly against her head.

Killing this bitch with a rusty spoon would be so much more satisfying, but a butter knife would have to do. There would only be one chance to free myself. This was it. I aimed, with all of my strength, straight for the strand of pearls. The serrated edge scraped against the silk thread, sending the beads in a cascade around the room.

The blade met the firm resistance of flesh, shooting me with a short-lived thrill of victory. Gigi's hand latched around my wrist. Pain rocketed up my arm as she wrenched me away and pinned my hand to the small of my back—and firmly pressed the muzzle of a small pistol to my temple.

"Where were you keeping that?" I panted. My heart felt like it was trying to claw its way out of my chest.

"I didn't spend all those years climbing the Ozmandrian ladder to be felled by a butter knife. Stupid girl." Her thumb pressed into a point in my hand. I involuntarily cried out against the flare of pain, and the knife clattered to the ground. With it, my hope plummeted. "You have no appreciation for what it took to get you into this room. The decades of planning."

She pushed me to the ground. My hands came down hard on the scattered pearls, the sharp jab of pain jolting up my arm and twining with the ache still fresh in my chest.

"I don't care about you or your plan." I spat in her direction, not close enough to hit her, but I didn't need to; the insult landed all the same. "I never did an Oz damn thing to you, and still, you carved my entire life apart until all that was left were scraps. You sit there on your emerald pedestal like you have some kind of right to call yourself queen."

Gigi straightened her jacket, adjusting the pleats of her stained blouse so that they were covered by the lapels. With a long sigh, she said, "I worked for your father; did you know that?"

The words I was about to say were sniped from my throat. My mouth shut quickly enough that my teeth clacked. Despite the hatred coursing through my veins, my entire body leapt to attention with that one simple sentence.

"I started as an intern for the Ozmandria prosecutor's office. They assigned me as personal assistant to the up-and-coming attorney. I watched as the man with a heart of gold rounded up the criminals, cleaning Emerald City one street at a time. In the beginning, I worshiped the man. He was my idol. When he ran for mayor, I wrote every speech and stood beside the podium as he took the spotlight. I didn't care that I was in the shadows so long as it was *his* shadow. The naive girl that ruled my heart told me we were changing the world. With his charisma, we were passing policies and changing lives."

I shifted, settling against the wall and wiping my sweaty palms against the legs of my jumpsuit. For all my blustering, I did want to know this. For my entire life, I'd wondered why me? If the woman condemning me had the answers, there was no option but to listen. I couldn't change my fate, but at least I'd be going to my grave with some closure.

Gigi smiled smugly at my obedience, eyes scanning the way I'd curled against the cement. It was almost enough to make me lunge for her again.

"The day Darren met your mother, we were campaigning for the Premiership in a small backwater town. It was the same day I saw him slip a check from the district's representative into his jacket pocket—Two million dollars. The next day, the bill he backed for tighter regulations on trafficking was never ratified. There was an unexpected shift in the votes." Gigi looked down at her nails, chewing on the inside of her cheek and shaking her foot as if the annoyance was still fresh.

"When he shut down the Witcher racket, Ozmandria all but demanded he take the Premiership. They had no idea that the same criminals he pretended to eliminate were the ones lining his pockets ... He won in a landslide."

"You're lying," I denied, despite the twist in my gut telling me otherwise. If what Eastin had told me was true, then my parents had millions of dollars to their name. It had to have come from somewhere.

Gigi lifted an immaculately shaped eyebrow. "Did you think it was by happenstance that your aunt had all the connections necessary to establish her *shipping* empire?"

I opened my mouth but couldn't find the voice to say anything. Em had very quickly set up Cyclone Shipping. I'd seen the paperwork. In only months, she was moving merchandise over the border. Within a year, she had every important politician in her pocket. Gigi was right. It was too convenient for there not to be an inside connection. The lump in my throat grew thicker.

"One day, two newly orphaned teenage girls came to his office seeking aid. They were too old for the paltry child services offered by the current government. He refused to speak with them, having security escort them from the building while he went to play golf with the very men who had taken their parents' place. I gave the girls every dollar I had and a number to call if they ever needed anything. Do you know what little Eastin said to me? 'You would think the king would understand that it's the other pieces on the board that do all the work.'"

Gigi leaned in like she was telling me a secret. "It was right then I realized the ideas that I idolized Darren for were never his. *They were mine.* He was only a talking mouth and a pretty face. You can't count on corrupt politicians to do anything but think about themselves. When a machine is broken, you remove the broken cogs and build it anew. I'm turning Oz into something better and more efficient."

"Better for who?"

Gigi shook her head. "You don't understand. I watched as Darren grew rich off the labors of lesser people, and for some reason, the country loved him for it. I vowed to do better. Slowly, a plan formed, one that would assure I had Oz's trust enough to enact real change. I headed back west, tracked down the Witcher girls, and connected them to another spurned woman bitter enough to do anything for a taste of power. A few whispered words here, a gentle nudge there, and the pieces of revolution fell into place."

"You're telling me you set Eastin and Westin to overthrow the Premiership and establish the Quadrants?" My eyebrows lifted in disbelief. Was there nothing she wouldn't take credit for?

"Among a few others. I'll admit, Mombi was a miscalculation, one I rectified."

The Northern Syndicate took the place of Mombi's reign. It was her beheading that launched Gigi's career. Or so I'd thought. Now, I was questioning everything I thought I knew.

— 3 —
DANNY

"**I**t stinks like shit down here."

Nick slid his hands along the stone wall, searching for the button we found on an old blueprint of the palace. "It's better than having to wade through *actual* shit. Remember that Quick City job we pulled?" He huffed, "*Ah aspetta,*[1] you don't, because you got to stay home for that one."

"Yeah." A chuckle rumbled in my chest. "Crowe got that tar in his hair, and I had to shave half his head." Sadness tugged my smile down. I missed Crowe's banter. It would have made this so much easier with him by our side. At the very least, his humor would distract me from the anxiety of what would happen if our mission failed.

"Got it." Nick pushed on a stone that was slightly smoother than the surrounding ones, triggering a hidden door to swing open.

We were deep beneath the palace, using the ancient sewer system to access the oldest parts of the building. These tunnels probably dated all the way back to Ozma herself, laid when she conquered this land—long before our ancestors deified her. The second Gigi settled her crown on her fat head, Gigi dusted off the old building.

We headed towards the Northern side of the building where she'd converted the entire tower into a high-security prison and the adjoining courtyard into her own personal execution grounds.

Just thinking about it made my blood turn to an icy boil. Our timing today had to be perfect, or our girl would pay the price.

We climbed the stairs, cautiously entering a chamber that smelled of stale air and dust. My headlamp illuminated the small room, cutting the darkness in stark white beams.

"*Che cazzo è sta roba?*"[2]

Lining the wall were racks and racks of skulls. Their yellowed bones were in varying sizes. "Some kind of forgotten altar?" I posited, bending down to inspect them.

"An altar to whom?"

My wrist buzzed with a message alert. *Keep moving.* I tapped the headset in my ear. "Do you read me, base?" The line was silent, not even a crackle of a partial voice.

I shook my head at Nick's questioning look.

"We must have ascended far enough to enable messages but not comms," he said, checking the seams of the next door to be sure there were no alarms.

At least the GPS would track our progress. We'd anticipated the iron in the stone to affect communication, it was why we'd built in the messaging failsafe. Hopefully soon we'd be in camera range and have real eyes on our progress.

"Fucking knew it." Finding a thin copper wire along the top edge, Nick slid a piece of metallic, conductive tape between the door and the frame to keep the circuit from disengaging and alerting someone of our presence in this forgotten part of the palace. "How old do you think this is?"

"It's probably not even hooked up to anything anymore."

"Doesn't hurt to be careful."

We ascended three more flights of steps before, finally, a thick wooden door blocked the top. Light leaked from the corners of the frame. I clicked off my headlamp, stowing it in the pocket of my uniform. We pulled off our boot covers and hip waders, tossing them down the stairs behind us.

---

2. What the fuck is this?

Nick scanned my jacket, pushing my hair in place while I did the same for him. I wasn't sure where Ginger managed to acquire a pair of uniforms for the new regime, but she had, and once again, I was grateful for my sister's newly found kinship.

Nick's broad chest pulled at the buttons of his too-tight uniform. Tattoos peeked above the high collar, but otherwise, he was a more than passable replica of the mindless automatons moving about the palace.

My wrist buzzed again, a countdown beginning synched with the security feed. The cameras on the main floors were timed on a fifteen-second sweeping rotation. I cracked my neck, rolling my shoulders in anticipation for anything.

The timer ticked down:

5 ...

4 ...

My heart beat in time with the counter. I took a deep breath to slow it.

3 ...

2 ...

Now

Nick pushed the door open seconds after a patrol of guards passed. We slipped into the back of their ranks, moving in tandem with their steps. The heavy door clicked shut with a too-loud thud. The Captain leading the group stopped, and the rows of men halted with him. He looked over his shoulder at the hallway. I lowered my gaze, hoping he wouldn't notice he had two additional men amid his soldiers. With a nod, he stepped to the side, commanding that we continue. His scrutinizing eyes scanned each row as they passed.

As the row ahead of us walked by him, he grabbed the collar of the man in front of Nick, hauling him out of formation. We kept walking, my breath tight despite the steps we took away. Sounds of the officer berating his man for improper dress echoed along the halls.

We followed the group as they continued into an adjacent corridor, the hurried sounds of the guard rushing to catch up clicked in a quick cadence. My watch buzzed again, and we dipped into a side door just as the man turned the corner. Through the crack, we saw him and his commanding officer pass, none the wiser that we had come and gone.

I watched the tension in Nick's shoulders lessen with each step the group took down the hall, and I finally let out the breath I had been holding. "Fuck, that was close."

— 4 —
THEA

"So, I get it. You had it out for my father and had dreams of a better world, but what does any of this have to do with me?" I played with the locket, sliding it up and down the chain to distract myself from my growing unease.

"You, my sweet, are the villain of this story."

"Me?"

"Every hero needs a villain. People innately trust heroes. What they have to say holds weight among the masses. Radical change requires either trust or fear, and fear is so unpredictable. Trust, on the other hand, is blind. It's what allowed Darren to abuse his position, and it will be what I use to mold this country into what it should have been all along."

"But why me? Surely, there was a more fitting person to take the fall for your delusions of grandeur."

"No one else had the means or motivation. You were perfect: orphaned, bitter ..." Gigi looked down her nose at me with a disgusted sneer. "... and desperate."

"YOU *made me* those things!" I shrieked it at her as the truth of her story settled in. *She* killed my parents. *She* gave me to my aunt and let her believe she had power. *She* gave Eastin and Westin the power to enslave masses of people.

"I did. I also put Danny's sister in your path and ensured that when you went to free her, your aunt would catch you. Who do you think tipped Henry off that you were in Em's system?"

A cold shiver coursed down my spine as I thought of his ruddy face as he stepped over the body of my one ally at The Farm. I could still feel his rough grip as he threw me to the ground. Pure muscle memory had me rubbing my palm over my bicep.

"Of course, I needed you to be twenty-one so that Darren's bloody fortune would be in your name. Revolutions aren't cheap, you know."

I shook my head. Disbelieving and understanding all at once. When I stumbled across her, Toto was isolated and in a place where I would definitely notice her.

"How could you know I'd kill Eastin? I'm not a killer," I said, the trembling in my hands finally making it to my voice.

"That was a pleasant surprise. I'd planned on killing her myself and tricking you into holding the weapon, but you did the work for me."

"And you hired YBR to collect me and send me to the Wizard, knowing she'd never help me without both Emeralds."

"This plan doesn't work while a meddling wizard is behind the controls. Danny's need for his family would ensure he kept you safe. The boys had the means to take down Westin; they just needed incentive. Tipping off King's team to your location at the bank and pushing the Wolves in the right direction helped them understand the urgency."

I closed my eyes. Crowe's heartbroken expression as I drove away from him blended with his stone-white complexion as he lost consciousness on the floor of the club. It morphed into Nick's agonized look when he realized there was no choice but to leave while Danny clutched the hard drive, kneeling broken at my feet ... it was all a part of Gigi's script.

I was going to be sick.

"You were both my weapon and my bait."

"And your patsy."

"I told you, a queen does not move into position without sacrificing some pieces. Oz accepts that I am what is in their best interest. They love me, and I will nurture them as the mother they deserved all along."

Silent tears fell from the corners of my eyes. *I was never leaving this jail.*

Like death's toll, outside, the clanging began again—the metal-on-metal clash of hammers driving spikes into the hard earth.

She'd accounted for everything, planned my entire life and death like I was simply another cog in that machine she was building.

There was a knock on the door, and a guard stepped in. "Your Majesty, they're here."

— 5 —
DANNY

The fifth floor of the tower was the most heavily guarded in Gigi's new palace. We knew we'd never be able to get up there, so instead, we waited for reports of Thea being moved with the hope of being able to intercept her. Weeks of hoping and planning crawled by until the truth finally settled in: The only time she was ever leaving that tower was on her death march.

It was like having a bit of my soul siphoned away with each passing day. My girl was locked alone in her tower while I couldn't do an Oz damned thing about it.

After she'd been taken, I'd paced the blown-out remains of Ciopriani Villa, racking my brain for a solution. We assumed that Gigi kept eyes on us, on occasion spotting a random drone hovering in the air on the hillside. Nick threw himself into rebuilding the Villa and removing all traces of his father from the premises. I spent long hours reconnecting with our YBR contacts. To Gigi and the cameras, it would appear like we'd moved on.

With every brick I laid, I thought of Thea. She'd been freed from one captivity, only to be thrown into another. The hard labor of clearing the rubble kept the anxiety at bay, mostly. I worked until my body collapsed, then fell into a restless sleep. When I closed my eyes, all I saw was the hurt on her blood-streaked face as I left her behind. If it wasn't that, it was replays of my own captivity. Only, in my nightmares, Thea chose King. Every time.

"Dan, you with me?" Nick's heavy hand landed on my shoulder. The compartment at the base of the stairs was cramped and dark, the perfect place for an ambush.

I blinked away the image of my Firecracker in chains, her spark all but snuffed.

"Yeah. I'm here." I clicked the display at my wrist. There was less than an hour until the televised broadcast of Thea's execution. "They should be bringing her down any moment."

On cue, sounds of descending steps echoed in the stairwell. Gigi was giving clipped commands, her voice sounding with an irritating amount of jubilance. "After the broadcast has ended, invite Ms. Rosen to join us at the banquet. We can discuss the new role Cyclone Shipping will be taking. It's critical that imports and trade begin again."

A man's voice responded, "Of course, my Queen. You know Emily is going to demand you reinstate her accounts. She's already petitioned several times for them to be transferred to her."

"She can make all the demands she wants. If Emily Rosen wants to do business in Ozmandria again, then she will do as I say. Or tell her she's free to join her niece."

Gigi walked past our location. My hand tightened around the grip of my pistol. Hidden by the shadows, I raised the gun. She was right there. When would we have a chance like this again?

Nick pressed down on the muzzle, lowering my arm and silently shaking his head. He was right, of course. Thea came first. There was only one way we were getting her out of this palace, and it wasn't by assassinating the newly crowned Queen. We'd be arrested and probably executed right beside Thea.

I leaned back against the wall, listening as the sounds of Gigi and her retinue disappeared. The haptics on my wrist buzzed again; Nick and I looked at our watches in tandem.

She's on her way down.

We moved into position on either side of where she would be exiting. My heart galloped, thumping against my ribs hard enough to hurt. Only minutes separated us. When we were on Westin's pleasure boat, I'd at least had the video to feel connected to her. Radio silence was infinitely worse.

Fuck, I missed her. When we got home, I was going to lay for hours and just look at Thea; an entire day of nothing but pillow talk and endless hours of staring at her angelic features.

The first thing I noticed was the rattle of chains. They clinked against the railings and the metal bumpers edging each step. A team of guards flanked a figure draped in a bright red jumpsuit. Thick strands of auburn hair obscured her face. Clasped tightly enough to turn her knuckles white, her hands were cuffed and linked to an identical set of shackles at her feet.

Nick rocked side to side, almost shaking with need. I understood the urge. I breathed through the impulse to run to her, counting the seconds as the group passed our location.

As the last man exited, I pulled the pin on a smoke bomb, quickly filling the confined space with a green fog. I dropped the man closest to me with a quick jab to his neck while Nick snapped the spine of another.

I lunged forward, locking my eyes on the mass of dark hair amid the cloud. I barely felt the blows I dealt on my quest to make it to her. Bodies collided, but all I saw was that one figure wreathed by smoke. My fingers wrapped around her arm. I tugged her slight frame back. She turned easily, falling into my embrace.

"Thea," I said, pushing the hair from her face at the same time I felt the muzzle of a gun press into my stomach.

Running my thumbs over her cheekbones I processed what I was seeing. Blinking back at me were two brown eyes, a crooked grin twisting a face that did not belong to the girl I loved. "Hello, Mr. Kalidah."

Nick let out a strangled yell. Three men, seeming to appear out of the fog like phantoms, wrapped around his arms, holding him back while he raged like a bull. The doors opened, flooding the landing with fresh air and light. The fog dissipated as quickly as it had come.

The Thea doppelgänger stepped back, tossing her wig aside and easily removing the cuffs. How had I ever thought she looked anything like the stunner that was Thea? She gestured down the corridor with her gun. "The Queen has been expecting you."

—6—
DANNY

They pushed Nick onto the balcony first, the glaring daylight making it hard to tell what I was looking at. Leaning against the balustrade, Gigi stood like the queen she'd crowned herself as. Her tall stature was refined yet strong. She waved at the crowd amassing in the stands and balconies surrounding the courtyard. There must be a thousand people gathering here today.

A television crew recorded her genially welcoming the people of Ozmandria. Two more cameras were mounted to the corners of the building aimed to the center of the grounds where a large, red guillotine stood, its oversized blade shining like a beacon.

"*Puttana di merda.*"[1] Nick fought against the guards holding him, doing all he could to shake them off. I didn't blame him. If I could, I would squeeze her throat until her eyes popped, then throw the carcass over the railing for the vultures to feast upon.

Gigi, still smiling and waving, looked over her shoulder at us. "That's enough, Bill. If you could please get some footage of the crowd, perhaps some pre-execution interviews, that would be lovely."

"Of course, Your Majesty." Bill tipped his hat to her, eyeing us as he rested his camera over his shoulder and hurried away.

The guards strapped me into one of two waiting chairs.

"I saved you a front-row seat." Gigi slowly walked towards us, gracefully waving at the guillotine. "Wouldn't want you to miss this historic moment."

"A guillotine is a bit barbaric, don't you think?"

"Sei una donna morta."[2] Nick spat, pulling at his restraints enough to cause the back legs of the chair to tip up.

Gigi gave him a contrite smile. *"Vostra Maestà. Siete una donna morta, Vostra Maestà."*[3]

Returning her attention to me, she continued. "This palace is full of all sorts of interesting antiques, especially if you know your history. Everyone knows about Ozma, but have you ever heard about the last Queen of Oz?" Gigi ran the pad of her index finger along my jaw. I leaned as far away from her as my bindings would allow. My obvious disgust spurred her on. "About four hundred years after Ozma established this Queendom, there was a woman who was revered and feared more than any who had come before her. Even Ozma hadn't seen the kind of loyalty she garnered."

"So revered you don't know her name?" I tried to keep my tone bland, but also realized that every minute I stalled was a minute Thea gained.

"Her name has been lost to time. Her usurpers scrubbed all mention of her from the history books and damned her memory. However, you can't erase the past, no matter how hard we try. Deep within the palace, we found many treasures that belong to this once fierce queen." She gestured at the guillotine. Its red lacquer shone in the sun like fresh blood. "Her preferred form of punishment was decapitation. I had this marvelous bit of history serviced and brought up. With it, I will revive her forgotten legacy."

"You're fucking psychotic."

"No, I'm driven and I understand the importance of symbolism. With sweet Dorothea Gallant's death, I will usher in a new age. The people of Oz will know prosperity unlike ever before. I will eliminate the dregs of this society until all of the Emerald City sparkles, even its shadows."

"Even if that makes you the biggest murderer of them all?"

---

2. You're a dead woman, Gigi.

3. Your Majesty. You're a dead woman, Your Majesty.

Gasping and pressing her hand to their heart, Gigi looked personally affronted by my accusation. Her expression never met her eyes, they stayed just as cold and calculating as always. "Murder is a matter of perspective. Do you see those people, hundreds of Ozmandrians?"

I followed the sweep of her arm. The balcony beside ours held dignitaries and a few members of Oz's elite that I recognized — and Emily. Fucking. Rosen. Thea's aunt looked like she was attending a matinee. She even held a small pair of silver binoculars.

"They aren't clamoring for clemency. They don't want a benevolent ruler. They want divine retribution for all of their suffering ... And I intend to give it to them."

–7–
THEA

I heard the crowd before I saw them. They buzzed like a hive of bees, churning about the stands. Chairs and risers surrounded the guillotine in a horseshoe while hundreds more watched from the surrounding balconies.

The structure in the middle was massive, a red lacquered stage consuming nearly half the grounds. At the center, an oversized blade hung ominously over the stockade. It could be my panic carrying me away, but I could have sworn the wood beneath the blade was redder than the rest.

Without meaning to, my feet stopped, forcing me to stumble when my escort didn't. Rather than descend into full blown panic, I focused on everything but the death machine before me. The gravel crunched under my feet and the heat of the sun beat down on my face. Pausing for only a second, I closed my eyes and bathed in it, knowing it would be the last time I'd ever feel its warmth.

"What was this space before it became an execution ground?" I asked. Even though I knew I shouldn't, I searched for three specific faces amid the sea of strangers.

The guard hauled me forward. He was an older man, maybe in his late fifties. The grey in his beard was already turning white. It contrasted against the green uniform, making him look kinder. Although the metals adorning his breast told me where his loyalties truly lay. "During the Premiership, this was where legislative sessions were held, and on occasion traveling performances to entertain the masses. Today, *you* are the entertainment."

The weight of the crowd grew as they became aware of my entrance. The sound surged with jeers and venomous shouts. Still no sign of my guys. Even with everything Gigi had shown me, I knew in my heart they wouldn't have resigned themselves to letting me die. I expected an ambush on the way here or ... I didn't know, a miracle? With those guys, they could have repelled down from a helicopter, whisking me into the sky. I looked up, imagining the fantasy despite the clear blue sky. The sinking feeling of hopelessness was creeping up on me.

These minutes were my last.

"Did you know my father?" I squinted up at him, blinking against the harsh midday sun, but unable to shield my eyes thanks to the chains looped around my waist and connected to my ankles.

"I did." His brows pinched together with what was either disgust or pity, I couldn't tell.

"Do you think he would have approved of a hall of justice being turned into this kind of spectacle?"

The man looked up at the balcony where Gigi was waving at her adoring crowd. A wicked grin curled her lips as her eyes connected with mine. There wasn't a trace of our earlier scuffle on her. Every hair was in place and her skin glowed. Dropping her hands to grip the railing, she looked like the drawings I'd seen in history books of victorious Roman generals parading in chariots before the people. Except, there was no-one at her back to remind her of an impending death. There was no memento mori for this queen.

Gigi glanced over her shoulder and ... my heart lurched. Danny and Nick were beside her, their arms chained to their chairs. Danny had a purple bruise on his cheek and the guards aiming guns at their backs proved that I was right. They had come for me ... *and failed*.

Nick yelled something, but the rich purr of his voice was swallowed by the hum of the crowd. Nausea hit the back of my mouth in a sour wave. It nearly drove me to my knees, except for the hold the guard had on my arm.

The guard followed my expression of horror to the two men looking like they would tear Oz apart the moment they broke free of their restraints. "I think he would have approved of The Queen's cunning. Premier Gallant fostered that in a lot of people."

I kept my eyes trained on Nick and Danny with every step I took until my toes hit the edge of the platform. The guard looked at me; his face was expressionless, but his hand squeezed my arm with reassurance. "Dorothea."

Still, I couldn't make myself look away. I felt a scream building in the center of my chest, and I couldn't breathe around it. Danny's green eyes were bright with hatred. His muscles strained against his chains as he roared at Gigi. Would they be next?

"Dorothea," he repeated, giving my arm a sharp shake to jolt me loose from fear's bony grip. The guard turned his back to the queen, blocking my view of Danny and Nick. "Thea, be brave. She only wins when they see you as weak. Don't give it to her."

"You could let me go," I whispered.

The lines around the guard's eyes creased, making him look decades older and completely resigned to what he said next. "You know I can't."

"I'm innocent." I could barely choke the words out. Nobody in this court-yard cared about innocence or guilt. They want blood. Hopefully it would only be mine.

I nodded, using all of my strength to force back the tears burning the corners of my eyes. Would she drag them down after me? I pulled against his grip, looking over his shoulder towards the Queen's balcony. I strained for a full view. Two chairs. Two men with guns to their backs. Where was Crowe? He wasn't there.

He. Wasn't. There. The realization hit me like a hammer to the heart. I flexed my hands, willing away the memory of his life pouring from his chest.

"Ozma, save us all," I whispered.

Would he be waiting for me in the next life? ... Unless ... I looked up at the platform, squinting against the bright light.

The executioner approached the edge, staring down at me with cold in-difference. Maybe ... A dark hood and mask covered their face. They wore a nondescript black uniform. It looked like the guard's, but his was more ominous without the green and red tones to it. Maybe still ... Maybe it wasn't an executioner at all. Maybe that hood was hiding a mop of straw-colored hair.

His black-gloved hand took hold of my chains and hauled me onto the platform. The executioner pulled me within inches of their face. The eyes behind the mask were a blue much paler than his. Their height was barely more than a few inches above mine and beneath the black uniform their build was too slight.

It wasn't Crowe.

Nobody else cared enough to try something as foolish as a jail break at the eleventh hour. There would be no heroic last minute saves where the executioner stopped the blade and whisked the damsel away.

A hope I hadn't realized I was holding on to vanished like ashes on the wind. Hundreds of people surrounded me. Yet, for the first time in my life, I felt truly alone.

He walked me to what looked like the world's worst bed. I swallowed hard, flicking my gaze up to where the blade shone brightly. It looked so much larger up close. And sharp. It was lucky really. A quick death was better than what many got.

"On the bed," the gruff voice commanded. "Stomach down."

The tremor that had been with me all day increased, making the chain rattle. Though I didn't want to show weakness, tears slid from my eyes anyway. I was powerless to wipe them away and so I couldn't stop them from coming.

As best I could, I climbed onto the stainless steel surface. The wheels attached beneath the bed were ready to roll away my corpse. The executioner grabbed my collar, shimmying me forward until my shoulders hit the wood of the stockade. Pulling back on my hair, they slotted my neck into the hole and angled my chin until my face tilted to the side.

My mother's locket hung loose before me, swaying like a pendulum, counting down the seconds. The blue stone flared with light. I took a deep breath, pretending its glow was her, here with me now. Swallowing hard, the muscles of my throat fought against the press of the wood.

With a thunk that made my entire body jolt, the top of the stockade came down, locking me in place. The chains around my waist and arms were removed, traded for straps that kept me secured to the table. I couldn't move, not a millimeter. My heart pounded out of control. Realization that this was, in fact, the end finally sank in.

With my limited view, I watched the black boots of the executioner move around the small channels built to direct the blood to a waiting trough. Occasionally they flicked or tugged at something until they were sure everything was perfectly in place.

The crowd hushed. I held my breath, waiting for the inevitable and praying that Danny and Nick weren't following me there.

-8-
NICK

K nowing what's coming doesn't make it easier to watch.

Thea walked to her fate like the queen she was. *Da quella lurida zoccola degenerata e succhiasangue.*[1] Thea had more grace and more poise in the face of fear than Gigi could ever hope to have.

I'd never loved Thea more than I did at this moment.

Gigi raised her hand, and the crowd instantly obeyed. She looked straight into the cameras. Her face was projected onto the screens suspended on either side of the courtyard. "Ladies and Gentlemen, people of Ozmandria. Today is the dawning of a golden age." She thrust her hand towards the restrained Thea.

The cameras flipped to Thea's tear-streaked face, making the crowd holler in response.

"With the death of this traitor, we will begin anew. I give you the land and the skies, I give to you everything I am, and I give you my word. From this historic day forth, in the heart of this great nation, we will meet the change we've waited for in this world and embrace it."

The fucking crowd ate it up, poison and all. They roared with support. Danny and I yelled, but our cries drowned amid the cheers. I pulled and rocked against my binds, knowing there was nothing I could do to change the next few minutes. I forced myself to watch each tear fall. Her lip trembled, but Thea never openly wept. She didn't scream or protest, not like we were doing.

Thea had accepted this fate, even if I couldn't.

"Executioner."

A figure clad from head to toe in black stepped to the edge of the platform, bowing to The Queen.

Gigi dropped her hand. "Off with her head."

The crowd went feral. The rush of blood pounded in my ears as the executioner's gloved hand wrapped around the lever.

"Gigi, I'll give you anything. Fucking anything," Danny screamed at her. "Don't do this. She's innocent, Gigi. She's innocent. Don't."

The lever pulled back, and the blade dropped like a streak of lightning, hitting the wood with a loud clunk that would haunt my nightmares for the rest of my life. To my horror, her head dropped, thunking against the wood and rolling onto the ground with a spray of crimson blood, her poppy red hair flaming in the sun.

The bellow of rage that tore from my chest was not of this earth. The air shook with it, my vision vibrating the grotesque scene before my eyes. The chair beneath me groaned, and my muscles screamed for release as I promised Gigi death in every language I knew.

"Show it to me," Gigi commanded, pointing a long, manicured finger at the severed head.

Beyond her, Emily Rosen gripped the railing, staring at the remains of her niece with relief painted across her bitter face.

I would slay them all.

The executioner descended the stairs, deftly taking a fistful of hair and lifting. I looked away, meeting the horror in Danny's eyes. It was impossible to miss what was happening when it was broadcasted on every screen around the courtyard. Every home in Ozmandria was looking upon her beautiful, blood-stained features.

Satisfied with the spectacle and roar of the masses, Gigi returned to us. "Well, boys, this has been fun, but it's over now, and I have a speech to give." She gave Danny's face a light slap, eliciting a feral growl from him like he really was part

Leone.[2] The queen snapped at the guards stationed behind us. "Let them stew for a while as a reminder of what true power looks like. It will be a good lesson for them."

"Fuck you, *Your Majesty*," Danny said in a low rumble. "I hope you choke on your power and drown in your blood-soaked fame. You better hope that's how you go. The day I lay my hands on you, you'll wish for something as merciful as choking."

Gigi tilted her head back and forth like she was truly considering his threat, then winked. "Actually, leave them here overnight. That one in particular looks ready to do unspeakable acts." She was talking about me, but my vision had long since turned red, and the sound of that blade falling was still echoing in my ears.

When Gigi regally descended to the dais erected before the guillotine, her flawless exterior was once again in place. Of course she would deliver her first speech in front of the body of her *enemy*. The fucking, unchecked hubris in that woman ...

The executioner draped a sheet over Thea's body, wheeling the gurney already in place out from under the platform.

My people. Heart of my heart ...

The black figure walked around front, picking up the chain that had fallen on the ground and gingerly placing it and her head atop her body. The squeak of the cart wheeling out the back of the grounds felt like when Eastin had carved away strips of my flesh, like a piece of me had just been tossed away like trash.

Together, we will sow this land with ...

The haptics on my wrist buzzed three times in quick succession. I looked at Danny, knowing he'd felt the same thing I had. His brows relaxed from the way anguish had tightened them into a single line.

It was time to go. I could work on getting my shit together later. I tugged on the loose thread hanging over my palm. A small laser scalpel fell into my hand. It was a miniaturized version of what my aunt Gabby had used to patch me up.

---

2. Lion.

It was usually used for precision surgery, but in this case was rather handy for escaping cuffs.

I glanced over my shoulder. The guards left to watch over us were already bored and discussing the previous night's ball game. Slowly, I drew the laser over the metal, careful not to slice my skin in the process. The metal heated. A tinge of pain radiated up my arm. It was nothing I hadn't felt and survived before.

Danny grimaced, his teeth sinking into his lip to stifle his impulse to curse. I couldn't help but shake my head in a silent chuckle.

He mouthed, "Dickhead."

With a lift of my chin, I whispered back, "*Cazzo.*"[3]

I caught the cuffs before they could drop and wrapped the metal around my hand. Danny met my eyes, nodding in confirmation. Simultaneously, we jumped up. I spun, swinging the chains into the head of the guard closest to me and pushing him into the alcove of the doorway before anyone in the crowd could become alerted to our actions. I slammed my other fist into his cheek, feeling the bone beneath my hand crumple something delicate in his face.

Sating the rage still boiling within me, I pummeled him with the chain and cuffs until the bruised face of the man was barely recognizable.

I stood slowly, sucking down a calming breath. Danny watched with appreciative horror. "Save some of that brutality, yeah? We're not out yet."

"*Si, tranquillo. Sto bene.*"[4] I glanced at Gigi, still delivering her speech and none the wiser to our escape. A balcony over, Emily Rosen was grinning like a fool, eagerly lapping up every lie Gigi dished out. I involuntarily shifted in her direction, the irrational urge to leap from the railing and tackle her making my muscles twitch.

---

3. Fuck.

4. Yeah, I'm good.

"Not now." Danny gripped my collar, pulling me further into the shelter of the doorway. "Nobody wants to claim her death more than me. Her time will come."

Fuck, he was right, but what I wouldn't give for a sniper rifle right about now. I tucked my shirt in and straightened my jacket, running a hasty hand through my hair to tame it. "Let's get the fuck out of here."

− 9 −
DANNY

S lowly, we made our way to the ground level of the palace. With every scuff of my shoes against the stone floors, I heard the swoosh of the blade in the air. With the thump of my heels, I heard her head hit the wood.

Now that some of the initial rage was subsiding, it was taking all of my focus not to vomit all over the pristine floors. While it would be satisfying to mar Gigi's beautiful palace, it probably would attract more attention than we wanted at the moment.

My watch buzzed.

"This way," Nick said, turning down a side corridor and into a narrow staircase. Five more turns and we were finally in the ground tunnels used to move unwanted waste to and from the palace. In this case, it was being used for the removal of dead bodies.

At the end of the long corridor, two figures leaned against the exit, one slightly smaller than the other. The taller woman was already changed out of her black uniform and into the white scrubs of a medic.

"Took you fucking long enough," she said around the hair tie in her mouth as she drew her long blonde hair into a high ponytail. "What'd you take, the scenic route?"

"Fuck off, Alice." I picked up my pace and lengthened my strides. My heart felt like it was running two steps ahead of me, and I couldn't keep up.

She rolled her eyes. "I would, but you haven't paid me yet."

"I'm not paying you for your snark."

Alice snapped the elastic in place. "No, you get that free of charge."

Pushing past the blonde, I ignored her smug grin in favor of the woman standing beside her. Her arms were wrapped around her middle like she couldn't figure out what to do with them. She tapped her fingers one at a time against her sleeve. Beyond that, she hadn't reacted at all.

I grabbed Thea's shoulders, pulling her into me and slamming my mouth over hers. Recognition slowly set in and her hands lifted to my arms. I tasted the tears falling from her eyes as she openly wept into our kiss. She smelled like death, and it felt like it was clinging everywhere, but fuck, nothing had ever felt this good. Thea was alive, and nothing else mattered.

Nick pushed in, drawing her from me and savoring the feel of her in his arms just as I had. Despite the tremor shaking his hands, he held her face gingerly.

"Non farmi rivivere mai più una roba del genere."[1] He turned her head from side to side, inspecting the bruise ringing her neck and the thin cut gracing her spine.

"Tell me this is real," she whispered and traced the line of his jaw with her fingertips. "Tell me I'm not dreaming, Nick. Please."

"It's real, Fiore Mio."

She melted into Nick until he was holding her upright. "I thought—"

"I know."

"I don't want to rush this truly touching reunion," Alice said dryly, eyeing the way Nick slowly kissed Thea. "But this would be better if we were anywhere but here."

Brushing the tears from her cheeks, Thea looked around. "Where's Crowe? He wasn't with you in the stands. Is he in the cab?"

"We can talk about it in the van." I reached out, caressing her face to reassure myself that she was really here.

"Damn it, Danny!" Thea whisper shouted, slamming both hands into my chest. "Where the fuck is he?"

"I'm sorry, Princess," I replied, knowing that I'd be apologizing to her for the rest of my days. "There was no—"

---

1. Don't ever make me go through that again.

"We need to get in the van, NOW!" Alice commanded.

Thea slammed another angry fist against my chest. "So, you *left me* and couldn't even *save* him?" Her words tore open my chest, exposing the raw guilt living there. I regretted so much of that impossible situation.

Thea glared down the tunnel like she could see Gigi through the acres of stone. "I'm going to tear that woman apart slowly."

Alice wrenched Thea away, twisting her so they were face to face, "I didn't save you from the blade, just for you to end up under another. If we get pinched because of this sentimental bullshit, I will hunt you down in hell and kill you again."

"You're right." Thea swiped at more angry tears, the collar of her red jumpsuit darkening when they landed on the fabric. "How are we getting out of here?"

Alice patted the gurney, inclining her head towards the double doors they'd been waiting beside. "We're going to walk out the door."

"The cameras are still blacked?" I asked, eyeing the camera pointed at the door.

"Of course, I'm not an amateur," Alice replied with a snap. "But they aren't outside. If we're going to sell her death, they need to see her being carted away. Now get changed already,"

I stripped out of my jacket while Nick did the same, and Thea laid back on the metal cart. Seeing her once again in that position sent a wave of chills down my spine. Alice draped the sheet over her sweet form, setting the scarily accurate decoy head at the top. We'd played this way too close for comfort. The assassin's plan worked, but fuck, I'd be having nightmares about this for years.

Shaking off the hair raising on my arms, I pulled out a velcro patch and affixed it to my shirt. It was simple, but effective. To the camera, our attire looked like a medical technician's scrubs. We were just three people doing their job and taking out the trash. We tossed our clothes under the sheet with Thea.

"Where's the original executioner?" I asked before we exited. Alice had said she'd handle the executioner and guillotine, but hadn't divulged the finer details of how.

She kicked off the brakes. The gurney shook, making Thea chirp in alarm. She had to hate being under that sheet. "He's currently sleeping off a hit of Morphia and a rather potent round of hypnosis. When he wakes, he'll believe that he played his epic role perfectly, and the newsreels will fill in the blanks for him. He's going to cover up our crime and he won't even know he's doing it."

I hated how brilliant that was. Of course, that was why she could charge so much. Nobody did covert like Alisandra Liddell.

Alice pushed the cart out the doors and into a waiting ambulance. The gurney locked into place next to another identical bed. The body strapped down to it was wearing a red jumpsuit identical to Thea's. However, this unfortunate woman was currently missing a head.

Nick slid into the driver's side while I climbed in the back with Thea and not-Thea. The severed head stared back at me with blank eyes. It was an eerie doppelgänger.

Nobody stopped the vehicle rolling off the palace grounds and onto the main road. As escapes go, this one was flawless. Alice turned and gave me a smug wink. She had pulled off the impossible.

Thea pulled the sheet from her face. "Pretending to be dead is at the tippity-top of the strangest things I've ever done list." She stared at the dead woman strapped beside her. "For the record, this experience is not one I would like to repeat."

"NO! NO! I SAW YOUR HEAD ROLL ACROSS THE GROUND!" Toto screamed, her hands still holding open the front door of the newly rebuilt Villa.

Every television in the country was set to play the execution live. My poor sister would have been forced to watch the entire charade play out in real time, having no indication of the truth. As much as it killed me to keep secrets from her, we couldn't afford to gamble with any part of the plan. Gigi had eyes on us and it was critical that she only saw what we wanted her to see.

"Hey there, Freckles." Thea gave a tiny wave hello.

"HEY THERE, FRECKLES? NO. Nope. No. I saw it. There was blood. *So much blood*." Toto whirled around, pushing an accusatory finger into my chest. "I saw you chained to a chair. Both of you." She glared with just as much ire at Nick. Rage trembled her petite body.

We'd be paying for this for a long time. I could already tell. "Sis, we—"

From down the hall, a voice yelled, along with several loud thumps sounding like the legs of a chair banging against the floor, "I could have explained it to you if you hadn't handcuffed me to this desk and left me back here to rot."

I chuckled. Served him right.

"You fucking handcuffed him?" Thea kicked me out of the way, hurrying down the hall. "He's recovering from major heart trauma and you *handcuffed* him?"

"He had it coming," Nick said, tossing our duffle bag of supplies on the ground.

"In my defense, it wasn't that major and he's an idiot," I called down, watching with amusement as she pushed open every door she passed.

Toto gaped at me. "Is somebody going to explain to me how she's running through this apartment with her head still intact?"

-10-
CROWE

I pulled on the edges of the desk, shifting towards the door and not caring in the slightest how my movements pulled at my still healing muscles. While most would hate the pain and the itch of healing, I welcomed it. That burn connected me to my last moments with Thea. Until now.

She was out there—my beautiful and fearless Darling Thea. Even knowing the truth of our ruse, the fake head rolling off the stand and onto the ground was hard to watch. I needed to see her and feel her to be certain she was still in one piece.

"Down here," I shouted. "Thea, I'm down here!"

Thea slammed the door open. Her wide expression was bright as her eyes fell on me. The prison jumpsuit was stained, and her hair looked like it hadn't been washed in days ... probably longer, but beneath the grime, she was radiant. Like a plant left locked in a closet, I felt starved for her light.

I pulled on my cuffs, straining with my entire being to move closer to her.

"You're alive." She rushed at me.

"That makes two of us."

"Danny said in the van that you were, but I didn't dare to hope until now," Thea's voice cracked. "Hearing it and seeing it are two very different things."

She had that right. Fuck, was it possible she became more beautiful in the weeks we'd been apart? Maybe it was the near-death experience or the terror of seeing her face rolling across the ground, but it was damn near impossible to breathe just looking at her.

Gingerly, she wrapped my head in her arms and pressed my face to her chest. I nuzzled into her and took a deep breath. The hidden panic, I refused to acknowledge, finally eased. Lifting up as much as I could, I commanded, "Kiss me."

"What about the cuffs? There must be a—"

"I don't want to wait." Lifting my arm for her to slide under, I said, "Now, climb on my lap and put your mouth on mine before I break free of this desk and claim it."

Thea tucked under my arm, the confined space of the restraints pinning her between the wood of the desk and my chair. I widened my legs, scooting forward until I could feel the warmth of her body against mine. The chain of the cuffs was just long enough to brush her lower back with my thumbs. The scratchy polyester jumpsuit was not nearly soft enough. I needed to feel her skin on mine.

"Are you in pain?" she asked.

I was, but I would never admit that to her.

Thea slid her hand into my partially unbuttoned shirt. Her fingertips danced along the small bandage that was still taped over my left pec. "I don't want to hurt you."

"I was shot, not shattered. I'm not going to scatter into a million tiny pieces the second you touch me."

"But—"

"Darling, if I'm not tasting some part of you in the next five seconds, I'm going to call Danny in here and have him spank your beautiful ass raw."

I was finally graced with a smile. It was slight, but it was there. Straddling my hips, she gently lowered her weight onto my lap. It was agonizing how careful she was being. Reaching up, she ran her fingers over the crow inked above my ear, tracing it exactly as she had that first night in the car. "You're really okay?"

"I'd be better if you would kiss me."

She grazed her lips over my jaw with one light brush after another. The fuzz of the beard that had grown in these past few days shifted with each press of her mouth.

"I fucking missed you, Beautiful. I missed you every cursed second."

Resting her forehead against mine, Thea looped her arms around my neck. The weight of her body finally sank against me.

"I missed you, too," she said over increasingly shaky breaths. Her sea green eyes glimmered with tears. "When I didn't see you on that balcony with the others ..." She clamped her hand over her mouth to keep from sobbing.

On instinct, I reached to pull her hand away, only to have mine yanked back. I looked at my wrists and then at the key Danny had left atop the dresser. She needed to be held. I could see the edges of her composure fraying. Thea curled against me, tucking her face into my neck and taking a deep breath.

"Dandelion Kalidah, get your stupid lion ass in here and uncuff me!" I shouted.

Danny poked his head into the room, lifting the small silver key in question. "She didn't take them off? The key is right here."

Nick followed him into the room, dropping into the armchair in the corner and untying his dusty boots.

"Listen, *Kitten*—" I ground out. It was his betraying ass that locked me to the desk to begin with.

Nick huffed in what I was sure was a laugh, or as much of a laugh as he did these days. Danny shot him a sharp glare.

"Just take them off so I can hold our girl." I pressed my cheek into her hair. "Then go run a bath."

"I'll get the bath." Nick made his way into the bathroom, shedding clothing as he went. "Everything still smells like *fogna*."[1]

Undoing the first lock Danny asked, "Anything else?"

"Nope. The only thing I'll ever need is right in my lap." I sank my fingers into her hair, finally lifting her lips up to mine. The moment we connected, the pieces of her armor broke. Sobs shook her entire body as my mouth continued moving with hers. Relief and gratitude poured through me, just as the emotion was tearing through her. If I hadn't been sitting, it would have driven me to my knees.

---

1. sewer shit.

Damn them all. Damn everyone who forced this grief on her. It was more than anyone should have to bear.

I murmured against her lips, "It's going to be okay."

After removing the second cuff, Danny ran his hand up and down her back. "Take a deep breath, Princess. It's over."

"Is it?" Thea looked at the ceiling, tapping her fingers one at a time against her thumb.

I frowned at the movement. Instantly recognizing it from when she was locked on Westin's boat. When the drugs King was shooting her with had twisted her perception of reality, this was exactly what she would do to reassure herself she was in the present. Touch was key to keeping her grounded in the present. We'd spent an entire week helping her through the flashbacks. Had she still been fighting the pull of delusion the entire time she was housed in the prison, forced to go through it alone? My heart broke for our girl a little bit more.

"How can you say that?" she continued, her desperation shifting to fury, all of it aimed at Danny. "Every time you make me promises, they end up *broken*. How is this any different?" More tears streamed down her cheeks. The red lining her eyes made them turn a rich shade of green.

He swallowed hard, taking a step away and letting his hand fall from her back. "That isn't true."

Thea straightened, huffing a laugh. In a deep voice, she mocked, "*Whatever we do, Thea, we do it together. It won't be like last time.*"

"That's not fair. Gigi put us in an impossible situation."

"No!" Thea swung for him, climbing from my lap and falling into Danny. "You want to know what isn't fair? I spent *weeks* thinking you'd abandoned me to my fate. *All of you.* Fucking alone and forgotten." She pounded fist after fist into his chest with every word, even as he wrapped his arms around her and pulled her close. "I walked across that courtyard knowing I was going to die. I laid in the guillotine thinking the two of you would be next." She circled her hand around her throat, like she could still feel the press of the stockade. "In those last desperate moments, my foolish heart didn't mourn my own death; it lamented that I was powerless to stop yours."

Danny smoothed a hand down her hair, combing the tangled strands away. "I told you I was coming back, and I did. If it wouldn't have gotten everyone killed, I would have torn you from the prison the day you arrived."

"Cut it kind of close, don't you think?" Thea shook her head with a disbelieving laugh, anger and grief raging in her expression. "How many times do I have to watch one of you die? What's stopping Death from really claiming one of us next time? We aren't cats. We don't have ten lives."

"Pretty sure that's nine lives," I said, trying to keep my tone light despite the ache thrumming in my chest. I hated seeing how dismantled she was and knowing I was powerless against it. Perhaps this was the first she let herself accept any of what she'd experienced these past few months.

Eastin. King. Gigi. Westin. Orin. Even the three of us had taken a piece of her.

"It's only a matter of time before some new horror reveals itself and takes it all away again. For all I know, none of this happened, and I'm still stuck in that Oz damned dream waiting for King to wake me up."

"Thea ..." Fuck, what did you say to that? I wrapped my fingers into hers, pulling her palm to my lips.

Danny's jaw tightened. He looked like he wanted to put a fist through the stone wall. "Maybe that's true. Maybe we are on our last life, but right now, the world believes you're dead. You got your wish." In complete contrast to the waves of aggression he was putting off, Danny pressed a soft kiss between her brows. "You're free, Thea. If you wanted, you could leave Oz right now, and no one would be the wiser."

"Free?" Bitter laughter mixed with her tears. "Freedom is an illusion, a fool's hope, and I was foolish to believe in it."

"Thea ..." I repeated. How could I promise to keep her safe when we so clearly had no control over the savage world around us?

"Bath is ready." Nick extended a hand to her, pulling her away from Danny and the heaviness of the room. I took a step away, fighting the instinct to steal her back. Nick had unique insight on having to piece yourself back together. He'd be good for her right now. "Let's wash away what's left of that awful place."

— 11 —
THEA

"**I** hate him," I grumbled, letting Nick lead me from the bedroom. I dragged along behind him like a puppy on a leash.

"You don't hate him any more than you hate me. That's the adrenaline let-down speaking."

Of course he was right. I was angry and hurt, and for once, I couldn't push my fear aside. There was no containing it. It was everywhere, even in this humid bathroom with the tub steaming and covered in a luxurious layer of bubbles.

I was terrified.

"A little brush with death will do that to you."

While I stared at the bath, Nick began unbuttoning my jumpsuit. It was the only one I'd been given for the entirety of my palace visit. The thing was filthy, barely even red anymore. I both looked and smelled like a drowned cat out of lives. Gigi reveled in how I slowly became more pitiful. Image was everything and the statement my bedraggled appearance made when she stood perfectly coiffed next to me was almost as politically charged as the execution itself.

"It was more than a little brush with death," I mumbled, watching the rainbows shimmer on the soap bubbles.

"Nah, you've only got a scratch on you. I've seen you take way worse." He pushed the fabric over my shoulders, letting it fall to the ground. Shedding it felt like a snake slipping from too tight skin. I closed my eyes and took a liberating breath.

"You've lost so much weight." Nick smoothed his hands over my ribs, inspecting my skin for signs of injury. "I'm going to have to feed you a straight diet of cheese and chocolate."

I tucked my arms around my middle, feeling oddly vulnerable beneath his scrutiny. "I don't want to take a bath."

Nick tilted his head to the side in question.

I shifted my weight, studying my toes as I traced the lines between tiles. "Westin kinda ruined the respite of being submerged in water for me. It's silly, but I see that water, and all I can feel is the ropes pulling me down." I ran my fingers over the faint scar on my arm from the rope burn. Fear wrapped its bony hands around my throat the longer I thought about it. I closed my eyes, but rather than the black nothingness of my lids, a reel played of Westin clawing at me and her eyes going wide as she sucked in that first drowning breath ... Or the shark tearing her arm free.

"It's going to be a very long time before I want to go swimming again." If ever. Who needed swimming anyway? Pools and baths were overrated, right? A tear tracked down my cheek. Fuck, I hated that I couldn't stop crying. If I wasn't crying, I was shaking. The self-loathing was almost as potent as the fear. I was nauseous with it.

Not taking his hands fully from me, he stretched to flick on the shower. "Then we won't take a bath."

"Can I ..." I chewed on my lip and looked at the ceiling. "I'd prefer to be alone."

Nick shook his head, pulling his shirt over his head with one hand. "Not a chance. If you're going to break, I'm going to be there to catch the pieces."

I thumbed at the jagged scar streaking through the tattoos on his side. It was still pink and red. It was a shame that the spear of wood had ruined the exquisite ink. Would he cover this scar, too? There'd been so much blood pooling on this family's kitchen floor. My memory of the stained tile floor shifted into dark wooden slats and the pig's blood dripping onto my cheeks through the cracks in my hidden compartment. Luckily, the cheering of the crowd swallowed what little noise I'd eked out in my panic.

It felt like eons that I spent strapped to the cold metal table, in the dark, and in a space so tight that it pressed in from all sides—with blood pouring over my face and filling my mouth and nose. Because managing two phobias wasn't enough, fate needed me drowning, too.

I shivered and goosebumps prickled along my arms. Nick coasted his hands over my forearms, chasing away the lingering chills. "Okay," I murmured softly enough that I could barely hear myself.

Kicking his pants to the side, Nick walked under the spray.

My head was so fucked right now. I couldn't even appreciate how intensely beautiful he looked with the water raining down on him. Locked in my tiny room, I spent weeks aching for this man. I'd lay on the hard plank of wood they called a bed and dream about the way his skin always smelled faintly of whatever food he'd been cooking, imagining his strong arms wrapped around me and the rumble of his voice vibrating against my back as he whispered words I didn't know but understood all the same.

Now, he was right here. All it would take was a single extension of my hand and I could run my fingers along every single flower and bone inked into his skin. Instead, I stood motionless as Nick closed his eyes to the fall of water.

I was so sure that I'd never feel the reverent touch of his hands again.

"Thea?" Nick wrapped his fingers through mine and squeezed. "Fiore Mio, you still with me?"

Tears blinked out of my eyes as they came back into focus. "Yeah." My voice caught in my throat like it wasn't sure of the answer anymore than I was.

"Come on. This will help. I promise." He gave me a tug, dragging me in with him before I could run away.

My head fell to his chest. I let the steady beat of his heart ground my thoughts into the here and now.

He started with my arm, lifting it in his large hand and dragging the loofah over the surface until it glowed pink. Nick pressed a kiss to each of my knuckles before lowering it gently back to my side. We stood in silence as, one limb at a time, he scrubbed away the weeks of filth. With each cleansed bit, he kissed it gently like welcoming me home one piece at a time.

When he was satisfied with the state of my skin, he moved onto my hair, lathering the shampoo into the knotted strands. The cap on my fear loosened as he worked his fingertips against my scalp.

"I don't know how to do this," I whispered and wrapped my arms around his waist.

"I'm not the authority on dealing with pain in a healthy way."

"Not an authority?" I looked up at him for the first time since entering the shower. Thick drops of water fell from my lashes. "Nick, you're the sovereign ruler of compartmentalization land. Compared to you, I'm a mere lowly peasant."

He met my half-hearted humor with a surprisingly gentle smile. "I'm going to let that slide because I had it coming. Tip your head back." He took the wand from the wall, spraying the suds down my back. "It helps to pick one thing you can control and focus on that."

My eyes closed to the spray, I leaned into his strength, choosing him as my focus. The feel of his breath rising and falling, the coast of his palm down my arm. He hooked the wand into the holder, then took my face into his hand, tilting my chin to press an achingly gentle kiss to my lips. "You will make it past this, Fiore Mio. We'll get through it together. *Insieme.*"[1]

My heart squeezed tight enough to cut the air from my lungs. All those days of feeling like there was nothing left for me but the sharp edge of a blade. All those days when they'd really been plotting my escape. The warring emotions bled into something unrecognizable. It was too much.

For just a few moments, I wanted the freedom of nothingness.

"Angel ..." I reached down, running my palms up his thighs.

Nick's eyes scanned my face, assessing me. "I don't think I've loved the sound of any word more. I've thought about that day in the kitchen more times than I can count."

---

1. Together.

"Me too." It was one of my favorite fantasies to disappear into. In my dreams, the bees never came. Nick and I slipped back to our room, and he fucked me slow in the shower, just as he promised. It was such a bittersweet lie.

His lips brushed my temple as he spoke, "Whatever you need. I'm with you. Go dark, and I'll be right by your side. I'm intimately familiar with rock bottom and I'm not afraid to go back there with you."

I didn't want to go anywhere. I didn't want to be afraid, or strong, or fucking anything. I didn't want to exist in my own head. For just a few minutes, I wanted to have my senses obliterated so that I didn't have to feel anything.

"Right now ..." I met the steel of his gaze, wrapping my hand around his cock. The studs rolled hard against my grip. Nick's mouth dropped open and an uncontrolled breath punched from him. I stepped forward, pushing with my palm at the center of his chest until he backed into the wall. "I want you to chase every thought from my mind until there's only you."

He closed his eyes, the fingers on my shoulders tightening. "Thea, you've been—"

I silenced him with a long pull from root to tip and back. The rise and fall of his chest grew shallow. He was worried about me, but this was the steadiest I'd felt all day. "I don't need your chivalry, Nick. You've never been that for me. I need you to fuck me—" I slapped the wet tile beside his head. "Against this wall. Slow. Hard. I don't care how you do it so long as the only thing I'm thinking about is the feel of your cock pounding into me."

"Thea ..." He closed his eyes as I increased the speed of my hand.

Was I about to use sex to escape instead of dealing with my trauma? Fuck yes, I was. I didn't care. The pain would come rushing back. I knew it, but that could be Future-Thea's problem. Present-Thea was taking his advice and focusing on what she could control. Him.

"Please, Nick. Give this to me." I tugged harder, causing his knees to involuntarily bend. When his tongue licked the water from his lips, I knew I had him.

Nick gripped a handful of hair, arching me backward into the spray. I held my breath, stomping down the need to panic at the water flowing over my face. His mouth closed around my pulse, kissing and sucking hard enough to kickstart my heart while his other hand teased at my nipple.

"You're sure this is what you want?" he asked, lifting my head from the downpour, eyes alight with desire.

"Maybe my demand wasn't clear enough." I dropped to my knees and smiled sweetly. "You said whatever I need."

Every muscle in his body tensed at once, even before I traced my tongue along the vines inked down the length of his shaft. His cock was even more beautiful than I remembered. I had to press my thighs together just looking at all those bars, the Prince Albert at the tip glinting hello.

"You shouldn't be kneeling for anyone right now." Nick sucked in a breath through his teeth, the grip in my hair tightening. I put the ball shining at his tip between my teeth and tugged lightly.

"Sei la mia rovina."[2]

Taking whatever he groaned as encouragement to continue, I wrapped my lips around the head and sucked while massaging the top several piercings with my tongue. I couldn't imagine how much pain he'd endured to make his dick this fucking tantalizing. It was definitely worth it. Every movement I made elicited a different, delightful response from my dark angel.

"Fuck, Trouble, you have no idea the number of times I've imagined this." He pushed down, forcing himself deeper. The piercing at his head scraped over the roof of my mouth, hitting the back of my throat. I breathed through the urge to gag as the muscles of my neck flexed around the intrusion. Each rung of the ladder pressed into the sides, making the suffocating feeling of fullness so much more intense. My eyes watered, and for the first time today, I welcomed the tears.

Nick brushed his thumb along my jaw. *"Bellissima."*[3]

---

2. This will kill me.

3. Beautiful.

I rocked, the hum of anticipation thrumming through me. Every harsh breath Nick sucked in shot straight to my clit. My confidence bloomed back to life with each pass and subtle word of praise. His cock grew harder and thickened until, finally, moments before I knew I'd finish him, he pulled me off with a curse.

Hauling me to my feet, he spun us so that I was pinned to the tile wall. His mouth collided with mine before I could take in a full breath. Life sparked in my veins. My body buzzed with need.

"Hold on to me," he said against my mouth, not slowing enough to break away. He hooked a leg over his arm, lifting me high enough that the toes of my supporting leg barely brushed the tile. The warm metal of his piercings raked against me in one shallow testing thrust before lining up and slamming in fully.

The stars that peppered my vision were exactly what I'd been aching for. Warmth flooded my system. My teeth pulled back with his lower lips pinned between them. I exhaled into his kiss. My need warred with my mind, hungry for more and loving the rhythmic way we ebbed and flowed together. The pull of each thrust blended with the pressure of his piercings, until there was nothing left but this moment.

Blissful nothingness.

We shifted from one wall to the next. My hand rocketed out, pulling down the rack holding the shampoos. The bottles scattered across the floor. I didn't know how long we were at it, but eventually, the water went cold. The icy spray hit my hot skin like tiny daggers. Nick turned us so that he took the brunt of the water. He didn't let it slow him at all. If anything, the new assault of pain and pleasure was enough to drive reason from us both.

The wave of my orgasm crashed over me like the pulling of a tide, surging with his in a collective cry of pleasure. It wasn't the earth shattering cataclysm of our last time together. This was more like the slow tango of our souls twining together. Even after the shock of release eased, we continued moving, the kisses deep and unhurried. It was the life affirming connection that I needed to face the world with my strength intact.

"*Ti amo, Thea. Tu sei il mio cuore.*"[4] Lowering me to the ground, he placed my hand over the center of his heart. "*Senza di te c'è solo silenzio dentro di me. Non lasciarmi mai più.*"[5]

---

4. I love you, Thea. You are my heart.

5. Without you, there's only silence within me. Never leave me again.

– 12 –
CROWE

I sipped on my beer, incredibly happy that we'd chosen clear shower curtains. I would never tire of watching that woman in ecstasy.

In a mix of shock and amusement, Thea's expression immediately met mine when she stepped out. "Were you just sitting here watching us?" she asked, bashfully tucking a towel around herself.

"Of course." I took another sip, scanning the freshly fucked flush to her cheeks. She was so mind-alteringly beautiful. Thea was the kind of woman that inspired epics and made men declare war. "I missed you, Gorgeous. You're lucky all I did was watch." I reached into the bag of chips beside me and popped one into my mouth.

"And you brought snacks?"

"Well, yeah. I was locked to that desk all day. I'm hungry." I aimed the bag at her. "Want one?"

"*Sei un'idiota,*"[1] Nick said, shaking his head and walking unabashedly naked from the room.

Thea watched him walk away with her lower lip firmly pinned between her teeth. She sidled up to me, wrapping her arms around my waist and nestling into the crook of my neck. I lifted her chin for a drugging kiss. Sitting on the counter put Thea at the perfect height for lazy kissing. That was my favorite kind. There was something wonderful about being able to linger in the unhurried moments.

When she finally came up for air, Thea asked, "How long were you in here?"

"Long enough to see you make the big guy weak in the knees when you tugged on his sparkly bits."

"All that time? Crowe!" She pushed away from me, trying so very hard to look offended.

There was a light to her expression that wasn't there before. It lifted a bit of the weight from my chest. I knew Nick would be good for her. It gave me hope.

A hint of wickedness flamed in her gaze. "Do you think if I got him sparkly studs, Nick would wear them?"

"For you, Darling, that man would wear a pink heart-shaped tiara if it put that smile on your face." I brushed a light kiss over her lips. "Are you hungry? Ya know, for something other than Italian sausage."

"I might actually hate you," she said in an attempt not to laugh.

"How about this? Let's throw something comfy on you ..." I slipped my hand beneath the edge of the towel to cup her ass. My fingers splayed as wide as possible before squeezing hard enough to make her squeak. Oz damn, she felt so good. "And then we can curl up on the couch, and I can feed you something decadent, like chocolate cake."

She scrunched her nose. "You have chocolate cake lying around?"

"No, but Danny is due for some penance. We can make him get us some."

Thea flashed me a devious smile, my unbreakable girl finally bouncing back. "Make it cookie-dough ice cream, and you have a deal."

I kissed the top of her head. "You got it. Then we can shop for rainbow glitter studs together. Also, Toto is going out of her skin waiting to see you. I think she's still not over the whole beheading thing."

Thea huffed a heavy sigh. "That makes two of us."

"You're saying that *wasn't* her head on camera!" Toto said, stealing a spoonful of ice cream from my carton. "That can't be. I saw her crying. Real tears fell down her cheeks. Thea called out your name." She pointed frantically at Nick, sending the ice cream flying directly into his nose. He winced and used his sleeve to wipe the sludge from his face. "How is that possible? Was it a video trick, like CGI, or is this one of those mass hysteria moments, and we all just imagined it together?"

"What?" Danny looked at his sister like she'd just suggested the moon was made of pizza. "That's not a thing."

"It is."

"It was a real head," Nick answered, preemptively stopping the two of them from getting in yet another ridiculous argument. "A really fucking realistic one." His gaze drifted past Toto, landing on Thea. I could only imagine what it must have been like being feet from that grotesque scene. Watching it on the security cameras had been hard enough.

"It wasn't just realistic. It *was* real," Thea said around the spoon I'd just shoved in her mouth. "Alice showed it to me while we were waiting for those two to catch up."

"Hey now," Danny sniped, looking personally offended. "We had chains to slip and guards to incapacitate, all while avoiding the attention of the couple hundred people beyond the balcony."

"That's right, Kitten, we're all very impressed." Thea winked, and I swear the color of his face shifted an entire shade darker. I pushed my tongue into the back of my teeth to subdue my snicker.

"Anyway, Alice used prosthetics to make it look like me. Trust me, there is nothing freakier than holding *your own* severed head."

I tightened my hold on her, pressing a kiss to the mark on her spine.

"But HOW?" Toto jumped up, waving her hands. If her eyes went any wider, they were going to pop right out of their sockets.

Danny pinched the bridge of his nose. "I need a drink for this."

Nick, seeing the new vacancy, moved quickly, sinking beside us on the couch. He didn't seem to care about the glare Toto shot his way. Deflecting, he gave Thea's knee a sympathetic squeeze. "We knew that breaking her out of the prison was as good as a death sentence for everyone. We'd never be able to break in and get her out without being gunned down a dozen times in the in-between. The security on the palace is too complete."

I added, "Even getting access to the cameras required a week of hacking, and I had to call in a college buddy to help me do it. That's actually how we ended up working with Alice. They're sort of roommates."

Thea twisted in my lap. "Alice has roommates? That feels so ... normal."

She wasn't wrong. Alice was as friendly as a caged Rottweiler. "It's more of a casual come-and-go thing. Alice isn't the kind of girl who forms real relationships with people. I only know because Maddox and I go so far back that I remember when he and Alice first met. Turns out he has a bit of a vendetta against Gigi, too, so he was all too happy to assist when I told him that we needed access to the entire palace security feed."

"Plus, it wouldn't matter if we broke Thea out of prison if the entire country was just looking for her again." Danny pulled the stopper from a blue glass decanter of scotch, foregoing the ice and taking a swig directly from the bottle. "Thanks to the story Gigi spun about Thea murdering half the Ozmandrian leaders, she would be public enemy number one. The only way to really get away with it would be to fake her death."

"Publicly, and in a way that would leave nothing to doubt," I added, skating my hand under the extra-large hoodie Thea was wearing, one of Nick's that he was always stalking around in. I smoothed my hand along her spine, making her shiver when my fingertips ran over her scars. Ozma bless it, I'd missed the feel of her so much. I didn't think I'd ever tire of touching her.

"That makes sense, actually," Thea said, examining her nails like the answers to all of her problems were there. After a longer-than-normal pause, she shook her head, leaning over the back of the couch to speak directly to Danny. "Alice did all the work of getting me out. Why bother risking your lives, too?"

"I suppose the fact that *we all* care about you enough to risk our lives doesn't factor in?" Danny ground his teeth, the bitterness coming out with a sharper edge than Thea deserved. He was probably about to say something stupid that would require me to kick his ass again.

Danny opened and closed his mouth twice before continuing. "Gigi never would've fallen for it. She's worked with us for too long to buy us giving up so easily. She was waiting for us to make a move, and we couldn't have her attention on Alice."

"You mean to tell me you knowingly walked into a trap? *You?*" Toto asked, walking over and slapping Danny's arm hard enough to make his scotch splash onto the counter.

"Damn it, Daffodil. I just poured that."

"You were a decoy," Thea said with slow understanding, reaching out to brush her finger along the bruise darkening Nick's cheekbone. "You let yourself get caught. For me."

I kissed her nose. "Exactly. Gigi was so pleased with herself. While she was grandstanding about her greatness, Alice was making the necessary adjustments to the guillotine."

Thea's eyes went distant, losing focus on the wall behind me. "I saw her. That morning, I watched the executioner set up and prepare the guillotine. They spent close to an hour testing the blade and hammering pieces in place. That was Alice."

"But the head?" Toto repeated, still perplexed by the public sleight of hand. "Subterfuge and what not is great, but how does Thea still have a head?"

"I can answer that." Thea climbed from my lap and laid stomach down on the coffee table, her hands flexing several times. Gesturing to her upper body, she explained, "The bed of the guillotine had a lower compartment. Alice twisted my neck so that it was in exactly the right position. When the blade fell, it triggered the drop. My upper body tilted down—" Thea slid herself forward until her upper body was bent over the edge of the table. "—and a box closed around my head."

I jumped up, scooping her back into my lap. The muscles in my chest screamed with the added strain of her body weight, however slight it might be. Seeing it once had been enough. I knew I was clinging to her again, but I really didn't care. She'd allow me this. I needed it and even if she'd never admit it, she needed it, too.

Danny added, "At the same time, the fake Thea head was released. The decoy drops down while Thea's is still intact. It's an old magician's trick."

I thumbed over the slash of red on her neck. That blade had been close, *really close*. "A blood bag at the top of the compartment sliced open, creating the perfect cover for the switch. All the cameras saw was a shiny blade and lots of blood. Nobody was watching her body when a severed head was rolling on the ground."

Thea tucked closer, her hand sliding into mine. "Gigi got the victory she wanted while we walked right out the back door." I was glad she finally understood. This was the only way it could have played out. This plan was why she was sitting here in my lap today.

A buzz sounded, making the screen at the security panel glow. "Who is it?" I asked Danny.

He clicked the panel, showing a camera feed for the outer gate. One of the first things we reestablished was the perimeter security. Now that we didn't need to feed Gigi our fake infiltration plans, the anti-drone security was in place, too. Anything unauthorized entering this airspace or coming within a mile of The Villa would be shot down immediately.

Danny zoomed in on the dark-haired beauty twiddling her fingers at the perimeter camera. "Ginger."

Toto sat up straight, "So soon."

"Ginger was getting new documents for Thea," I answered for him. "She's been faking documents for her little army of runaways for years."

"Hey," Toto snapped, then pursed her lips. "Also ... true. I'll be right back." She scurried down the hall, tugging her hair free of her ponytail as she went.

"What the hell was that about?" Danny said, staring at the disappearing silhouette of his sister.

I shrugged. "Who knows. With Toto, it could be anything."

Thea tried to get up, but I circled her waist and pulled her back while Nick lifted her legs into his lap and started rubbing the arch of her foot. The sound of bliss that our girl made as she melted in my lap was the thing of dreams. For the first time since she walked through my bedroom door, the stress lines etched into her face smoothed away. Maybe if we could relax her enough, she'd actually be able to get some rest. Holding her in my lap while she dozed sounded like the best idea I'd had in days.

Within minutes Ginger was escorted into our apartment by our new head of house. None of us trusted the former household staff, and Marcello's band of followers were just as spineless as he was. They abandoned the grounds instantly when The Crows arrived.

There wasn't much left to The Villa of our youth anyway. By the time Gabby had patched us up, and we were able to walk around, the ancient building was merely a skeleton of the proud estate it had been. Nick was content to leave the ruin behind, but that didn't change the fact we had nowhere to go. Large sections of Sal's stash were still intact, including the basement armory, and the few surviving members of his council quickly acknowledged Nick's right as heir to the entirety of Salvatore's operations.

It was a bitter pill to swallow. Despite everything he'd subjected his son to, Sal was still getting the heir he'd wanted. To his credit, the first thing Nick did was dismantle the Morphia production and burn the poppy fields. No doubt some opportunistic member of the old regime would fill demand sooner or later, but the Ciopriani's were done with the drug trade. Anyone who had a problem with that decision didn't need to stay.

"Well, if it isn't the notorious Dorothea Gallant, scourge of Ozmandria, alive and head firmly attached to her shoulders," Ginger said with a beaming smile that set off the umber tones of her skin. It was like the woman walked with her own personal ray of sunshine.

Thea winced, "Don't call me that."

"What, no, 'Hello, Ginger? Do you happen to have a new identity with you so that I can once again walk the streets of the Emerald City a free woman?'"

"That would be an oddly specific greeting."

She pulled a large envelope from her purse. "And yet, an accurate one."

Thea took the envelope, pulling out several papers. She held up the new ID, squinting at the picture. "What kind of last name is Gale?"

"The forgettable kind. You'll have to dye your hair, of course."

"What?" Nick sat up, pulling the license from Thea's grip. "No. Get her glasses or something."

Ginger whistled and playfully tapped his shoulder. "For the strong silent type, that was a very quick reaction. You got something against blondes?"

"I've got something about making Thea change her looks. She's gorgeous. She doesn't need to change."

Thea looked at Nick with bemused shock. Compliments from him were rare, but surely, she'd heard him tell her she was beautiful before. I had to make a conscious effort not to blurt it out every time I looked at her.

"This isn't about vanity, Sugar. Nothing changes identity like changing your hair. If you don't want her recognized the second she walks out those gates, then she needs a full makeover. The glasses aren't a bad idea, though. I'll call in for a dummy pair to be made up." Ginger narrowed her eyes, pinching Thea's chin and turning her face from side to side. "Hmmm. Cat-eye frames, subtle ones. Yes, those will compliment your cheekbones nicely."

Thea glanced back at me. "What do you think about the blonde hair?"

"No." Nick looked like he might burst a blood vessel. "You can wear a wig when we go out. I'll buy you a hundred wigs, in every color. Just don't change your hair." His voice dropped to a low whisper, "Please."

"Wow." I fought back the urge to laugh. Rabid dogs, a wild coyote, a pack of armed bikers. I'd seen Nick fight back a lot of deadly things. To think he could be reduced to begging with something as simple as hair dye. "A 'please' from Niccolo Ciopriani. How could you deny that?" I chuckled. He did have a point. I wouldn't change a thing about Thea, either.

"*Vai a fare in culo,* Vin."[2]

"Wigs could work. It feels like an unnecessary risk to me. You'd have to keep security here locked down tight. Although, I did have to go through three security checks to make it here, so you're probably fine on that front."

From down the hall, a bored voice said, "It *is* an unnecessary risk, and your security isn't that great."

We all turned, looking back in the direction Toto disappeared. Except, it wasn't Danny's sister strolling up the corridor.

---

2. Go fuck yourself, Vin.

—13—
CROWE

"How in the fuck did you get in here?" Danny asked. The scathing accusation pointed at me was hard to miss.

"Don't look at me. I locked this place down tighter than a noose over a shark pit."

Thea's jaw dropped.

I closed it with a single finger. "Too soon?"

Alice padded her way silently closer. She was like a phantom passing through the room. If she hadn't announced herself, we might never have been aware of her presence. "You are adorably stupid. Do you think I'd charge all that money if I couldn't bypass a little home security?"

I was speechless. *A little home security?* I had anti-aircraft guns, motion-sensitive cameras covering the entire property, and a perimeter laser grid small enough the field mice were setting them off.

"I'll give it to you, Thea, you know how to pick the pretty ones."

"Why are you here, Alice?" Nick, always one to get right to the point.

"I have something for Thea." A long silver chain dropped from the center of her hand, swaying beneath her palm like the pendulum of a clock.

"The locket," Thea whispered, involuntarily drawing back.

Alice tossed the delicate thing to her. I intercepted the necklace before it came into contact with Thea. She looked like the assassin had just thrown a snake at her.

"What is it?"

"It was Gigi's attempt at a failsafe," Alice said, climbing to perch on the back of the couch. "I had a feeling there might be something hidden in the structure of the locket and I was right. The guillotine sliced through the chain when it came down. I pocketed it when I retrieved the fallen head and brought the tracker with me to the crematorium. To Gigi's backup software, it will look like it and Thea's remains all went up in the same smoke. Maddox met me there."

Thea reached out with a hesitant finger, like the necklace might bite her.

"He disabled the tracker and mentioned that the stone is coded. Apparently, there is quite a bit of information stored in that heirloom."

Danny made a patronizing sound in the back of his throat. "And I suppose you didn't help yourself to a look around while you had it."

"Well, I had to be sure the Premier's cheat codes to the nuclear arsenal weren't in it."

"Oz has a nuclear arsenal?" Toto questioned, eyeing Ginger as she reentered the room and sat at the bar in the kitchen.

"Not a big one." Alice leaned forward, picking up the forgotten carton of ice cream and taking a big spoonful before making a disgusted face at it. "Gross, you could have warned me you were eating cookie dough."

Thea chuckled. I could have sniped at Alice for being so impertinent as to steal my food and then complain about it, but seeing Thea laugh was enough to make me want to hug the woman.

"What *is* on the locket?" she asked, turning the pendant over and over nervously in her hand.

"Photos. Some account information. Nothing exciting, but I figured you'd want it back. Seeing as you wore it to your execution and all. Memories."

Thea's fidgeting halted, staring down at the gleaming blue stone. "Photos?"

"Family ones, you know, birthdays and holidays, the odd swearing of oaths. Those kinds of things."

Thea was so lost to her thoughts that she didn't notice Toto taking her ice cream from her.

"Family," Thea whispered so softly that I thought I imagined it.

I took the necklace from her, not liking the harsh edge it returned to her finally softening features. I nuzzled her neck, whispering quietly enough that the others wouldn't hear me, "Are you okay?"

Thea didn't move for several long seconds. "It was my mother's." She took back the necklace, clicking open the locket and showing me the small picture of a family.

"Gigi told me a lot about my parents." She let out a long exhale. "They weren't good people. Or at least my father wasn't. He made Gigi the woman she is today. Once, she was idealistic and well-intentioned. Along the way, my father warped her perception of right and wrong to the point she actually believes that she's doing what's right for this country."

Thea snapped the necklace closed and tossed it to the coffee table. "Gigi's been orchestrating this plan for decades. She engineered everything from their deaths to Westin's. Even your placement, Toto." She nodded at Danny's sister. "She put you in my path, knowing I'd fall for your story and try to do something. Then she tipped off Henry, ensuring I'd be sent to the one person Em owes. My entire life, from start to finish, was planned for me to eventually take the fall for Gigi's coup. I was always destined for a blade."

I curled my arms around her.

"Get the fuck out." Toto dropped the carton of ice cream, the spoon clinking off the counter top. "You're telling me Gigi shut down The Chateau and pulled me from the line of girls so that you'd get caught?"

Thea nodded her head slowly. "I'm sorry, Toto."

"Don't be sorry, baby girl," Ginger said, walking into Thea's line of sight. "That bitch did heinous things. You didn't put Toto in that truck any more than you held the gun that shot your boy. Don't be sorry, be angry. She doesn't deserve your guilt, but she *does* deserve your wrath. Don't forget it."

Danny's phone rang. The buzz of it vibrating against the counter top was sharp in the silence following Ginger's declaration. Danny clicked on the speaker. "YBR Taxi Cabs."

I held a finger to Thea's lips, ensuring that she remembered dead girls don't talk. She silently nodded, wrapping her fingers into mine and lowering our hands to her lap.

"Hello, Dandelion."

Danny's hands tightened into fists, pantomiming punching the phone. "Gigi. You've a lot of nerve calling me after what you did to Thea."

"Indeed. Can't say I'm surprised you and Niccolo slipped my custody. There's a reason I always preferred working with you. It's why I'm calling now. I'm putting you on my payroll."

"Vai a farti fottere."[1] Nick said loudly enough to be sure the microphone picked up his voice.

"Attento alle parole, Niccolino."[2]

Nick cracked his neck, slowly rising to his feet like he could beat her down right here and now. "Of course the bitch speaks Italian."

"As I was saying, I'm putting you on my payroll. YBR works for me now—exclusively."

"There is zero chance we're agreeing to that. Not after today. As far as I'm concerned, Gigi, you're dead to us. I'd rather take a job for Emily Rosen than work for you, and she's essentially the devil."

"Noted." There were scratching sounds, like Gigi was taking notes. *"Oh, while I'm remembering, Dandelion, you're in violation of our agreement."*

"What fucking agreement?"

"In the club, I gave you a choice: leave or fight for Dorothea. Actions have consequences. Your sad attempt to free the traitor puts you in violation of that agreement."

Thea's complexion turned a sallow shade of grey.

"I'm sure you remember what I said the consequences would be if you crossed me. In case you need a reminder, check your messages. I've sent you a present."

Danny pulled over a tablet and flicked open the secure server we used to trade information.

"You bitch. I swear to fucking Oz, if you touch her—"

---

1. Get fucked.

2. Watch your temper, Niccolino.

"It's too late, Dandelion. Make all the threats you like; it's done. She was sent to him earlier today, almost immediately after your pathetic attempt to break into my palace."

Toto opened her mouth to balk, but Ginger slapped a hand over her lips.

"I'll be sending coordinates to you later today. There are a few facilities I need acquired. Niccolo and Vincent, your experience in the Morphia labs will be of good use."

Fuck, how could she pretend to be doing what's good for this country and at the same time condone the continued production of that poison.

"And if we refuse?" Nick said.

"That Villa isn't as secure as you think it is. Sylvan, while detestable, has never turned down an offer for fresh meat. Maybe I should go picking some Daffodils to go with my new bouquet of Daisies."

Toto. She was talking about Danny's other sister. Either we played along, or she made good on her threat to take his remaining family away.

"My people will be in touch." The line went dead before anyone could protest.

"FUCKING. CUNT." Danny bellowed, picking up the phone and hurling it at the stone wall.

"What was in the file?" I asked, holding out my hand for the tablet before he could smash that too.

Danny ran his hands through his hair, gripping the strands tightly. When he didn't let go, Ginger passed the tablet to me. Daisy's name was at the top of the file along with a transfer order to Sylvan Deveaux, dated yesterday.

"That bitch had her transferred before we ever set foot on the palace grounds," Danny growled.

Alice, who had been surprisingly quiet, jumped down from her perch at the back of the couch. She flipped open an archaic phone and pressed a single button. It rang once before answering. "I need you to send Crowe everything you have on Sylvan Deveaux and La Chasse ... No, everything. Oh, and their Villa needs an upgrade."

"It does *not* need an upgrade," I said loud enough Maddox could hear me.

Alice gave me a flat look. "No, it's pathetic. A toddler on a tricycle could bypass it." Into the phone, she added softly, "Thanks, Mads."

Danny and I exchanged a questioning look.

"You have a file on Sylvan?"

Thea asked, "What the fuck is La Chasse?

—14—
THEA

"**A**bsolutely not!" Danny gripped the chair back hard enough to make the wood groan beneath the pressure. He'd long since given up sitting. The rest of us were gathered around the kitchen table, what I'd come to calling the "War Room" over the past week.

We'd been at this for hours. Photos of Sylvan Deveaux's property were scattered across the table, not that you would know it. Each set of photos looked dramatically different: an old hotel, warehouses, homes, woods, and even a hospital. Sylvan didn't just own property; he owned an entire abandoned town. It was why we'd settled on this plan. Searching an entire town took longer than we had for our exit window.

"You're being unreasonable," Maddox's voice sounded tired over the computer speakers. His thin gold frames caught the light, their sheen a perfect compliment to his amber-brown complexion. Pulling them from his face, he used them to point at the camera. *"It's a good idea. You're not giving your girl enough credit."*

Danny threw his hands up, spinning in a circle before snapping back to Crowe. "You're seriously okay with this, after everything she's been through? Out of all of us, you're the over-protective asshole."

Crowe's eyes hesitantly shifted to me. He was probably gauging my reaction. "Thea is her own woman. She understands the risks."

Toto raised her hand, "I could—"

Danny swiveled on her, pointing an angry finger. "Don't you fucking dare."

"Someone has to go in and—"

"NO. We're going to get one sister out. I'm not about to lose another in the process. You have zero experience with this kind of thing."

Toto drew back, aghast. "And Thea does?"

"She doesn't. Why do you think I keep saying, 'No?' It's like you've all lost your Oz damn minds."

"I do have experience." I sat back, crossing my arms above my chest. "I know how these kinds of places run. I lived my whole life in one. Plus, despite being locked up, I'm in the best shape of my life. To keep my sanity during my time in the tower, I ran in place and did strengthening exercises."

Danny's eyes did a slow drop over my body and frowned. Fuck him.

Yes, I was thin—thinner than I'd been in a very long time. I hadn't missed my jutting collarbone or the way my hip bones felt like they were trying to skewer someone. That was mostly due to the lack of palatable food that I was provided. I tilted my chin in challenge. I could do this and his patronizing ass needed to get on board.

"I wanted to be sure that if I ever got the chance to make a run for it, weakness wouldn't be the reason I got caught."

"That's really smart," Nick said with a look of pride that made something low in my stomach flutter. At least he understood the value I could bring to our group.

"And you're just going to let her put her neck back on the chopping block? Next time, it might actually be for real." Danny glowered at Nick with wild eyes. I'd never seen him look so undone. Was this what people looked like before they spontaneously combusted? Maybe if I squinted, I could see smoke coming from his ears.

Nick placed his hand on my thigh. "I figured out the day she walked into YBR headquarters that we don't *let* Thea do anything. You seem to be the only one who hasn't caught on. She's going to do what she wants whether we permit it or not."

"Un-fucking-believable." Danny grabbed the computer, turning the camera on him. "Is Alice there?"

"You know I can't tell you that," Maddox said with a bored drawl, propping his head with the palm of his hand so that the twists of hair piled on top of his head shifted to cover his eyes. He idly spun the glasses in his hand by the stems.

"ALICE! I know you're fucking there. Get your judgmental ass on camera."

"Move aside, Mads. The big baby is calling for Mommy. Let me spank him a bit, and he'll calm down."

Danny blinked at the screen, finally silenced.

"Danny, you're not king. You don't get to make decrees."

"Stop being a bitch. Can you take the job or not?"

"WOAH!" Half of the room snapped at Danny all at once, Maddox included, who looked ready to push Alice off camera.

I picked up the closest thing to me, my pencil, and pitched it at him. The wood projectile flew with uncanny precision, lodging itself like a dart on a bullseye just below where his sleeves were rolled up. It was almost comical, especially because Danny was in peak asshole performance this afternoon. He pulled the pencil from his arm, snapping the wood in one hand and rubbing at the tiny grey mark it left behind.

Crowe shook his head. "Are you seriously so daft that you're calling her a bitch while begging for help?" He gave the blonde glaring at the camera a sassy wink. "Alice will murder you in your sleep."

"I wouldn't wait for him to be asleep," she corrected.

"Brother, for someone so smart, you really are a dumbass." Crowe cackled a laugh. "And ... that's not how you get back in Thea's pants. The women around here are practically their own army."

"Not helping, Crowe. Also, if *you* want in my pants, you'll stop talking about me like I'm not here." I threw him a side eye, then shoved Danny with both hands. "And you ..." I shoved him again, half debating on slapping him across his arrogant face while I was at it. Although, I did just stab him with a pencil, even if it was by accident. "Call another woman a bitch again and see what happens."

He narrowed his eyes, using all of his height to hit me with his most intimidating stare. "So, it's just you I can call a bitch, then? Good to know what the rules are."

Crowe pushed to his feet, but Nick pulled him back down. "She's got this. Besides, it'll be fun to watch her dickapitate him."

I tried really hard not to crack a smile, trading glances with Nick. He was referencing the knife job I'd done on King. I wish I still had that necklace. Unfortunately, Gigi had been smart enough to take it from me.

"I'm sorry." Danny took a deep breath, bracing my shoulders on both sides.

I blinked in surprise. Did Danny just apologize?

"No, actually," Danny's expression tightened. "I'm not sorry."

False alarm. Asshole mode was still intact. "You're not sorry?"

"See? Dumbass," Crowe laughed under his breath.

"No, I'm not sorry because I had to watch you be abused on that yacht for weeks. Every second of every minute of every day. I was there for every tear, scream, and look of horror. I know you don't remember all of it, and I thank Ozma for that because *I do*. Then, I had to watch you walk that yard, and I *screamed* for Gigi to free you, only to see the entirety of OZ cheer when the blade fell. Even if it was a ruse, it felt like my soul was being sliced apart." He lowered his forehead to mine. "I can't do it again, Thea. I failed you once. I can't just stand by while it happens again."

"*Because I respect your girl, I'll answer you,*" Alice interrupted before I could process everything he'd just said. "*No, Danny, I can't take the job. I'm booked. Getting Mads to give you his files is the best I can do for you. So, stop throwing a tantrum and be grateful for what you've got.*" Alice abruptly walked off camera, Maddox's dark eyes watching her the entire time.

Danny, finally relenting, flopped into his chair and scrubbed his face with his palm. "What's a little more regret? I'm getting so good at it."

"What do we know about this season's chase?" Nick asked, bringing us back on topic. "Providing we can get Thea inside undetected."

Danny groaned. If he kept tugging at his hair like that he was going to go bald.

Maddox slipped his glasses back on and tapped a few keys. The screen changed, showing a satellite view of Sylvan's town. *"There's nothing posted yet about the theme of this year, but I can definitely get the three of you invitations. I've been working for years on an in for this event. The exterior of the property is protected by an electrical field similar to the one you used on your compound. Anything that tries crossing the boundary will be fried. Except, unlike yours, this one covers air space, too. The only way onto the property is through the front gate. Here."*

A red circle indicated the edge of town, where a large iron gate crossed a dirt road.

Crowe sat up, "Wait. How do you know what my system was?"

A series of red Xs peppered a dozen buildings. Ignoring Crowe, he continued, *"These are where past chases have been held, but there's nothing saying that he won't reuse a building. This is also the fifteenth anniversary of La Chasse, so the buzz is that he plans to make this year special."*

"No, really, why do you know I had a perimeter field on the YBR compound?" Crowe repeated. "Maddox?"

"Special how? Like the fox chase will be hunting more than girls?" Nick asked, rubbing his hand up and down my leg. It wasn't like Nick to be so physically clingy. He might act cool about it, but this plan was definitely unsettling him. Fuck, for all my bravado, I was unsettled, too. His touch was the only thing grounding me as we discussed the finer details of this plan.

Was I really volunteering to be sold and hunted?

To save Daisy, yeah, I was.

"Hard to tell. I'd say be prepared for anything. We'll plan a few contingencies just to be safe."

Crowe added a set of pointy teeth to his notes. "At this point, it wouldn't surprise me for Sylvan to let a few lions loose in the town, or tigers and bears."

"Oh my ..." The skin at the back of my neck prickled. "I already had to fight off sharks. Please tell me I'm not going to have to take on all of the Emerald City Zoo."

Nick squeezed my thigh, "How long do we have?"

"La Chasse is next month. Sylvan is set to pick up his next order of foxes—"

"Foxes. Fucking hell, I'm going to be sick." Danny folded over and held his head in his hands like he was really trying to keep from vomiting.

"—from the newly reopened Ragbad Distribution Center on the Friday before."

"Hold-the-fuck-on!" I grabbed the computer. "What do you mean reopened? Gigi seized The Farm and all of Em's assets."

"She did. My take on the chatter coming down the line is that Em was reinstated as head of The Farm under Gigi's command."

"So much for a better Oz," I said, sitting back. "What utter shit. She did all of this to end Ozmandria's corruption, but she's just as bad ... worse, because the world actually believes the nonsense she's feeding them. She was right, make them love you, and they'll ignore the worst truths."

"Yeah, well, they're all reopened now."

Nick added, "She plans to restart the Morphia trade, too. Gigi had a courier drop off orders for Crowe and I to appropriate that drug den in Swing City. What's worse, we're to take the first round of product and give it to the dregs of Swing City for free. The people there are so desperate they'd do anything to escape for a minute or two. Free access to a designer drug will be too tempting for most to resist. If Gigi has her way, there'll be Morphia on every corner in Oz by mid-year."

Maddox bit down on his lip, holding something back. The man looked ready to commit murder. *"Her moment will come. Taking Gigi out is going to require some elegant planning."*

"That settles it. It has to be me," I said, swallowing my fear and thinking of the girl who looked so much like the man sitting before me.

Danny opened his mouth and I silenced him with a finger to his lips.

"One, it has to be a woman to get to where Daisy is held. Two, nobody knows the finer workings of the Farm like I do. Three, I've perfected the art of not being noticed. For years I walked those halls like a ghost. I know I can slip into that group without anyone noticing."

"The guards aren't exactly looking for people trying to get in. We could use that to our advantage," Crowe added, writing a note on the pad of paper beside the laptop.

"Exactly."

Toto, who had been unusually quiet, added, "It has to be after grooming. They pay too close attention to the girls during."

Danny growled. Actually growled.

Choosing to ignore the lion in the room, I continued, "Transfer's the only time that we could slip me in."

"*I'll hack the system and add you to the registry.*" Maddox quickly clicked away at the keyboard.

"You can't hack the Farm. I tried. It's a closed server." Crowe leaned forward clicking on the video feed. "Maddox, you hear me? I've tried, it's imposs—"

"*Done.*"

Crowe looked like he was going to punch the screen. "What do you mean, done?"

"*This isn't the first time I've had to get in there. I planted a Trojan horse a few years back. I don't always use it, but it does make things easier when I need to pull files.*"

Like a kettle boiling over, the anxiety rattling around in him finally exploded. Shaking me by both shoulders, Danny bellowed, "NO! We'll find anoth—"

"No?!" I twisted, knocking his hands away with such intensity that one slapped himself in the face. "It's not up to you. You insufferable prick. I can do this, and not a single person sitting in this room can do it better than me."

"*I could.*" Alice leaned into the frame on the computer. "*But like I said, I'm booked.*"

Ignoring her, I continued, "You three don't get to run around putting your lives on the line, but treat me differently. If it's a risk you're willing to take, then why shouldn't I? My life isn't worth any more than yours."

Danny took both sides of my face in his hands. "I would give my life a hundred times over to save yours."

The sincerity in his expression was stark enough to make my breath hitch. "What makes you think I wouldn't do the same for any of you? I'm doing this, Danny."

Slowly, he lowered back to his seat. For the first time tonight he didn't argue the point. Maybe I'd finally gotten through to the beast.

"*Thea ...*" Maddox cleared his throat and held up a vial. "*I have a new tracker that I've been working on. I'd like to try it out with you. I'll swing by the day before you leave and inject you with it.*"

"*Ohhh fermi tutti,*"[1] Nick said. "Inject her? What kind of tracker needs to be injected?"

My hand absentmindedly rubbed the spot on my neck where King would stick me. I wasn't exactly fond of needles anymore.

"*It's a nano-tracker I've been working on. It's perfectly safe; just hasn't been field-tested yet. What's more, it won't show up on any scans. It's completely undetectable, and the electro-field that disrupts the electronics within the barrier won't affect it either. Which is good because Sylvan is packing some pretty high-tech over there. I'm sure he uses a tracking system of his own, but I can't find a digital footprint for it anywhere.*"

Crowe shook his head. "I don't like it. Thea isn't some kind of guin—"

"I'll do it," I stated before I could chicken out. "Whatever it takes."

Danny jumped up, resuming his pacing. They were probably going to have to replace the tiles around the table after all was said and done. Shoving the chair aside, he made for the door. "I'm going for a walk."

Maddox rubbed the beard dusting his jawline. "*Whatever it takes.*"

---

1. Woah.

DANNY

An ominous premonition in the pit of my stomach gnawed away at my nerves. Thea's voice cycled through my mind like a banshee's wail.

What's stopping Death from really claiming one of us next time?

No, please. King, don't.

Alone and forgotten.

I kicked at the charred earth, climbing to the ridge of the hillside. The crunch of her following footsteps mimicked my own. It was surprising that she followed me out here. In the days since we came home, she'd been putting some excruciating distance between us. Every time she shied away from me, it felt like the barbed wire circling my heart cinched just a little bit tighter.

I only had myself to blame.

The sun set on the valley, and I listened to the rising chorus of crickets. The skies blazed above the once beautiful flower fields. Now, they were reduced to little more than singed earth.

"As a child, I was never the brave one," I said, sitting on one of the rare patches of grass left untouched by Nick's rampage. Some people took out rage by running or doing a few rounds with a pair of boxing gloves. Nick chose flame throwers.

"Children shouldn't have to be brave," Thea said, lowering beside me and resting her head on my shoulder. This was the closest she'd been in days. Her honeyed scent drifted on the breeze. I tilted into her, resting my cheek against the top of her head.

I missed her so much.

It felt like all I'd been doing for my entire life was missing her. I would do unforgivable things to rewind time and have her look at me the way she had that day in the safe-house, before everything went to hell.

"When I was eight, and Daisy was seven, she fell into the river beside where we played as kids." Thea sucked in a breath. I felt the movement all the way to my toes. "We were goofing around on a log, one we knew we shouldn't be on. That didn't stop me from daring my sister to walk across it and grab the string of honeysuckle dangling in the sun. My sister hesitated at first, proclaiming that our mother would tan us all if she found out we were playing by the river. Daisy always was the rule follower of our group. Didi heard my challenge and harassed Daisy until she had no choice but to walk the moss-covered log like a balance beam."

"Your older sister bullied the little one?" she asked, counting on her fingers. "She had to be at least twelve."

"Eleven, not quite twelve. You didn't have sisters. You don't know how evil they can be." I smiled to myself. Even at their most wicked, the memories had a warm glow to them. "When Daisy got there, the flowers hung just beyond the reach of her fingers. Didi or I could have reached it, but Daisy had always been petite."

Thea shifted. I opened my arm, allowing her to curl against me. My fingers hooked into the belt loop on her opposite hip. Fresh pain tightened in the center of my chest, throbbing like the heat of a burn. It pulsed with each of her shallow breaths, making me painfully aware of how close we were. I had to close my eyes against the pull to abandon everything and drown myself in the feeling.

"Her first jump brushed the petals. Random white flowers rained into the water below. I can still remember them catching in her hair. We heckled her, teasing that she was too small. On her second jump, she wrapped her little fingers around the vine and pulled. The tendrils from the stems locked in the branches of the overhanging bough, yanking her off balance and sending her straight into the rushing water."

Thea drew in a sharp breath. "What did you do?"

"Nothing." I continued, "Didi shouted, immediately kicking off her sneakers and leaping in after her." I blinked away the memory of her pink hoodie drifting down stream, her screams muted by the water engulfing her. "I was powerless to help then ... and I feel just as powerless now."

I picked up a random rock and chucked it as hard as I could toward the horizon. "I think about them all the time. It used to be thinking about our lazy days before the world crashed into us. Now, all I think about are those photos the Wizard sent, and the scars striping Didi's face. I wonder how she earned them, if it happened right away or slowly over time. Is Sylvan doing the same thing to Daisy right now? Will he do the same to you?"

Thea tilted her head up, her attention boring into me hard enough I could feel it.

"For the record, I wouldn't change my choices, but I can't deny that all of this is my fault. All of it. No matter which way I go, it's always in the wrong direction." I swallowed against the knot clogging my throat, ignoring the way my eyes burned. Regret and longing suffocated me. Even with my arm wrapped around her, the woman sitting beside me felt impossibly out of reach. "I'm terrified my next choice will be one we never come back from."

Not addressing my fears, she said quietly, "I always wanted sisters. Joking with Toto feels like what I imagined having a sister would be like. I was always alone. Not alone-alone, but I was the only child free to run the halls. You spend enough time on your own, you get good at it. I suppose that was how I kept my sanity while locked in the tower."

I tilted my gaze down to her. The warm rays of the setting sun made her hair glow, and the more understated golden tones of her eyes blazed. "How do you do that?"

She leaned back on her hands, putting enough space between us that I could breathe again. "Do what?"

"Roll with the hits like they don't take a piece of you every time?"

"They do. I'm just really adept at hiding the holes ..." She closed her eyes, squinting like they were holding back a sea of emotion. "... usually. My track record lately hasn't been quite as good."

I angled her face to mine. There were a lot of things I could take, but I couldn't stand her pulling away from me. Not any longer.

"I'm sorry you felt alone." I tried not to think of how many times I'd seen this woman cry. "I'm sorry I didn't choose you. I'm sorry I left." Fuck, I was sorry for so much. My regret was so thick I could taste its sour residue on the back of my tongue.

"Don't be." Thea played with the grass, picking a stray dandelion and popping the head into the air with her thumb. The discarded flower landed at my feet. I picked it up, crushing the yellow petals between my fingers. This was the most appropriate symbol of our relationship I'd ever seen. Most people made wishes on dandelions, while Thea chose to behead them.

"Gigi didn't give you a choice." She said all the right words, even though there was genuine hurt painted across her face—hurt I placed there and tears I was responsible for.

"It killed me leaving you. That was the longest elevator ride of my life."

Thea pinched her mouth shut, curling her arms around her knees and tucking into a tight ball. Using the heel of her hand, she pushed away the moisture gathering at the corners of her eyes. For a second, I wasn't sitting on this hilltop, I was chained to a tile floor, watching her weep in this exact position without anyone to soothe her pain.

I brushed the back of my hand down her cheek. "When we were locked away on that ship, seeing you was both my torture and what gave me strength. You were ... *are* my entire world."

Thea dropped her face to her knees like she'd lost the strength to bear the weight of her pain. She turned her cheek so that she was still looking at me, a barely perceptible tremor making her lip quiver.

At least she wasn't shutting me out. That was something.

"I want to pull you into my lap, kiss away your tears, and promise that whatever happens next, you'll be safe." If only everyone I wanted to protect didn't need protection because I failed them to begin with. The way I failed her. "Thea, I don't know how to make this right ..."

It hurt. My chest felt like if it wound any tighter, it might implode.

"You don't." She lifted her head. Her usual strength gathered firmly back in place. I hated that it looked like some of her warmth had iced over. It reminded me of the way Nick was never the same after Eastin's. "We can't change the past. Instead, we focus on what we can change."

Now she sounded like Nick, too.

"Like getting your sister out of La Chasse alive. What happened to me was awful. I scream in my sleep remembering King pin me to the wall. When I close my eyes, I see Crowe going limp in my arms. I can still feel the imprint of my cuffs on my skin. Just the thought of going underwater makes me want to vomit. It's all so overwhelming. Which is *why* I need to do something good. I can't stay here afraid of what's been done to me when there are people suffering the same or worse. Not when I know there's something I can do about it. Saving Daisy will give me back a piece of myself they tried to take away."

I hated how much sense that made. Thea had never been one to run away. She met her fears head-on. When they beat her down, she jumped back up swinging. It was who she was.

"I need it, Danny. I won't feel like myself again until I do."

"La Chasse." I heaved a heavy sigh. "I really don't want to think about people hunting you through some dark abandoned building. There are *so many* ways this plan can go wrong, Thea. So many." I couldn't stop imagining them all. What if they decided to test the merchandise before auction or realized they had more foxes than hunters and eliminated the excess? What if one of us didn't win her in the bidding war? Fuck, what if she was recognized and she ended up back in the very cell we'd just rescued her from?

I couldn't breathe. It felt like I hadn't breathed in weeks, the noose on my neck growing tighter and tighter. Eventually, I would snap beneath it. "I can't … I just can't, Thea … I love you too much."

It was weak, but I couldn't lift my eyes to see her reaction. It wasn't the first time I'd told her, except for some reason, this time felt so raw. My heart couldn't handle another rejection.

Thea's fingers unfurled against my jaw, and she cradled my face like I was the precious one between us. She didn't say anything. She didn't need to.

The setting sun winked out along the horizon, casting the valley in shadow. Small fireflies lifted one by one into the air, making the remains of the field glow like starlight. Somehow, in the wake of all the destruction and death that happened here, this beauty still remained.

"Well then, I guess you'll have to be sure to be the one who catches me." Thea sprang to her feet, running down the hill toward the forgotten flowers.

— 16 —
DANNY

T hea ran like there was fire licking at her heels. What I loved most about her was how easily she always snapped back. Sunken in misery to shrieking with joy in the blink of an eye.

I gave her a solid ten seconds, curious as to where she would go in the dark with nothing but rolling hills to hide her. She might make it to the woods if she went far enough beyond the flowers. I didn't really see her as the type to go traipsing at night through unknown terrain. Something told me she had very little experience with the outdoors.

I bounded down the hill. "Run all you like, Princess. There's nowhere for you to hide."

Her laughter floated back in answer. Fuck me, it was good to hear light in her voice again. It made some of my own shadows fall away. All at once, her silhouette disappeared. The purple expanse swallowed up her form until there was nothing there but the stars peppering the sky.

"Thea?" I picked up my speed. Charred stalks of plants and the remnants of dried seed pods crushed beneath my feet. She really was gone. I tried to keep the panic from my voice as I called again, "Thea!" What if she'd been spotted leaving the palace, and someone had been waiting for a moment when she was alone to snatch her?

How could I have been so fucking foolish?

"This isn't funny. Answer me!"

Cresting the place where I'd last seen her, I scanned far into the valley below. Even if Nick's massive black hoodie helped her to hide, I should have been able to see her from this vantage point. I turned, looking behind me and then back to the vista. Nothing.

"Thea!"

I took a step forward. The loose earth shifted beneath my soles. I was so focused on finding her in the distance that I hadn't looked down to see the irrigation trench at my feet. As I wobbled, a hand wrapped around my ankle, yanking hard on my supporting leg.

Before I could process what was happening, I was flat on my back. Thea leapt from her position pressed against the side of the dried-up ditch. Rolling with surprising ease, she straddled my hips and pinned my hands on either side of my head.

"Oops. Looks like I caught you instead." Soot darkened her cheeks from where she'd laid flat to the ground. Moonlight splayed across her nose and lips, while the rest of her face was shadowed by the hood pulled over her head. She grinned with wicked glee, an expression I hadn't seen on her in a long time. Maybe I'd never seen this playful side of her really unleashed.

"You're full of surprises, Firecracker." I lightly tested her hold on my wrists. She was putting all of her weight on them. The stones of the ditch were rough beneath the exposed skin of my forearms. I could easily throw her off. For now, I'd let her believe she had the upper hand. "What will you do? The moment you release my hands, I'm going to pounce. You have to know that."

"Did you know that in a pride, the lionesses are actually the hunters?" She leaned in, running her nose along my jaw, her hips rolling against mine. If I wasn't already hard, the throaty moan she made would do it.

"I did." In a low rumble, I added, "I'll give you five seconds to make your move."

She tilted her head to the side. The pink tip of her tongue swiped over her lower lip. "Then what?"

"Five ..." I rocked my hips counter to the way she was rolling. "Wait and find out. Four ..."

Thea wrapped her ankle around the inside of my leg. "Way out here, with no one to hear you roar. Where's the fun in that?"

"You'll hear me. That's all that matters. Three."

Placing her foot flat on the ground, she leapt over me with a victorious laugh. I caught her hips mid-stride and twisted her to the ground. She squirmed beneath me. Unlike when she was on top, there was no getting free of my hold.

Thea jerked her knee up. I caught it with my thigh, repositioning my hips so that I could pin her legs, too. "You need to get a new move. You're becoming predictable."

Her body relaxed with a delightful growl of defeat.

"Giving up already?" Narrowing my eyes in suspicion, I added, "How very unlike you."

Her breaths quickened, looking up at where her hands were securely pinned above her head. I transferred her wrists to one hand and drew the zipper down the center of her sweatshirt. One inch at a time, moon brightened skin glowed against the black fabric. Her breasts were gloriously full and heaving. A pink flush painted its way across her skin. She was the personification of every desire I'd ever had.

I pressed a kiss to the center of her sternum and breathed her deep. Then I waited to see if any of this incited panic. When she didn't protest, I circled my tongue around the tightening lines of her nipple and blew a stream of air over the tip. The evening was already crisp, but I doubted the goosebumps peppering her skin had anything to do with the temperature. I pulled the chilled flesh into my mouth and sucked hard. Fuck if I wasn't rewarded by her entire body bowing against my hold.

I let the tenor of my voice vibrate against the soft flesh of her breast. "I'm going to release your hands, and you will keep them there."

"Will I?"

"Oh, Princess." I ran my nose along the under-swell of her breast. "You will, or when I make you scream, it won't be with release."

Thea chuckled, drawing my gaze up. There was no way she was going to follow that command. None. She raked her lower lip through her teeth, eyes sparkling with mischief.

Deciding that the only one who should be biting that lip was me, I surged against her hard enough the air in her lungs pushed out in a throaty exhale. I drew her lip back until it was firmly planted between mine. She still tasted like the chocolate and wine Crowe was feeding her before our call with Maddox.

It had been too fucking long. Thirty-eight days apart, and I'd only kissed her that one unrestrained time. In the week since her rescue, Thea's pain had pushed me away, winding my nerves into this aching ball of frustration. I needed her, wanted her in every way she could bend. To taste and fuck and hold ... and love. I wanted her to let me back in so badly. We'd barely had our chance. Now, with her sweetness on my tongue, I didn't ever want to stop. Was it possible to want to completely consume someone—to devour them so absolutely that there would never be a way to separate us again?

Unwilling to break our connection for even a second, I gripped the back of her neck and used the other against her spine to lift her into my lap. Her legs bracketed my hips. The small stones and debris ground against my knees as we rocked together. The hoodie fell from her shoulders, landing discarded on the ground.

"Take my shirt off," I demanded. What felt like miles of lush skin rocked against me. I slid my hand beneath the waistband to grab her ass. The muscle flexed against my palm in a silent plea for more.

"Wait, no. First, your—" I leaned back. Thea shook her hair from her shoulders, arching against the hand bracing her neck and beaming a seductive smile back at me. What I was going to say flew from my mind, leaving only this vision in my lap.

She was stunning.

Thea ground her hips in a slow circle. The pressure against my cock sent a jolt of pleasure intense enough to make me question divinity. Framed by moonlight, she looked ethereal.

My girl coasted her hands over my shoulders. I'd fantasized about the feel of her countless times over the past weeks. My imagination didn't once do her justice. She fumbled with the buttons of my shirt until she made it halfway and grew too impatient to finish the rest. Thea gripped the collar, dragging it over my shoulders and sinking her mouth to my neck. Her warm tongue licked up the column of my throat. I swallowed hard against the warm sensation trailing behind it. I loved feeling my muscles move against her lips.

Her breasts pressed against my chest. I practically moaned at the feel of her hardened nipples dragging against me. They burned like the slice of a knife. Thea pushed harder at the shirt. It rolled into a thick band across my back and arms. The tailored cut was tight, bunching at my elbows and restricting my movement. The taut fabric pulled my hands from her waist, leaving them woefully empty.

"Thea?" I flexed against the silk. It dug into my biceps, and the top button jammed into my chest, not budging at all. Of course, I had to have a designer brand that used fancy stitching with reinforced buttons and seams.

"Now, what were those instructions again ..." Walking her fingers along the bunched fabric pinning my arms, Thea whispered into my ear, "You *will* keep them there."

The minx grinned, fucking grinned, and ran her tongue along her teeth. The things I would do to that mouth once I was free.

"You did this on purpose," I said in disbelief. I fell hook, line, and sinker right into being restrained by my own damn shirt.

"Maybe ..."

A shiver ran down my spine, and my cock pulsed in response. I'd never seen her look so predatory. Whatever it was, it triggered something brutal within me.

I tried to reach the center row of buttons. I only need one to pop. That's all it would take to get the leverage I needed—then Thea wouldn't know what hit her.

-17-
THEA

I couldn't tell which idea I liked more, fucking Danny or leaving him pinned out here in the dark. For as bitter as I was, none of what had been done to me was his fault. Most days, I had so much fear clutching at my heart that I had to remind myself it was still beating. I knew it was wrong, but it helped to have somewhere to focus all of that anger, and Danny's guilt so willingly held a target for me.

In some ways, it was easier when I was a prisoner on the Farm without any love or kindness. When you aren't given anything, there isn't anything to take away either. Truthfully, now that I knew what life could be like, I was terrified of having it all torn from me again. Seeing Danny on that balcony brought all of those fears into focus.

"This won't hold me forever."

Lust and wrath blazed in Danny's eyes, churning into a dangerous mixture. The full moon highlighted the toned curve of his shoulders. The straining fabric was stark against the black backdrop of the valley. He really hadn't expected me to pin him like that. It was embarrassingly easy to do. One simple kiss, and he was mine. I knew his tailored shirt would hold him; I just didn't expect it to work this well.

The question was, what to do with my new toy?

I ran my fingers through his immaculately styled hair, teasing it this way and that until it was wildly mussed.

"Princess ..." he growled the word through gritted teeth. Could it be I'd finally pushed this man as far as he could go? Maybe. Only one way to find out.

"Yes, Kitten?" I batted my lashes innocently and palmed the hard line of his dick through his pants. Involuntarily, his hips bucked into the touch, and he made a deliciously throaty groan. I snatched my hand back and stroked my lower lip with the same finger that had just grazed the full length of his cock. "Was there something you wanted?"

"Other than my hand cracking over your perfectly round ass?" Heat pulsed in a current through my body at simply the promise of that threat. He leaned in, dragging his nose over my collar. "You'd love that, wouldn't you? I bet if I sank my hand between your legs, your pussy would be weeping for me."

"Weeping? Hardly." Lies. All lies.

I popped the top button of his slacks, barely having to do much to the zipper. His cock pressed at the fly hard enough it slipped free all on its own. I tilted my head to the side and watched as it twitched in earnest. The sheer size alone was enough to make me smile. In fact, I wasn't sure which was the bigger dick, him or the thing pressing against my stomach.

I held up my palm to him. "Lick."

Danny blinked at me a few times before dropping his eyes to my hand and running his tongue from the base of my palm to the tip of my middle finger.

I felt every second of that touch between my legs. It most certainly wasn't making me picture all of the places that tongue had been.

I pressed close, bringing my lips to his ear. The hardened points of my nipples brushed just above the band of bunched fabric and sent a frisson of excitement down my spine. "Good boy."

"Pr—" Whatever warning he was about to snap was cut off the second I made contact with his cock. The smooth surface glided easily over my palm. He was warm and thick in my hand. The velvet of his shaft felt like coming home. Danny was the first man I'd ever fucked that saw me as an equal and made me feel like I was more than an object. It was impossible not to remember that feeling every time I touched him. Dragging my nails to the base of his dick, I fisted his cock and gave him a solid tug.

"Fucking hell, Thea." Danny's head dropped to my shoulder. He blew out a massive exhale that warmed my collar. The veins along his neck strained with barely contained control. I watched his rapidly firing pulse pound against the surface as a cavalcade of heated memories scattered all plans for revenge.

Danny and I connected in a way I never had with the others. He understood the harsher part of me, the side that needed a sparring partner. He'd never shied from that facet of my personality. It fed our passion, guaranteeing that whenever we came together, it was always explosive. I loved it. Riding the edge of that energy was addicting. It'd been too long since I'd tasted it.

Then, there had been those long nights after Westin's ship. When I'd only truly felt safe in his arms, knowing that I'd never need to hide from him because he already knew my secrets ... my shame ... and my pain. Danny knew how I felt and what I needed before I did. There was a freedom in giving myself over to his control.

"Release me, and I promise not to go too hard on you."

Then again, sometimes, he was an arrogant ass who needed to be reminded of how far that control actually extended.

"Too hard on me?" I circled my arms around his neck so that my breasts were only inches from his face. "Who says I won't be the one going hard on you? Maybe you should be begging me for mercy."

I silenced his disbelieving laugh with what should have been a quick kiss but turned entirely too indulgent. My thumb smoothed the bead of pre-cum around his crown until he was moaning into our kiss and thrusting against my hand.

Before I could give in to the temptation, I stood, grabbing Nick's hoodie as I went. I brought my thumb to my mouth, licking it clean. Danny groaned.

I laughed, zipping the sweatshirt closed and slowly stepping backwards.

"Thea, don't you dare." Danny raised high on his knees, cock jutting hard and abandoned before him. His muscles rippled with the effort to break free. Fuck, he really was hot enough to make my body sweat just thinking of all that power thrusting into me.

"This has been super fun—"

"I swear to Oz, Thea, you better not leave." Danny pushed abruptly to his feet, wobbling without his arms to help him balance. "I can still catch you like this." He lunged forward. However, his pants, already loose at his waist, no longer had anything holding them in place. They dropped to his ankles.

I watched in comical slow motion as he toppled forward, hitting the ground with a loud, "Ooof."

Unfortunately, his tumble loosened the top button. The shirt hung limply around his elbows. He lifted his head. The moment our eyes connected, his expression darkened. His nostrils flared and the curl of his lip made him look remarkably like a bull moments before charging.

"Something tells me I should be running," I said with a squeal and took off at a full sprint toward The Villa.

In all honesty, I really hadn't thought this plan through. It wasn't long before his shouts and thundering footsteps started gaining on me. I swerved between the rows of burned flowers, aiming for the sliding patio doors.

Danny lunged forward, swiping at me close enough his fingertips brushed my waist. I vaulted the patio couch. With both hands, I tossed the side table behind me. The telltale crash and subsequent torrent of cursing told me that I'd correctly thrown it into his path.

Flinging the door open, I slid into the hallway leading to the living room. I pushed a table into the entryway, then turned, running face-first into a solid wall of muscle.

"What the—" Crowe's amused eyes scanned my frantic expression.

"Hold her," Danny roared, rounding the corner only seconds after me.

"Why are you filthy?" Crowe said, titling his head at Danny. He laughed, "Darling Thea, what did you do?"

"Nothing." I spun around him, pushing Crowe at Danny. "Save me."

"Nothing?" Danny dodged right, reaching around Crowe and barely missing my arm. "Well, that *nothing* is going to make your ass glow bright enough to be seen from space." When Crowe blocked his path again, his feral gleam grew more sinister. "Two words, Crowe: Eiffel Tower. I'll even let you pick."

Crowe whistled, spinning back to face me. "Oh, Pretty Girl, you should have been running." The words Danny said registered just a bit too slowly. Crowe grabbed me around the waist, throwing me over his shoulder like I weighed nothing.

I screeched in surprise, fruitlessly kicking my feet. "Put me down, Crowe. You shouldn't be carrying me. No heavy lifting, remember."

"Your room or mine?" Crowe asked, ignoring my protests and turning toward the bedrooms.

Danny slowly stalked closer. "Mine's got restraints."

Crowe palmed my ass, "Yeah, but mine's got toys."

"Toys and restraints. What were you two doing while I was locked away in the tower?" I said with completely faked outrage.

Danny took my chin in his hand, tipping me up until I met the piercing emerald of his eyes. "Preparing."

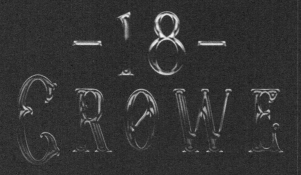

-18-
CROWE

I tossed Thea into the middle of my bed, ignoring the sharp burn at the center of my chest and hating that my muscles ached from carrying her the small distance to the bedroom. Technically, I had two weeks until I was cleared for strenuous activity, but Gabby also said that light exercise was encouraged. I could keep my part light. Maybe she'd let this count as my PT for the day.

Danny closed the door behind us with a velvet box tucked behind his back. Thea eyed it wearily, slowly backing away. With her lower lip firmly planted between her teeth, her eyes flashed at the door then back to me. I could see the wheels in her brain turning. She had to know she could never roll off the bed fast enough to make it to the door. Even if Thea could dodge Danny, it wouldn't matter. I'd grab her and pin her to the headboard before those dainty little feet hit tile.

Thea grabbed one of the pillows in both hands, hurling it at me with surprising force. The impact was a direct hit to the side of my face. Laughter rang out as she was sure she'd gotten the upper hand. With a second swing to my stomach, she was rolling to the edge. No wonder Nick called her Trouble.

"Nope." I snatched the pillow, tossing it out of reach. "You're done running." I loved the fire in her spirit. Part of me wanted to let her bolt so that I could have the pleasure of tracking her down, but it was the impatient part of me that latched onto her ankle and hauled her back into the middle of the bed.

"If you two are done with the pillow fights ..." Thea tracked Danny, ever watchful as he circled the bed until he was standing at her head. "I had a lot of time to consider this."

"Consider what?" Her voice was rough. She reached over her head, tugging on his shirt until he bent low to kiss her. Thea's fingers tangled into his hair and took from him despite the way he towered over her.

I hooked the elastic of her leggings and peeled them off. She was so focused on him I wasn't even sure she noticed.

Danny balanced the velvet box on her breast. "Open it."

Thea rolled over, pushing up until she was kneeling before the long case. "Is it another necklace? Gigi took the last one."

"No," Danny's grin grew with an amused exhale. "Nothing like that, although that can definitely be arranged. I liked seeing you in something of mine."

"It's a good idea. That necklace saved her life more than once," I added.

Carefully, she opened the box. Thea glanced at me over her shoulder. A pair of long silk scarves laid carefully folded within. They were sewn in two tones, one side black and the other side a deep crimson. They looked like something he'd have picked, expensive. It was always about the drama with Danny. He couldn't settle for something simple when there was the possibility of making her jaw drop exactly as it was right now.

Thea's eyes were wide as he gingerly lifted one long strip of fabric from the box. Danny rubbed it against her cheek before laying it in her palms.

"It's so soft." She ran it over and over through her fingers.

Danny stroked a long line down her neck until he reached the zipper pull of the hoodie. The sound of the zipper descending was loud in the silent room, ratcheting up my anticipation. He pushed the worn fabric over her shoulders. It slipped from her arms, leaving her beautifully bare.

The landscape of Thea's skin caught the light from the side table. It accentuated each dip and hollow of her stomach. I was mesmerized, watching it shift with every shallow breath she took. My blood burned hot with the need to touch her.

I wasn't the only one. Danny went straight for her chest, holding her firmly in place with one hand around the back of her neck and palming her breast with the other. He pressed a rough kiss to her throat, hard enough she would have tipped backwards if it wasn't for the grip he kept on her. Thea's breathy moan made my cock twitch painfully against the seam of my jeans.

Thea pushed with both hands against his shoulders, even though her body bent into his movements. When he didn't budge, her fingers slipped into his hair and pulled his lips up to hers. They fought and played, giving and taking in equal measure. It made me think of the footage from the bank Orin had recorded of Danny tossing her around the vault. If the way she came on a scream was any indication, Thea loved every second of it.

The lattice of red scars striping her back were bright against her pale skin. The memory of that night reeled me to her like a fish on a string. Shedding my clothing as I went, I climbed onto the bed behind her and kissed where the topmost mark curled over her shoulder. Tracing the scar with my index finger, her spine rolled beautifully in tandem with my caress. It felt like a lifetime since I'd seen these up close and in full light.

"Sensitive?" I asked in a low whisper while my hand explored the map work of her lower back. I hadn't been able to stop touching her since the day she walked back into this apartment with her head still attached. There was nothing like watching the love of your life's head roll to give you a newfound appreciation for the here and now.

Thea tightened her lips into a thin line, "Mmm-hmm."

Danny's eyes briefly met mine over her shoulder. I nodded in response to the question he wasn't asking.

"Give me your hands."

Hesitantly, she extended her arms to him, sitting back on her heels and leaning against me for support.

Danny lowered to one knee so that he was at eye level with her. "I'm going to need you to tell me if this is too much. Be honest."

Thea blinked slowly, watching the way his thumbs smoothed over the pulse points in her wrists. When Danny told me about his plans to buy new restraints, even soft and easily escapable ones, I'd been reluctant. Tying her up in Nick's shirt had been one thing. Was it hot? Certainly, but a lot has happened since then. None of us had been able to get her to talk about it, not in any significant detail. There was the very real possibility that this could be the thing that triggered her, or maybe, giving over control to us could be exactly the thing she needed to feel comfortable enough to open up.

"I'll be fine, just don't go strapping me to any guillotines." Her lips lifted into a smile, in total contrast to the visible shiver coursing its way down her arms.

"You can trust me, Thea." Danny placed a kiss on each of her palms, then repeated the action against the faint pink line circling her wrists.

Those were new. At some point between Head Shots and freeing her, she'd been cuffed for long enough to permanently mark her.

"You will always be safe with me even when the world around us is burning. I'm going to prove to you just how much, and I will keep proving it until the end of your days." Pressing her palms together, he wound the ribbon around and between her wrists. The thick fabric sat flush to her skin, finishing with a big bow.

She was the most beautiful little present I'd ever seen.

Thea gave them a tug, twisting and pulling against their hold. The ribbon stayed put, exactly as it should.

"Still good?" he asked, coasting his hands up and down her arms. "This will never grow tighter than it is right now. If at any time it gets too intense, you can always tug on the end, and the tie will instantly release."

She nodded. "It won't come to that."

"All the same, I wanted you to have an escape you could control."

Thea swallowed hard, looking down at the pretty black and red bow. The man might be arrogant at times, but Danny knew her on a level I didn't think the rest of us had quite tapped.

She circled her arms around his neck. All the playful fight coiled around them evaporated, exposing the raw love buried deep beneath the bravado. It was immensely intimate to watch. My heart swelled from simply being near it. I hated that he'd been shouldering the entirety of the blame. We'd all taken a turn down that particular road, but Danny refused to let it go. Even more than that, I hated seeing Thea scared and hurt enough to push him away.

All of us together was the way it should be. We were always destined to be together. As they gazed at each other for several long moments, I could see the love and trust were slotting back into their rightful places. Part of me thought it might be better to leave than feel like an intruder in my own bed.

Then Thea leaned her head back against my shoulder and gazed up at me with those big, beautiful eyes. "Kiss me."

"Now who's demanding kisses?" I teased, not that I could ever deny this woman. Cupping her jaw, I directed her mouth to mine. The slow dance of our kiss moved in tandem with the roll of her body. I sat back on my heels, pulling her into my lap with her legs framing my own.

Danny stepped back, running his thumb over his lower lip while scanning her very naked body. "Spread her. I want to see that needy cunt shine."

"With pleasure." Running my hands down her arms, I lifted them until I could loop her bound wrists behind my neck. She arched beautifully. The angle forced her high on her knees, her breasts lifting with increasingly rapid breaths. I rose with her, shifting my legs out and forcing hers apart.

"Fucking gorgeous. Wider."

Pressing a kiss beneath her ear, I parted her further. "Still with us, Darling?"

Her body rocked with a whimper, aching and unable to do a damn thing about it. "Don't just stand there, Danny, get over here and touch me."

"I guess that's a yes. I don't know why I'm surprised."

Danny's eyes flared wider for a second, then his smirk took over. "Be careful what you wish for."

Running a slow pattern along her hip with my finger, I nodded at the dresser beside him. "Top drawer, blue satin bag."

He pulled open the drawer and laughed a choked mix of surprise and amusement. "Oh, sweet Ozma."

"What?" Thea lifted as far as she could trying to see in the drawer, though I knew the position I kept her in wouldn't let her see any of the surprises I'd been amassing. Boredom and anxiety were not a good combination for someone like me.

Danny lifted the bag. "This? It's so small." The blue satin shined in the light, swinging from his finger.

"Trust me. What you're holding there is the Maserati of clitoral stimulators."

"The Maserati of what?" Thea tried to twist to look at me, but with her arms locked behind my neck.

"Is that a problem?" There was so much amusement in Danny's voice. He knew, just like I did, that Thea never backed down from a challenge. It didn't matter what he laid before her; she'd take it. "I thought you wanted me to touch you."

He pulled the sleek black vibrator from the bag, slipping the ring over his thumb so that the suction part of the device was pointing out. Clicking the button, it purred to life.

Every muscle in Thea's body tensed.

"Breathe," I whispered into her ear. On command, she let out the breath she was holding. "Have you ever used anything like this before?" I dipped my hand between her legs, smiling at how incredibly wet she was.

"No. I've neve—" Danny palmed her breast, centering the suction over her nipple. "Oh my ... Fuck."

Thea's arms instantly pulled at my neck.

"Do you like that, Firecracker?"

I dipped my middle finger as deep as I could. She clamped down on my hand, her legs pushing against mine. Her ass rocked against my cock in a fucking magical undulation. Indulging in the feel of her riding my shaft, I tilted my hips into her movements. Heat radiated from her pussy, hot and wet and the most tempting thing I'd ever touched. Unable to stop myself, I slid a second finger beside the first, drawing them back in a slow thrust. Her body seized around me, already quivering. The way she was rolling would choke the life from my dick, the same way she was trying to strangle my fingers.

"Feel the way that tiny device pulses and tugs." I held out my hand for the remote, and Danny placed it into my palm. I scrolled through the settings. "I can adjust suction, airflow, and vibration in a dozen different levels."

Thea made a tiny mewling sound, doing her best to hold back the open moan trying to force its way free.

Using my thumb, I rubbed her clit in tight circles. "Just imagine what that's going to feel like right here."

She pulsed around my fingers, clamping tighter with each pass Danny made. I pulled my hand away just as I felt her body tipping into orgasm, halting what I'm sure was a very wanted release.

Thea growled in frustration, tugging again at my neck. "Crowe, you edging bastard."

"It'll be worth it. I promise." I grinned, already knowing what I would do with the arousal coating my fingers. "Danny looks like he could use a treat. What do you think, Beautiful? Should we give him a taste?" I drew a circle around her nipple, making the tip gleam in the light like a beacon.

"Who could resist a temptation like that?" Danny leaned in, closing his mouth around her breast at the same time I increased the settings on the vibrator.

He groaned at the taste, or maybe at the way she moaned so perfectly for him. I was willing to bet that he could get her to completion just with the attention he was giving her tits. That would be a hell of a thing to watch ... except there were so many other fun things I could be doing.

I circled my arm around her hip and replaced the fingers I'd denied her. Thea sighed as they sank home, but before she could fully relax, I added a third. "You tell me when I've hit your limit."

Thea sucked in a breath that sounded like my name. Her entire body trembled, riding the edge exactly where I wanted her. Thea's quick little breaths rose her chest, showing off the way her flushed skin shone. With one word, I could tip her. I knew I could. It was killing me holding back, especially when I knew exactly how sweet she'd sound when I thrust into her—how tight and hot she'd grip me. It was a beautiful torment.

"What was that, Gorgeous? I don't think I heard you." I curled my fingers back and stroked the spot I knew would make her scream.

Danny licked his lips like he'd just savored a priceless dish. "I'm pretty sure she said, 'more.'" He hovered a kiss over her lips. Thea tilted up, trying to claim the kiss he was holding out of reach. Backing up, he laughed under his breath. "Is that what you want, Firecracker?"

She swallowed, trying to speak but losing the words as soon as they came when Danny dropped the toy between her legs.

The cry that she gave was pure sin. I fucking loved it.

"She doesn't come until I say," Danny said, removing the vibrator for a second time. My smile spread against her neck. The muscles of her back loosened then tightened, moving in time with the way she fought the urge to clamp down around my hand.

"Fucking evil bastard," she panted, staring Danny down. I knew he loved pushing her limits. Hell, we all did. The moment those scarves came out, she had to know this was where we were headed.

"Oh, I'm the evil one?" Danny palmed her breast, rolling the tip between his fingers while I slowly continued pumping my hand. Her legs shook, giving out so that I was completely supporting her weight.

"At least I'm not teasing you until your dick feels like it's about to explode, then leaving you painfully hard and pinned in the middle of a burned-out field."

"Savage, Pretty Girl, absolutely savage." I laughed, rocking our bodies together with each exhale. The image was too fucking good. Of course she played him. He probably chased her all the way out there, and she flipped the tables on him. It did explain why he looked rabid when he rounded the corner after her.

"I hate you both."

I kissed the base of her neck. "No, you don't. You love every tortuous second."

"You're so wet I can feel it slicking against your thighs." Danny dropped his pants to the ground, pulling Thea in for a slow kiss. "And I have a bargain to deliver on."

—19—
CROWE

"**F**uck yes." My heart rate spiked with simply the mention of an Eiffel Tower.

I don't know why I've been looking forward to this so much. It's not like we haven't tapped her together already, but for some reason, this checked a box on my fantasy Thea sex bucket list.

Danny lifted her arms, freeing her from the hold. She sighed, flexing her fingers and rolling her shoulders. Restrained in that position for as long as she was probably made her sore, even if it did place every beautiful inch of her body on display.

Pulling on the bow to release her hands, he added, "Heads or tails, Crowe?"

"I'm good here." I pulled my fingers free, slapping her ass hard for good measure and tugging her to make space for Danny to climb up with us.

"Okay, but don't high-five," she said, looking at me over her shoulder.

Oh, I definitely was going in for a high five. I couldn't keep from grinning like a goon, especially when she rolled her eyes.

Danny handed off the vibrator to me, pushing her onto all fours between us. He ran his thumb over her lower lip. "I had dreams about how gorgeous these lips look when well used. How close are you?"

"Not as close as I was," she said with a bitter laugh.

I stroked the length of her spine lightly, barely touching her. The corresponding shiver told me everything I needed to know. She was primed, so overstimulated that a light breeze could probably bring her to climax.

Reaching forward, Thea gripped his cock at the base, giving it a long lick that made my balls tighten with envy. I knew just what that felt like. She worked her tongue around his crown, and I could practically feel the warmth of her mouth on me. Thea sucked cock like she went at everything, with zero hesitancy and holding nothing back.

Danny kicked his head to the ceiling and gave a long sigh. "Fuck, that's good."

Thea wrapped her lips around the tip, sucking lightly in a way that was designed to tempt a man into insanity.

Palming the back of her head, Danny pulled her onto him until she bottomed out against the fist Thea had wrapped around his dick. Of course he couldn't simply let her tease him. Everything between them was always about the balance of power, and he just had to take control.

From the way his eyes flared, he was just as surprised as I was when she didn't put up any resistance. She didn't buck or fight. Thea barely gagged. Instead, the muscles of her neck flexed with a swallow. Leaning into the motion, her fingers dug into his hips, taking him even deeper.

"That's my girl."

I nodded with appreciation. "Yeah, Thea doesn't understand the concept of gag reflex. She just demands more."

Danny's eyes locked with hers in an unspoken war.

Thea pulled back with a hum before swallowing him down again and again. A light tear leaked from her watery eyes, and he wiped it away with his thumb. "Such a good fucking girl."

I looked down at my hand, where I'd been absentmindedly clutching the vibrator. How long had I been mesmerized by this scene? I slipped the toy over my index finger and changed the settings, making the frequency high and the suction hard. Thea had no idea what was coming for her when I pressed it to her clit. Shifting it until it locked into the perfect hold, and she moaned loudly around his dick.

She backed off, dropping her head to the mattress and pressing into me. Her voice broke as she tried to gulp down air; all power plays now completely forgotten. "Crowe, holy fuck. That's—" The muscles and tendons along her back tightened, her mouth opening on a silent scream.

128

Danny circled her jaw, lifting her attention back to him. "Not yet, Princess."

"Please," she said in a barely audible breath. Thea's body shook beneath the pressure of holding off what must be a tidal wave of sensation.

Danny's eyes met mine, knowing I'd held back for as long as I could. Not an easy feat considering she was rocking the slick heat of her pussy up and down my cock. Lining the head of my dick up, I paused, enjoying the sensation of her needy cunt trying to push back against me. The vibration of the stimulator buzzed through her and into me. When she finally detonated, it was going to be glorious.

I dug my grip into her hip, probably bruising as I leveraged all of my pent-up need. My pelvis crashed into her round ass with one devastating thrust. The heat was intense, all of the blood in her body must be centered around this one magical part. She pulsed around me with increasing intensity, gripping me hard enough my vision blurred.

"Sweet, fucking Ozma," I cursed, folding over her to keep the two of us from collapsing all together. "You feel like heaven, Beautiful Girl."

Thea was barely breathing. If she was feeling anything close to what I was feeling, then I understood the inability to draw in air. My heart was pounding against her back, or it would be if I had a pulse anywhere but in my dick right now.

The connection was everything I'd been missing. Whether Thea realized it or not, she'd held all of us at a distance, and we were a group of needy bastards. I especially had always been a physical creature. I needed that connection to feel whole. I loved her enough to be patient, but inside I was slowly crumbling.

"We come together. Do you understand?" Danny lightly massaged her jaw with his thumbs before gently sliding back between her lips. Every muscle in her body tensed the moment he hit the back of her throat.

Feeling her speared between us was everything we'd been missing. Electricity passed through us like a live current. Her moans blended with ours, becoming something primal. One hard stroke after another made her scream until her voice went raw. Thea's hand lifted to Danny's stomach, and her nails dug in hard enough to leave red tracks across his flexing muscles. She pushed against him to counter each of my thrusts. As a result, they hit harder and slid her farther onto Danny.

Thea was trembling hard enough to make my own thighs shake. The only thing keeping her upright was my grip on her hips. "She's at her limit," I said between heavy pants.

Danny circled her throat with a gentle squeeze. "Now, Thea. Take what you need."

The words had barely passed his lips when Thea's pussy tightened like a trap. All the pent-up aggression and emotion flooded from her, taking Danny along for the ride. He pulled her as far onto him as he could go, holding her there while groaning out his release. I slowed my pace just enough to ensure she didn't completely choke.

When he finished, Danny relaxed his grip and fell back onto the pillow, panting hard while staring at the ceiling. "Fuck, I missed this."

I pulled the pillow out from under him and shoved it under her hips. She was trembling all over, tiny waves of aftershocks making her tighten over and over around my dick — but I wasn't done.

I never said I wasn't a selfish bastard.

Hands on her waist, the angle completely changed. I ground deep against her, so fucking deep. With her senses already maxed out, it wasn't long before I was pounding her through a second climax, which then spiraled into a third. The sounds she made were laced in a drugging kind of sin. Our moans mingled together in near harmony. Or at least that's what it felt like my soul was doing.

Wrapping my hand around her throat, I pulled her back into my lap. Thea moved with me, rocking in slow, rhythmic time. Spare curls of auburn hair clung to her neck and chest. I pulled them free so that I could kiss my way from her collar to those tempting lips.

"Crowe," she murmured into the kiss. Her eyes closed with a blissed-out smile.

I pushed my hips harder, forcing her breath to hitch. "You can give me one more, Darling. Let me feel you free fall one last time."

Given how long it'd been since she'd ridden my cock, it was a miracle I'd managed to stave off coming with her for as long as I had. I increased our pace, letting memories of our first time together blend with the feel of her rocking with me. My name repeated as an increasingly desperate plea from her lips. I'd always been weak for her crying my name.

Thea reached behind her, clawing my neck to keep me close. Her spine arched and snaked in tandem with each of my thrusts. I clutched her breast, using it to direct her movements. The view over her shoulder was something else. Sweat slicked down her torso, making her peachy skin glisten. I was lost to the way her stomach flexed and feeling how each bow of her muscles cinched tighter around my dick.

I might have been able to draw things out. Then she opened those gorgeous sea green eyes, and I was hit with the full weight of the love behind them. I was a goner. My mouth closed over hers, and I let my body's instincts take over, driving us harder and harder through my release. I pulsed against her like my dick was trying to pull her apart from the inside out. For several long seconds, the intensity of my orgasm made the room wash free of all color and the sounds of her panting were drowned by the thundering of my heart in my ears.

"Fuck ... that was ..." she panted, sounding farther away than the beauty sitting in my lap.

"I know," I confirmed, already wondering when we could do that again.

"What happened to coming together?" Danny asked. He propped himself on one arm and stole a kiss from her puffy lips. She gave a contented moan that shifted into a chirp of surprise when he hooked her around the waist and pulled her into the pillows with him.

"I've never been good at following directions." I collapsed beside them, nestling her pliant body between us. "Zero regrets."

Danny pushed the hair from her face, using the position to lightly stroke her side. "That was perfection. You're incredible. Sexy and smart, beautiful beyond reason."

"That's true," I confirmed with a slap to her perfectly round ass.

He shook his head in disbelief. "When did I become the lucky one?"

"I don't know that our lives can really classify as lucky," she mumbled into his chest. Lifting her chin, she added, "I missed you. I missed this. I was beginning to feel like one of those massive rubber band balls. Each dark thought stretched over the last. It would only take one cut to make the entire thing snap. It's exhausting, feeling so much all the time. How did you know that was what I needed?"

"I know *you*," he said, kissing her brow. "Sometimes you need to lose control as much as I need to seize it. It's why we fit so well together." He leaned in, drawing her lips to his and not caring at all that our legs were all twined together. "I love you, Thea."

I pressed a kiss to her neck, taking a long, deep breath of her. The sated feeling of completion washed over me. "We both do."

Danny lifted a hand into the air, hovering it over Thea.

"What are you doing?" I asked, completely puzzled. Danny shook his hand in the air, and realization dawned on me. "Oh fuck, we never high-fived."

Thea laughed, curling deeper into Danny's chest.

Damn it. Mentally, I unchecked my bucket list box. No Thea Eiffel Tower. I brought my hand to his, slapping it mournfully. "Next time."

— 20 —
THEA

"On a scale of one to *'Oh fuck, get it out!'* How's that feel?" Maddox took a step back, dropping the high-tech-looking gun into its carrying case.

"Hear that a lot, do you?" Crowe snickered.

Playfully, Maddox turned, punching Crowe in the shoulder and making his coffee spill across his chest. "You're lucky you're recovering from surgery."

"Nick will never make me another cappuccino." Crowe frowned at his now mostly empty coffee cup. He pulled at his soaked shirt, then shrugged and sucked the caffeinated goodness from his fingers. Nick really did make a quality cup of coffee, so I didn't blame him for not wanting to waste a single drop.

"I swear you were born missing a lobe or two of your brain." The quirky tech guy was growing on me. I could understand how he and Crowe became friends. They had a similar devil-may-care way of looking at things.

I massaged the injection spot on my arm, secretly grateful he hadn't put the nano tracker into my neck. "Where does cold fit on your scale, and is it supposed to feel like ice trickling up my arm?"

"Yeah, probably. If it starts feeling hot, then we've got something to worry about. Cold is only like a two on the concerned scale." Maddox flipped open his laptop, displaying a satellite map of the Northern Quadrant. A tiny green dot flashed over the outline of the hotel we were staying in. "And we're live."

Crowe leaned over his shoulder, sipping on what was left of his coffee. Behind him, muffled shouting volleyed back and forth. Nick was on the balcony trying to talk down a pacing Danny. He was kicked out of the room after he nearly shot Maddox for trying to inject me with the tracker. You'd think getting laid again would have relaxed him, but instead, I think letting him back in was only winding him tighter.

I smoothed my hands over the nondescript T-shirt and drawstring pants, turning to look at myself for the 800th time in the mirror. The fringe of my wig tickled my cheeks. The blonde washed out my skin tone and made my eyes look less bright. There were strands of light brown and grey interspersed with the yellow tones, removing the golden luster and making the hair look flat and mousey. All together, the look was rather unremarkable, which was exactly what we were going for. Forgettable. Average.

Toto handed me a heavy pair of black glasses, then gave the wig a tug to be sure the lace was sewn in tight. It was critical that no one suspected the hair was anything but real. Sewing the wig to my scalp gave me the freedom to move and style the hair without the risk of it falling off or shifting unexpectedly. The throbbing scalp was just a bonus I'd have to bear.

I slipped the glasses on. Feeling self-conscious, I asked, "How do I look?"

Ginger squinted, slowly tracking up and down my body with her eyes. She tapped her lips with a pen, humming in contemplation. It felt like being dissected. Danny was right; this was a stupid plan. I was going to be recognized and either handed back to Gigi or shot on the spot.

"It'll work," she finally answered, getting up to adjust the way my hair fell over the frames. "People will believe anything, even when the truth is staring them in the face. Right now, Ozmandria believes you're dead. Nobody will suspect a thing. All they'll see is a pretty face and a tight little body ripe for the picking." Ginger dropped her hand, smacking my ass as she walked back to her place beside Toto.

I yelped in surprise.

"You need to work on those reflexes, though," she added with a coy smile. "Can't be squealing like that for the patrons, or they'll all be bidding on you."

"You've got the bidding system locked down, right?" Crowe asked Maddox.

Maddox nodded. "Like I told you the last three times you asked, I've got it. The three of you will win. Place your bids, and let me handle the rest."

"You're sure?" I asked, wanting to be confident in my decision, but my nerves were screaming to abort mission. Danny's tantrum wasn't helping.

The image of Daisy popped into my mind, reminding me why I volunteered in the first place. For all of Danny's blustering, I wanted to do this for him. I loved the big idiot and it killed me seeing the way the guilt ate at him. The girl was set to suffer for the sole purpose of being used as leverage against me, against the boys. How could I live with myself knowing there was something I could be doing to help and instead did nothing?

Danny came back into the room, somewhat calmer now but still looking like someone had stuck a knife in his heart. His eyes scanned me from head to toe and back again. "I don't like it."

Crowe lifted his fingers, "Eight." Danny started saying that he didn't like the plan so many times that Crowe started keeping count. He and Nick had a bet going to see if he'd make it to twenty before I got back. At the rate he was going, Crowe would be collecting before I even left.

Nick entered right behind Danny and asked, "Everything good to go?"

Maddox turned a screen showing not only a map with my location down to the room we were standing in but also a readout of my heart rate and blood pressure. "If these spike too high ..." He tapped on the screen. "Then I'll extract her, and we can try something else."

"How exactly will you do that? There's an electric field domed over the entire property," Danny sniped.

Tilting his head, Maddox smiled. One long twist fell from where it was tied at the top of his head. "The dome is only a problem if we don't want them to know we're there. There's no reason we can't set off a few fireworks on our way out."

"What does that even mean?" Danny shook his head, glaring with accusation at Crowe. "We are *not* entrusting Thea's life to this—"

"It means that I've got it covered." Maddox rose from his seat, stepping directly into Danny's space. "If things go wrong, I can get to her in five minutes, probably less."

"Five minutes?" Danny scoffed. "There's no way."

As unlikely as it sounded, Maddox's stare remained confident. Whatever tricks he had up his sleeve, I didn't doubt he could pull it off. "Yes. Give me ten, and I can get you all out."

Danny took a step back. "I don't like it."

"Nine." Crowe wiggled all but one of his fingers at Nick.

"Well, lucky for us, no one is asking you to like it." Maddox sat back in his chair, dismissing all of Danny's concerns with a click of a button. The hum of the speakers buzzed. "Thea, say something."

I swallowed, looking between my three guys. "If this works, we can all take a long vacation somewhere warm. Clothing optional." My voice played back on a ten-second delay. It was remarkably clear considering it wasn't coming from a microphone.

"That's spooky," Toto said with wide eyes.

"It could be tighter." Maddox chewed on his lip ring. "The nanobots pick up the sound waves reverberating through her bones and relay it. I haven't perfected it enough to be able to translate sounds beyond her body, yet. It's possible that someone speaking while touching her could be transmitted. At the very least, we'll have ears in Sylvan's camp."

"You're sure it's accurate?" Nick pulled me close until his chest was firm against mine, his large hands cupping my ass. He bent over me, claiming my mouth with a slow, drugging kiss. The kiss trailed along my jaw, moving until his lips whispered over my ear, "When all this is done, I'll keep you out of clothing for a full month. I don't care where we are, *l'importante è che io possa godermi lo spettacolo in mezzo alle tue game a qualsiasi ora del giorno* [1] ... and no more wigs."

On the screen, the readout of my heart rate spiked, and the oxygen count dropped as I failed to catch my breath. Nick looked over my head at Maddox. "Could you read that?"

Toto whistled in appreciation. "That's hot."

---

1. As long as I can enjoy that spectacle between your legs any time of day.

"Seems accurate to me." He clicked a button for replay, and the very faint recording of Nick's voice repeated over the speakers. "But wait, there's more." With a grin, Maddox clicked a second button, and the computer translated the Italian on the screen.

I don't care where we are, as long as I can enjoy that spectacle between your legs any time of day.

I could feel my cheeks turning bright red, spilling up to the tips of my ears.

"Keep the glasses though," Crowe added. "I've always had a thing for the sexy librarian look."

Toto pointed at Crowe. "That's hot, too."

"Fucking idiots, all of you." Danny pulled me from Nick, wrapping a protective arm around my shoulder. "How can you be thinking about your dicks when she's about to literally auction herself off to a room full of psychopaths?"

I looked through the binoculars at the large abandoned lot and the dozen people being offloaded from a Cyclone shipping truck. The deal was going down off of an easily forgettable stretch of highway on the far edge of the Eastern Quadrant. These were always the kinds of places that Em liked to do handoffs of this size. Under the cover of darkness made it easy to go unnoticed. It also hid our movements at the opposite end of the lot.

I scrutinized each face of the Cyclone guards, then gave the same attention to Sylvan's. "I don't recognize any of them. That's a good thing, right? Point one in our favor."

Three uniformed men with rifles urged the group of prisoners forward. They were a mix of men and women. One boy couldn't be much older than thirteen, if that. It made my stomach turn. I glanced over at Danny, who was stone-faced watching the parade. It was impossible to read him, but I could see the tendons in his jaw protruding.

I laced my fingers through his. He looked down at me, and a tiny bit of the frost in his expression thawed. "You don't have to go," he said in one last effort to persuade me.

"No, I do. I need to do this—for you, for Toto and Didi, for Daisy and every other person who has been moved through the Farm. We free those people, and then we take out Em."

Danny brought my hand to his lips, brushing a soft kiss over my knuckles. "You're the best person I've ever met, Thea."

"Nah. You broke into a heavily guarded palace and saved me from a very public execution. That trumps fox chase."

The corner of his mouth twitched up a fraction. "Don't forget the sewer. I had to crawl through an ancient sewer to get there, too."

"See, this is nothing. It's going to be okay."

Danny's grip on my hand tightened. "I love my sister, but if this goes sideways, then you get the fuck out of there. Hide until one of us gets to you. Don't be you—"

"Don't be me?"

"Yes, don't go running head first into trouble. There's always another way, but there's only one of you. Promise me, Thea."

I opened my mouth to argue, but Danny put his finger over my lips.

"No. Promise me you'll put your own safety first."

He looked deadly serious. Setting my playfulness aside, I nodded. "Alright. I promise."

He pulled me in tight, resting his cheek on the top of my head. "Fucking hell, I'm terrified."

"I know."

"I don't think I've ever been so scared." He was being so blatantly honest. It tugged at my heart.

"Me too." That was the truth. This entire plan was terrifying. It was also the best chance we had to get his sister out, and that meant we had to at least try.

Nick leaned between us. "You ready?"

"Yeah," I said with a confidence I didn't feel.

His eyes scanned my face, the only bit of concern showing in the tightening of his brows. With a light kiss to my lips, he said, "Try not to kill anyone too soon. I know it will be tempting to gut the bastard when you see him, but you've got to pick your moments."

"Yes, sir." I gave him a curt salute.

"Thea," he chastised, "I'm serious. Make wise choices. Be smart."

"Not you, too." Patting him on the chest, I added, "Don't worry, Angel. I'm not about to do something impulsive."

"You are the definition of impulsive." Danny scoffed, trying not to lose his shit—again. "One of us will be listening at all times."

"I know."

"We'll see you tomorrow night."

I twisted my hands together, doing a quick count of my fingers to ground myself. I cleared my throat, not able to look at either of them. "I know I joked about it before, but ... please make sure it's you that catches me first."

Nick grabbed my chin, forcing me to meet his eyes. "I'll murder anyone who tries to come after you."

"Not if I kill them first." Crowe climbed into position beside us, placing a swift kiss to the top of my head. "It's time. Give them hell, Beautiful."

I nodded in confirmation and prepared to jump from my hiding place.

There was a flash by the exit of the abandoned lot and the high-pitched sound of a motorbike peeling out. Both Deveaux's guards and The Farm's turned toward the sound.

"What was that?" one of The Farm's gunmen asked in surprise.

The leader of Deveaux's group, a tall man with a boyish look to his features, held up his hand to block the glare from the truck's headlights. "I think someone just photographed us."

"Fuck that. I'm not waiting around to be arrested." The Farm guards took off for their truck at a run while Deveaux's watched with gaping shock.

I took this moment to slide silently into the back of the line of prisoners. I watched the guards from the corner of my eye, looking for any sign of awareness, but none of them reacted to me at all.

"Son of a bitch. The boss is gonna kill us," the third man said, his mustache shaking with his exclamation.

"Well, don't just stand there," Tall Boy commanded, giving the middle guy a hard push. "Go after them."

"I've got this lot." Mustache grabbed the back of my collar. My stomach dropped like a lead weight. I used every ounce of my control to keep from screeching. With a shove, I was heaved into the truck, tumbling onto the dusty floor, and the door quickly shut behind me.

I pushed myself to my knees, losing my balance when the truck lurched forward. Doubt, panic, and a solid dose of fear turned my stomach. This was a terrible idea. The boys were probably losing their minds watching my racing heart on the monitor.

"I'm okay," I whispered, as much to reassure them as myself. "I'm okay."

Unlike Em's trucks, here, the captives weren't chained to the walls. They relied purely on fear to keep everyone in line. I plopped myself on the bench and leaned back against the bar. The walls of the truck were made from a soft canvas, making me think of the convoys in old war movies. Honestly, it would have been easy to escape. One well-timed red light and a sharp object would be all it took to slip free.

"Who are you?" The skinny man I'd followed onto the truck sat next to me. His pale blue eyes narrowed in suspicion from behind square wire frames. The carrot-colored hair, curled in a mop at the top of his head, dipped into his eyes. "You didn't come from The Farm. I'd remember you. Although, there is something incredibly familiar about your face."

I pushed his hand away before he could pull my glasses down my nose.

"I'm no one." I knew better than to be honest with him. At The Farm, there had been so many instances of prisoners turning on each other for a morsel of mercy. I'd seen it more times than I could count. Fear was Em's preferred method of population management. When prisoners were just as afraid of their friends selling them out as they were of the guards, then everyone stayed nice and docile.

"Come on, blondie, everyone is someone."

Blondie? He tossed me a smile, his eyes dropping briefly to my chest. Was he hitting on me? Here? This was not the time to be slinging pick up lines. Did he think this was some sort of *"You're gonna die, I'm gonna die, let's go out having some fun"* scenario? Fucking men.

"I'm really a nobody." I averted my eyes, taking a shallow breath to deliver the line Ginger and I had practiced a dozen times. "I'm not even sure *how* I got here. One minute, I was getting in a cab to New Munich, and then next thing I know some beefy guy is hauling me across a parking lot. These aren't even the clothes I left home in. What about you? What's your story?"

"I spent a year working in the mica mines, then a couple of us were traded. I'm pretty sure we're headed for La Chasse. When they shuffled us through the grooming rooms, I heard a couple of the guards trying to place bets on who survives." He lowered his clammy hand over mine.

Ew.

"My name is—"

"I'm gonna stop you right there. I don't need names. If what you're saying is true, then what's the point? Everyone on this truck is a walking corpse. It's simply a matter of time."

"I'd still like to get to know you better."

143

Of course he would. I imagined Crowe dialing up the volume and straining his ears to hear anything of note. Danny would be breaking the tile pacing around the desk, while Nick quietly seethed at the nerve of this prick.

"Yeah, well, I'm not looking to get to know anyone." I slid as far as I could to the edge of the bench, giving me exactly three inches of space, and prayed the rest of the drive went quickly.

Thirty minutes of fending off Mr. Handsy VonFeely and our truck finally slowed to a stop. I pressed my ear to the canvas wall, shushing the idiot beside me. The guards at the gate were discussing something. I could barely hear over the rumble of the idling engine and ...

"Could you please breathe through something other than your mouth?"

"Sorry," he whispered and promptly snapped his jaw shut.

From the opposite side of the truck, there was a loud ripping sound. Having the same idea I'd had when I got on, one of the other women seized the moment and tore the canvas wide. She crashed to the pavement hard, then scrabbled over the ground, slipping the grip of the guard closest to her and running at a full sprint for the tree line.

I held my breath, silently rooting that she got away.

The woman was a streak of light against the black backdrop of the night. Her panicked breaths were coupled by a wailing that grew quieter the farther she made it away, even though not one of the guards chased her.

I studied them and their casual lack of concern. One man shifted his gun, aiming the long rifle at her retreating figure. My fingers tightened around the edge of the bench, preparing for the crack of its shell firing. She crossed the edge of the road, stepping from the shoulder into the tree line.

One foot was all it took.

There was a crackle of electricity, reminding me of when a bug zapper went off. A very loud, very big zapper. The girl jolted and dropped to the ground completely motionless with a small curl of smoke lifting into the air above her. The smell of charred flesh carried on the breeze, making me feel sick.

"No fucking way," Handsy gasped.

This time, when he reached down with trembling hands to grasp my own, I let him. I bit down on my cheek to keep from screaming. I'd seen a lot of twisted shit in my life, but nothing left me unsettled quite the way this had. The desperation in the back of the truck was palpable. Across from me, a smaller woman put her face in her hands and openly wept.

Nobody was escaping this place.

— 21 —
THEA

"**S**on of a bitch," the tall guard from our truck cursed. "I'm going to have to explain why we're short a fox. Between that and the photographs earlier ... Fuck! Deveaux's going to kill me."

"Or worse, he'll make you take her place," Mustache added, climbing back into the cab,

With a lurch that almost made my stomach heave, the truck pulled forward. I watched the dark entrance of the town fade through the gash torn in the canvas. The dead woman, still sprawled along the edge of the woods, grew smaller and smaller until she was out of sight and nothing more than a memory. I stared at the toes of my plain white sneakers, wondering if anyone would mourn her death. If anyone other than me would ever remember her.

Slowly, the faint images of a town came into view, giving us a preview of the layout of this nightmare. I tried to memorize every detail I could, hoping that it might give me an edge during the chase. The town was dark. Building after abandoned building rolled by. Some had boards over broken windows, vines climbing the brickwork, and signs hanging crookedly from rusted hooks. Old leaves and scraps of paper accumulated in the corners of doorways.

Maddox had undersold the state of Deveaux's campus. This was a ghost town, like the kinds you saw in horror movies. I half expected a werewolf to howl at the moon when we passed the church and abandoned graveyard. One wooden door was splattered in a rusty stain that looked disturbingly like blood.

How many people had been murdered here? How many tormented ghosts still walked these dark alleys?

"Well, that's terrifying." Handsy draped an arm around my shoulder like the moron was actually giving me comfort.

Picking up his middle finger, I lifted his hand from my body before dropping it ceremoniously away from me. I didn't know what advantage he thought he might be getting by *befriending* me, but this had to stop.

"Listen, Josh or Phil, whatever your name is ... or maybe Brenden, you look like a Brenden to me ..."

"It's Kyle."

"Yeah, that tracks. Listen, Kyle. I was trying to be nice, but I've got a thing about people touching me when I don't want to be touched. It makes me want to throat-punch a guy. So, I'm going to say this in the kindest way I know how. *Keep your fucking hands to yourself.*"

"I wasn't—"

"Spare me. This night is gonna be hard enough without me having to worry about your bruised ego. I'm sure someone here has low enough self-esteem to sleep with you just because they're scared. Go find them."

Was that hypocritical? Probably. But also, fuck this guy.

"I was just trying to be nice," he muttered.

Before I could question his response, the truck eased to a stop. The backdoors were thrown open, the night feeling much colder than it had going into the truck.

"Let's go. Everybody out," Mustache snapped in a sharp command.

Being closest to the door, I was the first to clamber from the vehicle.

"These are the new foxes?" a man with a clipboard said, not looking up at the truck or any of the people nervously peering out at him. He flipped a couple of papers. "Did you get a solid head count before leaving?"

"See, boss, the thing is ..." Mustache palmed the back of his neck imploring with his eyes for his tall counterpart to save him. "One of the girls made a run for it."

"And ..." The boss lifted his eyes, looking over the rim of his glasses at him.

"And she was fried at the perimeter gate."

He folded the clipboard under his arm. "How the fuck did that happen?"

"We didn't get a chance to check them all before they went on the truck. She must have had something on her sharp enough to cut the side panel."

"Didn't get a chance? What does that even mean?"

Tall Boy cleared his throat. "At the pick-up there was someone photographing the exchange. We'd gotten almost all of them checked and loaded, when the photographer took off on a bike. I sent Simmons after them. I didn't think it was wise to compromise the entire shipment by waiting, so we hustled the remaining lot on board and took off."

Clipboard removed his glasses and pinched the bridge of his nose. "This chase is the largest we've ever had, thirty-two hunters. I was already doubling up."

Doubling up? Like two hunters at a time.

"Boss, I'm sorry. I swear we did everything we could."

Clipboard started counting the line of people, mouthing the numbers as he went. "Did Simmons catch them?" He squinted in confusion, then re-checked the papers on the clipboard. Mustache shifted uncomfortably. "What a nightmare. And Deveaux mentioned something this morning about the Queen and her retinue being in attendance. I can't afford to fuck this up."

"Gigi," I whispered, more out of shock than anything. Gigi was going to be at La Chasse? Wig or no, she would definitely recognize me. My heart rate spiked, pounding with a dull rush in my ears. Was she expecting Danny to make a move for his sister? Or was this simply the next stepping stone to keeping Ozmandria under her thumb?

"If one of the girls was electrocuted at the gate, why are there still twelve here?"

Fuck.

Mustache turned, scanning the line of captives. "I don't know. Maybe The Farm made a mistake. Emily's people didn't really stick around long enough to ask."

He lifted the paper, comparing what he had on his board with each person standing before him. His eyes traveled over me, moving on without a bit of hesitation. "It's the strangest, because it looks like what we have here matches my list."

"Maybe the runaway was the extra, and that's why she spooked so easily."

The boss tucked the clipboard back under his arm. "Small mercies. At least I won't have to tell Deveaux that you lost a fox in transit."

The tension in the back of my neck eased. I forced myself to unclench my fists and sent a silent thanks to Maddox for being able to fake the documents so precisely.

"But I want you to do a thorough check of them to be sure they aren't hiding any other surprises. Then get them tagged."

-22-
DANNY

"*Ma porca puttana.*[1] Will you please just sit down?" Nick looked like he was ready to strangle me, or maybe put his fist through something—probably also me.

I looked at the readouts and other vitals. "I don't like it."

Crowe lifted three fingers. "Thirteen."

I couldn't do it. I couldn't sit there listening to her answer questions about experience and act like nothing was happening. My heart was beating in my throat. I couldn't swallow, could barely breathe past the giant knot of dread. Any second, we were going to hear one of them forcing themselves on her. I fucking knew it was coming. Or worse, she'd be recognized. I'd have to watch her heart rate slow and hear the death rattle on a ten-Oz damn-second delay.

"*Ow.*" Thea's filtered voice cried out. Here it freaking came. I gripped the back of the kitchen chair with both hands, ready to throw the thing across the room. This was every single one of my worst memories and fears rolled into one. "*Fuck, that hurts.*"

"Relax, Danny. That'd be the tracker going in," Crowe remarked. When did he become the voice of reason around here? I was losing my mind, one heartbreaking second at a time. That's what was happening. Or I was having a heart attack. What was it you're supposed to smell seconds before a heart attack, burning marshmallows?

"Did you have to put the tracker in my neck? It's sensitive."

Calm as could fucking be, Nick asked, "Do you think they used a gun or a scalpel?"

Gun or scalpel? The wood groaned beneath my grip. I let go of it before I broke the thing and went back to pacing.

"Gun. It's quicker." Crowe made a note on the pad before him, recording the bits of info she was able to relay without drawing suspicion.

I was going to burn Sylvan's place to the ground. No, that wasn't enough. I was going to drop a city's worth of napalm on the town and incinerate the entire place right off the map. Then, I'd take the shards of charcoal and shove them right up Deveaux's—

"The new tracker doesn't affect the nanobot's transmission, does it?" Nick asked, leaning over Crowe to click on the satellite feed.

Fuck. Fucking fuck. Fuck.

I hadn't even considered that. If we lost her in that town, then this entire plan was fucked. We had a narrow damn window to pull Thea and Daisy out of there. The only way this worked was to use Thea's GPS to find them both. If she and my sister were hidden somewhere in an entire ghost town with no way to locate them, then we'd never find them in time. I paused my pacing long enough to see Thea's dot blink steadily in the same building she'd spent most of the night in.

"She's right there. Same as before."

Releasing a breath, I went back to walking my path around the living room. Twenty-two hours and I could see her again. Forty-eight, and this entire nightmare would be behind us—Ya know, if she wasn't shot, tortured, or raped before then. Not necessarily in that order. I put my hand over the ache in my chest. This was why I liked being the one in control instead of turning into this anxiety monster.

Crowe's phone rang, the incoming call projecting over the monitor. "Talk to me."

Maddox didn't bother with putting his face on screen. *"It's set. I'm sending over the entrance codes and invitations. Thea's picture's been uploaded into the betting system. From what I've seen, her profile is already getting a lot of traffic. I doctored up the photo a bit so it doesn't look exactly like her anymore, but you can expect her to be ... popular."* Of course she was. The woman was gorgeous. You'd have to be blind to miss it. *"Plus, we have another problem."*

I slid to a stop, my socks sliding over the tile from my abrupt change of direction. "Define problem?"

"Seems Sylvan is overreaching. He's invited more people this year than ever before. As a result, there aren't enough foxes for the hunt."

I hated that term. These were real people, not animals.

"The auction is still being held like always, but instead of one winner per fox, the top two get hunting privileges. There's only three of you and two girls. That means there's one loose cannon who will either win Thea or Daisy."

"I can take them out. Just tell me who it is and put me on their team." Crowe didn't blink. He'd retreated into that cold, detached place the moment Thea was thrown on the truck. Since then, he's been all business. It was possible that he was already planning his own brand of destruction for the entirety of Sylvan's operation.

"Yeah, except the rules are different this time, too. He's allowing player-on-player violence. If you can take out another hunter, then you can claim their fox in addition to your own. Crowe, there's some people entering into La Chasse with big appetites. If you know what I mean."

"Yeah, I'm one of them. This is nothing I can't handle. Just get me the info."

I pushed the heels of my hands into my eyes in a feeble attempt to quiet the static thrumming in my head. This was a stupid fucking plan, and Thea or my sister were going to be the ones who paid the price.

"One other thing."

I lost it, slamming my hands into the top of the table. "Fucking hell, Maddox. What happened to gaming the system, and this plan is smooth as a baby's knee?"

"Baby's knee?" Crowe's eyes slid sideways on one of his shit-eating grins.

"I never said either of those things."

"I don't fucking know. My mind is all scrambled from lack of oxygen. Shit, I'm starting to sound like Thea."

"You kind of are," Nick said with a laugh.

I ground my teeth. "Yeah, well, if you weren't such a thundercunt and actually listened to reason, maybe she wouldn't be getting injected with trackers, and Ozma only knows what else."

Nick's smile fell. That's right, fucker. It felt like I was the only one who cared anymore.

Maddox flicked on his camera. Behind him, the small bedroom was tossed like he'd been working from his bed. *"Danny, I'm starting to worry that your head won't be in the right place when the time comes. You're too invested."*

Of course I was invested. Thea was the single greatest thing to ever demolish its way into my life. There wasn't a single aspect of our lives that was the same since she arrived, and I stupidly loved it. I didn't want to go back.

"I'll be fine. Two of the most important people in my world are currently being held captive and about to be served up for Sunday dinner. If anything, you should be worried for the well-being of every person in that town because I might very well bring the entire thing down."

"That's what I'm talking about. What are you going to do when someone has their sights on Thea, or your sister? I'll tell you what— something reckless, and it's gonna blow the entire plan."

Nick pushed me aside. "You said there was something else?"

Maddox looked off-screen for a long second, eyes nearly glazing as he watched something we couldn't see walk by. Clearing his throat, he said, *"Yeah, and it's a big one."*

-23-
THEA

T he dormitories were more like a renovated barn. Bunk beds were placed in what I could only describe as stalls. The width of each was barely enough to provide room for climbing into the bed. Metal gates took the place of doors, making it even more obvious that this building originally held animals. I felt like a stray dog being forced into a kennel with all the other strays.

It had been a very long night. Being poked, prodded, and stripped, then poked and prodded some more, left one rather drained. Or maybe it was that all of the panic and adrenaline were finally letting up.

The biggest question mark in our plan was intake. We knew that the bidding happened with an online registry. Which meant photographs and descriptions of all the foxes. If I was going to be recognized, it would be then. Turns out, all they cared about was making me look marketable, not who I actually was or any semblance of the truth.

Skylights letting in the already bright morning light made the glare on the smooth white floors look like a serving platter; each of the prisoners staring out at me were on display like a buffet. I desperately searched each face for Daisy. She had to be in here. Most of the residents were awake. They hung on the bars, eagerly looking to see who was being added to their ranks. They were mostly women with only a few men spread among the group.

A guard hit the wall beside my head with a long pronged rod, making me jump. An electrical spark crackled at the end of the stick, sending a charge into the air that made the hair on my arms stand on end.

"Home sweet home, little foxes." He shoved me into the cell at the end of the row. "Be ready when I return." For emphasis, he made the rod spark again.

159

Mr. VonFeely was shoved into the cell right behind me because, of course he was. Twelve people, and he had to be the one forced into this tiny cubicle with me. Silently, I begged Ozma to throw me just one bone.

"Hey, roomie."

"We're not friends, Kevin." I climbed onto the top bunk, trying to keep the line of my shirt from riding up. Last thing I needed was this idiot thinking a flash of skin was an invitation to join me.

To make things worse, somewhere in this barn was the slap of flesh repeating at an increasing rhythm that was unmistakably the sound of sex. A loud male grunt signaled the end, but no sounds came from whoever he was fucking. The probability of it being non-consensual turned my stomach.

I'd been around this sort of behavior before. Knowing what to expect didn't make it easier to swallow. All of it made being forced into this confined space harder. I stared at the ceiling for a solid thirty seconds, counting my fingers in an attempt to contain the panic.

There were only so many fears a person could juggle at a time.

"Hey," Kyle whispered softly.

"Just leave me alone." I sat up, expecting to see his suggestive eyes, until I realized he wasn't talking to me at all. In the opposite stall, a woman lifted her head, her emerald gaze landing on Kyle. She didn't notice me at all, but I knew exactly who she was.

"Daisy?"

Her face lit up with surprise and fell just as quickly. It was definitely her. In the photographs, she and Danny looked similar, but in person, everything about her was familiar: the way her eyebrow lifted in question and the way her mouth tightened into an unforgiving straight line. Even the muscle ticking at the end of her jaw was the same. She was rounder than him, her heart-shaped face smoothing all of his hard edges into something beautifully feminine.

"How do you know my name?" she asked with the same scathing snap to her voice that Danny hurled all too often. I half expected her to call me 'Princess' next.

I couldn't mention her brother or the plan, not in a place as open and watched as this. So, instead, I said the only word that would trigger her understanding. "Dandelion."

The tilt of her scrutinizing eyes tightened in confusion. She walked to the bars, ready to ask for more, but then she glanced at the camera mounted to the ceiling and stopped.

I nodded slowly.

"Wait, you know each other?" Kyle asked, probably a bit too loudly, given the way sound traveled around the concrete walls.

"No. We've never met before. I just like flowers," I replied, rolling over on my bunk and feigning sleep.

"Wake up!"

Sound muffled in my ears, bubbling and gurgling incoherently. Dark water frothed in all directions. My limbs were pinned by the scrape of sandpaper shark skin.

"Wake up. *Please* wake up!"

Kyle shook my shoulder frantically. The yellow eye of a shark transformed into his blue, the underwater nightmare melting away. I untangled my limbs from the sheet and willed my heart rate to slow. Danny was probably losing his mind right now. Knowing he'd be panicked by the read-out made missing him so much worse

"I can't believe I fell asleep," I mumbled, still trying to get my bearings.

"Oh, thank Oz," he hissed. "They're coming. You need to be up. I just watched them use a cattle prod on the last person who wasn't ready and waiting for them."

"Fuck," I scrambled out of the bed. On the list of things I never wanted to experience, cattle prod was right below guillotine. Across the aisle, Daisy and her bunkmate stood against the wall, with their hands pressed flat to the stone. The girl beside Daisy was trembling so fiercely that the hem of her shirt swung back and forth.

The gate to our stall opened with a squeak, and a spindly man in a suit walked directly in front of me. His long and pointed features, much like the rest of him, were exaggerated by the coarse black hair tied tightly at his nape. He steepled his fingers before his face, tapping them one at a time in succession. When he hunched, he looked like a large black spider coming in to dine on a fly.

Unfortunately, that fly was me.

"This is the one?" Sylvan Deveaux asked, the tone of his voice just as menacing as his silhouette. There was a vague accent to his speech, something akin to a watered-down version of French. It made the darker notes of his voice seem to slither as he spoke. No wonder the girl across the aisle was trembling.

My mind, struck dumb by his entrance, was slow to process what he'd said. *This is the one?* The one what? There must be twenty people in here. Why was he coming for me specifically? I looked at the rifle in the hands of the man to his left and the cattle prod gripped by the man to his right.

"Yes, sir. Number 774." The boss with the clipboard from yesterday tapped on a tablet, flashing a picture of me at him. "She's already listing at 3.2 million."

3.2 million? ME?

Sylvan narrowed his gaze, giving my body a slow sweep. "You look remarkably like that girl the Queen executed." Using a pincer-like grip on my chin, he turned my face to the side. "Emily Rosen's niece. You could be her twin."

An involuntary gulp caught in my throat. My heart was beating hard enough that I was sure it would give me away. I'd met Sylvan before, twice. None of us had counted on him getting this close to me. I could feel his scrutinizing eyes traveling over my face and assessing each of my reactions. With each passing second, my terror ratcheted higher. This was the moment our entire plan fell apart. I could feel it in the marrow of my bones— Sylvan knew.

"No wonder they all want a piece. You, sweet thing, will be my biggest payday yet." His thumb ran over my lower lip. "The temptation to keep you for myself is enticing."

A scream built in the center of my chest. The effort of restraining it made my body vibrate in a way I was sure he could feel. I tried every trick I knew. I wiggled my toes and counted my fingers, anything to direct my focus from the way his eyes were cutting through me.

Flicking the end of my wig with his finger, Sylvan finally released my face. The blonde hair caught the harsh fluorescent lights, suddenly feeling way too fake for the examination it'd just undergone. With a last look, Deveaux turned to Clipboard Guy. "Dress her in something innocent to match that heart-shaped pout. Pick a few other show pieces to be brought down to the gallery. You have three hours. Guests are already arriving."

"Yes, sir."

Sylvan disappeared down the aisle as quickly as he'd come.

I blinked in astonished disbelief. Ginger was right; denial was a powerful thing. It reminded me of that country singer who entered a look-alike contest and lost to a drag queen. Nobody wanted to acknowledge that the simplest answer was the correct one. I looked like that girl because I *was* her. They just couldn't see past the dollar signs in their eyes.

I forced myself to let out a slow breath, covering my face with both hands, confirming, "I'm okay."

Clipboard gestured at Daisy and her bunkmate, "Bring them and the red-head from this morning."

The guard unlocked her gate, gesturing with the point of his rifle for us all to follow him out of the barn.

"Please, don't chase me. I can't do it again." I looked over my shoulder at the whimpering girl digging in her heels behind us. Coils of flaming red hair curled in a blaze around her shoulders. She was gorgeous, with doll-like features and alabaster skin. Like cracks on porcelain, a series of fine scars raked her arms. My heart broke for this girl, even more so as I realized the scars on her arms were a match to the ones strafing Didi in her photo. What the hell cut someone up like that? Danny's sister had been here for two years. How many times had Sylvan chased her through the ghost town?

"I have neither the time nor the energy for taming brats." Clipboard pulled open the door to a dressing room. "I don't care how much money your snatch brings in. If you try to run, I will have you shot in the knee. See how long you last in the chase when you can't scurry away."

"We're all going to die." Daisy's bunkmate made an audible gasp that transformed into a yelp. The cattle prod sparked and clicked. The sound alone made my muscles tense. Her body jolted into the air and came down hard on her knees. Fingers still twitching, she held her hand to her mouth and silenced any open weeping that might slip out.

"No talking. Now, get going to The Dollhouse. Unless, of course, you *all* need a little motivation?" I tried to make note of the man, the slope of his crooked nose and stubby jaw that made him look like a Rottweiler. When the time came, I would be sure to repay his kindness.

Racks of dresses lined one wall of the room, and opposite them sat a set of brightly lit vanities. It reminded me of the dressing rooms for actors in movies, or runway models. This definitely wasn't what I'd been expecting from a place like this. Women and men in uniforms similar to turn-of-the-century vaudeville ushers and cigarette girls scurried about.

One woman slowed as she strolled by, giving me a subtle wink and toss of her blue hair. I doubled back, sure I knew her from somewhere. These were probably the people Sylvan kept around as waitstaff, not the lucky ones who were the prime entertainment for this evening.

Maddox explained that the real money didn't come from the bets to win the fox you got to hunt, but rather which foxes would survive the night. The odds were against the fox 20:1. As the evening progressed, more and more money came pouring in from the dark net. If your girl gave the hunter the slip, it was potentially a massive cash haul.

Unfortunately for the $3.2 million in bets, I wasn't going to be finishing out the night. Our entire crew would be long gone by sunrise. Hopefully.

A tall woman with silver hair braided in a crown pointed at me. "Spin."

For a lack of what else to do, I spun in a small circle. Using the turn, I noted all of the exits and smaller details of the room—like the large fabric shears sitting at the alterations table.

"Mr. Deveaux specifically said to make this one look innocent."

She barely reacted to Clipboard's statement, drawing in large lines over the pad in her hands. When she was done, she handed an assistant the page and moved on to Daisy.

I stepped onto my tiptoes to try and see what she'd drawn, seeing only blue streaks. The assistant returned with a gingham dress in white and blue check, complete with a frilly white petticoat. Hanging the dress beside one of the vanities, she draped white thigh-high tights and two matching hair bows on the tabletop.

She couldn't be serious. How was I supposed to run for my life dressed like an Oz damn babydoll? Besides showing my ass to the entire world, I would stand out like a giant neon sign in the dark town. I'd never be able to hide the bright colors and absurd layers ... and fuck me, those were sequins.

"Get dressed. Hair and makeup are your responsibility. Make it look good, or you won't like the way I fix it. Do you understand?" Clipboard tucked his tablet under his arm.

I dropped my eyes to the ground. "Yes, Sir."

"Better." He strode away, and I waited a full ten count before lifting my gaze again. Fuck this place. Never in my life have I been so stressed by the idea of styling my hair wrong.

Knowing that Sylvan had asked for innocent, I opted for pulling the long strands of the wig into pigtails and keeping them in place with the bows. The ends were curled and shined, making the porcelain doll appearance complete. My makeup was simple. The apples of my cheeks were extra rosy and I used the bronzer to change the basic shape of my features into something softer.

Daisy's corset was a pink and yellow stripe, over a long golden skirt. Her look was more fairytale princess than my babydoll. Taking a bobby-pin, I plucked up a corner of her hair and moved in close to pin it. "Whatever happens, make sure you stay with me tonight."

"What about the rest of them?" she replied, faking a sneeze to cover her question. "Like Kyle."

"I'm not here for them." I shook my head, looking back at my *roomie*. He probably wasn't a bad guy, just unlucky and scared. Kyle pulled at the lycra hugging his thighs. Tiny golden gears were embroidered over the seams, making him look like a cross between a robot and a jester. There were even bells sewn into his cuffs. It wasn't just comical, it was absurd. Who did this appeal to?

"We sort of have history. He's as close to a friend as you get in these places," she said with big, wide eyes. That explained the sad way she'd looked at him when we arrived.

He kicked his foot, trying to dislodge the fringe that had snagged on the zipper of his fly. Bells tinkled, filling the air with sounds of tiny fairies. He was fucked if he had to try and be quiet. Kyle's pained eyes pleaded with us, mouthing, "Why?"

"Here, I'll help you," Daisy said, dropping to her knees and carefully pulling the lace free.

We were like the makings of a joke: A princess, a doll, and a jester walk into a manhunt ... Rolling my shoulders back, I prepared myself to face what came next. There was no fooling myself. The game had already started, and I'd be damned if I was going to lose.

-24-
DANNY

I flicked through the pictures on the complimentary tablet I'd been provided. We weren't allowed to bring our own electronics into the town. Everything had been taken and cataloged at the gate as we'd expected. Not our weapons, of course, just our way to communicate with one another. Hunters were allowed any weapon of choice. It was part of the appeal of these games. One man had an elephant gun strapped to his back. I cringed to think of the damage it would inflict. A shell of that size would tear a person in half. The idiot probably thought it made him look badass. I tamped down the instinct to laugh. Let him fire that thing and see how badass a dislocated shoulder was.

Maddox assured us that bypassing the technical issues of La Chasse's electrical grid was child's play. We each wore a watch specifically made for this job. It had minimal tech, but would allow us to see Thea's readouts and have basic messaging back to base. It simply required him recalibrating the signal once we'd passed through the perimeter defenses. So, while waiting for him to send his confirmation, I scrolled through the photographs of tonight's foxes.

Number 774. Blonde hair and painted on freckles. Fuck the devil, she was beautiful. Even beneath the costume, Thea made my heart stop.

We were tucked into an alcove, one that gave a view of the room but covered us in enough shadow that we weren't obvious to most of the other patrons. It was the perfect location to scout from. I watched Thea being escorted into the room and placed inside a cage—an actual fucking cage. With terrified eyes, she looked at the tight confines of the space, and her breathing shifted into shallow pants when she was shoved inside. It was too small to do anything but stand, the frilly edges of her skirt poking out between the bars. One man was already fondling the ruffles.

I squeezed the edges of the tablet. "Did you turn on the jammer?" I asked Crowe under my breath. One of our standard tools was a small device that emitted a pitch inaudible to human ears, but would record as static on any microphones pointed our way. Handy when you didn't want anyone listening in on your conversation.

"Of course."

Following right behind Thea was my sister. I recognized her immediately. She hadn't changed at all. With the long skirts and sleeves, Daisy looked like something from a fantasy world. In fact, each of the people being paraded around the room were dressed to fulfill a specific kink. "Good, because I'm about to start spitting a whole lot of death threats."

"What the hell is Thea wearing?" Crowe said, leaning into me. "And why do I find it so hot?"

"You think everything she does is hot."

"Because it is."

The problem was we weren't the only ones looking at her. The whole room was turned her way.

"I don't like it."

Thea pushed the thick black glasses up the bridge of her nose. The slight tremor to her fingers the only outward indication of the anxiety I knew was coursing through her. Why did he have to put her in an Oz damn cage?

"Seventeen."

"Will you cut it with that shit already? You're not helping my stress levels."

"Not a chance," he chuckled under his breath.

"Do I even want to know what you bet him?"

Crowe slowly raised his eyes over the edge of the tablet. "Fifty bucks and center bed privileges. For a week, the loser has to third-wheel it. I can practically feel her body curling up next to mine already. So keep them coming, Captain Broody."

"You know I've always hated you, right?" I said with an unamused, flat tone. "From day one, I had you pegged as a dick ... and look, I was right."

"Nah, you love me. I'm very lovable." Crowe leaned back on his bench, propping his arms on either side of the backrest. "Just ask Thea ... while we're snuggled up tight in the middle of the bed."

Didn't I know it. Our whole damn life Crowe has been getting away with shit the rest of us never could. Even at his worst, he had a charm that won everyone over. I both hated and loved him for it.

"Champagne, sir." A server stopped beside me. Her pastel blue hair contrasted brightly against her red satin uniform. She smiled sweetly. If not for the lollipop tucked into her cheek, I might not have recognized her.

"Aren't you missing your skates? Although, I guess things got a little dead around Head Shots."

She smiled coyly up at me, the glasses tinkling on their tray. "Can't blame a girl for taking jobs that pay. Did you want a glass of champagne? Something to celebrate with, perhaps. Or maybe your friend?" The server looked over her shoulder at where Nick was propped inconspicuously against the opposite wall. She was unnervingly perceptive, especially for a nobody we only met once.

"You seem to see a lot." I dropped a $100 onto the tray strapped around her neck. "When are they taking the foxes out to the town to get into position. I wouldn't mind a bit of a head start. If you know what I mean."

The server shoved the money into her bra, then looked from us to Thea and back. "Pretty. She looks so much like that girl who was with you in Head Shots. Is that why you're here, looking for a replacement?"

"That's not the answer to my question."

"My contract ends at ten. Beyond that, I don't know what's going on. I have one job to do. I'm just looking to do it and get out of here." The server didn't wait for more small talk. Instead, she moved on to the next group of men animatedly discussing one of the foxes on their tablet.

Crowe smacked my shoulder, pointing at the stripper pole in the corner. "At least they're together."

Daisy didn't go into a cage like Thea had. Apparently, our girl was getting special attention, just like Maddox predicted. Instead, my sister was tethered around the neck like a dog on a lead. A few of the patrons were already jeering and throwing out catcalls to her.

The whole thing made me physically ill. "I don't like it."

"Eighteen."

A spotlight shone directly on a small dais at the far end of the room, the music slowly dying away. Sylvan Deveaux ascended the small set of steps. He gripped the sides of the podium with his boney fingers. The overhead lights cast dark shadows in the hollows of his cheeks and eyes, making him look every bit the sinister villain I imagined him to be. "Good evening, I would like to welcome you to the 15th annual Chasse."

Sylvan paused, waiting for the polite round of applause. "This year, we have decided to do something special for everyone. As you know, traditionally, La Chasse is held in one of the buildings on my campus, and we theme the attractions to suit the location." He said "attractions" like he didn't mean torture devices and traps. Everything about this man, right down to his fake accent, made my skin crawl. "This year, the entire town will be the backdrop of the largest chase ever held."

The crowd murmured. Nick pushed his way to us through the crowd, no doubt connecting the dots for how this reveal royally fucked our plans. It felt foolish not to have considered it; dozens of contingencies, and this wasn't one of them.

Sylvan continued, "The foxes will each be strategically placed around the town and hunters will be given clues to their locations, but not exact coordinates. The chase begins at sunset, a siren will sound to announce the official start. No action is permitted before this time. Violations will be prosecuted swiftly and without impunity." Sylvan paused to let the message set in. "As always, you have until sunrise, 5:47am, to claim your prize, or they remain property of La Chasse."

Thea white knuckle gripped the bars in both hands. Her eyes were pinned on Daisy. We were supposed to be pulling them out together. If they were separated, it would be impossible to find my sister before our exit window closed. This town was simply too big.

"There are some surprises in store for everyone and treats placed throughout the campus." Sylvan waved his hand dramatically. A red velvet curtain parted behind him, unveiling a massive theater screen. On it were security feeds from every angle of the town: A hospital, a church, a hotel, a market, the woods ... even a lumber mill. Without meaning to, my eyes gravitated back to Thea, a knot of dread sinking heavy in my stomach.

"Each fox will have two hunters. It's your choice, if you'd like to team up in the hunt. Be aware that hunter-on-hunter acts will be permitted this year, should you and your partner choose that route. As always, you may chase your target to any point of the property. A barrier has been erected to help with identifying the boundaries. They are electrified and La Chasse will not be responsible for loss of life due to incompetence."

The cameras switched to feeds of the perimeter where tall white walls penned in the town. This was so fucked. How did Maddox miss that incredibly important fact? Our exit relied on being able to disrupt the electrical field. It would alarm the guard station, but by the time they made it to the breach, we would be long gone. An unscalable wall was an entirely different challenge; one we didn't have the time or the means to solve. My mind tumbled over everything I knew about electrical fields and came up blank.

Nick, finally reaching us, tapped Crowe's arm. *"Tutto okay?*[1] You look ready to murder someone."

I followed Crowe's line of sight. His features were cut hard enough to demolish whatever he was looking at.

"Fuck." My blood instantly began to boil. "She's going to recognize Thea." Gigi entered the room, flanked by an entire team of black-suited security. Her long blonde hair was pinned in perfectly placed ringlets and her tailored pant suit made her look like more of a mob boss than a queen. Sebastian Charles,

---

1. Are you okay?

her second in command and newly appointed Queen's Consort, pointed to my sister. If that asshole thought he was going after her—

"Stop staring at her, both of you, or they'll notice we're here," Nick hissed.

Gigi didn't look like she'd noticed anything happening on the floor, which was a small mercy, at least. She was deep in conversation with Sebastian, probably discussing which back to stick her knife in next.

"Now that we've discussed the rules ..." Sylvan continued, pointing to the red countdown clock over the dais. "We are in the final five minutes of bidding." On the screens, each of the sixteen foxes was projected, their stats below their photographs, and a ticking dollar count beside them. I recognized the eleven that had been loaded onto the truck with Thea, along with another three people who must have been survivors of previous seasons.

In the middle of them all, green eyes that looked so like my own stared back at me. The entire reason my sister's face was projected on that screen was because of me. The world wouldn't survive my wrath if this plan failed.

"*Cazzo*, Thea's number is high."

"Really fucking high," I confirmed, eyes locked on Sylvan. He licked his lips and stroked his jaw in contemplation, looking from Thea's value to her and back again. I didn't like it. The man was a wildcard. The longer I watched him, the sharper the temptation grew to tear out his throat like a wild dog.

"I swear on every sin I know," Crowe spat. "There are going to be a lot of people leaving here with missing appendages if I have to see her flinch one more time from a man putting his hand up her skirt."

"I know the feeling," Nick grumbled.

"Still think this was a good plan?" The "I told you so" wasn't nearly as satisfying as it usually was.

"Less and less every second. This is why you don't let me make plans, remember?" Crowe palmed the back of his neck.

"It was her choice," Nick said, like somehow he could ease the burden of guilt with one admission. "She knew people would want to fondle the goods. She knew there was danger and she stepped up anyway."

Thea glared at the man running his hand along the inner side of her calf. She gave him a little kick to jostle free of his grip. I mentally added his face to the list of people who would die tonight. "That doesn't mean I have to like it."

"But you should respect it," Crowe clipped.

I shifted my weight from foot to foot. "Why hasn't Maddox gotten in touch? It's making me jumpy cutting it this close to the final minutes without hearing from him."

Crowe glanced down at the all-but-forgotten watch at the same time my own buzzed. "He has."

"Finally." Reading his update, I typed a quick response.

M: "It's done."

D: "Need a new exit."

M: "Already on it."

The timer on the wall clicked down to zero, signaling the end of bidding. The screens switched from a running tally to a set of names beneath each photo.

I let out a deep breath seeing my cover name and Nick's beneath Thea's picture.

"Thank fuck," Crowe said on an equally loud exhale. His name was listed beneath Daisy's, along with Norman King. "I knew Maddox would pull it off."

I snapped at Crowe. "What was the name of the man Thea said tried to buy her virginity?"

He nodded at the obnoxiously boisterous ogre of a man. "Yeah, that's him."

Norman King was busy congratulating himself for winning a slight woman who would never be able to fight him off. Hand cupping his dick, the prick leaned back in his chair to get a good look at his prize and giving me a prime view of his companion for the night, Emily-fucking-Rosen.

Nick's hand pressed on the center of my chest just in time to stop me from walking directly to her. Curling my fingers into fists at my side, I imagined the pop of her vertebrae separating as I choked the life from her miserable veins.

Norman laughed again, "You were right to pick her. You always have the best taste, Emily." He lifted her hand to his lips while Emily did a respectable job of looking like she wasn't completely repulsed.

Sylvan's voice returned over the mic, "Ladies and gentlemen, say goodbye to your foxes. They're off to their new locations. In an hour's time, you'll be given information specific to your bid. In the meantime, please enjoy the libations and entertainment."

One by one, the captives were released from their displays. The hunter with the elephant gun winked at the jester-looking man, shooting him with a finger gun. The colorfully clad man tripped in surprise, crashing into the redhead before him. Together, they were shoved through the door. Daisy and Thea were the last to be removed.

Thea gave a long last look over the crowd, probably looking for a glimpse of us. I wanted to signal to her that she wasn't alone ... but we couldn't risk it. Sylvan noticed her hesitation and took the opportunity to snag her arm. The yelp of surprise she gave was loud enough to hear it over the din of the room.

Nick took an involuntary step forward, nearly moving into the light. I understood it. The same tether was tugging at my chest. Only Crowe remained motionless, flicking through the readouts of her vitals on his watch.

Sylvan twisted one of her pigtails around his hand, using it to draw her to him until his mouth was grazing her throat. Thea's face tightened, her breaths increasing in a rapid staccato that made my heart pound in a rush through my ears. My fist clenched tighter, resisting the urge to charge across the room and pummel the asshole for daring to touch what wasn't his.

"He's a dead man," Crowe cursed on a whisper, not watching the way Deveaux was fondling Thea but at the readout on the screen. Forcing myself to look away from what was happening, I glanced down at the watch. Written captions of what Sylvan was whispering into her ear scrolled across the display.

"Tell me, little dove..."

I looked back at Thea. I couldn't help the memories. Little dove was too damn close to "little bird." Flashes of King's hands holding Thea down filled my vision, his mouth moving over her skin and whispering to her like the poison dripping from his lips were words of affection. It hit me like a sucker punch to the gut. I couldn't breathe as I stared at the woman I loved suffering through the same trauma again. Thea's lip quivered. She closed her eyes tight and bit down on it to keep whichever emotion she was fighting from leaking out. Fear. Panic. Rage. I could see them all painted across her beautiful face.

"Do your tears taste as sweet as your scent? Will you cry for me?"

My vision ping-ponged between what he was doing and the captions on the screen. His tongue lightly traveled over her cheek, catching the single tear cascading down it.

"That's a good girl."

"A. Dead. Man," Crowe repeated through a clenched jaw. "Dead. In tiny pieces, never to be seen again."

Sylvan wrapped his free hand around her throat, tightening his grip enough that she struggled to swallow.

"Scream."

Thea shook her head as much as his grip allowed, her eyes still squeezed tight.

"That wasn't a request. I fucking said, 'SCREAM.'"

His last word was loud enough that I didn't need to look at the captions to know what he was saying. The whole room heard him. Several people turned to look.

"Scream. I want to hear just what it will sound like with my cock shoved down your throat."

Sylvan shoved her against the wall so that she was barely visible to the audience he'd now attained. It was only by chance that I was lucky enough to see him forcing his thumb into her mouth and the white flash of Thea's teeth as she bit down hard.

"Fucking try it. That will be the last thing your cock ever does."

And that was my girl, a fighter to the end. I waited to see him slap her or punish her for the disrespect. Thea was ready for it, too, lifting her chin in defiance and steeling her gaze. Hand to her throat and hair in his fist, yet she still managed to look down on him.

"You are delightful, 774."

Sylvan forced her to her knees, the babydoll dress fanning around her like the petals of a flower. Nick's sharp inhale shifted against my arm from where he was holding me back. I looked down at the indents his fingers were making into my chest. I hadn't even realized that I'd moved to rescue her or that he'd stopped me.

"Fly fast, little dove. I don't care who won your bid. Tonight, you're my prize to hunt."

"I'm no one's but my own."

Sylvan's spider-like fingers ran over the red spot on her neck. Right over where they'd injected her tracking device. Thea hissed in pain.

"That's where you're wrong. I'll always know where you are. You're already mine."

Deveaux gestured to the door, dismissing her like he was asking the man to take out the trash. A guard hauled Thea to her feet, dragging her from the room.

Nick took two deliberate steps back. "Show me the map, *in questo fottuto istante.*[2] I want to know exactly where they're taking her."

"He'd have to take you both out in order to claim Thea," Crowe said, like that was somehow a good thing.

"You really think he cares about *le sue fottute rules*?"[3]

I couldn't breathe around the pounding of my heart, made all the worse when I looked over at the table Gigi settled into. Sebastian had one of Sylvan's tablets in his hands, and they were looking at Daisy's stats. Gigi's pink lips curled up into a sinister smile. She was going after Daisy. I could feel it, probably because we ignored her demand to acquire the Swing City drug den.

"No," I said, too loudly for the cover we were trying to maintain.

---

2. Right fucking now.

3. his fucking rules?

"I've got your sister," Crowe said with icy confidence. "Norman will be zero challenge. Gigi is sly and knows how to play the game, but even if Gigi and Sebastian try coming for her together, I can take them."

Could he, though? What kind of surprises were out there that leveled the playing field? There were only sixteen foxes and this room was packed with people.

If Gigi tried harming her here and now, it wouldn't matter what plan we'd hatched or Maddox's claims that taking out Gigi required more planning, I would slay the bitch and damn the consequences.

"Someone help!" a woman screamed, "he's choking!"

The entire room went silent, directing their attention to Emily Rosen. She backed away from the table, knocking over a chair in the process. White foam poured from Norman King's mouth and his portly face was turning a deep purple. He pulled desperately on the tablecloth, falling to the ground and bringing the entire tabletop with him in a loud crash. The no doubt poisoned champagne flute rolled onto the ground from his meaty grip.

Gigi regally rose to her feet, waving her hand to gather the room's attention. "Mr. Deveaux, following the untimely passing of Mr. King, I would like to offer to take on his debts. My consort will act as hunter in his stead."

"You have to be fucking kidding me." There was no way this was by chance.

"Untimely passing?" Crowe huffed a disbelieving laugh. "The man is still twitching."

Gigi's look of mock concern and benevolence made me want to peel it from her skull. "If either of them touches my sister, then Norman King isn't going to be the only untimely passing tonight."

-25-
THEA

I gripped Daisy's hand walking from the showroom and tried to stay rooted in my purpose instead of lingering on the way I could still feel Sylvan's tongue gliding over my cheek. We climbed onto the waiting bus, and I dragged her into the back. Kyle and the pretty redhead sank into the seat across from us.

He immediately started tearing at his cuffs with his teeth. "These damn bells are as good as a death sentence," he said around the fabric in his mouth. "Did you see the size of the gun that man had?" The glittery gears that reflected the light couldn't be fixed, but getting rid of those bells would be a massive improvement. He was shaking so badly that his wrist slipped, smacking himself in the face. "Fuck, Daze. I'm going to die. I'm going to die because some damn safari hunter is going to hear these bells and blow my body in two with the biggest gun on earth."

Daisy's eyes softened "Here. Let me do it. How are you always getting yourself into these situations? This is like the beams in the mine shaft all over again." She took his wrist to her mouth and bit at the thread.

"I don't fucking know." He half laughed the line, but Kyle looked like he was two seconds from a complete meltdown.

"We'll figure something out. We've escaped tighter jams than this before." Releasing his sleeve, Daisy turned to me. "Speaking of ... It's time you started talking. How do you know my brother?"

The engine started up, making the entire bus rumble. Pushing as close to her as I could, I prayed the rumble of the engine would be enough to mask my voice. The other people on the bus probably already heard too much and I

183

didn't know how much time we had, but it couldn't be much. "Three things you need to know."

"Okay," breathed Daisy.

"I'm here to get you out. Your brother and his friends are tracking me. We counted on being released into the same area, but if we're placed separately, then we need to figure out how to get together. And we have about a minute to figure that out." I tried scratching the blacked-out bus windows to little effect. I flicked my mind over every bit of intel I could remember about the town.

"On the way in there was a church. It had a tall bell tower. We should be able to see the belfry from most parts of the town. The moment you're free, head there."

"I can do that." Daisy nodded, looking so much like her brother that my heart ached. "And then what?"

"Hopefully they're hearing everything I'm saying, if not, then the boys will follow my tracker and ..." I thought of those smooth white walls blocking our exit. "They had a plan to get past the electrical field; however, that was before there was a wall erected. I don't know, but they'll figure something out. They always do."

The bus stopped, throwing me into the seat back. The door opened with a hiss, and a guard with a rifle stepped on board. "Number 857."

The redhead beside Kyle started crying, her face in her hands. "I can't do this again."

"How many times have you done this?" I asked.

"857!" he repeated. Still, no one moved. The guard expanded the photo on the tablet, then scanned the rows of scared faces. He locked onto a woman with long hair scrunched down in her seat as far as possible. Shoving the muzzle of the rifle into her cheek, he commanded, "Up!"

The girl trembled, but didn't move. The entire bus collectively held their breath as we waited for something to happen.

"Fine." The guard gave an annoyed sigh. "If you're not conscious when your hunter finds you, then that's not my problem." He flipped the rifle around, slamming the butt of the gun into her temple. The girl crumpled into the center aisle. Her head lolled toward me, and her mouth hung open like she was screaming. Shouldering the rifle, he grabbed the back of her shirt and hauled the girl off the bus.

The redhead slid her terrified eyes away from where the girl had just disappeared. "Too many times. I can't remember life before all of ... this." She waved her hand at the bus.

I thought of the autopsy report that The Wizard gave us. Did she know Didi? Surely, no one survived this hell that long, right?

"Did you by chance know a girl named Dahlia? She went by Didi."

Daisy's head snapped to mine. There were so many questions in her expression. Questions that we didn't have time to answer. I gave her hand a sympathetic squeeze.

"She died in the chase nine years ago."

"Nine?"

Before Daisy could ask more, the girl said, "Didi saved my life." She ran her hand over the scars strafing her arm. "We were hiding in the storage shed at the lumber mill. When our location was discovered, she pushed me under an old bandsaw before they realized there were two of us. They pulled her out, and she never once mentioned me. The next morning, I walked back to town and she never did."

I pressed my hand to the center of my chest and whispered, "I'm so sorry, Danny." I didn't know if he was listening, but I couldn't get his heartbroken expression from when he saw that report out of my mind.

Kyle asked the question we should have been asking, "How did you survive this for ten years?"

The redhead frowned and her eyes distantly looked at the blacked out windows. "When they come for you, either hide or figure out a way to run very fast. Anything else and you'll join the ghosts, or worse." She gave me a sad smile. "Didi taught me that."

"What's your name?" I had to know. If I never saw this woman again, I had to at least know her name.

"Isabelle, Isabelle Crane."

"If I can, Izzy—" I reached across the aisle and took hold of her hand. "—I'll figure a way to get you out, too."

"No." She shook her head. The long curls swayed around her shoulders and caught the bus's emergency lights, making her hair look like it was on fire. "Nobody escapes this place."

"Yeah, well, you've never met me. I don't take no for an answer."

The bus slowed to a stop. This time a man of medium build didn't need to be asked twice to rise. He walked to the front of the bus like he had no fear. There was a level of respect that came from meeting your fate head on.

I sank back into the seat and pulled Daisy close. "There's something else you need to be aware of."

"There's some bad history between us and The Queen. She's been using you as leverage against Danny. She's here, and I have a feeling you're the reason why. Either she's waiting for him to try and rescue you, or she's planning on harming you to make a point. You need to be extra on guard. There's a better than good chance you'll be having more than just your assigned hunters coming for you. Crowe won one of the bids, he has long blonde hair with a crow tattoo on the side of his head, he's on our side. Trust him."

"How do I know I can trust *you?*" Daisy attempted to look out the scratch I'd made in the paint.

"Because I'm the one crazy enough to get into this mess for no other reason than to get you out." I played with the trim of my babydoll dress. "Also, I love your brother and you matter a great deal to him."

"Number 774!"

The bus only had a few people remaining. Daisy was pulled from me not long after we established our plan. Isabelle was taken two stops later.

Kyle gave me a withering smile. "Good luck, Blondie."

"You too, Kyle. Survive, okay." I gave him a tight smile.

He shrugged one shoulder. "I've made it this far, haven't I?"

That was the truth. Of all I'd been through, I survived when those who would seek to destroy me didn't. There were wrongs to be righted and I'd be damned if I didn't live to see Gigi answer for what she'd done.

Smoothing my skirt down, I pushed past the man with the rifle, noting the blood streaked along the butt. There was a flapping sound of fabric and the clink of a chain against metal. I looked up at a tall flagpole. Flying proudly against the pinking sky was the Ozamandrian flag, its emerald and gold design was covered in the center by a large red heart. Before I could fully take in my surroundings, a black bag was shoved over my head.

An instant wave of panic flooded my senses. I forgot every rule the guys taught me and clawed at the bag. I tried to inhale, but the scratchy fabric filled my mouth. My hands were wrenched painfully behind my back. I screamed and on instinct fought to get away. A strong backhand clapped my ear, making my head ring like a bell. Cold metal bands secured around my wrists and locked with a beep. I tapped my fingertips and took three deep breaths. This was not how I went out of this world. Fuck them and their scratchy bags.

"Walk," a gruff voice commanded.

The man shoved me through a doorway and into a room that echoed each of our steps. The air had the tang of chemicals, tinged by mildew. It was pungent enough that, even through the bag, I gagged.

"Careful she doesn't trip on the spikes," someone said and I was jerked to the side.

Spikes?!

I tripped into an unexpected staircase, coming down hard on my knees and shoulder when I couldn't catch myself with my bound hands.

The guard to my left pulled me onto my feet and commanded, "Climb."

We wound around several flights. The metal beneath our feet clanked and vibrated with every step. We climbed long enough that when we made it to the top I was panting and my legs ached.

"Watch your footing here. The path is very narrow," he said, using the barrel of his rifle to push me forward.

I felt with my foot, bumping it into several metal barriers, before becoming brave enough to move onward. It felt like we were walking forever. The sounds echoed around us, making the room sound impossibly large. I tried to imagine where we could possibly be, but nothing connected together in a logical pattern.

When we finally reached our destination, I was roughly shoved down onto a stool. The plastic of the chair was cold against my nearly bare ass and legs. Of course the frilly skirt did nothing to shield me. My arms were stretched behind me until they were hooked on something. After a few minutes, the guards' steps retreated, leaving me alone.

Short of breath and my vision blacked, I couldn't make sense of anything. Maybe there was a woman crying in the distance — Or maybe I was imagining the whole damn thing. It felt like I was back in the dream state, unsure of what was and wasn't real? I almost expected to feel the scruff of King's beard scraping my neck. It made my skin tingle, like any second I'd feel the sting of a needle.

I wanted to scream, but I couldn't draw in enough breath to do more than whimper.

A gunshot fired, the sound unmistakable. The crying I thought I'd imagined went silent. For the first time since this plan's conception, I doubted that we'd make it from this town alive.

-26-
THEA

A screech of speaker feedback tore through the silence. With a startled yelp, my whole body pulled at my already sore wrists.

"What the fuck!" I shouted, ignoring the dull ache pulsing in my shoulders from having them pinned at this awkward angle for the past hour.

There was a crackle before a faintly accented voice spoke from above, booming all around me like the voice of Ozma. "Dorothea Gallant Rosen."

Oh, fuck.

Sylvan Deveaux's pretentious accent was unmistakable. Even though I couldn't see an Oz damn thing with the bag over my head, I swiveled from side to side.

"It was a clever disguise. I haven't quite figured out why you would end up here, or how you're even alive, but I don't question gifts when they appear at my feet."

"I'm not her," I shouted, my voice disappearing into the void.

"Don't worry. You don't have to lie. I cut the feeds from this building. If Gigi realized you were here, then we wouldn't get the chance to play. Where would the fun be in that? And those boys who paid so handsomely to own you, I gave them a clue to somewhere far from here."

Double fuck.

"I didn't want us to be interrupted. It's just you and me, little dove."

I pulled fruitlessly at the cuffs, pushing with my legs in the hope that whatever I was sitting on might tip over.

The voice over the loudspeaker cackled. "You really don't want to do that. Even if it would be entertaining to watch. I'll tell you what, I was going to let

191

you simmer in your fear a little while longer, but I think I'd much rather get things started. Wouldn't you?"

With a beep and a click, the cuffs around my wrists released and fell to the ground in a loud clatter. I pulled my arms across my chest, stretching my shoulders as best as I could and sighing with relief.

Shakily pulling the bag off my head, I was hit with a wave of vertigo.

"Oh my fucking Ozma above!" I dropped to my hands and knees, the stool I was sitting on toppling over and rolling off the edge of a very ... very ... very high platform. Several seconds passed before the stool splashed into the dark water below. His stupidly accented laugh bounced around the aquatics center. I leaned forward, gazing down at the pool way below us. A large white 10 was painted on the side of the platform. I'd been sitting all that time less than a foot from a ten-meter drop. A very long thirty-six feet stood between me and a pool I didn't want to be anywhere near.

"What the actual fuck, Deveaux."

Sylvan's steps vibrated the platform as he approached the platform. "What has you trembling so deliciously?"

Showing fear to a predator was like scenting the water, and I'd already seen enough sharks around blood to last a lifetime. I swallowed down every emotion and rose to my feet. I brazenly ignored his question and faked a smile that said, *"No, I'm not scared tit-less."*

"Is it the height or the drop ... or maybe the water? I heard you've had some intense experiences in the water lately. I trust that won't be a problem?"

What did he want from me, to tell him that I hadn't been able to get in a bathtub for over a month, much less take a dip in the deep end?

For every step Sylvan took, I slowly inched back until the heels of my Mary-Janes bent over the edge. There were three more platforms above us, for the divers with a death wish apparently. The next level up, connected to a catwalk crossing over the pools to another set of diving platforms at the far end of the center. The stairs I'd struggled to ascend twisted down to the main floor, but all of those things would require getting past Sylvan first.

I had nothing.

Sylvan pulled a slender dagger from a sheath, spinning it in the palm of his hand effortlessly. "You could come here willingly. I'll take you from this place and you'll never need to worry about the water again."

"No, you'll just give me a whole new set of things to worry about."

Sylvan dipped his head and smiled with too many teeth. Pulling a second dagger free, he walked across the platform like it was the most natural thing in the world. The man wasn't fazed by the height in the slightest. I hadn't thought I was afraid of heights either, but being surrounded on all sides by such a drop was slaying my confidence. My heart was pounding so hard I couldn't think against the pain in my chest and the spots peppering my vision.

"I'll take it nice and slow." The rising moonlight from above set the shadows of his face into stark contrast, highlighting his brow and cheekbones. His eyes glimmered with predatory menace. "If you relax, you'll see that I'm not really the monster you think I am. Some women have found what I do to them to be quite pleasurable."

Fucking think, Thea.

He was only steps away now. The sweat gathering on the back of my neck cooled in the draft spilling in through the missing ceiling panels. I felt like I was standing at the edge of a cliff, being pushed to the limit by an approaching beast.

"There's nowhere for you to go, little dove. You're out of options." Light flashed off the blades, doing another revolution. In his hands, they looked more like pincers than knives. Deveaux would only need to take three more steps, and then he'd be close enough to strike with them.

"There are always options, Sylvan." Slowly, I toed off my Mary Janes, stepping on the heels so that only the very tip of my foot was in them. "Nick would tell you that I always take the path that causes the most destruction. Danny would say I make problems where none exist. I'm unpredictable on a good day, but back me into a corner, and I'm liable to do something truly reckless."

Kicking my foot hard, the shoe went flying at Deveaux, hitting him in the arm. In his shock, the knives he was spinning went flying into the distance. His stunned expression wasn't prepared for the second shoe that immediately flung into his vile face.

"I always have options," I said, throwing my arms wide and tipping backwards.

"NO!" Sylvan lunged forward, his fingers gripping the front of my dress in time to hold me hovering over the drop.

He curled his arm, fighting the pull of gravity. That trick was all I had. I slapped and scratched at the hand clutching the straps of my dress.

"That's enough! Naughty girl." He reached to his lower back, pulling free a smaller dagger. The edge looked wickedly sharp and I knew intimately the damage small blades could do.

As he slashed down with the knife, I twisted. The blade sheared through the fabric and the side of my stomach. Blood quickly soaked through my dress. It unraveled in his grip, tearing free of my body.

For several long heartbeats, I was weightless. I stared at the bloody scrap of fabric clutched in his hand. Then in a blink, I was tumbling into the air.

-27-
THEA

My back hit the water with the force of a freight train. Pain splintered its way up my spine, flaring hot at my shoulder. The momentum of my fall drove me deep into the water. I opened my eyes. The chlorine stung, and it was dark, but I was still able to make out the large steel spikes anchored into the bottom of the pool.

I twisted, barely able to rotate in time to avoid impaling myself. On one of the nearby spikes, a heavily decomposed corpse was skewered. Whoever this soul was had long since been forgotten. Pinching my mouth shut to avoid swallowing Ozma only knew what, I pushed off the floor of the pool and swam as hard as I could for the surface.

The fear of what lay in the dark distances of this massive pool pressed in on me. There were no sharks in here. This was just a pool. A forgotten, dirty as fuck pool, but still a pool.

My foot snagged on an invisible wire in the water. The irrational thought of being grabbed almost made the impulse to scream take over. I shook my ankle, slipping free but losing all of my upward trajectory. Several large harpoons shot through the water, exactly where I would have been if I hadn't slowed to free my ankle.

I needed to get out of this death pool. With that thought pushing me past the fear and pain in my side, I swam hard. My lungs screamed for release.

Breaking through the surface, I gulped down huge swallows of air and wiped the chlorine from my eyes. Sylvan was still looking down at me from the large diving platform. He was probably waiting to see if his torture pool did me in.

I waved good-bye at him and swam for the ladder. Sylvan ran across the catwalk far above. With a little luck, I could make it out of here before he made it down from his perch. My skirt fanned around me like I was a weird jellyfish. The front flap of my dress was half cut open and exposed the bra beneath it. At least I'd taken off my shoes before jumping in. I shuddered when I thought of how hard it would be to swim with the clunky things strapped to my feet.

Realizing the boys were probably freaking out and not wanting them to break from our plan, I said between strokes, "I fell into a pool. Sylvan is here. I'm okay. Get Daisy, she's in a theater … maybe." It was imperative that they got to Daisy first.

I climbed the ladder closest to me, ignoring the slimy green film on each of the rungs. Once out of the water, I scanned the room to see where Deveaux was. This place was huge, hosting three massive pools and large bleachers for watching the events. Movement clattered high above.

"Small mercies," I huffed and sprinted for the large glass doors on the far end of the atrium. Of course they would take me closer to where Sylvan was descending. Which was probably why he was headed on the catwalk to the other side of the pool. Staying here wasn't an option.

Halfway to the exit, I noticed the pool office. It was dark, with papers scattered over the floor. On the far side was a back door that looked like it went to the filtration system. What were the chances that there would be a loading dock through these rooms? Once upon a time, they wouldn't have brought parts and supplies through the main entrance. They would've had a way to tend to these discreetly.

Taking a chance, I broke through the office. My sopping body was probably leaving a massive trail through the building. It wouldn't take Sylvan long to figure out where I'd gone.

I gingerly felt my way around the massive pump in the back room. Any of the lasting light from outside was fully gone now. I was all too aware that if the pool was rigged, anything could be waiting for me in the dark. The air was cooler back here, making my already chilled body shake.

Somewhere behind me were footsteps. Sylvan wasn't far. This was a stupid fucking plan. I was like one of those dumb women in horror movies running into a dead end instead of making a break for the obvious exit. I never should have come in here.

The bit of the light spilling in from the pool area suddenly blacked out. Sylvan entered the room on quiet steps, stalking silently through the dark like it was second nature to him.

I pressed my body to the back of the pump, sliding into the narrow space between the casing and the wall. My cheek scraped the metal as I wedged myself into the cavity. I exhaled to compress my ribs enough to make it past the corner hump. Once I was into the slightly roomier space under the bulge of the tank, I gathered my soaking wet skirt to try and be as inconspicuous as possible.

A puddle already formed at my feet, but maybe, in the dark, he would assume that the water was from the leaky pump and not from me. My arm fell back, hitting the handle of something long and slender. Slowly it began to tip, and in slow motion my heart climbed into my throat. I wrapped my fingers around the handle, praying that my wet hands wouldn't let it slip. When my grip held, I let out a controlled breath. That was way too close.

Weighing the rod in my hand, I couldn't be sure what it was without getting enough space to fully look at it. Maybe a wrench or a crowbar. I wasn't picky, heavy metal was heavy metal. Either would knock a fucktart up, and my options for self-defense were in short supply.

Deveaux crossed the pump room to a door that I hadn't seen in the dark. If I had just felt around a bit more, I could have been running for my freedom. Instead, I was stuck behind this pump and waiting to be discovered.

Pulling on the handle, the door cracked open. Light and air spilled into the stale space. Sylvan ducked, squatting low as a large pipe swung down at head level. It slammed the door closed, its heavy weight ensuring that no one was going through that doorway again.

It was insanely unfair that he knew where the traps in this hell were. At this rate, I'd be lucky to make it out of the center, much less to the church to meet up with Daisy.

Sylvan spun in a slow circle, scanning each area as he passed. He stared directly at the pump, moving a step closer. His scrutinizing eyes narrowed on the space behind the casing. He had to know I was here. Where else could I have gone? I transferred the metal rod into the hand closest to the exit and pushed further into the tight space, holding my breath. If he came for me, I could at least get one quality swing in. Let's see how good he is at chasing with a smashed knee.

There's nothing here, you ugly maniac. Move on. Please. Please just keep going.

Sylvan's loafers scraped over the concrete floor, slowly moving away. The problem was that a man like him could and would be faking it. The old "you thought I left, but I didn't leave, surprise I'm behind the door" routine.

I eyed the massive pipe blocking my exit. If one door was rigged, chances were the others would be too. I needed an exit that even a psycho like Deveaux wouldn't think to try. I worked my mind over the details of the arena. Nearly the entire building was made of glass. It wouldn't be hard to break it. I thought of the breeze cooling my neck on the platform.

And then, I knew *exactly* how I was getting out of here.

Fuck. I was not lying when I told Sylvan that I was liable to do something reckless.

28
NICK

Dear Mr. Woodsman,
Congratulations on winning a place
in this year's chase.
You have won Fox Number 774

Please be aware that Mr. Leone has also won
hunting rights to Number 774*.
All Hunters must be ready at the
Central Plaza at 8PM.

Location Clue: Where minds awaken
and knowledge is found.

Best of Luck,
La Chasse Administration
*La Chasse is not responsible for loss of life,
damage to personal property, or bodily injury.

Leaning against the sculpture at the center of the cobblestone plaza, I stared at the message flashing on my tablet. Beneath the text, the photo of Thea stared back at me. I ran my fingers over it, wishing it was her and that we were anywhere but here.

Anywhere but here had been on my mind a lot lately.

Before Thea, I could spend days sitting in the quiet, alone and perfectly at ease. I preferred it that way, especially on days when my thoughts were loud. Danny and Crowe knew to let me be. They understood how important that quiet was to making my thoughts be quiet, too.

After Thea, I didn't think I could hate the quiet more. Surrounded by silence, I was reminded of just how much space she'd consumed and how gaping the hole of her absence was. I wanted my isolation from the world, but unlike before, I needed her to share in it with me.

Last night, I lay in bed—a very empty bed—contemplating what it would've been like to be just a boy with a girl he was crazy in love with. If I'd never left Italy and she was never orphaned. If we'd grown up average kids, with typical lives, in a normal town. Whatever normal was, I longed for how uncomplicated it must be. What I was looking at right now was as far from normal as it got.

Everyone was gathered in the center of town. The official sunset should be any minute. The nearly full moon was already high in the purple sky and the sun had long since dropped below the roof line.

Some of the patrons had changed from party attire to full tactical gear laden with weapons. I didn't know what they expected to find when the siren blasted, but it wasn't going to be a small army requiring full-body Kevlar.

A man in only simple jeans and a worn band T-shirt spoke easily with his companion. The pair had thick accents from somewhere south of Oz. Nothing about them looked like they belonged in a foxhunt, more like they were waiting to enter a concert. The one only had a bowie knife on his hip. I couldn't decide if that meant the man was lethal enough to be worthy of noting or dumb enough to come here so ill-prepared.

Sylvan was nowhere to be seen. I expected him to be here for the start of the hunt. That had my hackles rising. Sure, we knew where Thea was currently placed, but so did he, and it wasn't in the location that the clue pointed to. The clue clearly meant she was in a school, but the map showed her dot stationary in the middle of the massive Aquatics Center. There could be a dozen reasons for why Sylvan was purposely misleading us, and none of them were good.

"Tell me Daisy's clue again?" Danny asked for the third time.

"Where lies rise, and curtains fall." Crowe's attention was locked on Sebastian Charles. Gigi, it would seem, had stayed behind with her team of security, of course. She'd probably spend the night drinking champagne and laughing with the rest of Ozmandria's criminal world. In a way, it was appropriate for her to stay behind with the vultures.

"A hospital, maybe?" Danny guessed. "Life and death, with an exam room curtain?"

"How well do you think he's kept up on his fighting skills?" Crowe said, ignoring Danny.

Sebastian was double-checking his weapons. The various ties and cuffs on his hips proving that he wasn't going straight for a kill. At the very least, that meant we'd have another chance if we failed today.

I ran my hand over my mouth, considering the question. We'd done a few jobs together, enough for me to know that he wasn't someone to underestimate. "He spent years as an attack dog for The Northern Syndicate. Not only can he fight, but he'll know how to be covert."

"Maybe it's not a literal curtain," Danny said, still pondering the clue.

"It's a theater, Danny. A theater," Crowe said, never taking his eyes from The Queen's consort. "Daisy is in the theater."

"Ohhhh yeah. Lies—acting. Stage—curtain. Of course. Damn, when did you become smart?"

Crowe slid his eyes to the side, pinning Danny with a glacial stare. He didn't say anything, but the threat was communicated all the same. Crowe had gone full dark, moving into the mental space where he would do anything to get the job done. Even I knew better than to fuck with him when he was like this.

"Why couldn't they just tell you what building they were putting people in? It's a whole damn town. They could be anywhere."

"I'm pretty sure that's the point," I said, seeing the energy among the crowd beginning to ripple with anticipation.

"Yeah, well. I don't like it."

"Nineteen." Crowe dropped his head and grinned at me with truly possessed-looking eyes. "One more, *Cazzo.*"

"You're an idiot, *Vincen—*" My barb was cut short by the buzz of an incoming message, and then I didn't care about anything but what was on my screen.

M: She's not breathing.

Che. Cazzo. Stai. Dicendo?[1]

Crowe and Danny each looked at their watches, getting the same alert I had. While we were in the open, we'd been counting on Maddox to alert us if something happened with Thea. The last thing we needed was La Chasse's admin realizing we had our own form of communication with us. Even now, the three of us shouldn't be looking at our watches all at once, but a message like Thea not breathing was damn hard to ignore.

Thea's pulse was frantic, so she wasn't dead, but her blood pressure had skyrocketed, and the blood-oxygen level was bottoming out. Maddox was right. Whatever was happening, Thea wasn't breathing. There was no sound, no speech, no whispers in her ear—just radio silence and the rapid staccato of an out-of-control heartbeat.

"He's choking her, or she's suffocating." Danny turned, looking in the direction of where we'd determined the Aquatics Center to be. "Fuck this. I'm going for her now."

"If you leave now, those guards posted on the edges will shoot you before you make it ten feet," I said, pointing at Sylvan's guards stationed at the end of every street. Faking Sylvan's atrocious French accent, I added, 'failure to follow the rules will result in immediate disqualification and forfeiture.'"

"Oh, thank fuck." Danny said, letting out the breath he was holding in a massive puff.

Thea's stats all at once leveled out. Ten seconds later, text started scrolling across the screen.

"I fell into a pool. Sylvan is here. I'm okay. Get Daisy. She's in the theater on Main."

---

1. What. The. Fuck?

"See? Told you." Looking as calm as ever, Crowe said, "She's in the theater."

Danny sneered; provoking him when he was all wound up probably wasn't the wisest choice. "Sorry, I can't take anyone wearing a fanny pack seriously."

Crowe slowly tilted his head, making him look even more unhinged than he usually did when he got like this. "It's a hip pack. They aren't the same."

"Keep telling yourself that."

There was a better-than-good chance they'd end up shooting each other before the hunt began. Then I'd have to explain to Thea the story of their idiotic demise. At least I'd have her all to myself then. Silver linings.

"For starters, this is respectable. Fanny packs are something for pre-teen girls and old grandmas in kitten sweatshirts."

"Hey, if the fanny pack fits."

"I will kill you. Slowly."

Danny smiled for the first time today—which was probably a warning sign that he was about to crack. "Nick, tell me tha—"

"*No. Assolutamente no.*[2] I know better than to waste my breath on something so fucking inane as the fanny versus hip debate."

Crowe continued, "Not to mention this is fucking useful. I have to carry a lot of shit to keep you alive."

"Okay." Danny adjusted the weight of his rifle, pointing at Crowe's bag. "Still think it looks like a fanny pack."

"It's on my *hip,* fuckhead. My hip. Hip pack."

A beeping sound started, first slow, then getting faster and faster.

"Time to work, *cazzos,*" I said, snapping at the countdown projected beneath the clock tower ahead of us.

Crowe looked at me and then to Danny. "Take out Sylvan and get our girl. If I find out that either of you dropped your guard like last time, I will gut you."

Danny looked like he'd been slapped. That was a low blow. Even for off-balance Crowe.

---

2. No. Absolutely not.

"Along the way, I plan to take out as many of these fuckers as I can. Ya know, for funzies."

"Funzies? Now who's sounding like Thea?" I said, shaking my head.

Crowe's lips lifted into an unnerving smile, "See you thundercunts at the rendezvous."

The time clicked to 00:00, triggering a siren that blared loud enough there was no part of this town that couldn't hear it. A massive flock of startled birds took off into the sky.

Taking a deep breath, Crowe kicked his head back. Without looking, he drew his gun and aimed at the man to his right—the asshole who had spent the past half-hour recounting all the debauched plans he had for his fox. She was a sweet-looking thing, too, with innocent eyes and long curls framing her face. With a crack, Crowe pulled the trigger. The bullet tore through the man's neck, spraying the marble base of the sculpture behind him. The hunter had a second to clutch at his throat, before he fell to the ground dead.

Crowe winked. "Happy hunting."

-29-
THEA

S lowly, I crept from my hideyhole in the pump room. Every step I took sounded like a damn gong announcing my arrival. It was impossible to avoid the crumpled papers, broken glass, and random leaves—which had no business being in a pool, yet, for some reason, existed for the sole purpose of making it impossible to walk silently.

I couldn't see Sylvan, but I knew he was here somewhere ... waiting. A hanging sign pointed down a hallway indicating the direction of the locker rooms. In my panic, I hadn't noticed that the parking lot wasn't located outside the main exit. Now that I wasn't sprinting for my life, I had a clear view of the fountain and lawn spreading before the complex, meaning that somewhere in the back of the building there was a second exit.

My instincts screamed that Sylvan was waiting there for me. *Not today, stabby man.* I looked at the glass ceiling high above me. If all of the obvious ways in and out were rigged, then my only option was to take an unobvious one.

I padded my way back to the tall and winding staircase. Tinges of pain stung my feet from where the floor had torn open my soles, and I did my best to ignore it. A few minor cuts were the least of my worries right now. If the plan to enter myself willingly into La Chasse was a bad one, then what I was about to attempt was truly ludicrous. As quietly as I could, I ascended one flight at a time until I reached the 15m platform and connecting catwalk.

Air flowed freely up here, moving my hair like a fan was blowing directly on me. Chills coursed over my skin, making the wet dress feel like being wrapped in a heavy ice block. The metal floor was cold on my bare and cut feet. The longer

I lingered, the more the cold turned into shooting pain until each step felt like walking on needles.

Beyond the glass ceiling, it was a cloudless night with a large moon watching my movements and lighting the path for me. At least I wasn't attempting this in total darkness. I had to take my wins where I found them, right?

Just like I remembered, there were several broken ceiling panels scattered across the arena, including the one directly over the 20M diving platform. My escape simply required walking the catwalk, climbing onto the railing and up the supporting posts, then pulling myself over the broken glass and onto the roof. Simple. Like climbing the monkey bars ... except Em never took me to the playground, and the one time I tried climbing on the cages, I fell and fractured my arm.

Best not to think too much about it.

"This will be fine. Totally fine." Maybe if I kept telling myself that, I would begin to believe it. I definitely wasn't about to fall to my death or plunge back into a terrifying spike pool. Nope. *This would be fine*.

With already trembling hands, I leaned over the railing and looked down at the drop. Yeah, no. This was a terrible idea. Yet here I was stepping out onto the catwalk. The platform was narrow, barely wide enough for a single foot. This wasn't a simple walkway, it was a damn balance beam. The suspension wires acting as a guard along the sides did nothing to ease the vertigo spinning me from all angles. I placed one foot in front of the other, taking my time and gripping the handrails like they might actually save me from my own stupidity.

Reaching the middle of the natatorium, there was a small set of stairs ascending to an 18m platform, and beyond that a final 2m ascent to the final level.

"See," I said, speaking to whoever was listening in a foolish attempt to calm my nerves and feel a little less alone. At the very least, Maddox would be monitoring me. My hands shook uncontrollably as I climbed higher. The slice in my stomach burned with each ascending step as a reminder of what awaited if I didn't make it out of here. "This is child's play. Nothing scary about being up here." I couldn't catch my breath, needing to pant between words ... but I kept moving. I was certain that if I stopped, I would freeze and never leave this place. "Just one more platform and I'll practically be at the ceiling."

The final ascension was a ladder with bars looping in a safety guard around the rungs. "I can't believe there are people who do this for fun." I crawled onto the final platform, unable for many long seconds to get off of my hands and knees.

"Guys, if you're listening to this. Just know I tried to make the smart choice and, believe it or not, I think this is it. I'm going to exit via the glass roof. I have no idea if there will be a way down from up there, but it's better than the spikes of doom waiting down below. Not to mention the psycho with all those knives ... so, so many knives. Why does one man have that many knives on him? What happened to a gun? Not that I want him to have a gun either. Fuck, Thea, what are you doing here?"

It was probably a bad sign that I was now rambling to myself. I couldn't shut it off. In all my years of doing stupid shit, I don't think I'd ever reached a level of nervousness where I ended up rambling to myself.

There were several criss-crossing suspension cables connected to the ceiling rafters. I lunged for the nearest wire, attempting to keep my body weight as low as I could. The fibers of the steel were rough, biting into my palms when I latched my death grip around them.

"So I've learned some things about myself today. Like, I don't like heights ... or fake French maniacs." I poked my head between the wires and looked down, suddenly overwhelmed by the possibility that Sylvan might be climbing up behind me while I was busy babbling to myself.

Exhaling a long whimper, I relaxed slightly. There was no man stalking me in the dark, but there was a drop. The pool looked *small*. Like the toy version of the thing I'd jumped into earlier.

"Fuck me sideways. Yeah, I shouldn't have looked down. Danny, try to hold the lecture when I see you. I'm aware of everything you're currently cursing at me, and I agree. You're totally right, and the next time you try to talk me out of an idea, I will listen." I propped my leg onto the handrail, having to stretch as far as I could to do it. "Who am I kidding? I'll probably still do it anyway." Was

I hyperventilating? Damn it, I couldn't catch my breath. "But you can get the credit for being right."

I heaved myself up. "Fuck!" I whisper-shouted. My shoulder and back throbbed from the strain. My first fall into the pool must have messed me up more than I realized. That new bit of knowledge was not helping, especially as the pull of gravity swung my ass over the open air. Wobbling and twisting awkwardly, I eventually wrangled myself into something that resembled upright. I settled one foot on the solid handrail and my already aching hands clutched the wires.

All I had left to do was climb. "Here we go."

My limbs wouldn't move. I knew that I needed to hurry. It was only a matter of time before Deveaux realized I wasn't trying for any of the exits and came back. I bit down on the inside of my cheek hard enough to redirect all of my attention to the pain of my bite. It helped, giving me enough focus to catch my breath.

Extending my right leg out, I anchored the center of my foot between one of the wire intersections. A pair of bolts held the cables firmly in place.

Pushing my weight onto that foot, a howl of pain tore up my chest. I gritted my teeth, refusing to scream and alert Sylvan to what I was doing. The steel threads cut and pulled at my already torn soles. Tears fell one at a time from the corners of my eyes.

"You can do this, Thea. Just keep moving." Treating the wires like my own jungle gym net, I moved up my web, one painful juncture at a time. "It's not that far, really. A few minutes of climbing and this will be one of those funny stories you tell years later around a campfire. '*Gee, kids, did anyone ever tell you about the time Old Lady Thea climbed a net, suspended 30 meters over a death pool?*' I don't know whose kids these are that we're talking to at a campfire, but … Fuck, this is high."

Air from the open window buffeted my face. I wrapped my arm around the highest wire and leaned back to get a clear view of the ceiling brackets. The glass had mostly broken away, leaving a gap large enough to squeeze through, that is if I wasn't cut to ribbons in the process. One jagged piece in particular looked very menacing. I scowled at it. "Nobody likes you. Just stay over there and out of my stomach."

The smartest option would be to pull myself on top of the girder directly overhead. No, the smartest option was to stay at home wrapped in one of my boys and not placing myself in yet another death defying moment ... but the girder would have to do.

—30—
CROWE

Now Playing
The Hunting Season
8:32   5:47

Any other time I might have appreciated the humor behind making such a sign. Now, the only thing I felt was my pulse ticking in my neck. It hummed in time with the flicker of the marquee lights.

The ticket booths were clouded with years of grime. An open sign hung from a chain on the closest window. Oh, the irony. Naturally, a place like this would offer a creature like me an open invitation. The way I saw it, there was no harm in thinning the herd when the opportunity presented itself. I'd already dropped three people who thought I seemed like a worthy target, not including the man who was currently eating the heel of my boot.

He grasped feebly for the knife sitting a few inches too far away. Pity he only had another minute of life left in him. The way I'd staked him to the ground with his sword probably had something to do with that. Why did people always insist on wielding weapons they didn't know how to use?

The entrance seemed like an obvious way into the theater, but the curtains draped artfully over the entryway felt like a perfect place to hide a pendulum axe. I'd had enough experiences with guillotines for one lifetime. There was the possibility of climbing the outside of the building and entering through the service hatch for the marquee roof. Just the thought of scaling a building made my chest hurt. I'd leave that as a last resort.

Pocketing the deadman's knife, I slowly walked the perimeter of the theater. Most of the windows appeared normal, but a closer inspection found that they all had a small ring of explosives against the seams. It wasn't much, but enough to blow the hands and face off of whoever tried to open them. Guess that meant no climbing in through a bathroom window.

At the back of the theater, there was a fire escape snaking all the way to the roof. See, this was what fire escapes were supposed to do. If the Hotel Revolt had an escape like this, maybe we wouldn't have had to zipline. That being said …

I turned to the old pharmacy next to the theater. They were so close that they nearly shared a wall. Only a narrow alley separated the two, and that would be easy to jump. Peering into the window, everything inside was dark and quiet. It was possible that this wasn't set up as a hunting location.

There was no seal on the window, no trigger wires, and from what I could tell, no lasers to be interrupted. I pushed up on the glass, then jumped back and waited for something to happen. When a minute passed and I still had a face, I took it as a good sign that the window was clear.

Carefully, I climbed onto the window sill and pulled a small travel-sized can of dry shampoo from my hip pack. Danny arrived at a manhunt with his monster rifle. Nick opted for a simple pistol and a tactical axe. Turns out, admitting he loved Thea wasn't the only revelation Nick made that day in the hotel. I'd chosen to come prepared for anything. They were always expecting me to get into weird places, and you never knew what you might need. The small pack held everything from tinsnips to duct tape. My Desert Eagle was holstered, not that I'd needed it much. My suspicion was that the real hunters were biding their time and waiting for the riff-raff to take each other out.

Hunter-on-hunter violence was never permitted before, and I had to admit that there was a certain allure to stalking other predators. I didn't understand anyone wanting to go after the innocent bait spread across the town, but taking out someone who came prepared to kill? Now that attracted an entirely different kind of patron. It was probably why La Chasse was looking at its biggest payday in the fifteen years it's been hosting this event.

I sprayed the powdery aerosol into the surrounding air, being sure to check the ground. In less than a minute the cloud dissipated with no signs of a laser system or tripwires.

"Most people enter via the door," a smooth voice said, rising from a chair I hadn't seen tucked into the corner. Sebastian Charles leaned on the old-fashioned soda counter, no longer draped in the shadows he'd been waiting in. So much for getting the upper hand. "I did the same thing. Couldn't believe this building was clear. Were you going for the roof? That was my plan."

Sebastian placed his pistol on the marble counter with a soft clink and pushed it out of easy reach. It was an offering of temporary truce, although only a fool would believe that was his sole weapon.

I lowered into the room, checking the wall and the corners as I did. Missing one person was inexcusable, missing two would end up with me dead on the floor and I had family to save.

"Did you know that the first soda fountains were in pharmacies because people thought it was a wonder drug?" Sebastian said, lazily tracing his finger along the edge of the counter. "Early soda was loaded in sugar and caffeine, giving people an unexpected buzz."

"The cocaine probably didn't hurt any either," I said with an easy laugh. Casually, I sat my own pistol beside his. I'd always gotten on well with him. His death would be one that I'd bear the weight of for a long time.

"Crowe, I don't want to kill you."

"Well, that's convenient. I don't want you to kill me either. Problem solved. Why don't you pack up and head back to the palace like the good little lap dog Gigi trained you to be?"

Sebastian's smile fell into a tight line. "I didn't enter La Chasse to rid Ozmandria of a talent like yours. I'm not even here to kill Danny's sister."

What he was saying felt genuine. A part of me wanted to believe him, but none of what he said changed the fact that he chose to back Gigi's bid for power. "If you wanted to take Daisy back, why not order it? Surely *The Queen* can command anything she wants now."

"Not anything." Sebastian gave me a knowing look.

We'd refused her call to action. Nick was never going to start the Morphia trade back up again. After what she'd done to Thea, none of us would play any part in her dominion. If she wanted puppets, then she was looking at the wrong marionettes. We'd cut our strings long ago.

How could a man I respected side with a woman like Gigi? She didn't treat him as an equal. He was the Queen's Consort. Not King or Prince Consort, but the Queen's. He leaned into the counter.

"Tonight was about proving a point."

"What point is that?" I didn't bother masking my disgust.

Sebastian lifted his attention to something over my shoulder, and a sultry voice curled through the darkness like smoke, "That everyone has a line they will cross when pushed over it."

-31-
NICK

"This way," I said, glancing at the satellite feed. Turning down a side street, we aimed for the large Aquatics Center on the edge of town. According to Maddox, five people put bids in on Thea, but only two had won other foxes. In addition to Deveaux, we couldn't discount them as a possible threat. If they really wanted Thea, they'd need to come after us first.

I scanned the rooftops, glancing over the windows of each building as we walked. The new hunter-on-hunter rule was one the patrons of La Chasse were taking full advantage of. The streets of this ghost town had shifted into complete anarchy the moment the sun set. People were running and screaming in every direction. To my satisfaction, more than once, I'd seen foxes turning guns on their attackers.

My wrist buzzed with an alert from the app Maddox created to make it easier to track Thea. I wasn't exactly pleased with the voice commands required to operate the system, but they really pissed off Danny, and that made them easier to tolerate.

"Overlord General, show me Tight Tits," he said to his watch through gritted teeth. Squinting at the GPS, he added a relieved, "Good. She's still at the pool. At least she's not on the move. That makes this easier."

We passed Nod Hotel, the glow of the fluorescent sign painting everything in an inappropriately cheery shade of pink. A machine gun clattered from one of the upper floors. I felt awful for the innocents fighting for their lives in this hell, but there wasn't time to save them all.

My watch buzzed again:

"Just know I tried to make the smart choice, and believe it or not, I think this is it.

I'm going to exit via the glass roof."

"The fuck you are!" Danny scowled at his watch, scrolling through the readouts. "You're right, Princess, I'm going to give you fucking hell for this."

"*Cazzo!*" I shouted, seeing the display window of the shop on the other side of the street light up with three quick flashes. I grabbed the back of Danny's holster. Throwing him to the ground just as the wall blew apart. Chunks of masonry, glass, and flaming bits of wood rained down on us. Mixed among the rubble were stray pieces of what had once been a person.

"That'd be one of those treats Deveaux mentioned." Danny pushed my upper body off of him. I shouldn't have had to shield him at all, but his eyes were glued to the damn watch screen.

"Can you please get your head on straight? When I said Thea was a distraction that would get one of us killed, I fucking meant it, " I scanned the road for more signs of explosives. "I love her too, but I also know that I'm not helping her by obsessing over every rambling word and spike in her heart rate."

Danny pulled a string of charred flesh from his shoulder. "What are you trying to say?" His eyes widened. In a split second, he'd drawn his gun and fired it at the balcony across the street. A man in a designer suit toppled over the railing, snapping his leg on the cobblestone sidewalk. "Oh by the way, shooter three o'clock."

Presuntuoso di merda.[1]

He did a grand sweep of his arm. "Please, by all means, give me a lecture about keeping my head in the game."

---

1. Smug fucker.

I clicked off a pair of shots, ensuring the man didn't get back up. Whoever he was hunting had one less person to worry about now. "You—"

The rumble of motorcycles roared closer, cutting off what I was about to say and drawing our attention to the library at the end of the street. A woman with long, curly red hair rocketed down the front steps on a motorbike, her pale pink dress fluttering in the wind behind her.

She blew by us, a puff of exhaust pluming in her wake. A second bike followed closely behind. This one had a man with a white tank top and tactical pants. He was laughing like they were out on a joy ride together.

"When did libraries start checking out motorcycles?" Danny asked, just as confused as I was to see the vehicles tearing out of a building.

As the sounds of engines faded, I turned back to Danny. "I know being locked away fucked with your head as much as it did hers."

He looked down at his watch, frowning at what he saw. Whatever was happening to Thea, was making her ramble. The buzz of her speech alert was nearly a consistent hum now.

I smacked his face, not too hard, but enough to get his attention.

"The fuck?"

"You've got to stop obsessing about everything and accept that sometimes shit is out of your control. Failing to stop it or see it coming does *not* make it your fault."

"You're wrong." He pushed me away, taking off down the street. "*I* let her get taken. *I* let King get the jump on us. She was *my* responsibility."

I shook my head, jogging to catch up. "Yeah, and I was supposed to keep her safe, too. If you're taking blame for King stealing her, then so am I."

Danny scoffed, stepping into the shadows of an alley and pulling me with him. A brunette stumbled down the steps of the library, holding her side. A dark figure, with a heavy hood masking his features, calmly walked after her. In his hand, he held a tactical repeating crossbow.

"Shit, now that's a weapon," I whispered almost in awe of the modifications he'd made to it. "That's a Cobra Adder, but look at it: Scope, laser sight, extended magazine with extra clips on his belt. *Diamine*, I could get hard just holding a weapon like that."[2]

It looked like it held, at a minimum, twenty bolts. There was no way this should have been on the Ozmandrian market. The Premier made them illegal decades ago.

The girl screamed hysterically, running at a full sprint down the side road—in the exact direction we needed to go.

The archer calmly lifted the crossbow, notching the stock into his shoulder. The laser painted her back with a streak of red, then slowly lowered to her left calf.

"We have to do something," Danny said. Lifting his own rifle.

The archer pulled the trigger. The string snapping with a nearly silent '*shwick*'.

Danny fired in the same moment. His gun, even with the silencer, was thunderous by comparison. The bullet struck the golden bolt knocking it from its trajectory.

"Nice shot," I said, slapping his shoulder.

The archer snapped his head in our direction, cocking the lower level to notch a new bolt into place. Danny didn't move, the laser of his own rifle centered directly on the center of the archer's chest.

Like a wraith, the man leapt over the edge of the staircase and disappeared into the shadows of the side alley. The instinct to hunt him down was strong. I could see Danny warring with the desire too.

"You kept Thea safe, and it almost killed you," Danny said, thoughts still on that dreadful night at The Villa despite the interruption.

We quickly walked toward the Aquatics Center. Much like the archer, the girl he was stalking was nowhere to be seen.

"Nick, you took the blast from the bomb. Don't think I haven't seen the way the tattoos on your back have been shredded. That didn't happen while laying on your back, taking it easy."

---

2. Damn,

I smiled at the memory of laying on the kitchen floor with Thea grinding down on me, the glass shards cutting into my shoulder blades with every rock of her hips. I'd take those wounds a hundred times. "That's not exactly true. Besides, with the way that girl's a magnet for trouble, you'll get another chance to play hero."

-32-
THEA

I shimmied myself as high and tight to the ceiling as I dared. Small remnants of plate glass clung to the edge of the opening like the teeth of a shark—another unneeded visual right now. I tried to memorize where the largest bits were and swallowed my fear. Somehow, I managed to release the wire and braced my entire forearm on top of the metal girder. With a bit of luck, maybe I could avoid slicing my stomach open further and bleeding out on the ceiling.

Taking three centering breaths, I rocked up and down, priming my legs to give me the boost I would need to make it over the edge. It didn't matter how many push-ups I'd done while locked away in the tower. If I was hanging by only my hands, I didn't know that I'd have the strength to pull myself up. Seventy-five feet in the air felt like a foolish time to try testing that theory, and falling to my death wasn't exactly on my list of things to do tonight.

On the final breath, I pushed with all of my force, launching myself high enough that my upper body made it over the edge. The silky layers of my tulle petticoat caught on the bolts, slowing my trajectory and tugging me back down. I scrambled for anything to grab. My palms squeaked against the glass until my fingertips bit into the edge of the metal brace that held the panel in place. It wasn't much, but it was enough to counter-balance. I kicked at the snagged fabric until it tore free, leaving my legs dangling in the open air.

The insidious images of my body broken and drowning far below reeled through my mind while the strain on my hands ached for release. Silently screaming from the pain rioting around my body, I swung my leg up, raking my thigh over the shards of glass and using my hips to roll onto my back.

Staring at the moon, I spent several long minutes paralyzed from shock. My heart was beating in the sides of my temples, flaring over my stomach and thrumming against my palms. My entire body felt lit up by pain.

Pain was good. It meant that I was still alive, but I wouldn't stay that way if I remained here for too long. So, I gathered my strength and sat up. The cool air of the night instantly chilled my skin, the wet dress making my teeth clatter. Fucking hell it was cold out here, or maybe that was the shock seeping through my skin and making my bones rattle. I had to keep moving.

Taking inventory of my new surroundings, I looked around the sloping roof. It extended far in each direction. The building somehow felt even bigger from above.

The bells in the church tower rang, chiming the hour. The steeple was easy to see from up here. In fact, the entire village was visible from this vantage point. A street over, a woman sprinted in my direction. Her legs were a blur beneath her, turning into a side alley and cutting back in the direction of the Aquatics Center. A man with a crossbow ran after her, pausing his pursuit at the end of the alley to fire the weapon. Her scream was like the howl of the wind churning in the night air.

I only had one thought. That could have been Danny's sister, and my fear was keeping me from saving her. "I'm coming for you Daisy," I said, pushing to my feet. "Hey guys, I made it to the roof. I'm going to find a way down and head toward Main Street."

Leaning over the hole, the pool glimmered in the moonlight far below. I couldn't believe that I'd climbed up here. Thinking about it was like an out-of-body experience. I had no idea how I'd managed to pull it off.

Tentatively, I stepped onto the glass, testing its stability. On the opposite side of the roof was what looked like a lower level and, hopefully, a way down. I scrambled over the surface, zigzagging to avoid the missing or cracked panels.

Boom.

Ahead of me, a pane of glass exploded like a bursting star. The crack of the rifle echoed over the night. Its blast vibrated through the pane and into my aching feet.

"Fuck!" I screamed and scurried back over a metal bracket. Small beads of sweat rolled down the back of my neck, cooling instantly in the night breeze.

As much as I dared, I peeked through the glass. Beside the center pool, Sylvan stood against a stand. He held a long rifle, with an equally long scope attached—aimed at me. He pulled back on the bolt, cocking a new shell into place. There were dozens of shells laid out before him, waiting for his next chance to take his shot.

I climbed to the central ridge, where the steel girder was the widest. Wide was an overstatement. Even here, where the beams intersected, it was at most a foot wide, but it would give me some cover while I walked to the edge. But then what? He had to know I'd be climbing down, and wouldn't he be waiting for me on the ground?

Leaning over the glass a hair's breadth to see if he was still there, the glass beside my feet burst with another night-shattering crack. This time, his shot was close enough that I felt the heat of the shell graze my thigh, and a streak of tulle was melted along the bottom of my frilly skirt.

"Guys, if you're listening, I could really use some help getting rid of the very large rifle aimed at me in the pool, or I'm never getting off this roof."

Like the damned fates had heard my plea, a heavily accented voice called up, "Oy, girlie, what you doin' all the way up there?"

I blinked in surprise. Not one of my guys, but at this point, I wasn't picky and would take any advantage that slumped my way. I carefully inched my way to the other side of the roof.

The man standing in the grass beside the Center's walls waved jovially at me as if he'd found me sitting on the front porch sipping tea. He looked completely out of place in a nondescript band tee and jeans. The only visible weapon on the man was the large knife sheathed at his hip. Beyond that, he didn't look like he was armed at all. People didn't just go out for an evening stroll around here. Which meant he was a hunter, friendly expression or not. I was sitting here like a cat stuck up a tree. It didn't get much easier hunting than that.

"There's a ladder over thataway." My new-found buddy pointed down the building.

231

I chewed on my lower lip, debating my options.

"Never fret, baby girl, ole Chet will get you outta here." Ole Chet was too helpful to be good, but maybe I could con him into taking out Deveaux for me. I liked my chances with the bowie knife far more than the sniper rifle.

"Please. I'm so scared," I whimpered, trying to seem as meek as possible. I didn't exactly have to dig deep to pull out some tears.

"I'm sure ya are, pretty little thing." He flashed me a smile that was altogether too sweet.

"The gun. There's a man in there." I pointed toward the glass. "He tried to kill me. I don't know what's going on. Please, help me. Please." I sank to my knees, crawling as close to the edge as I dared. Using the most effective weapon currently available to me, I used my arms to press my tits together. Men were men, and right on cue this one's eyes fell to my chest. "Please."

"What man?"

"The one with the gun." My voice broke, becoming something sad and pitiful. The sob made my chest heave. I'd seen plenty of terrified girls begging for help in my days at The Farm, so I had a plethora of material to pull from. I should get an award for this performance. "Please. I just want to go home." For a bonus, I decided to add, "I want my mom."

"Don't you worry. All them frown lines are doing your face a disservice. Chet will get him for you, little miss."

Ugh. I tried not to outwardly cringe. There should be a special ring in hell for people who referred to themselves in the third person.

"Then we can see about getting you down from there and into someplace warm."

Chet moved toward the windows. Pushing to my feet I slowly walked backward. For a person who paid to be a hunter in this farce of a fox hunt, he had zero survival instincts. The man didn't hide his presence or watch his steps. No doubt Sylvan already had his sights on him. Which was fine, because if he was watching Chet, then he wasn't watching me.

As I moved closer to the end of the natatorium, I saw two yellow taped edges, indicating the access ladder. I'd have to thank Ole Chet for pointing it out. It would require crossing at least five glass panels to make it there. Five panels where I would be totally exposed to the psycho below.

I leaned over the steel beam. Sylvan was still there. My heart leapt with excitement. The spider's attention was solely focused on the man walking openly through the exterior floodlights.

To be sure both men were completely distracted, I glanced back. Chet clambered over the barrier fence, not bothering to check for booby traps. Idiot. His work-boots snagged a sparkly wire. He shook his foot, yelling, "Arggh."

Realizing what was happening, I turned for the ladder. A defining boom vibrated in the air, shaking the building. My sense of balance disappeared, the world spinning as my stocking feet slipped over the glass— just as a small arrow flew past my cheek.

No bigger than my forearm, a golden bolt clattered against the glass. Its surface shone in the moonlight. There were several long seconds where I didn't understand what I was seeing. An arrow?

"For fuck's sake!" I cursed.

A second bolt slammed into the glass by my hand. The arrowhead was wickedly sharp, gleaming with deadly promise. I didn't have time to question where these new projectiles were coming from. Or why, apparently, fate hated me. I picked up the arrow, tucking the metal into the elastic straps of my bra, and sprinted for the ladder.

Glass burst beneath my feet as I leapt from my panel, springing from one step to the next and praying that the ground would be there when I landed. I crossed the first two panes of glass missing the shot that shattered them. Pelted by tempered shards, I wove in time to miss the arrow flying for me and another that soared over my shoulder.

Stepping onto the third panel, the glass disintegrated beneath my feet. My stomach lurched into my throat as my body became momentarily weightless. Pinwheeling my arms, I flailed wildly, hoping to snag anything that could save me.

Wrapping my fingers around the metal seal that connected the panes to the girder, my weight slammed to a stop, causing my shoulder to wrench painfully. Forgetting everything but the pain and the drop below me, I screamed.

Panic slammed into me. I desperately kicked my feet, searching for anything to put them on, but there was nothing. No catwalk. No wires. No safety of any kind. The only thing beneath me was the drop and a massive pool. The palms of my hands burned, and the muscles of my fingers protested their hold as they slowly slipped from their place.

A voice in my head, that sounded a lot like Danny, said *Get it together, Princess! You're going to make yourself fall.*

I sucked in a necessary breath and then another, forcing my panic back into its cage. Fighting through the pain, I swung my other arm up, grabbing the metal bar. Immediately, the tension on my throbbing shoulder eased enough that the lightning streaking across my vision faded.

With a crack, the glass in the panel to my left exploded, followed by the one in front of me. With each shot, the bar in my hands vibrated and the bolts holding the metal in place bent. My body sank one terrifying jolt at a time until, finally the one at the end sprang free.

My palms, growing sweaty, slid to the very end of the bar.

"No. No. No. No." I prayed, whispering the word as if it could somehow save me.

-33-
THEA

One by one, the bolts tore free like buttons popping on a shirt that was too tight. With long terrifying sweeps, I swung over the drop, sliding lower with each deadly pass of the pendulum.

Bang! One last gunshot hit the bolt supporting my metal strip.

The piping fell ahead of me in a graceful spin, reminding me of seeds dropping from a maple tree. The water rushed up and a hundred panicked thoughts flitted through my mind all at once. I vaguely remembered something I'd seen on television about cliff divers and twisted body as straight as possible, hitting the surface feet first.

The cold water enveloped me, counter to the burning heat that blistered across my entire body. My shoulder, the gash in my side, my back and neck, the thousands of tiny cuts peppering my exposed skin—everything pulsed with pain like I was generating heat for an entire city.

My legs folded up like an accordion. I hit the tile lining the bottom of the pool with a slow-motion stop and the metal bars landed soundlessly beside me. Thousands of little air bubbles filtered back to the surface.

I was back in the fucking pool.

At least this one wasn't lined in spikes and dead bodies ... yet. Attempting to keep my fear from drowning me, I curled into a ball and pushed off the floor. I tried to swim to the surface, but my right arm wouldn't respond. When I lifted it, my vision momentarily went white from the pain. An involuntary scream broke from my chest, a bubble of air escaping with it.

Awkwardly, I used my upward momentum and one good arm to swim higher. Second after agonizing second, I kicked and thrashed my way to the surface, breaching the top just as I thought my lungs couldn't last another second.

Gulping at the air like a fish, I tread water, sinking beneath the surface occasionally when I couldn't keep myself afloat with my injured shoulder. None of that was my real concern. Somewhere down here, Sylvan was waiting for me. I scanned the deck, finding his abandoned sniper rifle and shooting stand.

"You really need to work on your flying, little dove."

I spun toward his voice. Deveaux leaned on a rack of rolled-up tarps, examining his nails.

Half floating on my back, I kicked away from him. It pushed me deeper into the pool, but I knew instinctively that I needed to be as far away from this man as possible. The fact that he'd abandoned his gun was as alarming as it was advantageous. That rifle could give me the upper hand I needed to make it out of this place alive. The explosion Chet triggered blew apart the side wall, and now whole sections of the glass were missing. It was an easy exit — if I could get past the killer hunting me.

"I wasn't sure you'd survive that last fall," Sylvan mused. He squatted down, his long legs folding beneath him, making him seem even more spider-like than usual. "Although, you don't really look intact either. My little dove had her wings clipped."

Like my shoulder could hear him, it throbbed in response. "I'm not your anything."

"I knew you'd be a joy to hunt. It will be most entertaining to see what you do next." He stood, brushing his slacks into place and straightening his shirt.

My heart rate spiked with warning. The opposite edge was so far away. I would never swim fast enough to outpace whatever he had planned.

"What are you going to do, Deveaux, release a hundred piranhas into the pool and watch as they nibble me to death?"

Sylvan barked out a laugh. "Now there's an idea. Would you mind if I stole it for next year's chase?" Of course he'd see that as a real possibility. He flexed his spindly fingers, wrapping them around the long handle attached to the end of the rack. "You might want to take a deep breath."

He pulled the lever, activating a noisy motor. It beeped three times in warning, before the giant roll of safety tarp slowly uncoiled. It was anchored on either side of the pool by large metal rollers.

"Son of a bitch." I swam as hard as I could, cursing that my stupid arm wouldn't respond. Slowly, the cover advanced. Pausing for only a second to look over my shoulder, the pool was already half covered. I was only about ten feet from the side, but the cover would reach me before I could make it there.

"Fuck." This was how I died. The rough surface of the heavy tarp scraped my legs. I pushed with my hands against the edge, hoping to somehow trigger a safety mechanism. I might as well have been pushing at bedsheets for all the good it did. I hung on the end, hoping my weight might slow it down, but all that happened was it bent in the middle, dunking me under the water.

Abandoning the bar, I scrambled for the edge of the pool. The tarp, like a weighted blanket, pushed me down while it continued to inch higher and higher. My fingertips brushed the tiled surface of the side, fighting back the pull of the tarp.

"Guys," I said frantically, knowing these seconds were my last. "I'm about to be stuck under the pool cover. Please, be fast. I love y—"

The cover pulled over my head, plunging me back into the much darker water. I pushed and slammed at the surface, hoping to force any amount of space between the wall of the pool and the edge of the vinyl. It didn't move. These things were meant to keep people from falling in the water. The was a macabre irony in that it would cause my drowning.

The black silhouette of two feet stepped onto the surface, standing directly above where I beat on the fabric. There was the faint outline of his toes. Of course a prick like Deveaux wouldn't want his expensive French shoes to get wet. I was going to die and the last thing I'd ever see was his ugly feet.

I beat against the silhouette. With each frustrating thump of my fist, a sharp pain scraped against my breast. I'd barely noticed it amid all the other aches. Hope sparkled golden in my mind and I pulled free the bolt I'd shoved in my bra. The arrowhead was sharp and fine like a scalpel.

Struggling to tread water, I braced the bolt in my one good hand. With all of my strength, I rammed the tip directly into the dark shadow above me. It hit the canvas with some resistance, but one at a time, the fibers gave way. I pulled back and did it again. This time I punctured through the fabric, directly into Sylvan's foot.

He cursed loudly. Drops of blood fell through the canvas. The light flooding through the hole lit up the red-tinted water. With satisfaction, I tugged the bolt free and used the tip to make the small hole larger and larger.

Heart beating in my ears, my lungs screamed for air. I brought my mouth to the hole, getting in one breath before his fist slammed into my face.

I recoiled, squinting against the pain and resisting the urge to cry out.

Deveaux tore at the hole, making it large enough to fit his entire hand. Fisting the bolt, I rammed the point into his palm. If he wanted it so badly, he could have it.

With a howl of pain, Sylvan pulled back, taking my arrow with him. "You're going to regret that."

I desperately pushed my mouth back to the hole. Instead of sucking in air, I bumped my nose into something hard and cold. The muzzle of Sylvan's gun hovered over the surface of the water.

This was it. The end.

—34—
CROWE

I twisted in surprise at the unexpected feminine voice.

Gigi walked across the room like she owned it. How long had she been in the room watching us? She wore the type of outfit expressly made for vanishing into the shadows and I'd walked right into her trap like one of those idiots out there in the street.

She lifted herself to sit on the counter directly next to where I was standing. The black suit she wore seemed to absorb the light from the entire room. As did the scarf tied around her usually glowing blonde hair. Even as close as I was, I couldn't make out the swell of her chest or the dip of her collarbone. When she crossed her legs and nearly disappeared against one another. It was like standing next to a void. At least now she looked like what I always knew she was, nothing.

"Where'd you get an ultra-black suit?" I tried really hard not to admire the ingenuity that must have gone into making something of this caliber.

"It's Vantablack, actually. Don't you love it? It's a fabric made from micro-carbon fiber, a gift from The Ozmandrian Aerospace Center. They were designing a coating for military vehicles at night. Planes that were impossible to see, even with the naked eye. Trucks that could roll through a town with no one knowing."

"A Vantablack suit ..." Damn, I hated how cool that was.

"This particular shade absorbs 99.9% of all light and is officially the darkest substance on Earth." She ran her hands over her thighs. "It's also bulletproof and more flexible than Kevlar. The applications for this tech are endless and *all mine.*"

The fucking hubris on this woman.

An explosion down the street shook the building, making dust from the rafters rain down around us.

Gigi sneered at the motorcycles buzzing past the front display windows. "You know I actually find these sorts of events distasteful."

"Distasteful is using the wrong china for a state dinner," I drawled, looking at my Desert Eagle and debating if I should make a move for it now. A bulletproof suit left a headshot as my only option. This close to her it would be impossible to miss. "These are innocent people being hunted. I think we've gone past distaste."

My watch buzzed. I closed my hand over the loop of continuous texts scrolling over the tiny screen. Thea certainly had a lot to say all of a sudden, but I couldn't risk paying too much attention to it. The last thing I needed was Gigi connecting the dots between number 774 and Thea.

She toyed with the jar of peppermint sticks next to her. "So what was the play here, Danny and Nick went after Sylvan while you freed his sister?"

"Something like that." I hated her. Plain, simple, pure hatred. Gigi had always looked down on us from a tower she'd erected, sure that she knew everything before the rest of the world. She assumed she was three steps ahead, somehow missing that we'd decided to leave the path entirely.

"This is the problem with Ozmandria. Too many people are trying to satisfy their own needs while ignoring the real problems at hand." Gigi flicked her wrist, shooing away the thought of the people she now ruled. "Case in point, If I wanted to, I could have Sebastian do anything to sweet Daisy. *But where is her brother?* She's at my mercy and he's off chasing vengeance. Its why Oz needed a strong hand to wield them back on track."

"You hear the hypocrisy in what you're saying, right?" I slipped my hand into the pocket of my hip pack, wrapping my fingers around a slender tube.

"Stop right there, Crowe." Sebastian, in a flash, retrieved his pistol and aimed it at me. "Hands out of your fanny pack of tricks."

"It's not a fanny pack." I rolled my eyes. "What the fuck is wrong with everyone? It's a hip pack. They aren't the same thing."

Gigi snorted. "It's definitely a fanny pack. I've always hated that thing. "

"It's clearly sitting on my hip." I pulled my hand free, pointing at the bag. For fuck's sake, this was a highly useful piece of tactical gear. It wasn't like I'd covered it in butterflies and glitter.

"Whatever you want to call it, I know the kind of shit you sling around in there." Sebastian cocked his gun, gesturing with the muzzle. "Keep your slippery hands where I can see them."

"Relax, Seb, it's just a pen." I opened my hand, letting the retractable pen fall.

"The problem is—" Gigi picked it up and twirled it between her fingers. "—people don't know what's best for them unless they're told what it is."

"Or maybe ..." I tapped the side of my head like I'd just had a novel idea. "People should be able to choose, rather than having every thought dictated to them. You can't do the thinking for all of Oz."

"Why not? Right now, their idiotic little brains do whatever the televisions tell them to. Why not me? Maybe if they follow what I say, then the world might improve."

"And if they refuse?"

"There's a hundred ways to thin a population."

She really bought into her own bullshit. I could see it on her face. Even when she was casually throwing around *genocide*, Gigi thought she was the hero in all of this.

"Forced Morphia addictions and trafficking innocents isn't what benevolence looks like."

She dismissed my concerns like they weren't valid. Pointing at me with the back of the pen, she remarked, "Those are a means to an end. Oz has a food chain, and there needs to be something for the people on top to feed upon."

Seizing my moment, I lunged forward, grabbing the wrist holding my pen. I twisted Gigi so that she blocked any shot Sebastian might have and shoved the tip of the pen against her neck. Throwing the full weight of my body into her, my sternum depressed the clicker.

Gigi gave a feral shout of pain when the quick release injection shot into her throat. She lifted her knee into my stomach, leveraging space between us to throw me back.

"I fucking knew you were up to something," Sebastian gloated.

Gigi threw the pen at me, the now harmless bit of plastic bouncing off my stomach. To the naked eye, it looked like any other ballpoint. All those minutes absentmindedly spinning a little wand of agony, and she never suspected.

"That was an underhanded trick," she spat.

I rubbed against the knotted scar over my heart. "You'd know all about those."

She hopped down from the counter, fury transforming her normally beautiful features. I transferred my weight to the balls of my feet, ready to react whichever way she went. Sebastian stealthily moved in my direction. If I wasn't careful, they'd box me in.

"What did you shoot me with?" Gigi rubbed at the injection site. Green veins were already spreading from the wound.

"You can't tell?" I licked my lips, waiting for the moment of realization to hit her. "Give it a second. It'll come to you."

"Crowe, the antidote—" Sebastian thrust his hand out. "Give it to me. You have to have one. You're too smart to deal in poisons without carrying it." A frisson of panic shook his voice ... as it should. Gigi was about to be in a lot of pain. Not enough, but a lot.

Gigi lashed out, moving to sweep my leg and driving a sharp jab at my solar plexus. It would have been a good attack. Except, her already slowing speed was easy to deflect. She threw up a high front kick, the spiked heel of her boot swiping through the air.

When her leg came down, it buckled beneath her. She crumpled to the ground like tin foil. The most satisfying scream I'd ever heard tore from her lungs. Gigi's spine bowed, her fingers curled, and her limbs contorted in opposite directions as all of her muscles contracted at once. The tendons and veins pushed against the barrier of her skin. Small capillaries burst around her eyes, turning them bloodshot and bruised. The green veins broadened, discoloring the hue of her neck into a sickly green. Covered in a mass of pinks, purples, and greens, she looked like a thrift store watercolor painting.

I drank down every second of the macabre display.

Gigi's tortured screams quickly turned into a choked and barely audible wheeze.

Abandoning his gun, Sebastian dropped to her side and pressed his ear to her chest. "Crowe, she's *The Queen*. You can't kill her."

I strolled to the counter, easily slipping my Desert Eagle back in my holster. "That's not poison." I couldn't keep my smile from rising. "Trust me, I want the bitch dead, but poison is too simple for the damage she's wrought. Gigi has a world of hurt ahead of her. I don't think she'll be going anywhere for a little while. You'd be smart to stay out of my way, Seb. So far, you haven't done anything wrong—besides screwing the devil."

"What did you hit her with?"

"Adder Oil, also known as The Green Dragon."

Recognition widened his expression.

"They say it feels like your blood is replaced with dragon fire." I hadn't planned on getting this close to Gigi. If I had, I might have packed better, more interesting things to do once the cytotoxin did its thing. She wasn't going anywhere. There'd be enough time to finish her off and save Daisy. Deveaux could deal with explaining to the press how The Queen ended up dead in the middle of a manhunt. This kind of opportunity would never present itself again.

"It's time for you to leave, Sebastian. In concentrated doses, Adder Oil rots flesh. If you don't go now, The Queen won't be the only one suffering from a touch of disfigurement."

Sebastian rose to his full height, taking a defensive stance but also completely aware that in his panic he'd left his gun on the counter behind him. "You know I can't do that, Crowe."

"I figured. You should know, I won't take any joy in killing you." I rolled my spine, hating how my too-tight abdominal muscles pulled at the vertebrae. That was another gift I had to remember to thank Gigi for.

Sebastian removed the dagger tucked into a sheath built into his sleeve. He flipped in backwards, so that he could maintain his fighting stance. I'd seen him take this approach dozens of times. Knife play was where he felt most comfortable. It was his strongest skill set.

However, it had one flaw—my gun.

I pulled my pistol, firing cleanly through his shoulder, forcing him to drop the dagger.

"Fucker," he cursed, clutching at the wound. He looked down at Gigi. I could see the debate warring within him. If Sebastian left now, I would let him walk out of here. He knew it. It was in moments like these when you saw what true loyalty looked like. This wasn't it.

"Okay." He dropped his head. "You win, Crowe."

A massive explosion shook the walls, resonating deep in my chest. Outside, several car alarms blared. Something massive must have been detonated on the edge of town. Involuntarily, I looked at my wrist. Thea was over there.

I pulled my watch to my mouth, hoping the mic would still pick up my voice over the cacophony of car alarms. "Overlord General, show me Tight Tits."

The map appeared with her dot still squarely in the middle of the Aquatics Center.

Before I could debate running to help, a thundering crash rumbled outside the window. It sounded like the roar of a waterfall. With several flashes of light, the central roof of the theater collapsed, the marquee falling with it into a massive heap of dust and rubble.

One of the hunters must have tried to get into the building, somehow setting off a chain reaction of the window traps.

Fuck. Daisy.

I never should have allowed Sebastian and Gigi to distract me. I looked down at the stupid fucking queen. The left side of her neck and face was a puffy mass of green, swollen flesh. Her eyes vibrated with all she couldn't express.

As much as I hated it, her words came back to me, *"She's at my mercy, and he's off chasing vengeance."*

"Son of a bitch." There was no time. Daisy was in that ruin. She could be dying in the seconds I was taking to decide what to do. Swallowing my wrath, I ran into the chaos of the street and left my chance at revenge lying on the floor behind me.

— 35 —
CROWE

The door to the pharmacy slammed behind me. The glass of the window was blown out by the explosion and shards crunch beneath my feet.

"Run!"

A crazed jester pinwheeled long limbs at me. Covered head to toe in torn lycra, he tumbled into me at full speed. The glittering gears of his costume hung at broken angles. It looked like he'd done battle with a blender and lost. His orange hair flamed beneath the streetlights, looking as wild as he was.

"Run!" he repeated, grabbing my arm and pulling me down the street.

"What?" I looked over my shoulder and had to blink twice to process what I was seeing. A massive panther prowled down the center of the road. His coat was black as the night sky, and his eyes glowed bright yellow like they had their own supernatural light. Leaping in one smooth bound, the cat perched on the blown-out remains of a car two streets down.

"Where the hell did he come from?" Sylvan really had lost his mind. We'd joked about wild animals, but I never actually thought he'd do it. The jester pulled me into the small alley that barely remained after the theater imploded.

"It's stalking me," he whimpered. "There was a can of something, and it sprayed me. It made the cat go all crazy like. He's been following me ever since." The jester pulled on the scattered bits of lycra, revealing the three massive gashes raking his abdomen. "I barely got away. The explosion startled him and he ran off, but I know he's still tracking my scent."

"Then why in the fuck are you dragging me along with you? Go be panther bait on your own, Jester Boy." I pushed at the hand death-gripping my arm. "I don't need you rubbing your sexy panther juice all over me."

251

"Because Blondie said you were here to help." His grubby fingers dug in harder.

I swear to Oz, if I ended up mauled because of some clown school reject ...

"You have a gun, right? Shoot it."

"Sorry, what did you say?" Did he say Blondie?

"Shoot it. With your gun." He made little pew-pew sounds.

"No. You said Blondie." He had to be talking about Thea. Then it clicked. This was the asshole trying to cop a feel on the ride in. I should leave him here for the cat.

"Yeah, Blondie. I heard her tell Daisy that you were here to get her out. Not a lot of guys running around with crows tattooed on the sides of their heads, know what I mean?"

The panther growled a low, dissonant rumble, leaping to the ground with an agile grace only large cats were capable of. He was close enough now I could make out the faint black-on-black striping in his fur. Was this actually a tiger? A black tiger. Fucking hell, I was right. There are lions, tigers, and bears in this nightmare.

"I'm not shooting the tiger. They're probably endangered or some shit." I pushed him further down the alley. Why the fuck I was going along with this? If he was sprayed with attractant, then he'd make a great distraction. I bet to a tiger he smelled like a kitty wet dream.

The cat stretched his jaws wide, the long fangs glinting bright white against the black shadow of his body. He roared in a warning that he was about to pounce. My muscles tensed, ready for him to close the space with a quick jolt of speed.

I rooted around my hip pack, pulling out a pair of blow darts. They weren't much bigger than a drinking straw, but they had enough tranquilizer to take down a large man. I just had to hope that they'd do the trick on a five-hun-dred-pound cat.

"Shoo!" he yelled, picking up a bit of rubble and chucking it toward the tiger. "Go on now, git!" The cat hissed, making the idiot dart behind me.

"Please don't do that again," I said through gritted teeth, pulling him off of me. There was no way I was playing human shield. "This cat is scary enough without you pissing him off."

"Kyle!" A girl whisper-hissed, emerging from within the rubble of the theater. "Kyle, over here." She propped open a door in the middle of a crumbling wall. Looking at her was like seeing a ghost. She was the spitting image of Danny, reminding me so much of what he looked like as a boy—before he cut his hair and the angles of his face firmed into something masculine.

Of course, any sister of Danny wouldn't need to be rescued. Here she was about to save us.

The tiger yowled. It echoed off the brick work, making every hair on my body stand on end. He was so large and nothing but muscle.

"Kyle, was it? You're going to run for the door."

"He'll catch me."

"That's a definite possibility, but I'm going to shoot this dart and, if you're lucky, it will take him down before he tears out your jugular. Whatever you do, if you make it into the hole, keep that door closed. It might take both darts."

"Okay." Kyle grabbed my arm. "Wait, what if it takes more than two darts?"

"Let's not worry about that. You ready?" I slid him off of my arm.

"No."

"Too bad. Go on three … two … one."

Squealing in fear, Kyle sprinted. Dust slipped beneath his feet on the start, but miraculously, he made it to the doorway. The tiger, on the other hand, did not slip. He leapt into the air, crossing half the distance in a single bound.

I crouched low, letting the cat soar past me. Taking a deep breath, I fired the dart into the thick muscle around his neck. The tiger slammed into the door, curling a paw around the edge as Kyle and Daisy screamed. He scratched at the wood, snarling and roaring his frustration.

I crept closer, moving so that I could get a clear shot at the raging animal. On my last step, my boot came down on a broken panel of glass. It crunched loudly enough to be heard over the growling and crying happening at the door.

With predatory precision, the tiger's head turned toward me. He didn't blink, didn't chirp in warning or roar, instead the cat remained perfectly still. The pair of us stood frozen, studying each other to predict our next moves.

With agonizing slowness, I lifted the dart to my lips. The tiger slowly stalked closer. I took a deep breath, firing the dart at the same time the cat pounced. Claws extended, his weight slammed into me. We slid into the wall of the pharmacy. All of the air rushed from my lungs.

The cat's paw raked the brickwork over my shoulder, gauging the terracotta and taking a chunk of my shoulder with it. I wedged the heels of my boots into the beast's stomach and heaved with all of my strength. Pain tore across my chest, and my legs screamed against the cat's intense weight. I craned my neck away from the snapping jaws. My thigh felt wet, the burn cutting its way down my leg telling me that the back claws had taken a piece of me too.

The tiger opened his jaws wide.

I twisted my head away and squinted my eyes shut. If he was about to devour my face, I didn't want to see it coming.

He blew out a gust of air on a loud yawn. The exhale blew back my bangs and smelled of blood. His big, sandpaper tongue licked out. It was wider than my hand and covered the better part of my face in a single wipe.

Slowly, his originally immovable presence shifted as the tension in his muscles eased, and I was able to press him back. With another loud yawn, he took a couple steps back and circled the pavement before flopping to the ground. He rolled from side to side, twisting this way and that with oddly contented sounds of relaxation. If I didn't know better, I'd have thought he was stoned. Eventually, the tiger curled in a tight ball, huffing out a final sleepy breath.

When he wasn't trying to maul me, it was easy to appreciate how beautiful he was. The sleek black, striped coat looked like midnight. His muzzle twitched. Tiny sounds escaped as he dreamed and one paw was ticking in time like he was walking in his sleep. He was probably dreaming of eating a jester ... or me.

"Holy fucking Ozma." I let an unbelieving laugh chuckle out of me. I just fought a *tiger*. A real, honest to Oz, jungle cat. I rested against the brick wall, holding my hand over my ravaged shoulder. It fucking hurt. Everything hurt.

After several long minutes putting myself back together, I climbed over the rubble to the wooden door. "Knock-knock."

"Who's there?" Kyle said in an absurdly fake voice. This fucker. My chest felt like it was torn in two, my leg had a cut deep enough to see the white of bone, and this idiot was making jokes. No wonder they'd dressed him like a jester.

"Open the door, Tiktok, or I'll feed you to the cat."

"I'll feed you to the cat, who?"

I actually laughed at that one.

Kyle pushed open the door, helping Daisy to climb safely over the debris.

"You're my brother's friend?" she asked, eyeing my tattoo.

"Yeah, that's me. Danny will meet us at the rendezvous. He's getting ..." I narrowed my eyes on Kyle. "Blondie."

"She's supposed to meet me at the church. Something about our exit having to change. I was on my way there."

I rose an unbelieving eyebrow. "Through a collapsed building?"

"Well yeah, the exits were all booby-trapped. How else was I supposed to get out? Who do you think triggered the chain reaction? It took a little bit of rewiring, but I made it work."

"That was you?" I shook my head, regretting it instantly when it pulled at the raw muscle of my shoulder.

"Sure. It's not hard." Her arrogant smile was all her brother, too. I thought of how Toto said they'd swap places, and I could see it.

"Fuck, you really are your brother's sister. None of you know how to do anything in moderation."

"I needed an out. It seemed like a good idea at the time." Daisy tilted her head, blinking in disbelief. "If I'm being honest, I didn't expect such a weak charge to do all of this." She gestured at the demolished building.

"You and my girl are going to be thick as thieves. I can see it already."

Daisy twisted her face in confusion. "Your girl? I thought she was with Danny."

Kyle coughed, way too invested in the conversation for someone who wanted to keep all of his teeth.

"We're a unit, a group package, so to speak. She'd never choose, and I'd never want her to." I directed my gaze at Kyle, letting my leash on the Scarecrowe slip a little just for him. I lowered my voice to barely above a whisper and dropped it an octave. "But if I see you put your hands on her again, then I will rip them from your arms. Understood?"

Kyle gulped, the fringe of his collar wobbling with the rise and fall of his Adam's apple. "Yeah, I never meant to. I mean, I was only—"

"Stop, Kyle. While you're ahead." Daisy patted his shoulder. "The man just fought off a jaguar for you. Don't make him waste that effort by killing you now."

"I don't think it's a jaguar," I said, crouching down. The beast let out slow, deep breaths. Slipping my fingers into the coat beneath his ear, I gave him a scratch. "He's got stripes, not spots. I think he's a black tiger. They must be incredibly rare. They used to have a white tiger at the E.C. Zoo, but I've never even heard of black tigers before."

I didn't look up at them, instead taking this rare moment to love on something as vicious as I was. In another life, I could have been one of these. Even if he had tried to eat me, I felt a weird sort of kinship to him.

"Well, let's go find your girl. I can't wait to put this town behind me," Daisy said, slapping dust from her dress. The flowing ends were torn in a jagged line at the knee. It was smart of her to shorten it. It'd take nothing to snag a skirt on a nail or a bolt.

"There's just something I need to do first," I said, saying my goodbyes to the beast. I really hoped Sylvan didn't do something stupid, like putting him down instead of corralling him back into a pen.

Main Street was surprisingly empty now. Smoke drifted from the hotel, casting an eerie fog through the street lights. The action from earlier in the night had died away, probably literally. I'd been waiting for this, the eye of the cyclone. A calm in the middle of the chaos.

Daisy and Kyle followed me into the pharmacy.

The empty pharmacy.

"Motherfucker!" I screamed, picking up a glass container and throwing it at the far wall. It exploded in a shower of shards. I didn't expect Sebastian to stick around or to leave Gigi behind when I wasn't looming over him as a threat. It didn't change the fact that this was our only chance. I felt it in my bones. Gigi'd never fuck up like that again. She'd have the Green Dragon's fire as a reminder.

"What is it?" Kyle searched the room with terrified eyes, thinking I saw something in the shadows that he missed.

"Nothing." I spun for the door. "What was here is long gone."

"So then we go get Blondie, right? At the church?" Kyle said like he was actually invited to this party.

My wrist buzzed.

"I'm about to be stuck under the pool cover. Please, be fast.

I love y—"

"She's not at the church." My voice felt hollow. The Aquatics Center was a mile from here. Even at my fastest, not half-mauled state, I couldn't sprint there in less than five minutes. Thea'd drown long before I made it there.

Where the fuck were Danny and Nick?

-36-
DANNY

Climbing the long road that led up to the Aquatics Center, Thea's silhouette was sharp against the moon. Seeing her in one piece eased the barbed wire knot in my chest. She was backing slowly across the central ridge of the building, looking through the glass at something down below.

Nick and I started jogging the second we got past the chaos of Main Street, but when I saw the words, *'very large rifle aimed at me,'* I started sprinting.

My watch was buzzing as she carried on a conversation with someone who must be outside. For all of my fear, Thea was as cunning as they came. She was trying to convince the new hunter to take out Sylvan for her. From the way she kept delivering line after line to him, she was succeeding.

With Nick keeping pace next to me, we made it to the Center's lawn in time to see the hunter she was talking to climb the fence lining the flower beds.

"He realizes that—" Nick's question was cut off by a massive explosion. The night turned momentarily blinding. A wave of heat rocketed us into the air. I landed hard on the pavement, my head knocking against the asphalt. The world spun as debris rained down. I barely managed to pull my arm over my face in time to block a massive chunk of wooden fence.

Beside me, Nick groaned and spat a bit of mulch from his mouth.

Thea sprinted across the roof. The glass burst beneath every step she took, echoed by the crack of a shotgun. Even with my concussed hearing making everything sound like it was underwater, there was no mistaking it. "We've got to stop him before he shoots her down."

Nick was already on his feet, but his attention wasn't on Thea. He was looking at the edge of the property—at the archer with a crossbow firing in quick succession at our girl. The laser of his targeting system cut across the night.

My next move was instinctual. I raised my rifle, aiming directly at the man I should have killed the first time I had him in my sights. When Salvatore first put a gun in my hand, he told me to never aim unless I intended to shoot. I hesitated earlier when I never hesitate, and now this fucker was firing that damned crossbow at the one pure thing in my life. My finger depressed the trigger.

Thea screamed. It was a sound that played on repeat in my nightmares. I woke to the sound of it every morning, like my own damn alarm clock. We both turned to see her silhouette vanish.

"NO!" As I watched her dangle from the rafters, everything else ceased to matter. I sprinted for the pool, forgetting that there was another hunter in our midst or that the ground was probably rigged with landmines.

Another shot boomed and glass sprayed around Thea.

"Danny, STOP!"

The hard weight of Nick's body plowed into me. We rolled over the ground, knocking against the hard metal jaws of a bear trap. The impact of my shoulder hitting the arm was enough to trigger the mouth to snap closed.

"What the fuck!" The trap was large enough that it could have snapped a man in half. Understanding finally catching up to me, I scrambled away from the thing. I looked up and into the gaping hole in the side of the natatorium. Thea dangled from the ceiling like a worm on a hook. The metal she was clinging to slipped, straining against the bolts holding them both aloft. On the ground, Sylvan was reloading his shotgun.

A golden bolt lodged into the grass beside my stomach. It was perfectly silent, appearing so quickly that it almost seemed to materialize from thin air.

Nick rolled to his knees, snatching my rifle from where it was resting in the grass. He clicked off three quick shots in the direction of the Archer.

Bang!

The metal gave way, and almost in slow motion, I watched Thea plummet into the pool, landing with a surprisingly small splash for the distance she fell.

Behind me, Nick was still firing the rifle, and he might have been shouting something, but all I heard was my heart beating in my ears. I couldn't breathe. This was the day by the river all over again, only this time, it wasn't my sister disappearing beneath the water; it was my entire world.

I couldn't make myself move. The water rocked, the ripples growing smaller and smaller with each second she stayed beneath. Bubbles of air popped against the surface until even they went still.

The breeze of an arrow flew by my ear.

"DANNY!" Nick's hand blistered against my cheek, the pain burning awareness back into me—just as Thea's beautiful face broke above the water. I blinked, sucking in a breath with her.

I grabbed his arm, pulling him back, a bolt flying through the small space between us. "She's ALIVE!"

"And we won't be if you don't fucking snap out of it."

Sylvan was walking the length of the pool, closing the distance between them.

Nick glanced back, seeing what I saw. "Go, kill that *figlio di puttana* for me. I'll cover you."[1]

He pushed me toward the pool, but I was already falling into a run, pulling my pistol from its holster. This time I'd be a hell of a lot more careful of where I was placing my feet. Bear traps and hidden explosives were probably only a scratch on the surface of what was hidden around this little slice of hell.

"Going somewhere, mate?"

I slid to a stop as a man appeared from within the shadow of the entryway. It was a bit surprising that the awning wasn't rigged with a catapult or something equally absurd.

"I know you," I said. "Think I saw a bit of your friend over there in the grass."

"Chet was a moron. That's why I let him go first." Other than a knife on his hip, the man didn't seem armed or ready for any kind of a fight for that matter.

---

1. motherfucker

"What does that make you?" This man was wasting precious seconds. I fired the pistol. It didn't matter who he was, or that he only had a sheathed knife, he was currently between me and Thea. That made him a dead man.

The bullet hit his chest with a bloodless impact, driving him back several feet. He stumbled into a backwards somersault. As he rolled, he pulled a Glock from an ankle holster and popped back to his feet. Apparently, shooting him had been the right call; just next time, I'd be sure to aim for the head.

"Now that was uncalled for," he stated with mock indignation. "I wasn't even armed."

"Doesn't really seem to be the case anymore," I responded flatly. Of course the man was wearing Kevlar under his faded band tee. The most menacing predators never looked dangerous.

From inside the center, a motor whirred to life along with the squeak of metal on metal rotating. I didn't dare take my eyes from the man in front of me to see what was happening. It couldn't be good. I knew that much.

The man tilted his head toward the pool. "She's pretty, looks a hell of a lot like the Premier's daughter. Is that why you paid so much to hunt her?"

"Fuck off are my reasons. Don't you have your own fox to chase?"

"Nah. We've moved on to bigger, prettier fish." His words were casual, like two friends sharing a drink and discussing the woman on the other side of the bar. Except his posture was primed to attack. The man didn't blink. The corner of his mouth lifted like he knew a joke that I wasn't privy to. "I was there the day of her execution."

My mind ticked over the day we freed Thea, of the few people we'd interacted with during our infiltration. All of them had been Ozmandrian, which this man clearly was not.

"I was in the delegates' box with the other dignitaries—directly beside the Queen's balcony."

The crowd of onlookers was massive that day. We knew Gigi used her power play to curry favor with neighboring territories. The delegates weren't the threat, so we'd never looked into them. The focus was on Thea and the plan, not who came out for the show.

"Most people were watching the execution grounds, but I was far more interested in the company the Queen chose to keep. The craziest thing happened; she had two men brought in and chained to the chairs beside her. Now, why would she do that?"

My hand flexed on the grip of my pistol. I should shoot him now. A clean head shot, and then I could go after Sylvan.

Sensing my thoughts, the foreigner tightened his aim. The muscles of his forearm tensed and his index finger slightly depressed the trigger, ensuring that if I fired, it would be signing my own death certificate.

The haptics on my watch buzzed, reminding me exactly what was at stake.

"I've never seen someone look so murderous. Then we get this invite to come hunt and who should slink into the shadows but the very man I saw offer up his soul to save her life. It must have killed you when the Queen waltzed into the club tonight. I bet you can feel the rage coursing in your veins right now. I can practically see it steaming off of you."

The rumble of the motor and grinding of metal in the pool stopped. The sudden silence made the thunder of my heartbeat that much louder. Fuck, why was it so quiet in there?

"Cut to the chase," I said, trying to sound bored. "I have a girl to claim."

"The chase is, that girl matters to the Queen enough to make her death a spectacle. That makes Dorothea Gallant uniquely valuable. It's not every day that a new, self-appointed monarch appears on the playing board."

"And you think having some look alike will give you power over her, is that it?" It was worth a shot. There were exactly eight people who knew Thea was still alive. He didn't need to be one of them.

The foreigner tightened his expression. "You and I both know she's not just a look alike. Or the fact that the pool went silent wouldn't be making you sweat so much."

"I can't let you take her."

"I don't need your permission." He raised his aim slightly and fired. The bullet cut through the awning. The support splintered, and the entire structure fell like dominos, one beam after another swinging down. The foreigner and I leapt in opposite directions. The metal pole above us swung down and knocked me to the ground. A second later, I was covered in a mess of vinyl sheeting.

"No!" I shouted, twisting against the hold of the awning. My gun was lost somewhere amid the wreckage. There was no time. "Fucking hell."

I disentangled my legs, watching as he made his way toward the opening in the glass wall. Like hell would I let another person take Thea away. I would die first. Weaponless, I jumped to my feet and leapt over stray bits of debris from the explosion. I gained on him with every step I took. Lowering my shoulder, I rammed into his side, tackling him to the ground. His gun flew from his hand and landed several feet away.

The foreigner was strong, and his lean muscle mass was quicker than my own bulk. Circling me from behind, his body bent around mine. One arm, and then another, twisted into my limbs. His elbow pressed against my throat, cutting off my airway as he forced me onto my stomach. I gagged and spluttered against the force. With each twist and buck of my body, he managed to grapple me further into the ground. For all our training and time in the gym, we'd never really covered wrestling. Boxing and some mixed martial arts training, but nothing that could counter the hold he had twisted me into.

Spots peppered my vision, a desperate realization taking hold in my final thoughts.

I failed Thea—again.

This asshole would kill me and take her. I didn't even know his name. No wonder the cunt had been so casual when he approached me. He'd sized me up and already concluded that he could outmatch me. I was too fucking arrogant to see it.

I craned my head the small fraction that his hold allowed. Beyond his shoulder, a figure dressed all in black pulled a lifeless body from the water. She was so small and fragile looking.

NO. My body revolted at what I was seeing. NO.

A surge of pure wrath poured through me. I hooked my leg around his knee and rolled to my back. Our momentum kept going until we were facing away from the pool. The new angle weakened his hold on my throat enough that I was able to wrench my head loose. I pushed our combined weight onto his arm, snapping it at the elbow.

The foreigner roared with pain, a sound that was cut off instantly.

His head kicked back, whacking into my shoulder before going limp in my arms. Protruding from his eye was a golden bolt. The metal shone bright in the light from the pool.

The dark mass of a figure rushed forward. I didn't want to know what had happened to Nick that the archer had managed to take a shot at us. If I lost him and Thea, the guilt would end me.

I grabbed the back of the foreigner's shirt, leveraging the dead weight so that I could use him as a shield until I could find something to dodge behind. The hard click of a magazine being slid into place and the crank of the leaver on the crossbow was loud against the silent night.

"You just going to lay there, *stronzo*, or do I have to do all the work?"

Throwing the body to the ground, I looked up at my brother. The relief of seeing him alive was quickly replaced by annoyance. "That arrow could have shot me. It was two inches from my face."

"Yeah, but it didn't. The calibrations on this deadly bit of craftsmanship are perfect." He lifted the bow and looked at it with eyes I'd only seen him give Thea.

"What happened to the archer?" I pushed to my feet, retrieving the foreigner's Glock and checking the remaining rounds. It wasn't many shots, but it would do.

"He's taking a break, with my axe pinning him to a tree. Figured we could go back and question him later." Ignoring whatever else he had to say, I took off at a run for the center. I didn't know who the figure was that pulled Thea from the pool. It wasn't Sylvan with his French designer suit or Crowe. So this was some new player I wasn't sure I had the mental energy to do battle with.

I just needed Thea to be alive.

The center was lacking the humidity you usually associated with pools, but an acrid chemical smell was pungent. The mix with mildew was enough to make me want to gag. Against the tile floor, Thea was a streak of white and blue tulle. She lay in a massive puddle, the water tinting red from the dozens of cuts covering her exposed skin ... and she was still. So very still.

"No. Thea!" I dropped to my knees, tilting my ear over her mouth, waiting for the slightest wisp of air to tell me she was breathing.

Nick pulled up her stats on his watch. "Her heart's still beating. It's really slow, but there is a beat. The blood oxygen is scary low, too."

"Find Sylvan, that fucker is here somewhere." Pinching her nose, I fitted my mouth over hers and blew. Her lungs expanded, the wheeze of an exhale a bit stronger than before. "Breathe, Princess. Breathe."

I repeated the breaths, each time her response increased until, with a final breath, her body sputtered, and water trickled from her mouth.

Pushing Thea to her side, the coughing turned to retching as her body rejected the water it had inhaled. When finally she calmed, I pulled her into my lap and held her cold and trembling form as tightly as I could.

I kissed the top of her head. Never in my life have I been more grateful than I was just then—not even on the day I ran free of the Farm and climbed into the back of the school teacher's car. Nothing compared to losing the love of your life and then being granted the gift of seeing them breathe again.

Nothing.

-37-
DANNY

Nick returned a few minutes later. He dropped to one knee and pushed the hair from Thea's face. He whispered low in Italian, ending his statement with a kiss on her temple. She hadn't stopped shivering and a cough shook her body every few seconds.

He sat a white box on the tile beside us, pulling from it a clear mask and a can of oxygen. "Help her hold that in place."

"Where's Sylvan? Scurrying away doesn't really feel like his M.O.," I asked, ready to tear him apart in about a dozen different ways.

"No, I found him." Nick's tone was hard to read. It was almost like he was confused. "He's not exactly a threat anymore. You'll need to see it for yourself to understand."

Nick prodded at the edges of her limp shoulder, forcing her to cry out until she bit down on her lip to silence herself. Sometimes it was amazing how fucking strong she was. "Thea, I'm going to need to put this back in place. We can't risk running out of here while your arm is dislocated."

"Just do it," she said, voice muffled by the oxygen mask.

"Maybe, *maledizione.*"[1] He pulled his leather belt free from his pants, folding it over twice before handing it to her. "Bite down on this. It's going to hurt like a mother fucker. Nothing you can't handle, but we also can't be attracting anymore attention than we already have." He redirected his gaze to me. "You're going to need to help muffle her scream."

269

We'd done this before. It was usually Crowe doing something stupid that got his arm ripped out. After the first time, it seemed to happen more and more. It was like he couldn't keep his stuffing sometimes.

Pushing the oxygen mask to the side, she bit down on the belt. I cupped my hand as best I could around her mouth and the leather strap while Nick braced her shoulder and her arm.

"Breathe with me, Fiore Mio." They took several slow breaths, on the third breath he jolted her arm back in place. Thea howled, breathing hard through her nose until the coughing took over again. Tears spilled over her cheeks and she buried her face into my chest.

"Thea!" Crowe climbed over the blown-out wall, half leaping over the glass in his hurry to reach the pool. "Holy fucking Ozma. She's alive."

He dropped to his knees beside us, panting so hard it forced him to cough. He looked like he'd been torn apart. The gash in his shoulder looked like someone had taken a literal bite out of him. When he could finally breathe again, he said, "I don't think I've ever run so fast. I knew I'd never make it in time."

Nick tore the top layer of her skirt free, using it to fashion a sling for her arm. I hated the way she winced when he positioned it in place.

"The question we should all be asking is, who saved her?" I said, telling them about the figure dressed in black that I'd seen pull Thea from the pool.

Nick pushed to his feet, scanning the center again for signs of our mystery hero. "That'd be the same someone responsible for what's left of Deveaux."

"What do you mean by 'left of'?"

Bending down, Nick scooped Thea up, carefully keeping her arm pinned between her body and his. "We need to get out of here. There's probably still half a dozen hunters loose in this hellscape. Follow me ,and I'll show you where Sylvan is strung up."

"Strung up?" Crowe added.

That was the perfect way to describe it. A massive net was stretched taut across the hallway leading to the locker rooms. Sylvan's limbs were tethered to it, like a spider caught in his own web. Several long cuts had been made, turning his expensive shirt to ribbons. One long cut ran low across his abdomen. From it, someone had pulled his intestines free and used them to tether his throat to the net.

"I might actually be sick," I said, feeling my stomach turn. The stench of the moldering pools were not helping.

Deveaux's head lolled to the side in a moan.

"You've got to be fucking kidding me," Crowe said, voicing my exact thoughts.

"Yeah, that's the other thing." Nick nodded. "He's not dead. At least, not yet."

"Who? How?" Shock hit me so potently that I couldn't form more than singular words.

Thea pulled at the mask covering her face. Her voice was soft and raspy when she said, "Someone pulled him off the pool cover right before he was going to shoot me. He had a gun pressed to the hole I was trying to breathe from, but then someone ran across the cover, and suddenly Deveaux was gone."

There was a loud crash of more breaking glass. I stepped back for a clear view of the room with the Glock already aimed at the window.

A battered jester slipped on the tile, caught inches from the ground by my sister.

"Daisy!" I exclaimed, probably louder than I should have, given there was an unknown attacker roaming the building.

I looked at Nick and then to Thea. She feebly pushed my shoulder. "Go."

Daisy gave me a tiny wave. With the exception of a torn skirt, she looked good and in much better shape than most of us.

"Hey, Dandy."

My sister skipped over the scattered glass and wrapped her arms around my middle. "I missed you, big brother."

Missed me? Like I'd been on vacation and our family hadn't been torn apart for over a decade? I hadn't just missed her. When we were children, Daisy was my other half. We finished each other's sentences and shared thoughts. For years, I struggled to exist from day to day. I didn't know how to function in a world where she wasn't following my every move. Not even fully a year my younger, we were as close to twins as two siblings could get without sharing a womb. I'd never truly felt like myself since that terrible day when we were torn apart. Without Daisy's softness and light, I grew into something harsh and unforgiving. Like Peter Pan catching his shadow, hugging my sister felt like bringing that missing part of myself back.

I held her tight, still not entirely certain that she wasn't a ghost. As I held on, the truth warmed me from the inside out. We'd done it. Daffodil was safely back in the hotel, and all we had to do was get out of here. I had my family back after years of dreaming and convincing myself this day would never come. Here it was. Tears fell from the corners of my eyes, like a dam of pent up emotion finally crumbling down. She was back.

Daisy pushed against my hold. "Come on. We need to get out of here."

"Right." I released her, keeping one hand on her shoulder. Much as I had with Daffodil, I was having a hard time actually letting her go. "Daisy, I would like you to meet the rest of my family."

She pointed at the nearly dead man hanging from the net. "Is he part of the family too? Because I've gotta tell you, Dandy, the man is a psychotic prick."

"No," Crowe said firmly, flipping what looked like a hunting knife. "Sylvan Deveaux is about to learn what it feels like to be taken apart slowly."

Daisy snorted, "Pretty sure he already knows."

Crowe flung the knife into the air, landing it perfectly in the center of the man's belly button.

Sylvan might be half dead, but he was alert enough to moan in pain. Crowe easily retrieved the knife, wiping the blade clean on Deveaux's pant leg before returning. He offered the hilt of the knife to me. "It's like darts. Fifteen points if you can get his arm."

"A child could hit his arm." I took the knife. The weight of the hilt was solid. With a flick, I lodged the dagger directly above his right breast pocket.

"A child could, huh?"

"I did that on purpose." I walked over, pulling out not only the dagger but also the business card that was tucked into the pocket.

Leaving the paper on the end of the knife, I handed it back to Crowe with one eyebrow raised.

"You're an ass." Slipping it from the blade. He looked completely puzzled and read it twice back to front, then handed it back to me. "The only thing written on it is a number, 10/6. It makes no sense."

"Hey." The guy who entered the center with my sister perked up. "I know what it is."

I turned toward the jester, wondering why in the fuck he was here. "Sorry, who are you?"

"I'm Kyle."

Crowe pointed to the jester. "Oh right, that's Kyle."

"So, there was this one year I had a roommate at the mica mines. She didn't stay long on account of her having a massive rack, and the guys up top decided she was wasted working below ground. Her name was Sandy. She was a bit shorter than Blondie, and nowhere near as pretty. But still, like I said, great tits."

"Blondie?" Nick looked with puzzlement at Crowe, speaking over Kyle, who still hadn't stopped talking. "Where did you get this *stronzo*?"

"Is there a point to all of this?" I asked.

"I'm getting to it."

Daisy waved her hands, "You just have to let him finish. It takes Kyle a minute to get there, but usually, his rambling turns out to be insightful."

"Aww, thanks, Daze." Kyle paused to give my sister a sweet smile. "Anyway, Sandy was obsessed with this radio series that played Sunday mornings on the E.C. Public Radio. It was a show about true, unsolved crimes."

"Okaaaaay and?" I drew the word out in question, still waiting for the point.

"And that's the calling card of The Hatter."

"The Hatter?"

"Yeah. He takes out a couple people a year. Each time, he increases the fraction on the card. It's like a tally. This must be the tenth kill of the year." Kyle scratched at the stubble growing on his chin.

I looked back at the card. "And what, he's been doing this for six years?"

"Exactly." Kyle moved closer to the net. "This looks like his kind of scene, too. A ... what do you call those things that look like a painting but are made with real people? Like time stopped."

"A tableau," I said, already seeing it. The kill was definitely staged, then left for us to do with him as we pleased like the killer knew we'd want to finish him off. There was even a light shining directly on him. "But why? The Hatter shows up to kill Sylvan, and also stops to save Thea along the way. It doesn't add up. I don't like it."

"Twenty!" Crowe leapt into the air and hip-bumped Daisy. "Fuck yes! Middle of the bed, here I come." He continued his celebration, singing his own fanfare and wiggling in victory. Kyle whooped and started dancing with him despite the moron having no idea why.

The rest of the group gawked at them like Crowe had just knocked over a casket at a funeral, but only Nick looked truly annoyed by it. Not that it mattered. I wasn't the asshole stuck being third wheel for a whole week.

Still tucked safely in Nick's arms, Thea shook her head. "Crowe."

It was only then that Crowe questioned his actions and realized that standing before a disemboweled man might not be the place for a victory dance.

Crowe cleared his throat, "Sorry, carry on."

"You should put that card back in his pocket." Nick lifted his chin to the card still in my hand. "Everyone will think The Hatter killed him. Gigi knows we're here, right?"

"Oh yeah. Trust me, she knows," Crowe replied, implying that we'd missed a lot while he was off on his own.

Nick frowned at him, picking up on the same tone I had. It was a classic, Crowe did something we'd all be paying the price for later. "Well, she won't be able to pin Deveaux's death on one of us. If anything, it will cement the fact that we were here for Daisy. Especially when she goes missing."

"I don't think that would stop her. Besides, the cameras will show the two of us using him as target practice." I pointed at the camera mounted to the ceiling.

Thea coughed, then said "No, they won't. He didn't want to risk anyone recognizing me, so he turned them off."

My wrist buzzed with a new message.

Back parking lot. Now.

"Time to go." I grabbed Daisy's hand and started pulling her toward the glass. The telltale sound of helicopter blades whomped in the background.

"Wait," Thea said, wriggling herself free of Nick's hold. She held out her good arm. "Give me a weapon."

Skeptically, I took the foreigner's Glock from my holster and placed it in her palm. "Princess, you don't—"

"Don't patronize me, Danny."

"I'm not." I shook my head. "It's just ... you're not a killer. You said so yourself."

"I am what they made me." Thea turned to Sylvan, keeping her hurt arm tucked close to her body. "Gigi wants me to be her villain. It's time I started acting like one."

"Wake up," she said, knocking on the top of Sylvan's head with the muzzle of the gun. "What I would fucking give for a cattle prod right now."

"Creative," Crowe crooned, dropping his eyes over her body. Someday, we really needed to check his blood lust. "Unfortunately, we seem to be short on cattle prods at the moment."

"This will have to do." She smacked the butt of the gun across his face like a gentleman declaring a duel. Hitting him with every word as she commanded him to wake up.

Deveaux moaned, eyes fluttering until they finally opened, glazed with pain.

"Ah, there you are, *little spider,* stuck here in your web," she spoke almost sweetly. What had he said to her in the hour it'd taken us to get here? "I wanted to leave you with a parting gift in honor of every girl you've ever chased down and mutilated." Her lip curled with a sneer. "Don't worry. I hear some people find pain *quite pleasurable.*"

Thea slid the muzzle of the gun between his lips. At first Sylvan was too dazed to realize what she was doing. She waited for him to understand what she was doing, and then she forced it as far down his throat as the pistol allowed.

Sylvan gagged, making drool leak from the corners of his mouth on a pathetic groan. He tried to swallow around the intrusion of the gun and gagged again. This time, his retching was violent enough the entire net shook. The tears that fell down his cheeks mixed with the blood and drool.

"Now, be a good little spider." Thea leaned in until they were almost nose to nose. "I want to hear you *SCREAM!*"

In moments like these, it wasn't hard to see how Thea and Crowe had gravitated toward each other. That same twisted kernel of malice festered deep, waiting for the right moment to seek retribution.

Thea dropped the gun between his legs and pulled the trigger point blank into the man's groin. The force of the shot kicked her hand up, catching Sylvan's chin and knocking his head back. Blood poured down his leg, pooling in heavy streams on the tile beneath him.

Sylvan screamed for her, a sound that continued on a loop until he finally passed out from blood loss.

Thea held out her arm, returning the pistol to me. There was a chilling finality to her expression. "Now we can leave."

-38-
THEA

We carefully exited the Aquatics Center. This must have been what Dante felt like crawling his way out of hell. The air felt cleaner and freer than when I'd gone in that pool. Despite the scattered bits of what was once Ole Chet, it was almost cleansing walking into the crisp night.

"We won't have long. That bird is going to attract a lot of attention," Danny said, motioning to the helicopter lowering into the parking lot.

"What happened to the no-go air space rule?" I asked, scanning the surrounding area for signs of security. Just because we knew Sylvan was dead didn't mean the rest of his campus did. As far as they knew, it was business as usual. "I thought the electrical field or whatever prevented approach by air."

"Maddox must have figured out a work-around." On cue, the electrical grid of the town below shut down. One by one, blocks of streetlights winked out. From the vantage point at the top of the hill, it was easy to see the town go dark.

The helicopter rotors blew the air, chilling my sopping wet dress and sending the blond ends of my pigtails flying. I leaned into the heat of Nick's body, trying to use his bulk to shield myself. He pressed a quick kiss to the top of my head.

I blinked up at the unexpected display of affection. His dark grey eyes softened. Maybe it was because he was always so guarded about showing his emotions that when he did show them it made something flutter in my stomach.

He gently nudged me in the direction of where the helicopter was touching down. "You go, I've just gotta grab something quick."

He jogged across the front lawn, returning a few minutes later with an unconscious figure slung over his shoulder. The hood fell back to reveal long blue hair and soft features that felt vaguely familiar.

"You've got to be shitting me. It was the waitress?" Danny looked more confused than ever. "How the hell did a waitress get into La Chasse?"

"Or afford a crossbow that is otherwise impossible to get in Oz," Nick added, sliding his axe into the sheath on his hip. "The real question is what to do with her? She knows about Thea."

Headlights cut through the dark town, climbing up the hill toward the center.

"Bring her," Danny snapped. "We can figure out what to do once we're far from here."

Piling onto the helicopter, Crowe pulled me into the seat next to him. Despite having a nasty injury of his own limiting his movements, he helped secure my seatbelt around my shoulder. The sharp pain from earlier had dulled into an aching burn, that for some reason made the chills shaking my body feel more extreme.

Nick secured our mystery archer before sitting in the seat on my other side.

Lifting into the air, I watched the hell of La Chasse campus disappear. My chest hurt with every breath, and I was covered in enough cuts that I probably looked striped, but we made it out.

I looked up at Crowe. "What happens to the prisoners now that Sylvan is dead? I made a promise to someone."

He pointed out the window to where people were flooding over the perimeter fences. With the electricity down, there was nothing holding the prisoners inside the town. "We'll make sure Ginger sends her people in to round up as many as she can. They'll be okay, Beautiful."

Nick threaded his fingers in mine, and I let their presence soothe the battered bits of my soul.

Daisy and Kyle shared the bench with her brother. As I watched her chatting with Danny, their mannerisms a mirror to one another, I knew that all of the aches and fear had been worth it.

A large shadow fell over me, blocking the midday sun.

"Here you are."

I let out a long exhale, sitting back on my heels and wiping the dirt from my face with the back of my arm. The handful of grass I'd just pulled dropped into the small pile of weeds beside me, and I squinted up at Nick. "I couldn't walk by this again, seeing the forgotten remains of this garden."

The large masonry and wood from the Villa's main building had been removed long before I'd escaped my death sentence. Expansions to the Villa were already being made for our steadily growing family. Toto, Daisy, and Kyle already had apartments being framed out along the far end of the building. The new villa didn't resemble the old one at all. I liked that about it.

The only thing left of the ruin was the outline of the foundation and the trampled remains of a small vegetable garden. For weeks, it had been largely ignored. Until small tufts of green leaves sprouted in neat rows amid the chickweed and dandelions.

Nick lowered to the ground beside me. "It's only been a few days, you shouldn't be pulling weeds ... especially without a brace. If Gabby catches you, she'll handcuff you to a bed until you're healed. Trust me."

I smirked up at him, raising a suggestive eyebrow.

Laughing, he picked up my discarded sling and slipped it over my shoulder. "It's not as much fun as it sounds."

Of course I knew I should be keeping it supported. "I didn't want to get it dirty and it's so hard to do anything with the dumb thing on."

"Do you actually *know* how to garden?"

"No." I let out an embarrassed chuckle. What the hell *was* I doing out here? "The desert surrounding The Farm wasn't exactly conducive for growing things."

I couldn't bring myself to look up at him. Instead, I poked at the small white pebbles of masonry that were still lodged in the dirt.

Nick shifted his weight so that he was sitting cross-legged beside me. He took my dirty hand in his and ran his fingers lightly over the rough lines cut into my palm. It soothed the ache thrumming in my chest and sent a wave of warmth up my arm. Nick was always able to make the smallest touches feel monumental. I loved that about him.

"I have a photo of you from The Farm."

That got my attention, and I snapped astonished eyes up at him. "Where did you get a photo of me from The Farm?" As far as I knew, there were never any taken. It wasn't like Em was collecting snapshots for photo albums and keepsakes.

"I took it off the assassin that fed you the pie. When you were gone the first time after King kidnapped you, I was hurt more than I was willing to admit. I lied to everyone, including myself, but at night, I couldn't stop looking at the girl in that photo. The landscape was so desolate and bleak, but you were a bright spot against it. You've always been that for me, this glowing beacon of bravery."

"Heh. Bravery, right." There wasn't a single part of me that felt brave.

"The way you refused to give in to the pain that first night I stitched you up, I fell for you. Right then. It's just like how you never gave up on our memory or how you didn't stop running in the pool. Even when it looked like there was nowhere to go, you found a way out. You've never let fear hold you back. That's the definition of bravery."

All I felt was fear. It was everywhere around me, like my own personal storm cloud.

"Why are you pulling weeds in the middle of the noon-day sun?"

I thumbed the waxy green leaf beside me. How did I explain what this felt like? It'd been two days since we returned to Ciopriani Villa. From the outside, I probably seemed well-adjusted. Inside, I was still drowning in the pool.

"I just ... I don't know. I saw these little baby plants and figured if nothing else, maybe I could help them grow. They didn't do anything to deserve this." I gestured emphatically at the sprouts. "All they were doing was trying to survive. Day to day they lifted their little leaves trying to take in the tiny bit of sunshine they were allowed. While we stomped all over them, tearing them to pieces until there was nothing left but mulch."

"The plants?"

Fat tears fell from the corner of my eyes and I cursed the weakness for bleeding from me. "It's stupid, but some part of me feels like maybe there's a bit of Nonna still in this garden. It would have been nice to have a Nonna's hug to return to ... after."

So much had happened.

I couldn't begin to unpack my feelings about all of it. A massive chunk of the time was altered from drugs, making it hard to distinguish memory from dream. There were still days when I had to ground myself in something tangible to be sure the world was real. Part of me accepted that I'd never be truly free from the hallucinations; the other part wanted to be hugged by someone maternal and told it'll get better.

After our return, I'd decided to start wearing my mother's necklace, searching for a connection I knew I'd never really get. In moments like right now, when I felt like I was adrift in a sea of emotion, I anxiously ran the locket up and down the chain.

Nick reached for the trowel, digging up a patch of clover and tossing it into my pile. "She had this funny hat she would always wear when she was gardening. It had a big brim tied with a scarf behind her neck, but with the top part of the hat missing." He reached past me to the small bundle of leaves at my knees. "These look like zucchini sprouts. Nonna loved *i fiori di zucca fritti.*"

"Fiori?" I scrunched my nose. "She'd eat the flowers?"

283

"They're delicious fried. When these grow big enough, I'll make it for you."

"And we can make a plate for Nonna," I added, sadly drawing little designs in the dirt. "I'm sorry I wasn't there when they told you. You must have been hurting so much."

He nodded, silently staring at the tiny plants. We'd talked a bit about how he'd focused his grief into thinking I'd betrayed them, but we'd never really gone into detail about any of it. I knew he still felt guilty despite already having my forgiveness.

"It still hurts," he responded quietly, reaching his hand down to squeeze my knee. "Having you home helps. That's enough. Time will do the rest."

"What about Crowe? He's been a bit more ... unhinged lately."

"Yeah." He looked over his shoulder toward the remodeled south wing. "There's that, too."

Since we returned from La Chasse, he and Maddox had been working day and night to find a chink in Gigi's armor.

I think seeing the delayed message of my goodbye in the pool had shaken him more than he was admitting. He doubled the perimeter security in anticipation of her counter-strike. Sometimes at night, while the rest of us were piled into a big ball on the bed, I'd wake to find him staring out the window— waiting.

Nick grabbed my chin, turning me to look up at him. "Don't look so worried, Fiore Mio. He'll be okay. We all will." With his thumb, he brushed away the single tear falling over my cheek. *Ti amo, Thea.*

"I know." I said as more tears began cascading down. "I don't know why I'm crying." I felt ridiculous, kneeling in a beat up garden, crying like a child. "Sometimes it's like there's too much of ... everything. I used to be able to push my emotions into their boxes. But now, I think I've run out of boxes, and I don't know what to do with all of these feelings."

"Then let me carry some of it for you. It's okay to let go. I already told you, I'm not going anywhere." He gently tugged me forward until I fell into his lap. I tucked my cheek into the sweet spot of his chest, where this one divot seemed to have been made for me to rest my head.

Nick stroked my hair, running his fingers through it and looking at its dark color glow red in the sunlight. I'd missed this. You don't realize how much you need human touch until you've been truly isolated.

We sat in the garden until my tears had all dried up and the tightness in my chest loosened. Over the next hour, we worked together to remove all of the debris and weeds from Nonna's vegetable patch.

"Are you two seriously gardening?" Danny asked, Crowe walking by his side.

"Well, I'm not baking a cake," I snapped.

"Was cake an option?" Crowe asked, looking hopeful.

I shook my head, "You really don't want me to make you cake."

Nick gathered the gardening tools. "I can confirm that."

"Well, you *are* caked in dirt." Crowe helped me rise to my feet, brushing away the debris on my knees for me. "When you said you were going to find Thea, this was not what I expected at all. I mean, I expected you to be tending to her garden, just not literally."

"Ew." My face scrunched, physically repelled by the term. "Don't ever call it that again."

"Yeah, I heard it as I said it," Crowe added, looking more amused than anything. "Anyway, we've got an idea to lure Gigi out of her palace, and you're really going to like it."

"I am? Gotta tell you, I think I'm taking a break from the suicide missions for a while." I lifted my slinged arm to emphasize my point.

"Thank fuck!" Danny exclaimed, throwing his arms in the air. "Took you long enough. I tol—"

"Dandelion Kalidah, if I have to hear the words 'I told you' again," I propped my one good arm on my hip. "I will put you back in time out."

Crowe snickered, tucking me into his side. These boys.

Danny pushed his tongue into his cheek, visibly shaking from the effort of restraint. "Princess, you haven't begun to hear me lecture you on all the shit you pulled in there."

I narrowed my gaze at him. "Let me save you the effort." I cleared my throat, trying to pull out my best gravelly asshole tone. *"Princess—"*

"Oh, this is going to be good," Crowe said with too much joy.

"*You climbed a wire 70 feet over death spike pools. Do you have any idea? I told you this would happen. I should teach you how to listen or some other equally vague threat. Blah grumble blah.*"

Crowe held his breath, making his face turn bright red in an attempt to contain his laughter.

"There. How'd I do, Kitten?" Was it insensitive? A little. I knew the entire event pushed him past his limits, but he'd been such an insufferable asshole about it since we'd returned.

Nick, ignoring Danny's visibly rising blood pressure, asked, "What do you mean by death spike pools?" He held open the door to our apartment for me.

I slowed, giving his nose a little boop as I passed. "I mean, pools with spikes in them."

Lengthening my strides for the bathroom, I ignored Danny's glare. I didn't need to look at him to know that he was staring at me with enough intensity to shoot lasers from his eyes. Just because I knew it would rile him further, I added, "The sharp kind. With decomposing bodies impaled on them."

I closed the door to the bathroom behind me and pressed my back to the wood. My nails cut into my still raw palms. I focused on that pain rather than the memory of the bloated body in the pool with me. Fuck him. Fuck Sylvan and those people who had no problem with torturing innocent people. Fuck them all.

The shower taunted me across the brightly tiled floor. The whole room was decorated in cheery shades of teal and coral. I stared at the clear curtain. It was still, and I hadn't touched it since we returned, but I knew exactly what that vinyl sounded like. The memory of the sliding pool cover was potent, the squeak of the old metal wheels and the shush of the fabric unrolling. The tiny hairs at the back of my neck stood on end and a cool sweat broke across my brow.

"Fuck you, too," I whispered at the shower and snatched a washcloth from the basket next to the sink.

It took some struggling, but I was eventually able to get out of the dress shirt I'd stolen. Danny's shirts were the only thing that I could reasonably get on with my shoulder the way it was. It helped that they were unbelievably soft ... and smelled like him.

Fucking hell, I was a wreck. My shoulder throbbed in response like it was agreeing with me.

I soaked the washcloth and started slowly cleaning the dirt from my skin. Who needed showers anyway? Sinks were a seriously under-appreciated fixture.

The door swung open, smacking against the wall with a loud clatter.

"We weren't don— " Danny bit off the end of his own sentence. His green eyes connected with mine in the mirror for a second before I returned to cleaning my injured arm. "Why aren't you using the shower?"

"There's this thing called knocking," I snapped. I didn't owe him an explanation. He'd chosen to barge in here, that didn't mean he could start demanding answers.

"Is it the water? Is that why you aren't bathing in the shower?"

"Let it go, Danny. I don't want to get into another argument with you."

"Thea," he slowly turned me to face him and took the washcloth from my hands. His brows pinched together, and the sharp line of his jaw softened with something that looked too much like pity. "I could get some nice soaps. Something that smells good and maybe—"

"I said, let it go." I pulled the washcloth from his hands and shoved him toward the door with my good arm. "What is it with you three? You're practically super-glued to my ass. I only need a minute to clean the dirt from my arms and face ... by myself."

Danny's face dropped, but at least he wasn't looking at me with those mournful eyes anymore. "But what if we—"

"Fucking Ozma!" I cracked the wet cloth against the counter, then flinched when it sounded too whip-like. Of course, he saw that, too. "Go, Danny. Five minutes, and then you can show me this master plan of yours. Now get out of here."

He reluctantly stepped away, giving the shower a long look on the way out.

-39-
THEA

"Why is she here?" I pointed at the woman with her feet kicked up on the table, braiding her long blue hair into pigtails. The guys wouldn't let me be there for questioning, and after Gabby had covertly fed me a round of painkillers, I was so tired that I didn't put up a fight. That was a couple of days ago. Since then, they hadn't mentioned a word of it.

"We've come to an agreement," Danny said simply, like that somehow explained why a woman, who tried to kill us both, was sitting at my kitchen table. "Marley won't be trying to kill anyone in this room again. Isn't that right, Miss Jacobson."

Marley slung her feet down, flipping the chair around so that she was straddling it. "That's right. I've got debts to pay, and I'll dance like a chicken if it means you can get Ben off my back." She looked at me with an emotionless smile. Bitch was lucky I wasn't trying to put an arrow through her face. "Sorry, I tried to shoot you. It wasn't personal. For what it's worth, your aunt's a bitch, and I didn't want to take the job. That's not really my call, though."

"Maybe those painkillers Gabby gave me were stronger than she let on, but it sounded like you just said Em hired you to kill me."

"Not just you. Them, too." Marley nodded at Danny.

"How is that better?" I pinned Danny with a *"What the fuck?"* expression, then turned to face Marley directly. "I'm going to make this very clear. I will bury you and walk away to the muffled sound of your screaming if you try coming anywhere near me and mine."

Crowe slowly approached behind me, resting a hand on the back of my neck. I couldn't tell if it was in warning or to be ready to restrain me if I decided to go for her throat right here and now.

Marley's expression lifted, her eyes flicking up to him. "You know, I am really glad I didn't kill you."

"Princess, maybe try saving homicide for those who deserve it. If you'd slow your bloodlust down a bit, you'd realize that we'd never allow you within a hundred miles of Marley if I even suspected she was a threat to you."

Seriously, Danny had so much asshole in his reserves he could probably start bottling condescension. Even if I knew he was right. The man had been raging about my safety for weeks. That wouldn't simply stop because we were home again.

"How does Em even know I'm alive?" I asked, still in disbelief that the guys didn't seem the least bit fazed by Marley hanging out like she was one of the gang.

"She doesn't. I took the job a few months ago." She snapped her fingers at Nick. "Hey big guy, can I get a drink? Something fizzy."

Nick raised his eyebrows in surprise. "Danny might have chosen not to kill you, but I'm still deciding."

"Fine," Marley huffed in annoyance. "But only because the whole brooding and tattooed thing you've got going is really working for you. You get the pretty pass."

Crowe's muted laughter traveled down his arm to the hand resting at my nape, obviously delighted by Marley's candor. I twisted to look up at him, and his smile instantly dropped.

"She left the contract open on them, probably out of spite." Marley pointed at the guys. "Then I saw you at The Chase and realized I could actually get the full payday if I popped you, too. I needed the win. Shifting targets was a no brainer."

"I had a couple of smaller contracts that night. There's a thing about getting all of Oz's scum together into one convenient cesspool that always attracts someone like me. Should have been a really profitable night for me, except for the whole taking an axe to the side of my head thing."

"That's a lie. You were fox hunting. I saw you shoot down a girl. You're just as bad as the rest of them," I snapped. She may have fooled the others, but I'd never forget that girl running down the street.

Marley folded her arms over the chair back. "No, sweetness, I'm worse. However, for the record, the girl I was chasing down wasn't a fox, she was another hunter. A wolf hiding among the sheep with a bounty for 500K—" She glared at Danny. "—Which I won't be collecting thanks to you. Some other asshole probably took credit."

"You can bill me," Danny drawled, cueing up a map of Ozmandria. It had six big circles on it. "Marley has some pretty key information she's parting with in exchange for clemency."

"Clemency?" It was like I'd ended up in some inside-out version of Oz. Since when did Danny give mercy to anything?

In his most placating tone, he explained, "In addition to being on Em's payroll, Marley's also on Gigi's. Unfortunately for them both, Marley's loyalty ends at the threat of a long and painful death."

"And you trust her?" I scanned my eyes over the completely relaxed woman before me. She was probably a couple of years older than me, and there she definitely had the aura of someone who knew how to wrangle demons after being to hell.

"Not in the slightest, but her intel checks out. Particularly the bit where Emily Rosen is now the front for all of Gigi's illicit dealings."

"Really? After all of those years of carefully keeping her name off the books?"

"She is," Marley confirmed. "I spent some time among the palace waitstaff. You'd be amazed what people in power say around waiters and busboys. These days, Emily is signing all of Gigi's checks. Should something unfortunate happen, say the outing of a trafficking ring in central Emerald City, the Queen can come down hard on the criminals without her reputation or bank account having to take a true hit."

Danny continued, clicking the screen to a new slide of a processing center that I recognized immediately. "Marley very helpfully identified all of the new locations and using her access codes we can begin systematically wiping out every Morphia lab and Farm distribution center across all of Ozmandria."

Like a doberman with its ears pricked, I could feel my need for vengeance come to full attention. I've wanted to see those centers reduced to rubble my entire life. Without them, Em has no working network within Oz.

Marley smiled wide. "Those locations have more holes in their security than a cheese grater. It will be easy to exploit them and make the failures appear like poor management." She definitely struck me as the kind of person who thrived on chaos. "This will actually be fun. It'll be nice change to be swinging for the good guys."

"I like the sound of it ..." I side-eyed Marley. "Mostly."

Danny continued, "I worked with Gigi for years. She can't resist a chance to strut around like an overhyped peacock. We hit her enough times, and Gigi'll come out of hiding, if only to watch Em grovel. When that happens, we'll be waiting."

Crowe banded his arm around my chest, until his mouth brushed my ear as he spoke. "Marley is our ticket in, and then, Beautiful, you can sate that need for violence as much as you want."

"And if I want a blood bath?" I breathed back, leaning into him.

He pressed his lips to my neck, "Then we can bathe in it together."

The unexpected crackle of the intercom sent a kick to my chest. *"Sir, there's a courier here with a delivery for the main house. Scans are negative. Should we send it up?"*

"It's here," Crowe whispered into my ear with a tone of mischief I hadn't heard in weeks.

Nick went to the comms, holding down the button, "Yes, Simmons. We'll meet you at the door."

"Sir... It's quite large."

Nick's brows knit together, which would alarm me, except Crowe's body was already shaking behind mine. I looked over my shoulder at his goofy grin.

"Just wait." It was good to see him looking so relaxed. This was the first I'd seen him resemble anything of the easy-going man I fell in love with. Even when he was in full Scarecrowe mode, he had a dare the devil to dance way of doing things. Since we'd returned, he'd been nothing but obsessed with security.

"I'll meet you at the door." Nick motioned to Marley. "Time to go back in your box."

Marley rolled her eyes. "If I must."

Hand tucked in mine, Crowe and I followed Danny to the front door. When he opened it, there was a massive shipping box blocking the exit.

"What in the name of Ozma is ..." Danny said, squeezing through the tiny space between the doorframe and the box. Turning his head to the side he read the brand stamped on the cardboard. "A Snuggle Sac? Crowe?"

"Why do you think this is my doing?" Crowe asked with a mock surprise.

Nick quickly rejoined us, barking a laugh the moment he saw the box. "Describing this as 'quite large' was underselling it a bit."

"Because you're the only one of us dumb enough to order something with the word 'sack' in it."

Nick pointed to the shipping label. "Actually, Danny, it's made out to Kitten Kalidah."

Crowe looked way too amused right now.

"The fuck you say?" The daggers Danny shot Crowe could have cut down a tree. "I think I actually hate you right now."

With a skip to the door, Crowe pushed Danny out of the way and brandished a razor like it was a paintbrush. Tearing the box apart, the outer layer fell to the side revealing a massive grey cushion.

"What is that?" Danny stared at the thing like it was a personal affront to every bit of his cultured style.

I tilted my head to get a better look. "I'm going to say it's a really, really big beanbag."

"This, my friends—" Crowe tore at the protective plastic, making the contents of the cushion rustle. "Is the height of reclined comfort, and large enough to fit four." Squishing it so that it would fit through the doorframe, he rolled the beanbag into the main living area.

"That is not staying."

"You don't make the choices here, Dandy." Crowe evaluated the current living room furniture. "Over there is perfect. Lots of natural light and a great view of the television." Smirking the entire time, he pulled Danny's leather smoking chair away from the window. "Do you know what I had to do to get this? With cyclone shipping out of commission there's no one crossing the wastes anymore. I had to wrestle a nun for the last *Sac*."

Satisfied with its position, Crowe returned, lifting me into his arms and tossing me into the center of the cushion. I instantly sank into the foamy center. Normally, I hated anything of this nature. It was too similar to the sinking feeling I'd suffered through as a child. However, my initial panic was immediately driven out by Crowe's pure joy. It was infectious and any latent fears that might have dragged me down were quickly forgotten.

I attempted to push myself onto my elbows. "Did you say you wrestled a nun for a sack?"

"This is such horse shit," Danny grumbled. "Thea, do not listen to him."

"Not literally. It was online, and there was no nun. But this was the last they had in stock." Crowe stretched his arms and leapt with a perfect swan dive next to me.

I shrieked with surprise when, on the rebound, his weight bounced me several inches into the air.

"Come here, you beautiful temptress." He wrapped me up, rolling us until I was completely enveloped by him. I didn't realize just how much I needed this. It was impossible to keep my delighted grin down.

Danny tapped his foot against the tile. "Crowe, look at me. This is not staying. It takes up half the damn living room."

I pushed at the space between us, climbing my way free until I was fully reclined and no longer sinking to my death. There are few things that surprise me anymore. I've seen and dealt with so much shit that I take the crazy as common sense these days. What I didn't expect was to see Nick toeing off his shoes.

"Oh no," Danny blustered. "Are you serious? You can't be entertaining this nonsense."

Nick shrugged. "I know better than to fight against Thea when she's so obviously happy. I figure I might as well get the space beside her before you cave in."

"It's literally called a sack."

"*Sac*," Crowe corrected with an atrociously fake French accent. "It's a Snuggle *Sac*—imported directly from France, probably. You make it sound so undignified when you say it like that. Snuggle Sack. Ugh, have some class, Dandy."

Danny's face hit a new level of crimson, a shade I'd only seen in crayon boxes.

Nick crawled into the space beside me, grabbing my shoulders and notching me against him. I liked it, the more weight that was on the bag, the less I sank. It was like cuddling on a gigantic marshmallow. All that we needed was a blanket and snacks.

"I could stay here all day," I said with a contented sigh, nuzzling my head into Nick's chest while Crowe pulled my legs on top of him to remove my shoes.

I held out my hand, beckoning him closer. "Come on, Danny. Think of all the skanoodling we could do."

"What does that even mean?" His eyebrows lifted into his hairline, drawing his face tight. "Nevermind. You three skadoodle. I refuse—"

"Skanoodle."

"What?"

"Skanoodle. Skadoodle is just plain ridiculous."

"I completely agree, ridiculous," Crowe interjected.

I snorted a laugh. "How would we be able to skadoodle in a Snuggle *Sac*? That's the opposite of what I want to be doing."

"I'll tell you what I want to be doing," Crowe said, wiggling as close as he could. "And you can call it whatever you want, just so long as the end result is your pussy on my face."

"Fuck." Danny's eyes flashed, scanning my body quickly before remembering he was pissed. "No. The sack thing goes."

"No?" I sat up, pushing on Nick's stomach to get upright. He let out an unexpected groan, muttering a curse in Italian. "Sorry," I mouthed. It seriously was hard to maneuver in this thing.

"No." He crossed his arms over his chest, looking down sternly at the three of us.

"*Idiota.*" Nick shook his head.

Crowe agreed, "That was a mistake, Danny."

"Fine." I straightened my spine a bit more, feeling the strain in my abs from holding the position.

"Fine?" He raised an eyebrow in question.

"If you're so fond of the word, no. Then you can hear it a whole lot more, since you can't lower yourself to join in on a quality cuddle puddle."

Danny waved us off and stormed down the hallway.

"Why is it so cute when you speak in rhymes?" Crowe asked, cupping my neck to pull me in for a languorous kiss. Nick snaked his arms around my waist.

I sank into them, luxuriating in what it felt like to be truly safe and loved. Crowe's happiness was one of my top five favorite things, and I realized that this might be the first time I'd ever truly seen it.

"Can we do something normal for once? Like watching a movie while you casually cop feel?"

"Anything you want, Darling Thea. But I should warn you, it probably won't be so casual."

−40−
NICK

"A re you sure this is enough?" Thea asked, scrunching her nose at the small wad of explosives.

With a small screwdriver held between her teeth, Daisy raised onto her tiptoes. Even standing on a crate she was still humorously short. It was like Danny had taken all the height from his sisters. How he turned out to be such a giant, and them so petite, was a wonder of genetics.

Daisy inserted the wires connecting the plastics to the electronic trigger. Speaking around the tool, she said, "Oh yeah."

"You're sure?" Thea slapped the basement's steel supports, making a tinging sound. "It's so small."

Daisy hopped down. "Sis, I spent ten years as a blaster before Gigi snatched me from the mines. I know my explosives. This RDX expands at 27,000 feet per second. 27 thousand! She'll cut through this steel like it wasn't more than a blade of grass."

"See this?" She plucked the taut wire. "This here is a daisy chain. We put charges on these three basement supports. When we detonate them, they will trigger the other two on the floor above us. This baby is gonna fall faster than a virgin on prom night."

"Daisy chain?" Thea ran her finger along the connecting wires.

"They're kind of my specialty," she grinned, making the corners of her eyes squint so much that I could barely see the green in them anymore. "It was my nickname, back in the mine."

"I like it," I said. These past few weeks, Danny's spitfire sister had really grown on me. Thea, too. She, Toto, and Daisy had spent long hours doing girly things that made zero sense to me but seemed to make my girl happy, and that was all that mattered—even if she did put what seriously looked like mud on her face.

"But ..." Thea pouted her lips, looking at the sea of concrete as if she could see through the ceiling to the floors above us.

Daisy clicked the remote, turning the light on the trigger from red to green. "Gravity does all the work. We're simply giving it a boost. Just wait. It's gonna be *so cool* to watch. I've been dying for us to find a building big enough to do a proper implosion."

Kyle and Crowe came into the room. Their neck gaiters were pulled high over their noses. Kyle's orange hair looked brighter against all of the black tactical gear. If it wasn't for how handy he was with a sledge hammer and a stick of dynamite, we'd probably have left him at home. Kyle's knowledge of explosives was nearly as good as Daisy's.

Danny's sister beamed up at the pair.

"Hey, Daisy Chain." Kyle wrapped an arm around her with the kind of familiarity that came from knowing someone for a long time ... and intimately, if the way his hand was tracing her shoulder was any indication. I wondered if Danny knew that was a thing. I should probably warn Kyle. He was a likable oddball, and it would be a shame for Danny to throw him off a roof.

"Everything's set upstairs," Crowe said, dipping down to give Thea a brief kiss. "Ginger has them all loaded on the bus."

"Do they seem okay?" Thea asked nervously. I knew she worried what state we would find people in.

Emily Rosen had been covering up the people we freed, and word of our activities wasn't making it to Gigi. After we took down the first two centers, the care of the prisoners decreased. They were crammed into smaller spaces and often were beaten. With her sources depleting faster than she could replenish them, Em was resorting to more extreme methods of acquisition. There was no time to trick people onto the back of a truck when you had quotas to fill.

Since loss of income wasn't enough to get Gigi's attention, we'd decided to up the ante. Imploding a few warehouses was Daisy's idea, mostly. Kyle suggested the explosives, and Daisy explained how we could do it so that it looked like user error instead of arson.

Crowe played with the end of Thea's braid. "The people are mostly scared. I think a lot of them are still in shock. Marley and Toto are working with some of the more distressed prisoners. They're alive and free. That's a start."

"Oh, hey." Kyle bounced on his heels, pulling a large brown candy bar from his tactical vest. "Does anyone care if I take this?"

I shook my head in disbelief. "Did you pull that out of your mag holster? You know that's for keeping your spare clips, right? Not snacks."

"Where did you find a chocolate bar?" Thea asked in surprise.

"Over there." Kyle pointed to a side room, and his face lit up. "It's A Mallow Time Bar. They're my favorite. This one time, the guard that worked the lower pit brought one in his lunch. He was always bringing these elaborate-looking lunch pails that his wife would make him. You wouldn't think that hired thugs went home to a wife and kids, and dogs, probably a cat or maybe a bunny. Oh my Oz! I bet he named him Marshmallow since he liked Mallow Times."

"Kyle," Daisy said, steering him back on track.

"Oh right. Anyway, he let me have what was left of it when he was done with lunch one day. So, does anyone care if I take it?"

The room was silent for several seconds while we all processed the phenomenon that was Kyle.

"Nah, buddy," Crowe said with a clap to his back. "You go right ahead. Enjoy every damn second of that bar."

We all turned toward the scuffing behind us. A dozen men were zip tied and gagged in a line on the floor. The wolves branded into their necks proved that Em was finally catching on and putting more competent people in charge of her facilities. They still weren't good, but they were better than the dollar store version of security she was hiring.

The man on the end was attempting to inchworm his way toward the exit. Where he thought he was going, I had no idea. "What do you want to do with them?"

Thea squatted down to eye level with the oldest looking man of the group. His salt and pepper beard was a clear indicator of his age and the emblem sowed into his collar told me everything I needed to know about his rank. "Hello, Donald."

The man was silent. He lifted his chin, but his eyes were vibrating with rage. His teeth bared against the gag in his mouth. Given the chance, this man wouldn't hesitate to kill her.

Crowe stepped behind her, allowing Thea to take the lead but still being present if she needed the support. "That one had his own personal stash in the back of the command room."

Disgustoso.[1]

"Remember that time in the Underground when I cried and you told me to choke on it?" She flicked his Adam's apple, triggering the man's gag reflex. Blood-tinged drool dripped from the corners of his lips. "How's that ball feel in your mouth, Don? I bet it doesn't smell like sweaty man ass." Thea leaned forward, her knee pressing into Donald's broken one. The man hollered, the gag muffling the sound into something akin to a donkey's bray. "They're all Wolves? You're sure?"

The man's eyes shifted from anger to pure fear, realizing she wasn't the weakling he'd taken her for. No one was stopping her. Thea could cut him to pieces right now and there was nothing any of us would do about it. Cazzo, I'd even give her my knife to do it. He probably thought his elevated status among Em's ranks afforded him security, if only on the basis of information. Unfortunately for Donald, we had all the intel we needed.

"They are," I confirmed.

Thea looked down at the row of guards with none of the expected rage or self-doubt. "Every one of them swore an oath to my aunt, knowing the viper she was. If they're all so eager to get in bed with a snake, then they can stay in the den."

"If that's what you want."

---

1. Disgusting.

"They're waiting for us. Let's make this quick." Thea turned for the stairwell, taking the stairs out of the basement two at a time.

I met Crowe's eyes across the room. Thea's indifference was striking a hell of a lot of alarm bells. She wasn't the type of woman who approached anything numb, much less killing a dozen men.

"Is she always like that?" Daisy asked, slinging her tool kit over her shoulder.

"No," Crowe and I said simultaneously.

We had earplugs, but I cupped my hands over Thea's ears anyway. She was calm as we looked down at the empty holding grounds, save for the fine tremor vibrating beneath her skin.

"I love this part," Daisy said enthusiastically, tapping her steepled fingertips in a gesture that was pure Danny. I had to bury my face in Thea's hair to keep from smiling.

Thea flinched when the first explosions on the middle floors echoed. I folded her into my embrace. A puff of concrete and probably asbestos spilled from the windows. The building imploded in a spectacular display. The walls folded in on themselves with very little rubble scattering over the site.

"There's always a bit of unpredictability with explosives. RDX is pretty safe, but you never really know how a building will blow. That's what makes it so thrilling." Daisy beamed with excitement.

Eyes locked on the settling dust cloud, Thea asked Crowe, "Did Ginger make it to the shelter safely?"

"Yeah. Danny just checked in." He took her hand, raising it to his lips. "Of the forty-three people housed here, they all seem physically fine."

Tension leaked from her shoulders. This was the one thing Thea had been clear about. Her first priority was getting the people out. There was always time for vengeance, just not at the expense of the innocent. Especially when we learned that the guards' newest instructions were to put down the *merchandise* at the first sign of intrusion. Emily Rosen was such a vindictive cunt that she'd rather kill her victims than see them freed.

Thea knew someone at each of the four sites we'd already shut down. Although, Donald was the first time she openly confronted one of them. It was hard to swallow how much these people had abused her, or at the very least ignored the abuse. It was even harder to see it etched into her features. I knew Crowe was struggling with it, too. He was itching to slay every last one of her demons. That wouldn't truly help her, though. Not in the way she needed.

Which was exactly the reason why Danny had been grounded to the cab. At the first center we'd broken into, Thea ran face first into one of Em's lieutenants. The man instantly recognized her. His statement about how he hasn't had his cock sucked properly since was cut short when Danny blew a five-inch hole through the man's face. The shot triggered the entire compound's alarms. Instead of being able to covertly remove the guards one at a time, we had to cut our way through them all at once.

Now, Danny stays in the car.

She craned her neck to meet my eyes and pulled me down for a slow kiss that I was more than happy to indulge. With each building that fell I saw Thea's confidence returning.

—41—
DANNY

"**D**anny!"

There was a crash from down the hall. Followed by another harsh yell. "Dandelion! Fuck!"

I tossed down the gear bag I was unloading from the van and followed the sounds of Thea's hollering. I leaned in the doorframe of the bathroom and spent several long seconds trying to make sense of the mess she was making in the shower.

"Do I want to know why you're screeching my name like that stupid parrot video Crowe keeps making me watch?"

Thea screamed in surprise, jumping high enough to catapult her body straight into the showerhead and knocking the wand to the ground with a loud thunk.

"Fucking. Ozma. Above. Dandy. What the hell are you doing creeping in the doorway like a damn ghost?" Thea pushed the strands of her hair out of her face, scowling at the wet faucet like it had personally offended her.

"What *am I* doing?" I bit back the desire to laugh. Nevermind the fact that she literally screamed for me to come down here. "Why are you in the shower fully clothed, surrounded by dozens of empty bottles? Expensive empty bottles, I might add."

"Fucking typical," Thea scoffed in disbelief, popping her hip out and tapping her fingers against it. "Because, Danny, Ozamandria's entire supply of soap, scrubs, and fizzers are in our shower? Do you even know what a shower fizzer is, because I don't? But there are 30 of them stacked in that corner!" She jutted an accusatory finger at the offending pile.

"The consultant insisted you needed them."

Thea ran her hands through her hair, looking like she might cry, or burn the house down. Honestly, with my Firecracker, it could be both.

I bit down on my lip. This was definitely not the time to laugh. Thea was a tight little bundle of adorable fury. She was a complete 180 from the girl who emotionlessly ordered the death of a dozen men only a couple of hours ago.

When I still hadn't answered her, she huffed, "Fuck it. I'll get Crowe to help me clear this shit away."

"He and Nick are reviewing the day's reports with the Villa's security team. They'll be back soon." I made my way closer, pulling back the shower curtain. Thea's body curled into itself like a snail hiding in its shell. Under the guise of inspecting the rainbow swirl of soap, I pushed the curtain all the way to the wall, just to be certain. Sure enough, she flinched like the curtain had whipped her. "I take it you didn't like my surprise."

"You could say that." Thea dropped the arms wrapped around her waist and balled her hands into fists like she was preparing for war.

I raised an eyebrow at her and pointedly looked back at the rainbow carnage. Something was obviously wrong and if she thought she was avoiding this conversation ...

"It's nothing. I'm fine." She kicked at the many empty bottles on the floor, slipping on the well of soap.

Before she could injure herself more than she already had, I grabbed her good arm and hauled her out of the shower.

"Danny!" she protested. "Release me."

Lifting her by the hips, I sat her on the counter so that we were eye to eye. Then, securely caged her in place by planting my hands on either side of her. "No."

"Why do you have to be so ..." Thea wiggled and pushed feebly in the center of my chest. Finally, once she accepted she wasn't going anywhere, she cracked a smile. "Infuriating?"

I stole a kiss from her perfect lips, happy that they were no longer pouting. "Let's play a game."

"A game? You don't play games, Danny."

"I'll play this one." I knew Thea, probably better than she knew herself. She would never open up if she wasn't coerced unless she was getting something in return for her candor. "I'm going to ask you some questions, and for every honest answer, I'll reward you."

"Reward me? Like a puppy. Are you going to give me treats, too?" she clipped, hiding her fear behind a solid dose of snark.

"No, like a good girl." Taking her thighs in hand, I spread her legs until I had enough space to rock her hips into mine. "The better the answer, the better the reward."

"Danny," she whined.

Palming the back of her neck, I drew her in. "Either we can talk about it this way ..." I ran my free hand up her thigh. "Or I can tie you down and force you to answer me. You've hidden long enough, and you should know by now that you could never truly hide from me."

I nipped at the tender flesh at the base of her throat, lingering with a kiss in the hollow of her collarbone. "I see you, Thea. You are more than a collection of bruises and scars. Beneath them, the woman I fell for is still there. I'm willing to do whatever it takes for you to see her, too."

She loosed a surrendering breath. "You just had to go and be fucking sweet. I like you more when you're being an asshole."

"I'm only being honest." I brushed my lips over hers lightly.

"Fine. You win. Ask your questions, but I'm not answering anything I don't want to."

"You underestimate how persuasive I can be. Don't forget, I've made mafia bosses sing like canaries. I can make you sing, too, Princess."

"There's no version of this world where you would hurt me." Thea straightened against my grip, as if it did anything but press her closer to me.

"Oh, Thea, I don't need to hurt you to make you beg." I thumbed at the top button of her shirt until it slipped free. With her shoulder hurt, she'd taken to stealing my dress shirts. The bottom was tied in a knot, and the too-long sleeves were rolled until they sat mid-forearm. I fucking loved it.

"First question: How long have you been avoiding the shower?"

"Not—"

Only one word into her denial, I tilted my head to the side and tightened my expression so there was no doubt that I knew she was lying.

"Danny, please. Let's go. I promise to suck your cock until you go blind. Can you just leave it, please? Please?" Her eyes were large, the redness in her cheeks spilling down to her chest.

I waited patiently, lowering my hands back to her thighs. However tempting her offer might be, she wasn't squirming her way out of this. Thea may still feel like the girl trapped in the tower, but she needed to understand that we weren't going anywhere. She was hurting, and I loved her too much to watch her suffer alone.

She worried her lower lip as she scanned my face. "Since La Chasse."

"That's my girl." I palmed the back of her neck and pulled her close enough to press a soft kiss to the sweet spot just beneath her ear. Thea let out a soft sigh and melted against me. The next two buttons allowed the shirt to fall off her shoulder. The soft fabric clung to her breast, barely hanging in place. I ran the tip of my index finger along the swell of flushed skin.

She sucked in a breath through her teeth, and tiny goosebumps stippled her skin. I loved this about her. It didn't matter how lightly I touched her, she always reacted.

"What is it about the shower that has you so triggered?"

Her vision shifted to the stall behind me at the same time her pupils blew wide enough to swallow the sea green that I loved so much. Whatever it was that had her spooked, it was bad. Really bad. I hadn't seen her this jumpy since the day we came home from Westin's boat.

"I ... I ..." Thea's voice caught in the back of her throat. "I don't want to play anymore."

I smoothed my thumb over the soft surface of her inner thigh. I knew her thin leggings were doing little to block the full heat of my touch. I also knew that it was grounding enough that her defenses were already unraveling.

After Thea was released from the isolation of the palace she'd been considerably more sensitive to touch. I'd more than once seen her seeking out one of us solely to be close to someone. It was usually Crowe. He was clingy on a normal day, so he'd been soaking up the extra attention. Now, while she was so obviously anxious, one simple stroke of my thumb was all she needed to remember she was strong.

She looked at the ceiling. "I don't like any part of it."

Grabbing her chin, I lowered her eyes back to mine. "The shower?"

"The curtain." Bingo.

Her body rocked with a heavy breath, like the admission had lessened a weight on her chest. I tilted her head to the side and kissed my way from her jaw to her collar. Her breast was heavy against my palm, the hardened point of her nipple pressing into the brushed cotton. Her spine arched with each slow touch.

"Keep going," I whispered against her skin. "You're doing so good."

"It sounds like the pool cover … and the feel of it … It's too similar. I don't like it."

Keeping my hand on her waist, I leaned to the side and gripped the vinyl. "This curtain?"

"Yes." She sounded so small.

I yanked the sheet from the rod with one hard tug. The plastic tore free, making the muscles beneath my palm tighten. When I looked at Thea, she was trembling.

"Done. Curtain gone."

Small tracks of tears cascaded from the corners of her eyes. "It's more than that." She swiped at the moisture gathering on her cheeks. "Fuck." Thea took several heavy breaths, getting faster and faster as she fought the panic. "It's everything. It's the water running down my face or even the smell of the moisture. Beneath the water used to be the one place I could escape. Em was a spiteful bitch, but she never came in the room when I was bathing. King stood outside the door, but even he always let me have that space ..." She ground her teeth, baring them in pure loathing. "I *hate* that Sylvan took that from me. I hate them all."

The remaining buttons of her shirt came free easily. I carefully slipped it and her brace off until her upper body was bare to me. The sight of her was something that would never cease to make me pause. Thea's body was a road map of all she'd conquered. Reverently, I traced the ghost of a bruise along her side.

"And the soap?" I paused, lifting my eyes from the path I was drawing against her skin.

"I don't need you running to my rescue." Her voice dropped to barely a whisper. "I don't want to be saved."

"You've got it all wrong. Thea, you walked into our lives, blowing it apart. In the aftermath, we'd saved each other. You save me from myself every damned day."

Thea pushed at the corner of her eye with the heel of her hand. One by one, the tears fell faster. "When I came to clean the building dust from my skin, I saw them all there. It was like each of the bottles were my insecurities given physical form." She gave me a sheepish smile. "I thought, if I could just wash them all down the drain, maybe they'd go away, and I could be done with it. It's stupid."

"It's not."

"You all don't need to worry about me, Danny. I'm holding it together, but I'm done with showers and baths. My friend, Mr. Sink, and I are doing just fine." She patted the counter. "You can feel free to leave now. I'm aware of how pathetic I am."

She wrapped her good arm around her middle, subconsciously cradling the injured one.

I took her chin, lifting it from where her expression had fallen. "No part of you could ever be pathetic. You are the strongest and bravest person I've ever met. If pouring body wash down the drain makes you feel better, then let's do that. Fuck the expensive imported soaps."

Scooping under her ass, I lifted her into the air. She screeched with surprise and reflexively wrapped her legs around my waist. "Danny, what are you doing?"

I walked us into the shower stall. Reaching with one hand, I grabbed the faucet and turned on the spray. Thea immediately crawled up my body.

"No. Turn it off. You're dressed. There's water going everywhere, and I ... I ... I—"

I silenced her with a hard kiss, crashing my mouth into hers until she was forced to surrender. Seeing her fight this, and being embarrassed about it, wasn't something I was willing to accept. "Listen to me, Thea. I don't care one bit about wet denim or that the bathroom is flooding. The beginning and end of what I care about is you."

Thea's eyes shook. Before her face broke with more tears, I pushed her against the wall of the shower and kissed her slowly, reminding her of the woman she was in my eyes. The same one that lit an entire construction yard on fire. The one who vowed to do her worst. The one I loved. "You trust me, right?"

"Of course. I mean, I'm terrified right now, and you've got that scary eye gleam thing that you get sometimes, but I trust you."

"Scary eye gleam thing?"

"Yeah, it's somewhere between committing murder and eliminating the entire world on the quest to rid me of my shower fears." Her expression lifted. It wasn't much, but it felt like the clouds parting. "I don't want that kind of responsibility."

"Then let me be the responsible one." I eased her onto her feet and picked up the closest plastic-wrapped disk. I dropped the thing into the middle of the soap puddle. It instantly fizzed, filling the air with the scent of lavender and lemon. "Heh, so that's a shower fizzer."

"I love you," Thea said on a disbelieving and relieved exhale. She grabbed the closest bottle, dramatically popping the lid. "And I love that you understand my tortured logic." Upending the bottle, the stream of red soap dripped like a spray of blood against the white tile. I flicked open a creamy blue one. In a single shot, I painted it across her chest.

313

Thea's shock quickly turned to mischief, slashing her red soap at me with an enthusiastic burst of wicked laughter. Swapping the blue bottle for a green one, I fired the body gel. She threw up her arms to block. Opening a jar of scrub, she scooped a handful, tossing it at full power at me. The glob landed thick in my hair.

I lifted my hand to the mess. The strands were caked with gritty paste.

Thea bit down on her lip, restraining a laugh. It was the most beautiful thing I'd ever seen. There was light in her eyes where there had just been such sorrow. It made my heart feel like it had wings and it fluttered against my ribs.

"So that's how you want it?"

Thea laughed with a squeal of mock fear. "You've got that scary eye gleam thing again."

I took hold of her stomach and pushed against the wall. "I'm thinking very scary eye gleam types of things." I reached over her shoulder and spun the lid off of a jar. Keeping her pinned, I upended the entire contents over her head. Thea scrambled her hands behind her, grabbing a bottle and squeezing it between us so that it shot directly into my chin.

It caught me by such surprise that I released her and spluttered against the bitter taste of soap. The laughter shared in that moment was almost magical. It banished every dark thought and emotion. Her smile was broad, the absent weight of her fear making her giddy. Together, we emptied the entire stock down the drain. By the end, she didn't care that we were in the water and that suds coated every inch of us or about the absurdity of what we'd done.

When I kissed her this time, the powerhouse I knew was in there kissed me back. Every press of our lips, and the way her tongue demanded more as it flicked against my teeth, reclaimed a bit of my Firecracker's spark. The heaviness of just how much I cared for her slammed into me. I felt hot with it like a fire was building between us. There was nothing I wouldn't do for this woman. Nothing. I hadn't lied, Thea was both my end and my beginning.

Holding her in my arms, I used the wand to rinse us clean. When we were mostly soap free, I ushered her out of the flooded bathroom, discarding our sopping clothing to the floor as we went.

The second her leggings were free, I lifted her against the wall. "I want you, Thea. I will never stop wanting you," I vowed. Her body was slick against mine. I notched the tip of my dick against the heat of her pussy and memorized every breath she took as I sank into her. Her body wrapped around mine, drawing me deeper and deeper. I felt the connection in every one of my muscles.

"Show me," she said over our shared breath.

"Yes, ma'am." Turning her around, I angled her body so that she leaned against the full-length mirror mounted to the back of the door. "Keep your eyes on me." Slowly, I pushed into her, the new angle hitting something deep that made her clench hard enough that lightning rocketed down to my toes. I ran my hand down her spine, grazing the scars that striped her back. Thea whimpered, pushing her ass into my hips and pleading for more.

Pulling back, the fire in her gaze was nearly enough to send me over the edge. It begged to be obliterated. Her skin, still dewey from the lingering oils, sparkled in the light from the bathroom. She looked delicious, and perfect, and so fucking mine.

Cracking my hand against her ass, I slid from her and dropped to my knees. "Dan—"

Using my hands to spread her wide, I licked her from clit to ass.

"Fuck," she breathed, my name melting into a barely coherent curse.

"Come on my face, and then I'll consider giving you back my cock."

"Why are you such a commanding dick?" She pressed her cheek to the glass of the mirror, bending to give me more access.

"You assumed ownership of every part of me the moment you accepted I was yours." I circled the ring of her ass with my thumb, pressing deep. "Commanding dick included."

Her legs shook, growing more violent as I tongued at her clit. She mumbled, unable to articulate over her building orgasm.

I fucking loved when she was like this. Thea fought so damn hard, then it was this moment when she gave herself over. Right here was where she became truly mine for the taking. I would take her over and over again until she couldn't remember a life where she wasn't mine.

Her body rolled against the mirror, making the glass fog with each panted breath.

Like pulling the pin on a grenade, I slid two fingers into her pussy and curled them back against the press of my thumb. I counted to three before she detonated. Every muscle in her body strained against my hold. I sucked her clit between my teeth and watched as she did it again. There would be nothing left of that scared girl when I was done with her.

Her palm slammed against the glass, barely audible over the way she screamed my name. I fucking loved when she did that, too. There was no part of this woman that I didn't crave.

"That's right, Firecracker. Louder." I increased my speed, changing the position of my hand so that the soaking fingers from her pussy slipped easily into her ass, stretching her wider. With a hard crack of my hand, the beautiful lines of her body contracted, tumbling her straight into a third climax. "Let the house know who is currently owning this luscious ass."

Her legs gave out, and I took her to the ground with me. I didn't wait for her to regain her senses. I didn't want her to. Body quivering in the most satisfying way, I sheathed her over my cock and groaned with satisfaction at the heat that swallowed me down. Thea ground her hips in a circle, making her breasts sway hypnotically.

"You're so beautiful, Thea. Fucking perfection." I should install a mirror on the ceiling so that I could watch her tits and her ass riding me at the same time. Not to mention, it'd be hot when one of them was fucking her with me. She took cock like a dream, and I had dreamt of it. Often.

Gripping her hips, I took over her speed, lifting to meet each of her descending thrusts.

Like they'd been summoned by my fantasies, the light from the hallway spilled into the room, broken by the shadows of Nick and Crowe. Who knew? Some dreams do come true.

Thea lifted her gaze, looking at them through the reflection in the mirror. Her lids drooped, becoming veiled by lust. She rocked harder, sinking far enough to make her mouth part with a silent moan.

I reached up, coasting my hand over her breast and circling it around her throat. At the same, time she clenched around my cock, making my balls tighten with each rise and fall of her pelvis.

"Your pussy just got so hot it's bordering on painful." I followed the line of her sight to Nick fisting his tattooed cock, and looking just as ravenous as she did. "Is it because you're thinking about what it would be like to swallow down all those studs?"

Her eyes fluttered closed. All the confirmation I needed.

"Darling Thea," Crowe's voice crooned.

Her eyes snapped open. He propped himself against the headboard of the enormous bed, lubing his dick in preparation for her. Thea's eyes went wide as she saw in the mirror what I was seeing.

"Come over here and sit on my dick, Beautiful."

"Let me get that for you," Nick said, lifting her clean off of me. Any protests she might have made were silenced by his mouth crashing over hers.

"I wasn't done with that," I said, pushing to my feet to follow after them.

-42-
THEA

Nick's embrace hit me like a hurricane meeting the shore. He swept me effortlessly into the air. My head spun from the quick change of position, and with his mouth locked over mine, I couldn't draw in breath. I didn't exactly care about either. I secretly loved when they threw me around and came at me like our lives depended on joining in that very moment.

My heart pounded in anticipation, drowning out what they were saying to each other. It wasn't until he was swinging me down to Crowe that I realized how much I needed the three of them. Planning coups and infiltrating manhunts required a lot of preparation. Since returning from the tower, one of them was always coming or going. I was never alone, but we were never together either. After the toll of these past few days, I needed the world to feel like it wasn't careening over a cliff and taking me with it. The solidity of their presence restored a piece of what had been taken from me in that pool. Feeling my body leave Danny's, passing to Nick, and settling against Crowe reaffirmed the connection we all shared. The bodies surrounding me were solid, present, and completely devoted to being mine. Nothing was more real than that.

"Get the spare brace from the dresser. The one with the stabilizer built in," Nick directed, taking my hips and easing me onto Crowe's lap so that I remained facing him.

Crowe snaked around my waist, palming my breast. "Hey there, Gorgeous." He wasted no time, licking a line along my neck so that chills shivered down my spine with each of his breaths. "You're going to feel like sweet bliss."

The head of his cock pushed hot against my ass, giving me enough stretch to make me ache for more. I closed my eyes, focusing all of my attention on all of the points where our bodies connected. It would only take one deep thrust to make me see stars.

"We could hear you panting from the front door. How many times did Danny make you come? Once? Twice?" When I didn't answer, he pulled me an inch lower, causing my breath to hitch. "Three, really?"

"Sounds like we have catching up to do." Nick kneeled between our legs, giving my injured shoulder a kiss before slipping the sleeve onto my arm. It had been long enough that Gabby said I didn't need to be wearing it constantly anymore. I usually only put it on when I knew we were in for a long day or the ache was becoming a distraction.

"I hate that thing," I muttered, doing my best not to flinch when he tightened the first strap. Nick noticed it, because the man notices everything. "I can't move with it on."

Hoping they'd get sidetracked and forget the brace altogether, I rocked my hips in an attempt to sink down. It didn't work. Crowe kept me supported and all I did was tease myself more.

"That's the point. The two of you know better than to be bouncing around without one." Nick said, tightening the last strap so that my arm was securely fastened to my waist. I'd never tell him that it felt better to have the pressure off the joint. Without the added pain, sensation heightened over my skin in a wave.

I arched my back against Crowe, letting my head fall onto his shoulder. Every brush of their skin against mine sent goosebumps down my arms. I rocked my pelvis, trying to force more friction.

Nick whispered in my ear, "You're lucky I'm not restraining both arms as a reminder." He took control of my hips, sinking me onto Crowe one tortuous inch at a time. The air vanished from my lungs as I both fought and welcomed the invasion. He watched my expression, stealing a kiss when I could finally breathe again. "It's not even my cock you're riding, and I still love seeing how beautifully you take it."

Crowe nuzzled against my neck, biting at my shoulder when I tested our new position. A sound, somewhere between a hum and growl, rumbled in his chest.

"You keep doing that, and we won't be able to play with the others." He gave my ass a hard swat. I jolted, arching into Nick while his grip on my hips kept me solidly in place.

Danny called over to Crowe, "Next time I get tails."

"I'm good with head, too," Crowe replied casually.

Nick pushed my back fully against Crowe's chest, letting him support us both as we laid back into the pillows. Abandoning my hips, he moved to my breasts. "Besides, look how beautifully this brace serves up your chest in offering. It's like dinner on a platter."

"Thea has the best tits," Danny confirmed, reclining on the chaise with one hand slowly stroking his cock and the other propped under his head.

Nick's mouth was hot against my skin, moving in a burning trail from one nipple to the other. His hands hooked my legs on either side of Crowe's so that he could keep them spread.

"*Cazzo*, that's a sight. Are you seeing this?" Nick leaned back so that Danny could have a clear view. He dipped two fingers into me. The pressure sent heat coursing over my body before returning to pool at the tips of his fingers. He curled them forward like he was pulling out the moan in my chest straight through the center of my body. "Have you ever seen anything so inviting?"

A devilish smile spread over Danny's lips, our eyes locking. "Oh, I see it."

Crowe's hands splayed over my stomach, keeping me anchored as he very slowly pistoned in and out. Together he and Nick wound my pleasure higher until I was a writhing mess between them. His lips passed over my ear and settled against that sweet spot just behind it. Against my skin, he said, "Tell Nick you want more."

Nick dropped his lips to mine, claiming a kiss with such intent that I could barely think beyond it. He slid the hard ridge of his dick against my clit, one bar at a time. My wetness coated his length with each teasing stroke. I closed my eyes, picturing what it would be like to feel those piercings thrusting in and out of me while I already felt so tight. "Are you ready for me, Trouble?"

"Always," I whispered against his lips.

"Take a deep breath with me."

Crowe's hand slipped over my hip, stroking my clit in slow and feather-light circles. My body pulsed in time with his movements, my muscles clenching and relaxing in anticipation. "Relax, Thea. We've got you. He's going to feel so damn good."

One breath at a time, Nick pushed in. My skin was alight with sensation. Sweat beaded against my neck and cooled with every breath Crowe took with us. With the added pressure of his cock filling me, the piercing at the head of Nick's dick dragged over a new point that left me keening for more.

"More, Angel. I need more." I fought against my brace, ignoring the way the action shot pain into my shoulder. I was desperate to drag my nails down his back and pull him to me or to thread my fingers into his hair while I held his mouth to mine. Anything, so long as it meant that I got more of him.

The sadist in Nick smiled, withholding that final sinking thrust despite how I writhed with need beneath him. He'd never looked more like that dark angel.

With my free hand, I reached for the velcro. If my pleasure was going to be withheld, then I would take it for myself.

"No." Nick slapped my clit.

I cried out. The sudden spike of pain rocked my senses, the wave nearly triggering me to fall headfirst into another orgasm. I arched, pushing my shoulders into Crowe and rocking against them both. Nick pulled back slightly, easing off the pressure so that my release went with him.

Nick's voice crooned with dark promise. "That stays on. Or, I don't care how sweetly you beg; I will spend hours edging you and then leave you in a wanton puddle."

"You're all cruel." Although, I still debated on ripping the thing off. Hours of edging could be fun. Torture, but fun torture.

Crowe chuckled, "Only because you love it."

"Please, Nick. I'll leave it on. Just, please."

"There she is, my good fucking girl." Nick drew back, sliding far enough that I feared he was leaving me. Gripping the headboard over Crowe, he said, "*Respira, Fiore Mio.* Breathe."[1]

The punishing hit of his hips slamming into mine was enough to make the three of us collectively groan. It was everything I wanted. There was no time to adjust to our new position. His biceps strained, the tattoos inked along its surface rippling as he used the bed frame to leverage the pump of his hips with increasing aggression.

To the side I could hear the slide of Danny's hand as he stroked in time with Nick's thrusts. I turned my head, meeting his emerald gaze. I curled a finger at him, beckoning him closer.

"Fuck, that's hot." He prowled to me. "You're sure?" He propped one knee on the mattress, sweetly brushing away the hair clinging to my face. I wrapped my hand around his cock, stroking until he finally gave in and pressed the head to my lips. I ran my tongue around the crown before opening my mouth and taking the full, hard length into my mouth. There was no stopping my moan from the tangy sweetness that still coated his cock. The intensity of our moment in the shower flooded my mind along with the feel of the three of them surrounding me.

I watched his expression, studying the lines in his neck and the swell of his biceps as he found his way into the natural rhythm of the three of us. He was beautiful. His normally styled hair was a disheveled mess, with a hint of oil still coating their strands.

The rapture consumed me. Our combined undulation commanded my body, playing me like the sounds of our fucking were composing a symphony. It was bliss, and I let myself float away on it. We weren't four people in the throes of passion but one entity that rose with the tide, climbing with the pounding my body was eagerly taking.

My vision went hazy, the overload to my nerve endings mixing with the knowledge that this was mine. Every inch of them belonged to me. I let go of

---

1. Breathe.

my fears and gave everything I had of myself right back to them. It was a mutual claiming in the most primal of ways. Nick grabbed my leg, hitching it over his shoulder and angling his body to reach an entirely new toe-curling angle. The muscles of my stomach seized, sending my orgasm crashing through me in wave after wave, one climax flooding into the next like there was no end.

My scream of ecstasy was muffled by his cock, but the sound was enough to tip Danny over with me. He spilled down my throat with a final hard thrust that pushed the barriers of the back of my throat. When he pulled free, he dropped to my still buzzing lips. The kiss was raw and filled with passion. His tongue stroked against mine like he was relishing the feel of all the ways we came together. "I love when you taste like me."

I smiled at the sentiment, scandalized by how filthy it was and demanding he never change. As Danny kissed me slowly, Nick's movements increased until he was pounding his release into me, too. He pulled away, giving the inside of my knee one last kiss before climbing from the bed.

Once Nick was free from between our legs, Crowe rolled us to the side. He lifted my leg, hooking it over his and rotating us so that he was supporting my weight. Our new position took all of the pressure from my suspended shoulder. He cupped my throat, drawing my face to his.

Danny slid beside me, settling comfortably at my stomach. While Crowe shifted to slow, impossibly deep strokes, my lion peppered kisses down my exposed body until his breath was cooling the throbbing heat of my pussy.

I didn't think it was possible to come harder than I had with all three of them fucking me, but Danny tonguing at my cunt while Crowe maintained each earth-shaking thrust sent me reeling into an entirely new state of ecstasy. Crowe's cock thickened, driving harder with his finishing thrusts until I thought the man would tear me in two if he could.

The room spun. I couldn't take in air fast enough and it felt like my heart was beating somewhere in outer space. It was almost impossible to tell which way was up until Danny rose to my lips and anchored me to him.

Crowe rolled me into Danny's arms. He slipped out from under us, giving the base of my neck a kiss and the globe of my ass cheek a solid love bite on his way out.

The room became surprisingly quiet. The stillness made every touch we shared feel monumental. This kiss was in complete contrast to the normally demanding way we fucked. No part of me was lashing out, and the only fight left in us was to pull one another closer. The pace was slow, like time no longer existed, and we had forever to stay in the moment. Usually, I walked away from Danny feeling owned and the pain lingered for days as a reminder of every place he'd touched me. This time, the only thing I felt was cherished.

Loved.

-43-
CROWE

I stared at the ceiling. The shadow of a cypress tree swayed in the wind outside our window. Slowly, I ran my hand up and down Thea's spine, counting the raised lines. With each scar I passed, flashes of her taking Eastin's lashes filtered through my thoughts. The memory of her on the security feed mixed with the way she'd clung to me that night when Nick stitched her up. Every time I returned to the unblemished small of her back, she made a tiny, contented whimper and melted further into my chest. Her slow and measured breaths drifted over the still healing welt above my heart. For once, she didn't seem like she was fighting anything in her dreams.

Nick slept with his arm wrapped around her waist, molding his hips to hers while being careful not to crowd her so much that she woke feeling trapped. I hated that there were still mornings when she would wake stuck in limbo with her nightmares. They were fewer now, and she seemed to be resting easier with each center we closed.

"She isn't going anywhere," Danny whispered from my other side. Thea's arm was stretched over my stomach, with her hand tucked safely in his. He blinked sleepily, shifting slowly so that she didn't wake.

It was early. Far earlier than either of us needed to be awake. Of course, I hadn't actually slept at all, so waking early wasn't really an issue. "We can sleep when we're dead, right?"

"You keep pulling all-nighters like this, and you will be."

"I'm fine."

"Yeah, we're all fine. That's why I keep baiting my sisters into a fight, Nick cooked enough food yesterday morning to feed a small city, and Thea's gone spookily quiet. We're all processing this shit. So don't try to lie to me and say you're fine."

This was the problem of being as close as we were for so many years. We'd taken enough of each other's shit to know when one of us was slinging it. I took a deep breath, filling my lungs with Thea's sweet scent. Even after cleaning up, she still smelled like the massive array of soaps that Danny bought her.

"Why hasn't she done anything?" I asked.

"You're going to have to be more specific. We've pissed off a lot of shes lately."

"I shot Gigi with Adder Oil, Danny. She has to be furious."

"That shit probably fucked her face up good. Maybe she doesn't want the public to see her until the team of plastic surgeons can make her look less disfigured."

"I should have killed her instead of fucking around. I should have killed her." I flattened my hand over Thea's scars, squeezing her tight. If anything happened to her now, that would be on me. "I should have shot her and been done with it. If she gets the better of us again—"

"She won't." Nick lifted his head, voice deep and gravely from sleep. "*É troppo presto.*"[1]

"We're ready for her," Danny continued. "We took the upper hand, and she knows it. Maddox wiped La Chasse's footage. It's like Thea was never there, and all intel points that Gigi still has no idea she's alive."

Never there? Fuck, that was the grossest understatement of the century. I could still feel my heart beating as I pushed myself to make it to that pool. My legs still ached from it. The wound in my chest pulsed in time with each of her breaths just to remind me that for a few precious minutes, she'd stopped breathing. Never there?

"She's safe, Vin," Nick said, pulling Thea's hair from her neck and pressing a soft kiss between her shoulder blades. "*Smettila di preoccuparti.*"[2]

---

1. It's too early.

2. Stop worrying.

"I'm not worrying."

"You really think I'm going to let Thea walk into another trap?" Danny asked. "Last time, Gigi got the jump on us because we weren't ready for her. That will *never* happen again."

Danny rolled onto his side, checking that she really was still asleep. The adrenaline let-down from the raid hit her hard this time, and through it we drained every ounce of energy from her. She hadn't moved since we all collapsed into a massive heap. While our dynamic was still new, we'd fallen into it like this was the most natural thing in the world.

"There's something we haven't really discussed." The muscles along my neck tensed in preparation for whatever he was about to disclose. "Earlier today, I asked Maddox to check the footage at the pool again. Just in-case we missed something, but he couldn't find anything on the cameras."

"We already knew that. He and I reviewed the tapes together weeks ago. The feed shuts off right after Thea is placed on the diving platform." If it was possible to disembowel a man more than once, I'd be considering it right now. To no one's surprise, Thea still hadn't told us half of what happened.

"Whoever they are, they pulled Thea from the pool before she drowned. I saw it."

I tried really hard not to consider the fact that without this guardian angel, none of us would have made it in time.

"What about Kyle's theory of The Hatter?" As much as I didn't want to think about that dumbass while Thea was laying with us naked in bed ... "He seemed pretty certain."

"The Hatter's an urban legend. If anything, it's a pretender."

"We should try recruiting him," I said absently.

"Who says it's a him?" Nick mumbled into his pillow.

"Whoever they are, they took out Sylvan with zero signs of a struggle."

"And quickly ..." Danny added, voice drifting off with whatever memory was haunting him.

"I wonder if Maddox could figure out a way to track him. We could use that kind of efficiency."

"Something tells me this ghost doesn't want to be found."

Thea stretched her back, eyes squinting against the darkness. She took a sweeping look at the three of us and scowled. Tucking her face back into my chest, she mumbled, "No plotting in bed. That should be a rule."

Danny's face softened, releasing her hand to cup her cheek gently. "Go back to sleep, Firecracker. It's still early."

An idea clicked in my head, snagging on something Danny'd said, *this ghost*. I rolled Thea into Nick's arms. "Take her." I pressed a kiss to the center of her brow, before climbing off the end of the bed.

Thea glued herself to him, clinging like a baby sloth. She was so adorable sometimes, especially with the little pout her lips were making. Slipping into my boxers, I added, "Try to get her back to sleep, if you can."

"I'm up," she mumbled, the words slurring as she fought the pull of sleep.

"She needs more than she's been getting lately."

"Are you the pot or the kettle in this scenario," Danny remarked, sliding into the space I'd just vacated.

Nick pulled the blanket around them all, tucking the ends under her chin. "He's the burner—"

"Shut up. I think I just figured out the answer to all of our issues. I need to go wake up Maddox. He's going to hate me, but I know exactly what we need to do next. Then, I promise to drag her sweet ass back to bed with me for a long snooze."

"A snooze. Right." Danny snorted a laugh. "I don't think you actually know what sleeping looks like, but I'll give you a hint, it doesn't involve knocking the headboard against the wall."

"I'm here. Are you happy now?" Maddox stalked past me, pushing his way through the front door and down the hall.

I spun on my toes following him. "What, no good morning kiss?"

"I actually hate you right now. True unadulterated hate, the kind that makes me want to drive tiny needles into your toes."

"So, that's a no to the kiss, then?" I shoved a cup of coffee into his hand as I pushed open the command room door.

"Fuck right the hell off." He bent over, plugging a long power cable into the wall socket. "At least you have a proper office now and aren't working out of your kitchen like a heathen."

"You work from your bedroom." I couldn't deny that this was a quality upgrade. After La Chasse I poured all of my energy into breaking through the Palace's upgraded security. Two days in, I decided our apartment in The Villa either had to be expanded or one of the bedrooms had to go. It wasn't like I was doing much sleeping outside of Thea's room anyway. Giving up my space was an easy sacrifice.

Plopping himself into my oversized desk chair, he leveled an unamused glare at me. "Only because Harrison already claimed the spare room in our apartment for all of his books. And I know that you already knew that because you helped him do it while I was out of town."

I chuckled at the memory. "Yeah. That was hilarious. You were so pissed."

"You moved my *entire* gaming station into the bathroom! How am I supposed to react when you put my desk *over* the toilet?"

I scratched at the stubble growing along my jaw. "Some of my best work, really. Do you think I should grow a beard?"

Maddox jumped up, stomping toward the door. "Never mind. I just remembered what a dick you are. If I wanted this level of abuse, I could have stayed with Alice."

I slid into his path, holding up my hands in surrender. "Woah. Not so fast. I know how we're gonna get Gigi out of the palace."

He chewed on the inside of his cheek, considering his options while furiously tapping his toe. I had him, and he knew it. "Fine."

I snapped my fingers in victory.

"But only because that bitch murdered my sister and she deserves to die in terrible, horrible ways for it." He returned to the chair, opening up his own laptop. "And your skill set is particularly good at creative homicide."

"I have other skills, too."

"Sure, if you want to call your mid-level hacker ability a skill."

"Mid-level?" I blinked at him slowly. "That hurts. Truly."

Maddox tapped his pencil against the glass desktop. "Well, despite my better judgment, I'm here. Care to tell me what was worth driving at the ass crack of dawn for?"

"Do you remember Mirage?"

His face was a blank slate of indifference.

"It was a program that digitally masked images. It started as a joke filter on social media, but then quickly became an issue as people started using it to alter evidence and surveillance footage."

"I guess I remember it. I've never cared much about the social media fads."

"A year later there was buzz that the program was applying the same tech to video footage, allowing you to manipulate the video and audio feeds to make people say and do anything. It was believable, except for the fuzzy halo around the edges of the figure — giving it the nickname, Ghost."

"Where are you going with this?"

"What if the way to get rid of Emily Rosen and Gigi is to pit them against each other? Not just bait Gigi to come out of the palace, but really set them against one another."

"Go on."

"What's the one thing that Gigi would never allow to go unchecked?"

"Indentured servitude, oh wait." Maddox grinned like he was hilarious, but tricking people into slavery wasn't a joke.

"A direct attack on her ego. She acts tough, but she worked damn hard to create her image. The first sign of a challenge, and it gets stamped out before it can be seen as a weakness."

"So you want to what, use Ghost to make her look like she's doing one of those stupid dances or an old-fashioned sex tape? You just said that the halo was a giveaway of the tech."

"I want you to adapt the program to apply to live footage, masking a living person without the halo."

Maddox rapped his fingers on the desktop, clearly debating something. "Fuck it, I already have a program like that."

"Why would you already have a program like that?"

"I've been running it for a few years now. It doesn't recreate a specific person, rather it uses AI to alter features in real time, but it would be easy enough to adapt with the right source material."

"Good, because Emily has been dumb enough to cover up the way we've been systematically shutting down her cash flow. I think it's about time she tells Gigi all about her plans to upset her reign."

"Emily is making a play for the throne?"

"No, but Gigi doesn't know that."

-44-
DANNY

I squinted at the monitor. "Turn to the left."

A perfect likeness to Emily Rosen turned so that her head was in profile. The long line of her beak-like nose gave her a silhouette akin to a vulture.

"Now, back to the right." She turned in the opposite direction. The masking was flawless. Even her cropped blonde and grey hair swayed naturally. There were no glitches or seams in the animation. "Try moving quic—"

"I'm not a performing monkey here for your amusement, Danny," Thea snapped. Except it wasn't Thea's voice, it was Emily Rosen's. It was realistic enough that chills trickled down my spine.

"Say something Emilyish," Crowe said, reaching over to tweak one of the knobs on the panel.

Maddox slapped his hand. "Can you stop touching my shit for five damn seconds?"

"So you want cold and unyielding?" Thea asked. I shivered again. Hearing Emily's hard voice over the speakers might as well have been a bucket of ice water being dumped over my head. "How about ... Dorothy. Dorothy, where are you? Worthless girl, I'll have you hung by your thumbs if you don't show yourself this very instant."

The entire room went still, staring at Thea through the sound booth's glass panel.

I tightened my fist until my knuckles popped, feeling incredibly guilty about deliberately calling her Dorothy for all that time. No wonder she hated the name, if that was what it sounded like.

"Your thumbs?" Toto asked. "Please tell me you're being facetious."

"Yeah. I am," Thea added lightly. "Aunt Em was too lazy for all that. Why would she bother when throwing me in the crawl space was just as effective?"

Nick palmed the back of his neck. "So, when we get to the Farm, which one of us gets to kill *la vecchia zarra*?[1]

"Thea chooses what happens to Emily," I said firmly. Crowe nodded in agreement.

Thea walked to the glass of the sound booth, placing her palm to the glass and mouthing, "Thank you."

Emily Rosen may be responsible for ruining the lives of half the people in the room, but Thea was the only one she'd directly hurt. I knew she needed to confront her aunt if she was ever going to be free of the woman. Until then, the trauma of her past would follow Thea around like a shadow. She put it firmly behind her, but I recognized too well what it's like to have it lingering at the edges of your vision.

"Thea, think you're ready?" Maddox asked.

Refusing to look at the screen, I focused all of my attention on my girl. Thea picked at a stray thread popping from the cuff of Nick's hoodie. It made her look so small. Crowe's expression was laced with concern as he joined me from across the room. The smaller Thea became, the guiltier he looked.

He rapped his knuckles on the divider, startling Thea from her thoughts. "You don't have to talk to Gigi if you—"

"Don't coddle me, Crowe. I'm not some child that's going to burst into tears just because I have to talk to the woman who engineered my entire shitty life."

"I didn't say you would."

"Good." She flicked a switch. The recording light over the glass blinked on, cutting out the general feed from outside the booth.

"So, now that's settled. I'm glad I didn't just waste a month's worth of my time recoding an already perfect program for nothing." Maddox clicked a few

---

1. hag?

buttons, transferring a live feed for the phone call onto the screen in the sound booth.

"Why *did* you have this program?" I asked, thinking over how familiar it all felt.

"I've been using it for years. Anonymity is a hacker's greatest weapon." He pushed down on the intercom button, "Whenever you're ready, Thea, I'll dial in the number to her secure line."

"Maddox ..." I quickly cataloged the equipment. It was professional grade, top of the line. The lens on the camera alone had to cost thousands of dollars. "Whose face do you use when you mask in a video call?"

While I waited for him to answer, I watched Thea move on screen wearing a face I loathed. The software mutated her beautiful features so that they were indistinguishable, then reformed them into something flawless in its disguise. The modulation of her voice had clarity specific enough to fool any vocal recognition software. The synchronicity of it all made it impossible to detect the original figure behind the camera. There was only one person I knew of who wielded a live feed this way. One person that, up until this moment, I was sure was dead.

"It doesn't matter. Can we focus?" Maddox continued, pushing back on his chair to the spare computer with Gigi's information already waiting.

"Answer my question." I pulled back on his shoulder.

The hacker froze, looking slowly down to where my hand laid. "You're going to want to take your hands off me." Maddox's face tightened, the hostility in his eyes looking completely unlike the simple computer nerd I'd always dismissed him as.

Nick edged closer. Even Toto's expression grew concerned as the electricity in the room began to spark.

"First, tell me this ..." Maybe my instincts were wrong. The way my stomach was tightening could have nothing to do with him and everything to do with the steps we were about to take against Gigi. Maddox had grown on me over the past couple of weeks. I wasn't a man who kept friends, but I could see someday counting him as one. "Have you ever called *me* from behind that camera? Or better yet, have you ever called *her*?" Without looking, I pointed toward Thea.

Maddox rose from his chair, easily meeting me eye to eye. "And if I did, what are you going to do, Dandelion?"

"You motherfucker." I swung hard, my fist connecting with his cheek before cocking my arm back for a second hit. Nick caught me, denying me the satisfaction of cracking his skull open. "My Oz damn car was in that garage!"

"No. Your ego was in the garage. I'm trying to keep tyrants from running this country into the ground, and all you're thinking about is yourself."

Nick threw me back, forcing me to stumble into the glass wall of the sound booth. With a hand to the center of my chest, he pinned me in place. "Stay there, *cazzo*, before your temper fucks everything up."

"Thea almost died. *You* almost died." I swatted his arm away. "He *played* us, Nick."

"Yeah, well, you tried to double-cross me. So I'd say we're even," Maddox spat.

"To be fair, that was all Nick's doing," Crowe said, leaning against the door like this was nothing more than a squabble between children. "Also, if we're keeping track of losses. I'd like to add my fish to the list."

Maddox ignored him, pushing into my space until Nick was holding us both back. "All you lost was a house and some over-valued vehicles. Gigi took *my* *sister* from me." He shook off Nick's hold, the fury in his expression twisting into a pain I knew too well. "My twin. Losing Maggie was like having a piece of my soul amputated. So you and your self-righteous ass can fuck right the hell off."

The rage poured off of him in waves, causing his chest to rise and fall with hard panting breaths. Maddox's fists vibrated as he reined himself back in. I knew he had to be harboring something against Gigi. He was so singularly focused on taking her out.

It wasn't until now that I truly saw his resemblance to the dead girl at Head Shots. My thoughts drifted to the last moments of her life when I was sure she was handing me the answers I'd been searching decades for. I could still feel the blood that had soaked through my pants when Gigi drove me to my knees with the impossible choice of Thea or my sisters. A choice he was never given.

"Your sister was never the Wizard, was she?" I asked, biting back a confusing mix of rage and grief.

Thea pushed open the door to the booth. "What the hell is going on out here?"

Crowe wrapped an arm around her. "Danny is throwing a tantrum because Maddox is The Wizard. The real one."

Thea's jaw dropped to the ground.

"Technically, my sister and I were *both* The Wizard." Looking to Crowe, he added, "You never met Maggie. She ran the club while I took care of more delicate business."

"Like extortion?"

"Not just extortion, blackmail too." He lifted one corner of his lips in a failed attempt to joke.

"Your best friend is an assassin, and you didn't think to use her instead of an innocent woman just looking to get the hell out of Oz?"

"It was too hard to get into Westin's yacht. You saw what those schematics looked like. Thea was the one person she'd be so eager to see fall that she'd forget all of her usual protective measures. Your girl was perfect bait and I knew you three would never let any harm come to her."

"Except a whole fucking lot of harm came to her." The vein at the side of my temple pumped hard. I couldn't process all of this right now.

"Danny." Thea's hand was soft as it slipped around my already throbbing knuckles. "We need him, just like he needed us."

"No, I need to murder him. Right here and now." He was damn lucky that I didn't have my gun on me.

"Danny," she repeated, taking my face in both hands and pulling me down until my forehead was resting against hers. "I don't approve of his methods either, but we have enough enemies. Maddox doesn't need to be one of them."

"How can you always be so forgiving?"

She rubbed her nose against mine. "Because I've seen what a life without compassion does to a person, and I refuse to become one of them."

It was impossible to argue with her when she was being so gentle. I gave her a chaste kiss and took a step back, pinning Maddox with a glare. "You owe me a car."

***

The phone rang three times before Gigi answered it.

Thea didn't show any of the anxiety that I knew was coursing through her. Instead, she flawlessly picked up her Aunt's clipped condescension, never once breaking her demeanor as The Queen appeared on screen.

"Is there a reason you're calling me, Emily? I was very clear that all messages were to go through Sebastian." Gigi looked thin, making her head look like an apple balancing on a toothpick. Her eyes were sunken, and a greenish hue moved in patches from the side of her throat to cover half of her face. Gigi pulled on her blazer, attempting to cover what was clearly impossible to hide. Even her fingers looked boney as they clutched the fabric. In the nearly ten years that we'd worked together, I'd never seen her look so unkempt.

For the first time since we returned, I saw a bit of the guilt Crowe'd been harboring lift from his shoulders. His smirk was smug as he leaned in to study the finer details of her complexion. Adder Oil was a bitch. No doubt, the still infected patches of skin ached. It was a good start, but none of us would be happy until the bitch was six feet under and in tiny pieces.

Thea moved her hands to her hips and tapped her fingers with impatience. She silently marked one blemish after another, purposely letting her gaze linger on each. "You look like you lost a fight with the ass end of a slug."

I had to bite the knuckle of my fist to keep from laughing. Gigi's face turned red, except where the skin was already discolored. The contrast made her look like a bloated corpse.

"Mind your tongue. Remember, there's nothing to keep me from ordering it removed and pinned to my desk as a paperweight."

I cringed at the thought.

"It's adorable that you think your people are actually loyal enough to you that they'd follow such an order." Thea was cool as an iceberg, the flat indifference of Emily's voice clearly carrying the threat. "Do you know what the problem is with buying allegiance and killing the rest?"

Gigi lifted her chin, making the veins curving over her jaw turn a sickly shade of white.

"They're only as loyal as the money that fattens their wallets. It's a shame you haven't been paying them. Don't worry. I've taken care of that for you."

"What?" Gigi's eyes flicked to where Sebastian was standing not far away.

"You heard me. I've ... Forgive me, what did you call it? Seized your assets?"

Fuck, she was good.

"You don't have the—"

"Authority?" Thea barked a fake laugh. "I don't need you to bestow authority when I can so easily take it. See for yourself. There's nobody left to stop me."

This was a bluff. Maddox modified the records days ago. When she snatched a tablet from Sebastian to look at her accounts, Gigi would see that nothing had come in from any of her locations for weeks. Her eyes widened as she watched what once looked like flush wallets turn empty.

"Where did my money go?"

"You mean *my* money? That was never yours for the taking, and no, I don't think I'll be giving it back."

Gigi turned to Sebastian, placing a hand over the mic to muffle it, but I was still able to hear the panic in her voice. "Get Andrews on the phone. Right now."

"Don't bother, Sebastian." Thea shifted her weight, leaning with both palms flat on the desk before her. She pushed play on the console. On the video feed, each of the strongholds, centers, and labs that we'd destroyed streamed to Gigi one by one.

"This is a lie. These videos ..." Gigi's jaw dropped, at a loss for words.

Sebastian stepped away, calling a number, while watching the implosion of building after building. It was a beautiful thing to see the way their faces fell into abject shock.

"While you've been licking your wounds, I've been taking back what's mine. Did you really think that you could double back on our deal and there wouldn't be consequences?"

Sebastian shook his head, focused fully on what he was being told over the phone. "What about the others?"

"What Andrews is not telling you, Your Majesty, is that for the past month, I've been quietly dismantling everything you've worked so hard to steal. My people masked the intel and doctored reports to make it look like all was well in your Queendom. Hell, I even had them inflate the numbers a touch to make it look like you were having a record breaking quarter."

"Give me the phone." Gigi held out her hand, snapping at Sebastian when he was still staring at the screen.

"Don't go too hard on the man. It's not his fault. Andrews didn't notice I was changing your books because he was too busy skimming off the top of them."

It was beautiful the way Gigi's mouth hung open like a dead fish. Thea was playing her part perfectly, delivering one hit after another.

"How would you have ever known the truth, hiding in your palace, afraid to show your face? Not that I blame you. Any broadcasts you made would have needed a disclaimer to keep from scaring the elderly and small children. Who knew that boy of my niece's would turn out to be good for something after all?"

Gigi ground her teeth hard enough to hear them over the microphone. The criminal empire she'd so meticulously constructed was crumbling to dust right before her eyes. Politically, she had no allies, and financially, she no longer had a way to pay the ones who might have stuck around. A month of not being paid closed a lot of doors for a woman like Gigi.

"Oz is no longer yours. It hasn't been for weeks. I'm only here now to inform you that your services are no longer necessary. "

Crowe clamped a hand over his mouth to keep from cackling. Through the glass, I watched Thea's spine straighten, her chin lifting in challenge. Oz damn. When I'd called her Firecracker, I was right. She'd just blown Gigi's fucking mind. It was surprising that small bits of brain matter weren't splattered on the wall behind her.

"I *will* kill you for this," Gigi ground out through her clenched jaw. "You might have closed a few drug dens and killed a few whores, but I have Oz-mandria's entire armed forces at my disposal. Your pack of untrained dogs are nothing. *You* are nothing and you'll all die screaming beneath my feet ... just like your niece."

Thea looked at her nails, taking several long seconds to examine them. I'd give anything to be in her head right now. Was she silently screaming, or holding back maniacal laughter? Her blank mask of indifference gave nothing away.

"I know it's hard to admit when the better woman has won." Thea finally flicked her eyes up to the camera, the rest of her remaining eerily still. "Don't worry, you'll get there."

Before Gigi could answer, Thea ended the call. The ghost of Gigi's livid expression lingering as the screen went dark.

-45-
DANNY

The cab hit a set of rumble strips as Nick exited the bypass and turned onto an old and never used highway. I pulled Thea tighter to me so that I could look over Crowe's shoulder at the seat back computer. On the screen, dozens of Sand Crawlers slowly traversed the deadliest desert on Earth. The live feed was from a satellite Maddox requisitioned, positioning its eye in the sky over The Farm. We didn't ask how he was able to hack into a supposedly top-secret surveillance satellite, or how he'd fooled an entire foreign government into thinking they still had control of it.

After Thea's stunning performance, it didn't take long for Gigi to mobilize her people. Maddox and Crowe discretely redirected her calls and looped video feeds so that anytime she tried checking on the status of life beyond the palace walls, all Gigi saw was the devastation our girl had promised.

"Take your next left. The road doesn't have a sign or anything, but you'll see it." Daffodil leaned forward to rest her elbows on the front dash. "It's not much farther now."

"Wow. That was a big one," Thea exclaimed, and Crowe zoomed the camera in.

On the screen, a massive puff of sand plumed into the sky like a geyser. One of the Sand Crawlers tipped into a freshly opened sinkhole. Armed men jumped from the vehicle, scrambling along the shifting ground. It was ultimately a losing battle. The ground swallowed them all whole while Gigi's fleet never slowed. Not a single person went back to save them.

There was a reason why we'd never considered going after The Farm directly. Even in my darkest days, we knew it wasn't possible. Emily Rosen fortified herself in the most uninhabitable place on the continent. I still couldn't believe Thea'd grown up in that hell. With every passing day, the respect I held for her grew.

Moving over the terrain was slow. The dunes hid quicksand pits that were impossible to detect until you were sinking beneath them. Emily Rosen had mapped a very precise route through the landscape, one she wasn't sharing. It was how she cornered the import market. Few had the ability to move large quantities of goods in the way Emily's modified Cyclone trucks could. There were only two other, equally arduous, routes in and out of Oz. With them, there were a couple of smaller import corporations, but none of them could match the speed at which Cyclone Shipping moved.

Travel by air was even more dangerous. The mica that gave the Emerald City its luster also came with heavy ore deposits. The magnetic fields in the shifting sands surrounding Oz were responsible for downing more than one plane.

Daffodil clapped her hands enthusiastically, pulling on Nick's arm so that the cab swerved. "We're here." The winding dirt road curved its way over the crest of the hill, giving a clear view of the rows of barn-like buildings forming a sprawling village.

Thea propped herself between the front seats for a better view. "Toto, what is all of this? I thought we were headed to one of Ginger's hotels."

"Oh, no. A hotel couldn't possibly hold everyone. This is the Army of Revolt's home base." Daffodil twirled a lock of red hair around one finger.

I sat back in my seat, pulling Thea back with me. "Army? That's a bit much for a group of runaways. Don't you think?"

My sister scowled at me, just like she had hundreds of times when we were children. "She brings in those pop-up houses as more people find their way to her."

Crowe closed the monitor and flipped up the computer into the back of the front seat. Then, grabbing Thea around the waist, he hauled her onto his lap. "We probably have half a day before Gigi's people make it to The Farm. They're progressing slower than we anticipated."

"That's good. It gives us more time," Nick said, looking at us in the rearview mirror.

"What about my Aunt?" Thea asked, fiddling with the IV hook on the back of the seat.

Crowe took her hand and laced her fingers through his. "She just got her third denial to move operations inland, followed by a cut to The Farm's budget, specifically Em's personal take from the Ozmandrian Morphia labs."

Thea laughed, covering her mouth with her hand to hide her glee. "Sorry, just the idea of her having to ask for permission is the funniest damn thing I've ever heard."

Crowe smiled conspiratorially. "She'll be fuming by the time Gigi's people arrive."

I stretched out my legs, taking advantage of the extra space in the backseat now that Crowe had commandeered Thea. "That's the plan. Maybe we'll get lucky, and they'll wait to tear each other's throats out until after we get there."

"Aunt Em deserves to feel the underside of a boot for once. Has she tried tapping any of her connections? The office vault has blackmail material on half of Oz."

Crowe pulled her fingers to his lips. "For some reason, she hasn't had much luck with reaching anyone. It would appear that Emily Rosen has turned into a bit of a pariah."

"I fucking love that."

"Yeah, well, I fucking love *you*. Darling, I told you there was nothing I wouldn't give you, vengeance included. You have a few people you want me to slay for you while I'm at it?"

Thea pulled his lips down to hers. "You say the sweetest things."

"Can the two of you cut it with the mushy shit?" Nick pulled the cab beside a large airplane hangar at the edge of Ginger's compound.

"Yeah, well, not all of us can wax Italian poetry when we think no one is listening," Crowe's patronizing laugh was cut short when Thea went in for another kiss.

Ignoring them, I leaned over Thea and Crowe to get a good look at the building. From the outside, it was completely nondescript. The building could be housing anything.

Daffodil flipped down the visor mirror to check her hair, running her fingers through it and flipping it from one side to the other. Then she pursed her lips, blowing her reflection a kiss.

"What are you doing?" I asked.

"Checking my hair before I get out, why?"

I frowned at my sister, then looked out the window to where Ginger was waiting in a fully decorated flight suit, including a white scarf and goggles holding back her long sleek hair. The form hugging uniform and partially buttoned top made her look like she'd just walked out of a vintage pinup calendar.

"That woman is a menace," I grumbled.

Thea slapped me playfully. "Shhh. Ginger's great, and you know it."

Ginger waggled her fingers in greeting.

Daffodil rolled the window down, leaning half out the frame to wave back with her entire body. It was like watching flowers turn toward the sun.

I looked at Thea, completely perplexed. "What is happening right now?"

Thea cringed, biting her lower lip. "Danny, there's probably something you should know."

"Stronzo." Nick put the vehicle in park, "Sometimes you really are oblivious."

"Hey, Totes," Ginger said, leaning against the doorframe.

My sister didn't bother with the door. Instead, she climbed through the widow, and right into Ginger's arms, latching onto the woman like a spider monkey.

"No, really what's happening right now?"

"Ya, know what?" Thea said with a laugh, "I think you're about to find out."

Daffodil took Ginger's face in both hands and went in for a kiss so indecent that Crowe whistled with appreciation.

"That's my sister." I grabbed Thea's arm, pulling her out of the way so that I could slug the catcalling moron.

"I mean ..." He laughed, rubbing at his shoulder. "You've got to appreciate anyone who goes at it with that kind of enthusiasm."

Ginger sat Daffodil on the hood, pressing close enough I'm sure there were tiny angels fainting somewhere. I banged on the window to get the women's attention. "This car costs more than both of you combined."

"Don't worry, Dandy." Crowe opened the door, taking Thea's bag for her. "They have to come up for air eventually."

I glared at Crowe. "It's like you *want* me to shoot you. You know I will."

"Nah, you can't shoot me. Thea loves my dick too much. She'd never forgive you."

I sniped back at him, "You can't keep using that excuse."

"Nobody likes a prude, Dandelion," Ginger chided, squeezing two large palmfuls of my sister's ass before stepping away.

Climbing from the car, I pulled my sister to the side. She didn't look the least bit embarrassed. "Were either of you going to mention that this was a thing? Because I can think of about a dozen ways I would've rather discovered your relationship, and about half of them involve my eyes being gouged out."

"It's not like I need your permission, little brother." Daffodil laughed, giving my cheek a patronizing squeeze.

"Need my permission? Your ass marks are on the hood of my car!"

"Our car," Crowe corrected.

"Oh please, I've heard you and the guys tearing Thea apart more times than I can count. This was pretty tame by comparison."

Crowe snickered. "I can guarantee that's not going to stop, either."

Using a single finger to fix the edge of her lipstick, Ginger remarked, "If you two are done with the sibling squabbles, I've got everything set up. We can be in the air within the hour. We just need to do one last brief with the teams going in with us."

"I thought planes were useless for crossing the desert? The dial doodads don't work or something like that." Thea asked, giving Nick a puzzled look.

"Dial doodads?" he replied, trying not to crack a smile. "Is that the technical term?"

Thea smacked him in the chest. "Shut up. You know what I mean. The controls don't work right."

"Which is why we aren't taking a plane." Ginger gestured to where a man and a woman were pushing open the large hangar doors.

Inside were a fleet of hovercrafts. They looked like a cross of something between a tank and spaceship. Each was painted in varying shades of tan, with three massive, bladeless turbines mounted on the back.

"My mechanic, Al, has been working on these for the past month. We'll be able to move over the desert in a straight line for The Farm. Shouldn't take us more than an hour to get there."

A man approached us with a wave. His long dark hair was tied back with a bandana. He pulled it free and used it to wipe away the streaks of engine grease mottling his russet skin. Stuffing the scarf into his pocket, he held out a hand. "I'm Al. You all must be Toto's crew."

"Toto's crew. That's cute." I took his hand, accepting the firm shake before he moved on to the others. As we followed him into the hangar, I grabbed the collar of my sister's shirt and pulled her back with us.

"Now we're your crew?"

Daffodil shrugged. "I'm a very fair boss. Three weeks paid vacation and hour lunch breaks."

"So you're going to be the one paying for all the operation costs, too?"

She licked her lips. "I mean, I was considering outsourcing. Interested in the job?"

Our group slowed to a stop by the nearest of the hovercrafts. "Remind me again why I looked so damn hard for you?"

"Probably has something to do with loving me." My sister went up on her tiptoes and pressed a kiss to my cheek.

Al slapped the vinyl base of the first craft. It sat about four feet off the ground, with a rope ladder used to climb up and down the side when it wasn't in use. "These are quick as the devil and, for their size, have excellent maneuverability. Air moves through the turbines using a cyclone technology, making them both fast and silent. We can load up to twenty people on each. With luck, we grab the captives and get them out before anyone has realized we've come and gone."

Nick broke away from the group, using the ropes to haul himself onto the main deck. "This is some seriously high-tech you're slinging here. Is this a Sunlink sat-nav?" Nick pointed to the sleek plating elevated on an angle above the cockpit.

Al's face lit up. "It is. I was told that we'd be connecting to our own satellite in order to navigate the magnetic fields."

"And solar panels, don't tell me you made them electric?" Nick jumped to the end of the vessel, poking his head around the engine panel.

"With integrated energy conversion, so she's also self-charging," Al added, trying to appear casual and not like he was bragging for the first time to someone who appreciated the technology for what it was.

"This is some of the sexiest electrical work I've ever seen." Nick looked straight at Al, bouncing a bit as he asked hopefully, "Can I drive one?"

"He looks like it's his birthday and every other holiday all rolled into one," Thea said. Her eyes seemed to glitter as she watched Nick's unbridled joy. "It's kind of adorable."

Crowe nodded. "Bets on how long it takes for him to start humping it?"

The man and woman who had opened the hangar doors approached Ginger, handing her a clipboard. They wore a uniform similar but not quite as adorned as hers. "Al had all of the vehicles loaded. The ranks are waiting for a last brief in the meeting room, and then we can leave."

"Brilliant. Thank you, Al," Ginger responded, flashing the mechanic a bright smile.

Al waved down but was otherwise focused on showing Nick the ins and outs of the turbines. Nick looked like he was one spark plug away from coming all over the pistons.

Ginger flipped a couple of pages, then filed the board against her chest. "Thank you, Hans. I expected nothing less from you both. You've done a bang-up job managing the troops. I was very fortunate the day the two of you found your way to me."

Hans beamed with pride at the woman standing beside him.

"Troops?" I leaned into Crowe, whispering from the side of my mouth. "She realizes that she doesn't actually have an army, right?"

We followed Ginger and her team through the meeting room doors, joining the fifty uniformed people sitting in neat rows. The majority of them were women, with a few men peppering the ranks. Regardless of gender, they all looked at their General with adoration as we entered the room.

Crowe shook his head. "No, I think Ginger absolutely has her own army."

"Let me introduce the Army of Revolt. These are about a quarter of the people who serve under me." Ginger walked down the line of people. "I've been planning for a day like today for a long time." She paused, adjusting the collar of one of the women in the front line. "In many ways, I should be thanking Gigi. She eliminated a large chunk of my competition in her own bid for power."

"Technically, that was Thea," Crowe pointed out.

"Not all of it." Ginger smirked, "Sorren was a bit of a thorn. She was too interested in what was happening down here, so I made sure to acquire the Southern Quadrant before all of the others. It took a lot of work to ensure Gigi didn't suspect anything when Sorren went missing."

"It was you who killed her?" Crowe asked, eyeing the woman with renewed appreciation.

"Killed? Gracious, no. The woman was already dying. I found her a specialist outside of Oz and made her a deal." Ginger snorted with a wave. "What do you take me for? I'm not some cutthroat looking to conquer the Emerald City for a few jewels. I'm in it for the people."

"So, that's your endgame then? You want to be Queen?" I asked, uneasy with the idea of my sister tying herself to someone with such lofty ambitions.

The leader of the rebel army scanned over the people who followed her movements with pure devotion. Her features melted into pride when she met the eyes of the people staring back at her. To many like my sister, she was their savior. The lost people of Ozmandria found her when they had nowhere else to go. Maybe she would be good for Oz. Maybe Ginger would protect the nation the same way she'd protected the abused and underappreciated ... Or maybe, like every other person in power, she'd lose focus of the bigger picture and see only her own ambition.

"Not Queen, per se, but Ozmandria has been long overdue for a change, and Gigi isn't going to be it. There was a vacuum of power in this country, and too many people suffered because of it. There needs to be infrastructure in place to support more than the criminal base."

"What kind of skills are we working with?" Nick asked, rejoining the group.

The woman working with Hans answered for her, "Everyone standing before you has had months, and for some of them years, of firearms and hand-to-hand combat training. They're all aware of what's at stake."

Thea nodded in appreciation. "Well, I can certainly get behind that."

"There isn't a single person in this hangar who doesn't want to see The Farm burn."

–46–
THEA

The sun was low on the horizon, sparkling like fire on the sand. Our hovercraft slowed to a stop at the base of a dune. In the distance, the sound of gunfire and explosions echoed in a symphony of war. I couldn't help but smile at the chaos we'd invited to The Farm.

Everything was about to change.

Ginger and Toto climbed down from their own nearby hovercraft.

"Hoooooooly fuck." Crowe slapped Nick's shoulder enthusiastically. "Are you seeing what I'm seeing?"

Nick frowned at Crowe's pestering hands, which were still tapping at him for his attention. "If you mean Ginger walking toward us with an Anti-Tank Rocket Launcher strapped to her back, then yeah, I do," he said, dropping to the ground and turning to help me down.

"It's pink." Danny thumped to the sand beside me. "I'm pretty sure that's a crime against weaponry."

"When do I get a rocket launcher?" I said, batting my lashes up at Crowe.

"Oh, hell yes. Fuck, that's hot." He lifted me up for a kiss. "Darling, I will get you one in any color you want if you'll shoot it in that lacy black thong set that I like."

I tilted my head to the side in question. "The one with the satin ties?"

"Yes." Crowe's eyes went wide with delight. "That one. Then afterward, I can unwrap you like a snack."

Toto cleared her throat. "Ummm. Don't we have an attack to coordinate or something? You two can make weapon sex plans some other time."

"Probably for the best." Crowe put me down, giving my ass a hard slap. "Nobody wants a hard-on while wearing kevlar. The chafing is brutal."

Together, the six of us climbed the hill, keeping the sun to our back.

"I never thought I'd be back here again," Toto said somberly.

In the growing shadow of the valley, lay the desolate place that had been my childhood home. There was only one mountainous collection of stone in this desert, and like a parasite, Aunt Em covered the canyon base in concrete and steel. Smoke poured from the outer wall, where several chunks of the metal were blown apart. The rattle of machine gun fire paired with the flashes of small-range explosives. Danny had been right, Gigi's ego chose a full-on frontal assault.

How very convenient for us.

The line of Gigi's Sand Crawlers was parked in the distance, largely abandoned by her people.

Daisy climbed up the sand next to me with Kyle not far behind. "Wow. That's bigger than I remembered."

"Yeah, well, it's small when it's your whole world. Smaller when you're kept in a cage." I swallowed hard, the dry air already making me feel parched.

Danny pulled out his binoculars, scanning the action. "No fucking way." He lowered them and checked the settings, then looked back through them a second time. "I don't believe it."

"What?" I moved closer, shielding my eyes to try to see what he was seeing.

He handed over the binoculars. "Look at the guard building by the south gate."

"Okay ..." It took my eyes a second to adjust to the lens. There was only one person on guard by the gate. We knew that Em had repurposed a large portion of her people to the few remaining locations she still had in Oz. Everyone else was firing at Gigi's people over by the main gate. Nobody was worried about the back shipping entrance that was rarely used. Nobody but us.

Danny moved close, pressing his back to mine and pointing over my shoulder. "Do you see the balding man whose gut is slightly too big to fit the vest he's wearing?"

"Yeah. That's umm …" I had to take a minute to think of the man's name. He wasn't always on-site, usually manning one of the centers in Oz. Times really must be dire if Em was putting him on a security detail. "Johnston, or Johns, Jones … something like that."

"That's Silver Tooth. That's the man who kept me locked in his office."

"What?" Crowe stole the binoculars from me, zooming in on the fat fucker who had chained one of the loves of my life to a radiator and thought it was fun to terrorize a child with scorpions. My heart ached when I thought of all Danny had endured as a boy.

"He's obviously older now, but his face is burned into my memory. I'd know him anywhere."

Crowe gritted his teeth, his upper lip curling back in a sneer. "That fucker. He's a dead man. I mean, they're all dead men walking, but this one in particular has ugly death written all over him. I promise, brother."

"I never thought I'd get the chance." Danny stared at the valley like he could still see the man from this distance. The muscle in the side of his neck twitched as he ground his jaw.

Over our comms Maddox's voice crackled to life with an update. *"Heat scans show the most movement by the main gate. As anticipated, the south gate shows minimal activity."*

"Sounds like it's time to party." Crowe handed off the binoculars back to Danny, pointing Daisy at the line of Sand Crawlers. "See those weird-looking ATVs? Those are how Gigi got here."

"I see them." Daisy hiked her duffle bag higher on her shoulder.

"None of Gigi's people are leaving this desert. You two up to that?"

"If there's one thing we're good at, it's fucking shit up," Kyle said, tightening the straps of his backpack and looking down at Daisy.

I shook my head with a laugh. Kyle was like the mold in bleu cheese. It grew in unexpected places, in theory sounded gross, and yet, somehow made it better. Beyond all logic the guy made awkward work for him. Daisy was certainly taken by it. She told me bits and pieces of their history together at the mines. The main takeaway I had from her stories was that Kyle always delivered when it counted. It just might not be in the way you expected. It was that quality to him that kept drawing her back. Mostly, I liked that he made her laugh. We all needed to laugh more.

"I still don't like that you're going off on your own," Danny grumbled.

Kyle held up his hand. "She's not alone."

That only served to make Danny's brows pinch closer together. "Same thing."

"Nobody will even know we're there until you give us the signal," Daisy said, holding her hand out for the binoculars. "Don't you remember? I'm the hide-and-seek champion."

A loud explosion rocked one of the guard stations, the metal sheeting of the roof blowing into the sky with a flash. With it the din of battle grew more frenzied.

"*Front gate is fully breached. Gigi's forces are advancing.*"

Ginger turned to the fifty women and men standing at attention behind her. "B Team moves on Hans's command. I'll be leading a covert group going after The Queen. It's imperative that we take her alive so that she can be brought back to the Emerald City to stand trial. Does *everybody* understand that?"

Crowe made a sound under his breath, clearly not agreeing with Ginger's attempts at justice.

Ginger continued, "The YBR crew will be headed to the Underground to release anyone held there. If asked, you are to provide support as necessary. Your primary concern is getting out as many innocent people as possible. Escape crafts will move in shifts at the extraction point." She gave them a stiff salute, and they all returned the gesture.

"Now how about we pop open this can of worms?" Ginger swung the rocket launcher off her shoulder and slid open the back. From a bag on Toto's hip, she pulled a shiny red tipped missile. Down the side, she'd written, "*Hello*" and painted a bright smiley face with Xs for eyes. "Kiss it for luck, baby cakes."

Danny groaned. Whether it was for the fact Ginger had decorated her warhead or for calling his sister "baby cakes," I don't know. Probably both.

Toto leaned forward, leaving a pretty pink kiss mark on the tip of the rocket.

With a click, Ginger secured the missile in the back and lifted it onto her shoulder. She squinted one eye to look through the scope. "Okay, folks where do you want me to aim?"

Danny met my eyes. He was a serious man even in the lightest of moments, but right now, death stared back at me. "I know exactly where."

I nodded, the corner of my mouth tilting up. It wasn't every day you got to blow your demons apart. By the time we were done today, the skeletons hiding in our closets would be ground to dust.

"Aim straight for the shiny head of the man standing guard at the south gate." Danny moved close, pulling my back into his chest and resting his chin on my head.

"Chrome dome, I see him." Ginger flicked a safety latch and cocked back on the trigger. "Whenever you're ready."

Nick looked behind us, taking note of all the people waiting to move. "It's a good day to die young."

The Farm echoed with violence. Somewhere in that maze of rats was my aunt and I was coming for her.

"Someone is dying today, but it's not going to be us," I said confidently, knowing there was no turning back once that smiley rocket made impact. "Fire."

The launcher echoed. The vibration shooting behind the weapon shook the sand at our feet in a wave. The missile zoomed in an arch for the south gate. It hit its target, blowing apart the gate and the man in one impressively bright blast.

At my back, Danny took a deep and slow breath, his arms tightening around my shoulders.

I tilted my head up to look at him. "I love you."

He leaned over me, grazing my lips in a soft kiss. "I love you more."

Ginger fired a second missile, this one designed to instantly cover the entire valley floor in smoke. With luck, the people below wouldn't be able to see us advancing down the hill, and we'd be able to evacuate the innocent before Em or Gigi realized there was a second attack team on site.

Ginger handed off the rocket launcher to Hans's counterpart. "Greta, wait here for my cue. If something should happen to me, mission command goes to Dandelion."

His head snapped up. "What?"

Ginger gave him an easy smile, snapping a gun holster over her uniform. "I don't know why you're surprised. You're easily the best strategist here. You're coming with me after Gigi while the rest of your crew goes into the Underground after Emily. Making you my second is the logical choice."

Danny opened and closed his mouth twice before speaking, his eyes dropping to ,who stood slightly behind the woman. "The Army of Revolt is impressive."

"That sounds very close to a compliment." Ginger kicked her hip out, placing her hands on them.

Danny smiled. "Don't get used to it."

Climbing over the blown-apart gate, I pointed toward the dormitories. I took shallow breaths through my neck gaiter to keep from choking on the smoke.

Following my direction, Hans waved on his team. They pushed at the front of the group. Several of B team had packs of weapons on them, ready to arm anyone who was able and willing. The dormitories housed the people ready to be relocated. Of the prisoners here, they'd be in the best condition and the most likely to be itching for retribution.

"I've got eyes on Gigi," Maddox's voice crackled over the heavy hitting boots running by us. *"She just entered the front gate. Looks like she has a team of six flanking her. I see Sebastian with her, too."*

Ginger's grin was feral and ready for a fight.

I pressed the button on my headset. "Maddox, what about Em?"

Around us, Hans's team was already bringing the first wave of people out. The whirr of a hovercraft grew louder behind us. Al came zipping in and out with the largest transport craft before anyone could stop them. Seeing the dozens of people escaping lightened something in my heart. I'd imagined freeing the souls in these buildings so many times. To see it happening was immensely empowering. We were going to win this fight. I could feel it in my bones.

"She's on the catwalk, facing off with Gigi on the ground."

"Typical," I said, pushing my tongue in my cheek. "She's always looking down on people, why should Gigi be treated any differently?"

Ginger looked at me. "You're sure she'll be headed to the underground?"

"That's where the emergency escape route is." I nodded. "Em's a coward. It doesn't matter how pissed she is at Gigi. If it looks like her Wolves are losing the fight, then she won't face off against her. She'll run, and I'm going to be waiting for her."

"Alrighty then," Ginger shifted her attention to Toto. "Lead the way, sweet cheeks."

Toto answered for me, "Past those buildings over there, but if we go around the dining hall, we can come up behind her."

"Have fun rat catching in the maze. I've got a queen to dethrone." Ginger waved goodbye over her shoulder, Toto following close behind her.

Danny looked at where Ginger and Toto were disappearing into the smoke, then back at me. There was so much concern on his face. "I don't like leaving you."

I pressed a kiss to his cheek through the soft fabric of my gaiter. "We planned on this. Ginger can't take them on her own and I've got these two looking over me. Who knows, maybe Gigi's people will see an all-girl army and go running."

Danny's lips tightened into a thin line.

"We're leaving this Ozma forsaken place together. Go on, before you lose them in the smoke." I gave Danny's shoulder a push. "I promise to drag Em up here by her hair so that you don't miss a thing."

"Be safe." He kissed the top of my head before taking off with a jog into the smoke.

"So when you didn't want to go into the basement that first night at the YBR compound, it wouldn't have anything to do with this place, would it?" Crowe asked.

I pulled open the gate to the service elevator at the back of the garage. "In my experience, good things don't really happen to people when they go below ground."

"What exactly is down here?" Nick pushed the only button on the control panel, sending us silently down.

"Staff quarters, long-term residents, and employee benefits."

"Employee benefits?" Crowe lifted an eyebrow, but I could tell from the way his face went tight that he knew what I meant.

"You didn't think my dear Aunt Em kept her employees loyal because of her pension plan, did you?"

He exhaled in that amused yet pissed-as-hell way that he had. "A slow death is in that woman's future."

"lenta e dolorosa," Nick agreed.[1]

"Out here in the desert, guards can't really go for a run to blow off steam. Em always said that a bored guard was a sloppy one, so there are varying forms of entertainment to keep them happy. Usually, she sends the acquisitions that require more intensive breaking in before they can be shipped to a buyer."

"In lots of little pieces for the dung beetles to feast upon," Crowe continued.

The doors silently opened. Nick and Crowe swept the hallway, but I knew it would be empty. Everyone was up top fighting.

"Be careful down here," I warned. "The Underground is like an ant colony spanning the entire Farm. It's really easy to get lost. There is a white strip on the bottom of the hallway pointing toward the nearest exit. There are a few of them, if you need it."

Nick nodded, leading us down the main hallway and checking each intersection.

"The fifth door on the left is a control room. We should kill the power. Em won't be expecting to exit the elevator into the dark. She hates the powerless feeling of having your senses limited."

Crowe put a hand on my shoulder. "How do you know the layout so well?"

I stopped walking. Did I want to tell them that I'd been forced to spend an entire year of my life down here?

"Thea?"

"Don't ask questions you don't want to hear the answers to." I pushed open the abandoned office door. "Kill the power and open the cells. People can get themselves out." I scanned the monitors for lingering guards and anyone who

---

1. slow and painful.

might be too broken to walk out on their own. When I didn't see anyone trussed up as a human punching bag, I let out a breath. I wasn't really prepared to handle it, even if I was pretending like I was. It took me a long time to not be sick by the smell of blood after doing cleanup down here so many times.

Nick hit the release mechanism on all of the door locks, while I flicked on the announcement button, bringing the microphone to my lips. This wouldn't just broadcast in the Underground, I knew that much. The entire campus would hear my decree. "Attention. The Farm is officially closed for business. Get out of this hell, or burn with it. This is your only warning."

The sounds of bare feet running down the halls slapped as person after person fled. I don't think I'd ever heard anything more satisfying.

"Savage and beautiful." Crowe's bright eyes gleamed with satisfaction as he pulled me in for a sinful kiss that trailed down my neck. "You're the whole fucking package."

"Save it for later." Nick flicked the breakers. One at a time, the different wings of the Underground were plunged into darkness. The hum of the air filtration system went silent, making the basement feel infinitely creepier. The last room to go dark was ours.

I counted the seconds, pacing my breaths with each number to keep myself calm. Fear was only an illusion. It had no power over me unless I allowed it. By the count of twelve, the red emergency light in the corner came on. It cast the control room in a glow similar to what I imagined old darkrooms were like. Good for night vision and murder scenes alike.

"It won't be long now. Who wants to go hunt a bitch?"

—47—
DANNY

The smoke billowing around the buildings glowed with each newly set fire. I peered around one of the larger buildings, spying on the scene playing out in the central yard. It was the perfect vantage point: close enough to hear and see but still blocked from their direct line of sight.

Gigi, always relying on her ego to shield her, stood dead center. She glared at the upper catwalk. "You always were a spineless cunt, Emily. I remember the way you used to follow your sister around like a puppy. Must have really hurt the day Darren chose her over you."

"That's funny, Gigi. I remember him turning down more than just me." Emily Rosen gripped the railing. The four red dots painting her chest showed just how powerless she was to retaliate. "Don't forget that you came begging for *my* help when you wanted to take him down, not the other way around. Without me, you never would have known about their ski trip to the lake house."

Sebastian slowly climbed the stairs leading to Emily. She hadn't noticed him yet. Neither had the men standing on either side of her.

"And I paid in full for that bit of information." Gigi waved at the surrounding buildings. "I think you made out alright with our arrangement."

"I did until *you* decided to overplay your hand by fisting it around my business. How many times in the past months have you shut me down?"

"Shut *you* down?" Gigi laughed, kicking her head back.

The guard to Em's right fired toward Gigi, hitting her square in the chest. I'm sure he thought her distraction meant there was a window of opportunity,

367

but I'd done enough jobs with her to know that woman was always aware of her surroundings.

"Ow. Damn that stings." Gigi stumbled back a step and looked down at where the bullet was lodged in the body armor covering her chest. "Was that really necessary?"

Without pausing to look, Gigi lifted her pistol to the side and fired a shot directly into the guard's head, followed by a second equally fast shot to the man on her left. Simultaneously, the men tumbled over the railing, landing in the smoke with a thud.

With Emily's guards gone, Sebastian made his move. He lunged up the final few stairs, twisting Emily's arm behind her so that her own gun fell harmlessly to the side. Digging his hand into her hair, he pulled her back and pinned her against his chest.

Gigi's eyes flared with satisfaction, and she retrained her gun directly at Emily. "I don't know how you ever thought you could take *my* crown."

I almost laughed at Emily's confused expression. "I never wanted your stupid tarnished crown. Why would I?"

Ginger tapped my shoulder. She motioned to the three men standing behind Gigi. I looked to Daffodil, checking that she was really okay with what we were about to do. I'd done it more times than I could count, but taking a life was never easy. I didn't want to think of how that stain would change my sister.

She held up five fingers, waggling a sixth thumb with a question. I glanced back, counting again and realizing she was right. Gigi only had five guards with her, but Maddox had said there were six. I scanned the yard. There was no sign of the missing guard. My stomach twisted in warning. I hated having an unplanned variable when making plays like this.

"String her up and toss her over the edge. She can watch The Farm burn from the end of a rope."

Releasing his hold on her hair, Sebastian pulled a coiled wire from his belt, looping it around her neck. He was oddly prepared for this eventuality. Had they planned to hang Em from the rafters, or did Sebastian always carry a noose on him these days? Emily thrashed, fighting against his grip. When kicking backward like a donkey did nothing, she attempted to bite him like a feral dog.

Using the commotion of Emily's fight, I pressed down on the comms. "Maddox, do you have eyes on the sixth guard?"

"Hold, please, activating the heat trace."

Sebastian slammed Emily's face into the railing to get her to quit fighting. Stunned, blood flowed from her nose in a stream as he looped the wire over her head.

Gigi looked completely amused, holstering her gun and foolishly relaxing. Dumb bitch really thought she'd won. She probably thought all the noise in the back of the compound was her people claiming control.

Sebastian lifted Emily into the air. She screamed, a throat-rending sound strangled by the press of the wire into her jugular.

"It's now or never," Ginger hissed under her breath. Fuck, she was right. It wouldn't get better than Gigi distracted with a holstered weapon.

"Now," I affirmed, giving the girls the go-ahead.

I stepped out, aiming at Sebastian. "She's not yours to kill."

His eyes met mine just as I pulled the trigger and sent a bullet through his left hand. It sprayed his face with blood. Sebastian dropped Emily to the ground, the echo of the steel catwalk screeching beneath her howl of pain.

In slow motion, Gigi turned toward me. Her cheeks were ruddy from the desert onslaught of riding on the Sand Crawlers for hours.

I winked at her, quickly popping the two men standing to her side. "I told you I'd be back. Unlike some people, I keep my promises."

Ginger and Daffodil moved behind the officers standing in the back line. They were all so busy being shocked by my entrance that they easily went down.

"Stop right there, Your Majesty." The hard barrel of Ginger's gun pressed into the back of Gigi's head. "Hands in the air."

"I like what you've done with your look, Gi." Keeping one hand trained on Sebastian, I waved at the discolored skin spreading up her neck and over her cheek. "Green skin is a bold choice, but I'm sure Oz will label it avant-garde or some equally vain shit. Just watch, by spring sunburned and scarred will be all the rage."

Gigi sneered, making the brutalized skin stretch taut.

Seeing the power shift, Emily threw off the wire and sprinted in the opposite direction. My smile broadened, thinking of her ending up face-to-face with the rest of my family. Thea would make good on every vow she'd made. Emily Rosen had a world of hurt coming for her, and she was running straight at it.

Like my thoughts had summoned her, the speakers mounted in the corners of the yard screeched to life. Thea's voice echoed, proud and strong. *"Attention. The Farm is officially closed for business. Get out of this hell, or burn with it. This is your only warning."*

"Well, aren't you full of surprises?" Gigi said slowly, raising her hands.

Ginger reached forward, pulling Gigi's gun from her holster and tossing it away. "Georgiana Grace, you're under arrest for crimes against the Quadrants. The whole world is about to learn the truth of your deceit."

A strangled scream squeaked behind me, making my heart leap into my throat.

"Move," commanded a gruff voice.

Daffodil stumbled forward with the missing guard's gun pressed to her temple. His meaty arm wrapped around her neck, keeping her body between us. I directed my entire focus on the soon-to-be dead man using my sister as a shield.

Gigi spun, simultaneously disarming Ginger and turning her pistol back on her. Sebastian leapt over the stairwell railing, landing only feet from us with his gun pointed straight at me. Blood from his wounded hand dripped from the gun's grip.

Just like that, our upper hand had slipped away as fast as we'd seized it.

-48-
THEA

I heard her panicked breaths first. Nick and Crowe were waiting in the alcoves outside of the room while I watched from my place behind the door.

My aunt stumbled into the panic room, tripping in the dark over the chair and table in the center of the room. She hobbled with a limp to the escape hatch. Using the back of her hand, she wiped away the blood leaking from her swollen nose. I took great satisfaction in the way the red glow of the emergency lights exaggerated the grotesque quality of her battered face.

"Fuck Gigi and her ungrateful, backstabbing, cunt ass. I'm going to get the fuck out of here, and then she won't know what hit her," Aunt Em grumbled. "I'll hire every assassin and cutthroat in Oz. There'll be a price on her head so large they'll have to wheel it in on a crane."

I had to bite down on my lip to keep from cackling.

With an enthusiastic tug, she pulled on the handle. Her entire body lurched when the door didn't budge. She shook the handle, rattling it several times before giving up.

"What the—"

Emily bent over, pressing the locking mechanism. Small bits of white foam leaked from the cracks of the lock. Filling the mechanisms with quick-setting insulation foam was Crowe's idea, one that worked in spectacular fashion.

My aunt pulled her fingers away, wiping the sticky substance on her pants, only to have them stick to the fabric. She cursed several times before the reality of her situation sank in. There was no magical escape route to save her this time.

In the hallway, Nick pulled the pin on a smoke bomb. It hit the concrete floor of the hallway with a clank, making my aunt spin around in alarm. She couldn't see me in the shadows. I was sure of it. Her whole body trembled as the smoke slowly crawled over the floor. It caught the red glow of the light, making it look like the fires of hell were rising up to claim her.

"Who's there?" she asked with an unsteady demand. The responding silence was thick, only making her shake more. "I have a gun."

A lie, one that would be clear to anyone seeing what I saw now. I studied the way her movements became hesitant. For the first time in my life, my aunt was cracking. It took surprisingly little given how many times I'd seen her break someone else.

"Hello, Auntie Em. I'm home," I said low, stepping from the shadows and into the light. The smoke billowed around me.

Em screamed, scrambling away from the doorway.

"You look like you've seen a ghost." I tilted my head to the side, "Didn't you miss me?"

"No. No. You're supposed to be dead. I saw your head roll," she said with disbelief, stumbling away until her back hit the sealed hatch door. "I saw it."

"I bet." I placed one foot in front of another in a slow stroll across the room. "Crazy how I've been in front of you so many times, and you've never really seen me. I bet you're seeing me now though, aren't you Em?"

"Dorothy, I don't know what you—"

"Ugh. Shut up." I spun the dagger Crowe had given me before he left. It flashed bright red in the emergency light.

Em snapped her mouth shut.

"You're so boring. There isn't an original thought in your body. How many years have I had to listen to you go on and on?" I pushed the table and chair in the middle of the room out of the way. The chair tipped over, clattering loudly in the small space. I smiled wide at the way it made her jump. Then I smiled wider when she winced from whatever had happened to her ankle.

"I've thought for years about how this would happen when I finally got the chance."

"Dor—"

"No! If I wanted you to speak, you would know because I would ask for it. Until then, keep your venomous, lying mouth shut. I'm *done* listening to you. Instead, you're going to listen to me for a change."

Em nodded her head slowly, "Are—" Eyes locked on the knife in my hands, she stopped her question.

"Are you worried about this?" I held up the knife, letting the reflection of the metal shine in her eyes. "We'll get there. So, like I was saying. Before I killed Eastin—"

A pathetic, squeaky sound left her lips.

"Interrupt me again, and you'll *really* not like what I do. All these years, you've done a great job educating me on *all the ways* a human can suffer. I have so many to choose from."

The bitch's lip quivered.

I scoffed, watching a single tear drop from her eye. "Don't disappoint me by crying now, Em. We both know you don't actually have emotions."

Em wiped at her cheeks, hissing when she hit the bruise at the bridge of her nose.

"Eastin told me some very interesting facts. Mainly that the money you stole from me was used to fund all of this." I used the knife to point to the whole of the room. "Then you let me believe that my parents died, forcing my life into your hands." I kicked my head back and laughed. "When I think of the number of times you beat me because of how much *I* cost *you* ..."

I lowered my eyes back to her. "When did you decide to kill them? Was it before you met the Witchers? Because before I killed Westin ... " I winked at Em, purely because I saw how reminding her of the woman she'd forced me to become scared the shit out of her. Pulling free the gun holstered at my lower back, I moved closer. Em mouthed a silent prayer and closed her eyes. It made her appear so pitiful, nothing like the woman I'd feared for so long. I shoved the barrel of the gun under her ribs until she gave a pathetic gasp. "... she said something about how this vendetta went back all the way to my father securing the Premiership."

Using the flat edge of the dagger, I tipped my aunt's chin up and forced her to look at me. The brown of her eyes looked impossibly dark, their dull surface shaking in fear. "So, I'm wondering, was it your idea or theirs to kill them?"

"It was Wes—" I slapped her across the face with the flat of the dagger. It left a long slice across her cheek. Small drops of blood rained onto her blouse.

"Why?" she whimpered.

"We've been through this. I'm done listening to your lies."

"But you—"

I backhanded her, the blade leaving a matching gash to the first on her other cheek.

"Blah, blah, blah. Stop. Talking. Your words mean nothing to me. I don't want them."

I took a couple of steps back, getting a full view of the powerless woman before me. She was pathetic. I slid my finger over the trigger of the gun, knowing that I could end her life here and now. Except the lives she'd destroyed deserved more than this woman bleeding out in a basement.

Em's tears came faster now, her body descending into silent sobs.

"Did any part of you ever love me?"

The old woman opened her mouth to answer and lifted her arms as if she actually expected me to be dumb enough to come in for a hug.

I waved her off. I didn't need her to lie to me to feel better.

"I'm going to give you the chance you never give anyone else. I'm going to let you make a run for it. If you can make it to the surface before you're caught, then I'll let you live."

"You are?"

I nodded. "Watch out, though; I'm not down here alone."

Right on cue, the boys howled like wolves. I appreciated the irony. How many times had her wolves howled while dragging a runaway back. I loved that they got me enough to realize how much joy this tiny detail would bring me.

Em moved toward the doorway. "How much time do I have?"

"Mmm, I don't know." I looked at my make-believe watch. "How about a minute? Oh, and Em, from one girl who's been hunted to another—lose the shoes. Heels are murder on the feet when you try to run in them."

She looked down at her sensible pumps.

"Better run, Auntie Em."

Em kicked her shoes off and sprinted from the doorway. Her hurt ankle instantly rolled and threw her into the frame. She kept going though, the smoke in the hall swirling as she hobbled away.

Nick emerged from his position. He strode into the room and immediately pulled me into his arms. He didn't say anything but rested his cheek on the top of my head, holding me tight. I gave myself one minute to let the weight of what I'd just done settle. When I got my heart rate back under control, I looked up at him.

"Thank you."

"Ready?"

Crowe leaned in the doorway. "Can we chase her down now?"

"Be my guest." I gestured to the doorway.

He spun, stalking in the direction she'd disappeared, and started whistling. The sound echoed off the walls, along with the occasional tapping of his gun.

"You closed off the ends of the adjoining corridors, right?"

"Sealed up tight, Fiore Mio. She'll have no choice but to head up the stairwell we chose."

"Good. We can wait there. Let Crowe have fun driving her toward it. He's earned it."

-49-
DANNY

Sebastian wrenched my arms behind my back. "I really didn't want it to come to this."

The sounds of fighting dissipated. People slowly filed into the space, dragging with them several of Revolt's soldiers. Some of them looked beat to hell.

Smoke drifted over the yard, obscuring most of the buildings. Yet, I knew there was no one lingering in the shadows coming to the rescue.

"Deposit the prisoners over there. We can bring them back to the Emerald City to be tried for treason," Gigi commanded. "It's been a while since we've had a nice mass execution. It could be good for morale."

Gigi's people looked like they hadn't even broken a sweat taking us down. We were fucked. As much as I loathed to admit it, our best-case scenario was to shake them off and make a run for it. I hated feeling like a coward.

"It was always going to come to this," I said, watching Gigi push Ginger to her knees. "You picked her side."

"Crowe said the same thing," Sebastian said contemplatively.

Gigi made a disgusted sound in the back of her throat. "Your problem is that you've only been able to see your own needs. Sebastian sees that Ozmandria matters more than the needs of any one of us."

I rolled my eyes, not willing to engage in her bullshit propaganda.

"You'd think by now, you'd have learned your lesson. I just need to find where your undead girlfriend went so that I can finish the job I started."

I tightened my jaw, breathing heavily through my nostrils. If she got anywhere near Thea again, I would tear her to pieces. I'd gladly take the bullet if it meant stopping her.

"Your Majesty, we have secured the grounds." A man with a badge on his arm threw Hans at her feet. Ginger's squad leader was unconscious. The massive head wound staining the ground red was clearly the reason why. At least he was breathing. For now. No doubt Gigi would use his execution just like she'd tried to use Thea's.

"No. Ow!" A scuffle of boots over the rubble and a woman shouting redirected everyone's attention to the yard entrance. "Let me go!"

"Fuck," I cursed under my breath.

One of the guards dragged Daisy across the ground by the back of her collar like an errant child. Another man had Kyle's arms pinned behind his back and kicked him in the ass to push him forward.

"Found these two scurrying under the trucks like mice." The royal officer deposited Daisy before us, a bruise already blooming over her cheekbone from where he'd hit her.

My sister immediately jumped up, aiming a kick for the man's shins. I had to give it to her. Daisy was scrappy and apparently fearless.

"Well now, a Kalidah family reunion. How sweet." Gigi's voice trailed off as she looked between my sisters and finally settled her eyes on me. "The question is, which sister's death will finally get the message across?" Gigi waved the gun back and forth between them like the swinging of a pendulum, settling her aim on Daisy. "We only really need to keep one for leverage."

"Don't you dare touch her." Kyle fought against the grip on his arms.

"Kyle, don't," Daisy warned, but it was too late. He had the queen's full attention now.

"You, I don't need." She quickly shifted her aim. The bullet flew, perfectly centered between his brows, blowing apart the back of his skull and spraying blood and brain matter across the concrete. The guard holding him jumped away, wiping at the viscera sticking to his clothes. Kyle's lifeless body fell to the ground with a muffled *thwap*.

Daisy screamed, falling to her knees and shaking her head in disbelief. Her vocal cords scratched as a howl of pain ripped at her. The sound tore me in two, summoning the memory of Thea falling to her knees in an eerily similar puddle of blood. Kyle was a bit of a moron sometimes, but my sister was obviously fond of him. He deserved better than one of Gigi's carelessly fired bullets.

"You know, I think I'd rather keep you around. Something tells me you'll be more fun to play with." Gigi redirected her attention to where her guard still had his gun pressed to the side of Daffodil's head.

"For someone playing the long game, you're really short-sighted," Ginger said, pushing herself as high as she could on her knees.

"What?"

Ginger gestured with her chin to the horizon. "Does it ever feel like you're banging your head against the wall, expecting the bricks to change and not for your head to crack?"

A shadow slowly blotted out the setting sun. Gigi lifted her hand to block the glare, squinting at the hundreds of people lining the top of the dune—the true entirety of Ginger's Army of Revolt.

Ginger batted her eyelashes and smiled wide. "Hammer-head."

A blaring airhorn sounded over the hill. Like a floodgate being released, Ginger's second wave charged.

"Sebastian." The queen swung her head to her consort, for the first time looking rattled. She hadn't accounted for Ginger or that the people she had used as an expendable commodity might be capable of overthrowing her carefully laid plans.

I kicked the stone at my feet at Daisy. It rolled through the puddle of blood where she was staring blankly at Kyle. "Daisy-chain."

She blinked at me, forcing fat tears to roll over her cheeks.

"Daisy-chain," I repeated.

She blinked again, and Daisy's eyes took on a new, brutal clarity. Giving Gigi the same look I'd given her the day I watched Thea walk across the execution grounds, she pulled a small device from her pocket and, without hesitation, hit the button.

A three count later, the first Sand Crawler in the line at the top of the opposite hill exploded in a ball of flames, followed by a second and a third. A thick sense of pride filled me as the entire line of Gigi's escape vehicles sent flames into the darkening sky.

Ginger reached forward, pulling Gigi's feet out from under her. She came down hard on her back. The gun she'd taken from Ginger slipped from her hand on the impact and went skidding across the concrete. Together, the women grappled for control.

I stepped backward, ramming my elbow into Sebastian's stomach. The breath whooshed from his lungs in a surprised wheeze. Looping my arm under his, I heaved his weight off center, flipping him over my shoulder. As the man went flying, I saw Daffodil stomp on the arch of her captor's foot, simultaneously knocking his gun behind her. She took his wrist, wrenching the firearm from his hands and turning it on him in one decisive movement.

Daffodil didn't wait, firing point-blank at the man before he could wrestle it from her again.

Ginger's army came storming through the front gates, clashing with Gigi's in explosive fashion. Greta at the lead, fearlessly cut through Gigi's ranks in an attempt to get to the unconscious body of Hans.

As I expected, Sebastian fell in a practiced roll that brought him back to his feet with ease. He hesitated like he wasn't sure if he actually wanted to fight me or not.

"Come on, Sebastian. Put 'em up." I lunged forward, closing the space between us before Sebastian could pull his weapon on me. He dodged my right hook and swept beneath my punch. I doubled down on the motion, stepping into the strike and hooking his leg. The sweep brought us both to the ground, but it was worth it when I heard the snap of his leg.

Slowed by the pain, Sebastian was easy to immobilize. I wrapped my arm into a choke hold while keeping his broken leg pinned to the ground. As the flow of blood to his brain slowed, the struggle quickly fled his limbs.

I craned my head over my shoulder to take stock of our current circumstances. The Army of Revolt was clearing the yard in a clean sweep. We outnumbered Gigi's guards three to one. Many of her guards were disarmed and cuffed, while several others were shot in the struggle. I would never again doubt

Ginger's Army. The unexpected second wave won us the fight in a matter of minutes. Gigi just hadn't realized it yet. She had nowhere to run and no way out of this desert.

"Gigi, it's ov—" The words clipped in my throat. Ginger and Gigi were heatedly exchanging blows. For a would-be queen and con artist, Ginger's form was perfect and almost a match for Gigi's years of special ops training. She was a bit slower, which Gigi was using to push tightly into Ginger's space.

Ginger must have been aware she was losing, because she changed tactics. Rather than spinning into a kick or punching, she ducked low. Her shoulder rammed under Gigi's ribs and sent them both tumbling forward. In one last hit, Ginger fitted her bespoke military boots against the queen's hips and launched her far into the air.

As Gigi skidded across the concrete, Ginger rolled and grabbed the small pistol from her boot. The mother of pearl gleamed in the rising moonlight. It was the same beautiful gun she'd once pulled on me. Popping back onto her feet, Ginger exited the somersault with her gun perfectly aimed at the prone form of the queen.

"It's over, Georgiana," Ginger stated. "Give up."

"Ginger, your gun!" Daffodil shouted and darted around her opponent.

Hearing her name, Ginger shifted her attention to my sister's mortified expression.

The courtyard lights flared silver off of the barrel of Ginger's earlier discarded gun. The same one Gigi landed on. As she climbed to her feet, the queen kept her back to the yard, concealing the pistol so that Ginger was still completely unaware that she was armed.

I dropped Sebastian, moving too slowly to stop my sister from running for her lover.

A loud crack echoed around the grounds. It shouldn't have sounded so clear amid the chaos of the battle, but the gunshot was the only thing I heard.

Gigi slowly lowered her gun. As her once beautiful features shifted into a menacing smile, I heard the thump of a body landing behind me.

In the distance, I registered Daisy's anguished scream. It felt like it took eons to turn. My body twisted, and it took several breaths for me to register what I was seeing.

Daffodil was sprawled on the ground, surrounded by an expanding halo of blood. The pink quickly drained from her cheeks, leaving them a ghostly shade of white.

A hole the size of a quarter was torn through her stomach. She looked like a fallen angel.

"No. No. No." Ginger pulled Daffodil into her lap, elevating her body and pressing her palm against the wound. "Greta! Greta, get a medkit!"

"This isn't real," I said in disbelief. Memories flickered in my mind, distorting the truth of what I was seeing: My sister pulling me in a wagon on our way to pick wildflowers, the horror of our last night together before our family was torn apart, seeing her surprised expression the day we were reunited, the hug she gave me when we returned from the palace. All of them played out in the blink of an eye.

Gigi looked quickly at Sebastian, knowing this was the only moment she would get to flee. Like the selfish bitch she was, she abandoned the man who had stood at her side this entire time and made a run for one of the smaller Cyclone trucks parked by the garage.

From across the yard, Daisy shouted. Rage twisted her features. She ran in a full sprint for Gigi. Ginger's gun was still in Gigi's hand. If Daisy attacked, there would be no reason for her not to take a second sister from me tonight.

"Stop, Daisy." I intercepted her in only a few strides and knocked her to the ground before she could do something rash.

Daisy roared in frustration, clawing and slashing at me despite the detonator still clutched in her hands. "Dandy, you asshole. Let me go. She's getting away."

"No!" I glared at her and slammed her hands back into the ground. "Help Daffodil. I'm going after Gigi." Before she could argue, I took off in pursuit of the queen.

"Dandy, wait," Daisy called after me, but I wasn't stopping. I increased my speed, pushing my body as fast as I could. The bitch wouldn't get to escape her fate for a second time. "Dandy, the bomb."

Gigi ripped open the door to the Cyclone truck, throwing herself into the cab and quickly pulling the door closed behind her. The engine rumbled to life, and then blinding light rocketed the truck into the air. The body of the vehicle rotated, before landing upside down. The body of the truck crumpled like tin foil.

The concrete trembled beneath my feet. Fissures radiated out from the base of the explosion, snaking over the ground like cracks in a frozen pond.

Then, all at once, the world was falling.

-50-
THEA

The underground shook with a rumble that I felt at the center of my chest. The walls swayed around us like they were made of putty. I squeezed my eyes tight, refusing to let panic take hold with the thought of being trapped in this subterranean hell. A second tremor, this one larger than the first, vibrated beneath my feet.

"Fuck, Nick." I was going to be sick. I pressed the heels of my hands against my eyes. "Tell me I'm not dreaming. Right now. Tell me."

"You're not dreaming, Thea. This is really happening." He pressed a kiss to the center of my brow. "We have to get out of here."

"Earthquake?" Crowe asked, the semi-conscious body of Aunt Em slung over his shoulder. He'd hit her hard enough that it didn't simply daze her as he'd intended. Her constitution was so weak it had knocked the bitch out. Her arms were zip-tied behind her, and drool leaked around the gag I'd made from a spare towel.

"No, that was an impact tremor. Something big must have blown up top," Nick said, placing his hand against the metal door of the elevator for signs of heat. "*Cazzo*. We can't take this."

Large black cracks spiderwebbed over the ceiling, accompanied by a rainfall of small pebbles and dust.

"The building is coming down." I held up my arm to shield myself from the falling debris. The elevator groaned, the light on the panel blinking out. "Closest stairwell is around the corner."

We turned to run in the opposite direction when the hallway before us disappeared. The ceiling dropped, filling the space with two floors worth of concrete.

I coughed against the dust, pulling my neck gaiter over my nose and blinking to keep my eyes clear. A massive hole gaped above us, with half of a truck wedged on its side across the freshly opened space. Above it, the twilight sky twinkled with inappropriately happy-looking stars.

"That must be the truck that was being loaded outside of the garage," Nick said, pulling me so that I wasn't standing directly beneath the vehicle.

The door of the truck groaned, buckling beneath the pressure and swinging open. The driver screamed, catching the steering wheel before she fell from the cab. Her black jumpsuit looked nearly white from the ash and dust coating her.

"Mother-fucker! That bitch," Crowe exclaimed. "Only Gigi could survive an explosion and a cave-in."

"Maybe she'll fall into that mess of rebar," Nick added, pointing at the torn pile of concrete and steel.

"Fate doesn't like us that much," I said, pulling my gun from the holster at my lower back. I shouted up, "Gigi, you're a dead bitch. A lucky one, but fucking dead all the same."

"Shit!" She looked over her shoulder at my pistol pointed directly at her. Her feet scrambled to find purchase, panting and huffing with each swing of her legs.

I fired a shot into the center of the cab, barely missing the swing of her leg. "Damn it."

Nick came up behind me, wrapping his arms around mine and whispering in my ear. "Take a deep breath and aim. You have all the time you need. She's not going anywhere."

After my shoulder had healed enough to get the okay from Gabby, we'd spent a solid chunk of time going over gun safety and working on my aim. I wasn't good by any measure, but I felt safer armed. At the very least, knowing how to fire a gun properly made me more confident. I'd never been more grateful for that training than I was right now.

Gigi hooked her foot into the window of the door and pushed against the frame until she could leverage herself onto the passenger seat. The truck groaned and the wheels shifted as she yanked on the steering column. If she kept turning that tire, it might not be only Gigi who came tumbling down.

I closed one eye, sticking my tongue between my teeth in concentration.

"Exhale, then pull the trigger."

Letting out a slow breath, I fired. The bullet zinged past Gigi's shoulder. The Queen howled in pain but didn't stop her slow ascent through the car. Her torn sleeve fell open, revealing a large gash on her bicep. She'd been shot, but it was only a graze.

"Damn, that was so close," Crowe cursed. Over his shoulder, Em groaned. He swung her around, letting her head bash off the wall. "Sorry, Emily, what was that? I can't hear you."

It took two tries, but Gigi pushed open the passenger door. The truck shifted, and the axle supporting the weight of the cab bent with every step she took. The rubber of the tire was the only thing keeping the entire frame from buckling. Chunks of concrete came loose and tumbled down the cascade.

"Try again, Beautiful. Third time's a charm, right?" Crowe winked, completely amused by the game and not at all worried that a truck might come crashing down on us.

Hefting her upper body out of the doorway, Gigi pushed up, screaming when it strained her injured arm.

I licked my lips, determined to make my next hit be on target. Closing one eye, I looked down the barrel, adjusting my aim to account for the natural curve of the shot.

"A little higher." Nick's breath drifted over my neck as he looked down my arms with me. His voice shouldn't sound so sinful, and gunning down a woman definitely shouldn't be making my chest feel so warm. "Good girl," he purred. "That's perfect. Fire when you're ready."

Muffled groaning filtered out from beneath the rubble at our feet. "Is somebody there?"

I dropped my gun, instantly recognizing the voice mumbling beneath the rocks. "Danny?"

"Fuck, tell me that's not Danny under all that rock." Crowe dropped Em like the worthless sack she was and moved quickly to pull away the bigger debris littering the ground. With each piece Nick and Crowe hauled away, more and more of Danny was revealed.

He brought his hand to the back of his head and hissed. "Fuck, that hurts." His palm came away bloody. Several gashes tore apart his arms and legs that would need stitches, but he was breathing.

Danny quickly sat up then immediately flopped back to the ground.

"Woah, slow down," Nick said, dropping to one knee to look at his head wound.

Realizing that Danny's unexpected appearance had completely distracted me from my mission to pump Gigi full of holes, I looked up in time to see her foot disappear over the doorframe.

"Fuck!" I carelessly shot at the cab, hoping a lucky bullet would fire through the metal and hit her anyway. The car shifted beneath her weight, the holes piercing the side making the frame weaker.

"Stop shooting. You're going to bring the whole damn car down," Danny said, pushing to his feet and wobbling as he took hold of Nick's shoulder.

Metal on metal screeched with every step Gigi took running the length of the truck. Stones tumbled free in bigger and bigger chunks until, finally, the front axle snapped. Sounding like a freight train careening off its tracks, the entire vehicle dropped. It tore through the hole, bringing down more concrete and steel with it. It landed with a deafening crash, completely obliterating what was left of the front cab and sending a tire flying toward the elevators.

Crowe threw us flat against the wall while Nick pulled Danny to the side, narrowly avoiding both the car and the rocketing tire. I twisted my face from the crash, keeping my eyes shut until the worst of the dust had settled.

We looked around at the thoroughly enclosed space, realizing our only option for escape was to climb up the same route Gigi was climbing.

"At least now the hole is free of the car," I said while examining the bits of steel rebar and mesh that poked out from the edges like a ghastly version of a ladder.

Danny walked up to my aunt and used the toe of his shoe to turn her slack face toward him. The dust had settled over her like she was coated in flour, making her hair and eyelashes look ghostly white. "You really were bringing her up to me, weren't you?"

I shrugged like my answer was obvious. "Of course. I said so, didn't I?"

"We need to get back up top, now. We can't let Gigi get away," Danny said, adrenaline making his expression clearer and less dazed than a few minutes ago. "That bitch shot my sister."

"Wait, what?!" Testing the rocks, Danny grabbed the highest hand hold that he could reach and pulled himself up. I snatched the back of his shirt and pulled him back down. "What do you mean shot? Was it Toto or Daisy?" My heart lodged itself in my throat, dreading the answer no matter who he said.

"We don't have time for this, Thea. With every second we waste, she's getting away," He snapped and heaved himself over the first pile of rubble.

"Hey Dan, take it easy. I want to catch her too, but you just took one hell of a blow to the head," Nick said, watching as Danny clambered over the fallen remains of the truck. "You're not going to do any of us any good when you fall to your death because of an unexpected wave of vertigo."

"Danny!" I shouted. "Who's shot? Are they alive?"

"I DON'T KNOW!" He roared back at us before disappearing behind the wreckage. "I don't fucking know. Stay if you want, but I'm going after the bitch."

"What do we do about her?" Crowe asked, giving my aunt a kick to the ribs. She bent at the stomach and groaned, the only indication that she was still alive beneath the film of dirt.

"Bring her. She deserves to see her empire burning," I said, not exactly sure how one of them would manage to climb out of the hole with an extra 150 pounds of dead weight.

Nick pried apart the partially open supply panel of the fallen truck. A long vinyl strap with ratchets at the end tumbled out, along with a box of hand tools and a tire iron. He kicked a fallen piece of metal sheeting. "Strap her to one of these panels, and we can haul her up one floor at a time."

Climbing the shaft was slow work. Nick followed me, bracing my ass anytime I slipped. Whenever we reached a place with solid footing, the guys heaved my aunt higher. I got a bit of grim satisfaction every time Em banged against the wall and moaned in pain. The woman had nearly broken my ribs before restraining me to the inside of a truck for two days, a few bumps and the occasional impaling of rebar were nothing.

I gripped the exposed bar of steel, using it to pull myself up like a ladder. My mind kept wandering toward the invasive image of the earth swallowing us whole. To avoid hyperventilating and falling to my doom, I focused on picking a spot to put my hands and Nick's words of encouragement as we continued to climb.

"Brava, continua così dolcezza."[1]

---

1. Good, keep going sweetheart.

The process was slower than I'd hoped, but eventually, we crawled out of our hole like ants. I rolled onto the ground. The concrete floor outside the garage was covered in a web of cracks. It was entirely possible that there were other weak spots as a result of the explosions.

I pointed at them and the line of burning Cyclone trucks. "That's got Daisy Chain written all over it."

The Farm was barely recognizable. Fire raged through the buildings surrounding the yard. Vehicles in every direction crackled with sparks, and the air was thick with the smell of destruction. The sheer number of people lying on the ground was staggering. The injured or the dead were everywhere. I bit the inside of my cheek, praying that someone I cared about wouldn't be among them.

Together, Crowe and Nick lifted Em's sled over the edge. She wriggled when they undid the straps. The journey brought a bit of the fight back in her—not that it did much with her legs and arms bound. My dear, sweet aunt wasn't going anywhere.

I looked for any sign of where Gigi might have slunk away to, but there was too much smoke. Even with the gaiter, it was hard to take more than shallow breaths.

"Thea!" Daisy came running through the smoke, latching onto my hand. My heart lurched as I realized Toto must be the one who was wounded somewhere in this mess. "Thank Oz, you're alive."

"Did you see Danny?" I looked over my shoulder. "He was right ahead of us, but I don't—"

She interrupted me. "Where's the infirmary? There has to be one."

"It's a couple of buildings over."

"Good, take me."

"Wait." I pulled back on her arm.

"There's no time. We have to find a doctor or a nurse. Somebody with a degree."

"Daisy," I lowered my voice, trying to calm a bit of the manic energy she was exerting. "Em doesn't keep them on site. She has a nurse and a surgeon that she keeps on staff, but only when shipments are incoming or if there's an emergency. There won't be anyone here. Besides ..." I looked over my shoulder at the bonfire. "There's nothing left of the infirmary. Whoever was on the fire brigade really took their work seriously."

"*No.* There has to be someone who can save them!" Daisy buried her face in her hands. "We only just found each other. I can't go back to being alone."

"Them? Daisy, who else is hurt?" When she didn't respond, I wrapped my hand around her forearm and dragged her behind me in the direction she'd come from. The smoke was thinner over here, a breeze from the open gateway blowing it into the compound.

It didn't take long to find them, and when we did it felt like being sucker punched with a crowbar. Even with Danny's warning, I wasn't ready for what I saw.

Ginger was sitting propped against a barrel, with Toto in her lap. Blood soaked through her fancy uniform, and her no longer white scarf was wadded against a wound in Toto's stomach. The puddle beneath them both was nearly black in the firelight. Danny knelt beside them with Toto's hand in his, buckled over at the waist, and letting his forehead rest on her shoulder.

As we approached, I could make out the gentle murmur of Ginger whispering something into Toto's ear. Silent lines tracked through the blood and grime staining her face. She ran a bloody hand through the wild strands of her hair in an attempt to ease the pain Toto was obviously in.

"Gigi's gone." Danny lifted his eyes to me. There was so much anger and pain in them that it made the carnage around us seem pale by comparison. "That bitch killed one of the hovercraft pilots and *fucking got away*. I made it in time to see her and Sebastian disappearing into the desert."

I shook my head in denial. This wasn't happening. Toto wasn't dying. Gigi didn't get away. THIS. WASN'T. REAL. It couldn't be. Daisy pulled free of the grip that I still had latched on her arm. I watched her running to her family in what felt like slow motion. This was a nightmare. It had to be a nightmare. Someone would shake me out of it. I closed my eyes and rocked against the horror of it all. "Wake me up. Please wake me up." Any second ...

The heavy weight of Nick's hands gripped my face. Without opening my eyes or hearing his ,I knew it was him. It was always him. Any second now ...

"Fiore Mio." His thumb gently stroked my cheek. "You're not dreaming."

"No." I fought the hold he kept on my face.

Crowe's warm palm braced my lower back. The heat of his body pressed against me. "Open your eyes, Thea. You need to go to her while she's still awake. You'll regret it for the rest of your life if you don't."

I swallowed down my rising nausea and looked at them both. It was the sympathy in their expressions that confirmed it all. This nightmare was my reality and there was no escaping it. Beyond Nick, Toto weakly patted Danny's cheek. I was so like her to comfort others while she must be in agony.

Crowe gave me a gentle push in her direction, and Toto smiled at me as I fell to her side. Fuck, she looked so sallow, worse when she struggled to cough and ended up choking instead.

"Hey there, Red."

Tears burned the backs of my eyes. "Hi yourself, Freckles." For a second, she wasn't dying on the ground, but we were huddled together in the back of a truck and pretending not to be scared shitless. I never told her how much being with her on the journey kept me calm. I've never told her how much her friendship has meant to me these past couple of months. She didn't know how fucking amazing she was or how much I loved her. She didn't know, and every time I tried to open my mouth to tell her, nothing came out.

"What do you think of my new look? I'm going for GSW Chic." She grinned with blood staining her usually brilliant smile.

"I'm pretty sure GSW was last year's trend." I forced a lightness into my voice that seemed impossible based on what I was looking at. "You might as well try something new. How about Near Death Experience instead? We can just call it a night and head on home to The Villa."

Toto laughed, triggering another coughing fit.

"Easy, baby girl." Ginger pulled back the hair that fell in Toto's face. The tenderness in her touch made the lump in my throat impossible to breathe around. They had so few days together. "We need to save that energy for when the doctor gets here."

Toto stretched her hand out to me. The tips of her fingers were purple from a lack of circulation.

I lowered her hand into my lap and held down the button on my earpiece. "Maddox, tell me you have a chopper incoming with Gabby on it, or another of your Hail Mary miracles."

"Gabby is on a hovercraft, but she's a minimum of thirty minutes out." I looked down at Toto's blackening fingertips. Thirty minutes was a long damn time. *"I'm sorry, Thea."*

If anyone understood how bad this stung, it was him. I'd had a frontrow seat to his sister, Maggie's death. Nick came behind me, resting his hand on my lower back and providing me with support in his own gentle way.

Toto used her free hand to tousle Danny's hair. "You worry too much, little brother. You always have. You know, we were never your responsibility. Remember the rabbit, *Qui craint de souffrir, il souffre déjà de ce qu'il craint.*"

Danny shook his head.

"I haven't thought about that book in years." All of the manic frenzy was gone from Daisy. In its place, she now wore a blank mask of shock. She spoke almost as if she was in a confused trance. "It's the title of an old fable our mother would read to us. We probably only had three or four books back then. It means, 'Whoever fears to suffer, suffers from what he fears.' It was about a rabbit that was so afraid of the plow that he starved instead of going into the field."

"You speak French?" It seemed like such a silly thing to focus on when everyone around us was openly grieving. Daisy was sharing deep philosophy, and here I was, stuck on this facet of Toto I knew nothing about. What else about this amazing woman would I never get to know?

"Of course I do. I spent years in a place called Le Chateau." Despite death's knell, my friend grinned with mischief. "I speak Italian, too. I can tell you, the mouth on that man," Toto weakly pointed at Nick and half whistled at him over her cracked lips. "The things he whispers to you are downright filthy."

I glanced up at Nick. He shrugged unapologetically. Of course I knew he was making dark promises that I couldn't understand. That was half of the appeal.

"That's how I know I'm leaving you in good hands. Any man who promises to lick you until you scream has my blessing."

I sank my teeth into my lip, refusing to acknowledge the word "leaving."

Toto leaned away from Danny to rest her head on her sister's shoulder. As she shifted, Daisy and Danny settled closer to Ginger until their bodies were holding up Toto's weak form nearly as much as Ginger was. The four of them looked like one of those Renaissance paintings with all the people lamenting the fallen in a scene so sad that even the angels wept.

"I'm sorry about Kyle, baby sis."

"Kyle?" I asked in surprise. Ginger's already sullen expression dipped further and she tilted her head toward the center of the yard. Behind them Kyle's red hair was bright against the concrete, a fine layer of ash had already settled on his still body. No wonder Daisy looked shell-shocked.

This was fucking hell on Earth. It just kept getting worse. Every time I thought my heart couldn't handle another blow, fate rammed a new knife into it. What was next, a meteorite falling on the desert to smite us?

"Who knows? Maybe I can track him down in the next life and keep an eye on him for you." Toto wheezed a small laugh. "Ozma knows that boy needs it."

Tears flooded over Daisy's cheeks, following in the already cleaned streaks from the crying she'd done earlier. In her panic earlier, I'd missed that fact. Although it felt so obvious now.

Toto's lids drooped, staying closed as she spoke. "We managed to find each other after all these years. I'll find you again on the other side."

"Daffodil, hold on a little longer," Danny pleaded. "Gabby is almost here. Just a few more minutes. Please." He dropped his head back to hers, murmuring. "Please, please."

It was his begging for time that cracked me all the way open. Time was the one thing I couldn't give them. I turned into Nick with a violent sob, letting him hold me like the cage of his arms could protect me from the inevitable.

Every good thing in our lives always ended soaked in blood and coated by ash.

I hated it. Toto deserved better. We all did.

"Gabby is fifteen minutes out."

Except, it was too late. The tension in my best friend's face drifted away, leaving only the carefree expression that even death couldn't take from her.

-51-
THEA

A ball of torn canvas swirled in the small dust storm outside of the exterior walls of the Farm. I watched it rise and fall with each gust of air like the fabric was breathing.

Danny had dragged Daisy and me out here a little more than an hour ago. The recovery team was too frenzied and too loud for how hollowed out my chest felt. So now, the three of us sat in silence, propped against what was left of the cold metal wall.

It helped that the dry wind of the desert whisked away my tears as they fell. It allowed me to lie to myself. Without the physical presence of my grief, I was able to pretend that I wasn't actually as devastated as I felt.

Daisy sat on Danny's other side, wrapped around his arm and resting after her own well of tears had finally dried up.

Every once in a while, I could hear Ginger barking commands at her people. As you would expect from a leader, she threw herself into managing the army and refused to acknowledge her loss while there was still work to be done. Her teams cleared the grounds and tended to the wounded.

Maddox had known when he told me where Gabby was that there was no possibility of her making it to The Farm in time, but she was currently working hard to save as many of our team as she could. With every person she saved, they were loaded on a transport back to the Army of Revolt's base.

I watched the last of the hovercrafts disappearing into the horizon and tried to take solace that not everything of this day had been a loss. We rescued so many people. Ginger's team would get as many of them as she could back to their families. For the ones she couldn't, she would give them a place to belong. It was what she did.

"It's done." Crowe stopped before us with a grave expression. "Everything is set up exactly how you wanted."

"Good." He helped me up to standing, pressing a kiss to my temple that felt like a balm to my aching soul. "Let's finish this so we can get out of here. I want to go home."

The desert and the buildings surrounding us may have been where I'd lived for my youth, but it was never home. The rolling hills and fresh paint of The Villa were home now. A place that my family built.

"Anything you want, Beautiful."

I walked with heavy steps into the main courtyard, refusing to look at the stained concrete from where Toto had bled out. In the center was a platform, constructed from the charcoal remains of the holding tanks where so many lost souls had met their fate. The dead bodies of Aunt Em's guards were propped around the base. Many of them still donned their wolf masks.

"Dorothy!" My aunt called when she saw me enter the yard. She gripped the bars of her cage, reaching with one hand through them toward me. "Dorothy. Tell them to let me go. Tell them."

I tilted my head to the side, considering how I'd walked by those very bars and had to ignore the unfortunate people behind them pleading in exactly the same way. I'd eventually brought this place down, but how many people had suffered under her hand before now?

When I didn't answer her, she continued pleading, "Dorothy. We're family. I raised you."

I blinked in disbelief. "I know there's no way you're trying to play the loving aunt card, not now."

"Dorothy, I do love you."

"I know it because you told me so many times how little you loved me."

She shook her hands, straining for me to come closer. "I never said I didn't love you, sweet girl."

"Maybe not in words, but in actions. You beat me, scarred me, took away my ability to ever carry a child of my own, locked me away, and gave me to your friends to abuse in any way they liked. *YOU SOLD ME.* Those aren't acts of love, Aunt Em."

"There was more than that, too. There were times when I was kind—"

I held up my hand. "Well, let me repay you with the same kindness you showed me."

"You can't kill me. Dorothy. You can't."

"I'm not going to kill you, Em. You don't deserve to die in this place. You deserve to have to live in this hell. These bars are all you will ever know until your last breath."

"What? How long is that?"

"That really depends on you." I picked up a bucket of water and sat it beside the cage just within arms reach. Even out here, it rained often enough to keep her alive. Probably.

I turned to walk away, taking a deeply satisfied breath.

"Wait, Dorothy. Wait. I'll starve in here. It's the desert. The sun and there are animals ... and ... and ..." She panicked, realizing there was nothing she could say to manipulate or barter her way free.

I walked as close to the pile of the dead as I dared. "You're right, Em."

"I am?" The dumb bitch actually looked hopeful for a second. She eyed the lock like I was about to set her free.

"You *will* starve. You'll become so hungry that you'll debate doing unspeakable things. The sun will blister your flesh, and those bars will become so hot that you won't dare to touch them."

Em's mouth flapped like the hinge was broken.

"The coyotes and the scorpions will come. I'm sure the festering bodies around you will smell like a five-star meal to the scavengers. Count yourself lucky that you made that cage so damn well. It won't keep out the smaller critters, but it'll keep the big ones from taking too big of a bite."

She looked at the bars, finally realizing that she was standing in the same cage that she'd damned so many souls to.

"No, Dorothy. I'll do anything. I'm sorry. Don't leave me here. I'm sorry. I'm sorry."

There it was. She was finally begging. Em even managed to drag up some tears. I studied the woman, taking in her haggard appearance and committing the look of desperation in her eyes to memory.

"Did you know that you once left me in the crawl space for five days? When I was finally brought out, it was only because *Henry* realized I was missing. You forgot about me, and I plan to forget you, too."

I turned my back on her.

What was left of my family, my true family, waited for me by the gate. Together we loaded the last hovercraft, and I bid farewell to The Farm and all its terrible memories.

— 52 —
THEA

Four weeks later ...

Daisy locked her arms around me. These past few weeks, she and I had grown quite close. There was something about our shared loss that bound us together. We'd sat and talked, and healed. Now, I was truly going to miss my friend.

"You're sure you want to leave?" I asked, pushing away a stray tear.

Her green eyes crinkled, and for a second, with the freckles painting her cheeks, I saw a bit of her sister in her. It made my heart squeeze.

"Yeah, I'm sure. With her new position calling her away from base so much, Ginger needs someone to help the new residents acclimate. More and more people seem to be finding their way to her now that the centers are all closed. Helping is what Toto would have done, and in its own way, it makes me feel closer to her."

Danny grabbed his sister's shoulder, and pulled her into a tight embrace. "Just know that you always have a home here."

She looked between us. "Is this where you tell me, there's no place like home?"

"There isn't," he agreed, "and, I'll build you a whole fucking house if it means you'll stay."

"I'd need a whole house with the way you four go at it all the time. Trust me, an apartment on the far end of the building is not far enough. I'll be back to visit soon." Daisy stepped up on tiptoes and ruffled Danny's hair. "Try to let loose every now and then. Life's too short to spend it so wound up."

She pulled the door open and gave us one last look before skipping down the path to the waiting car.

Danny and I stood on the doorstep until the cab was completely gone from view. He looked down at me. "What now?"

I gave him a kiss on the cheek. "I need Crowe to look at something for me. It's important. But, maybe later, we can do something terribly boring."

He raised an eyebrow at me. "Boring?"

"Yes, something that doesn't involve any guns or running for our lives. Like playing chess or putting together a puzzle."

He hoisted me up by my ass so that I could wrap my legs around him. "Or, I have a counter-proposal." Danny grazed his lips over the center of my chest, just above where my mother's locket hung. "I'll give you a hint. It involves you wearing considerably less clothing and the new cords that came in the mail yesterday."

"Ooo, tempting." I wiggled free of his grip. "But I know for a fact that you have a video conference with the E.C. Bank for that security contract in less than an hour. Come find me when you're done."

Spinning from his grip, I disappeared down the hall toward Crowe's office. I slid the locket along the chain wrapping my neck, and opened the office door. All that remained of the massive war room was a simple desk and computer setup. Well, simple by Crowe's standards.

"Hello, Gorgeous." He swiveled to face me. His smile was brilliant. Everyone had been lighter these past couple of days. There was no sign of Gigi or Sebastian. Maddox followed them on the satellite all the way to the Ozmandrian border. They were gone, and all evidence suggested that Gigi wouldn't be returning. If she did, Maddox's facial recognition software would know immediately. When that happened, he assured us that he would handle it.

Ginger had been sworn in as the new Premier last week. Since then, it felt like the world was settling into a new normal. We were able to breathe and life had been blissfully boring.

"Can we look at these?" I unhooked the chain and handed the locket to Crowe.

"That depends ..." He pulled me into his lap. "There's a tariff on crystal readers these days."

I laughed. "Oh, really? And what is the crystal tax?"

"It's pretty steep." He dipped his lips to my neck. "Some might even call it priceless."

"I could just ask Maddox for help. Maybe his fee won't be so expensive."

Crowe gasped. "And I'm sure he wants his legs to remain unbroken."

"So possessive," I teased.

"With you, always." He delved his hand into my hair and pulled my lips up to his. The kiss was delicious and deep, drawing a moan of pleasure to mix with the breath we shared. It was always like this with Crowe, like every kiss was our first, and any one might be our last.

He grabbed my hips, sitting me on the desk and spreading my legs so that he could push closer. Crowe hooked my shirt, pushing it up to nuzzle between my breasts before moving to the button of my shorts. "Lean back."

I arched my spine, letting my head fall back and lifting my hips so that he could pull my clothing free.

An amused voice cleared his throat. "Important things to look at, huh?"

I lifted my head and smiled at Danny. My blush burned all the way to the tips of my ears.

He leaned in the doorway, running the knuckle of his fist over his lower lip. "I thought after the monitor incident we agreed no more sex on the computers? That was your rule, Crowe."

Crowe pushed my legs further apart. His breath was hot against my inner thighs. "I've reconsidered my position on the matter."

The first long drag of his tongue sent a wave of heat sparking over my skin. I slid my hands over the desk, looking for anything to grip.

"Fuck," I breathed, pushing my hips further into his mouth and chasing the feeling of his tongue. Crowe's thumbs dug into my thighs.

"Okay, but you should know that Thea's hand kicked on the camera, and you're currently dialing Maddox."

"What?" Crowe's head popped up, eyes going wide when he looked over my shoulder. "Fuck."

The ringing stopped, connecting the call.

"Hello? Vin ... Why are you ... Is that ... Please tell me that you didn't call me so that I have to watch you eating out your girlfriend."

My cheeks flamed hot with embarrassment and I tilted my head back. "Sorry, Maddox. That was my fault."

"Call you later, Mads." Crowe flicked off the camera then redirected his attention to me. "You, pretty girl, are in so much trouble."

He lifted me off the desk and swatted my bare ass with a sharp crack.

"Rule stands. No sex on the computers."

I grabbed my shorts, pulling them back on, barely getting them buckled before Danny yanked on my wrist in an attempt to steal me from Crowe.

"Wait. Wait. I really did want to read the locket." I hip bumped Danny out of the way and retrieved my necklace from the floor.

"The locket, really?" Danny's eyebrows rose in surprise, and he dragged another chair over. He patted his thigh in a clear gesture for me to sit down. "Why didn't you say? That's a big deal."

I handed the necklace to Crowe. He dropped it into a scanner and glanced up at me, all playfulness gone from his expression.

Danny played with the ends of my hair. "Are you sure?"

"Yeah. It's time." I took a deep breath.

"Thea?" Nick dipped his head into the room. "Here you are. What flavor did you ... what are you three up to?" He walked into the room, seeing the locket open on the scanner.

"We're going to look at the files Maddox said were on my locket."

He grabbed the stool in the corner and rolled it over.

"And apparently, this is a whole family event now." I shook my head.

The folder opened with a gallery of photos. Crowe clicked on the first couple. There was one of me as a baby. I had a white bonnet tied over my curls.

"Awww," Nick leaned forward with a goofy smile. "You were adorable."

I gave him a puzzled expression. Cooing over a baby photo was about the least Nick thing I'd ever seen him do.

His grin dropped, bringing back his much more average scowl. "What? I'm allowed to say babies are cute, especially when they're you."

"Of course she was. Thea probably didn't even have an awkward pre-teen phase." Crowe leaned over, stealing a kiss.

He flicked through a few more photos. I pointed in the background. "Oh my Oz. That's Gigi. Right there."

In the background, Gigi was whispering in the ear of the man beside her while he handed her a folded piece of paper.

"Well, that looks shady."

He flicked through more, and now that I was looking for them, I noticed that either Gigi or my Aunt Em were in every single photograph. A few even featured the Witchers as young women.

"What's that video?" I pointed at the video file at the bottom of the folder, titled, "For Thea."

He clicked it. The video opened with a large image of my mother.

"Thea baby, I'm recording this hoping one day you'll know the truth ..."

I reached forward, tapping the spacebar to pause the video. I looked between the guys.

"What is this?"

-EPILOGUE-
GIGI

"We're here," Sebastian said. Rain poured in sheets over the small sedan we'd stolen at the first waste-side stop we'd crossed.

I looked down at the stitched-up gash across my arm. I still couldn't believe that girl had played me so completely. Someday, I'd learn how she managed to survive being beheaded—a mistake I won't be repeating.

We knew that we couldn't return to the Emerald City. Ginger and her army of misfits had secured the borders by the time we'd made it there. So, instead, I headed to the only ally I had left. To avoid detection, it'd taken weeks to drive this far north, but we'd finally made it through the tunnel. Passing under the mountain always felt like you were traveling straight through the center of the Earth and out the other side.

The hotel sign before us flickered, *Wonderland*.

I hated this place.

"You're sure she'll help us?" Sebastian asked.

"My sister is the only one with the resources to get me back my crown," I said, climbing from the car. "She's a necessary evil."

The lobby was surrounded by several identical doors, all of them leading to varying levels of depravity. I went to the farthest door, not bothering to waste time checking the others. Overhead, the fluorescent lights buzzed. It was otherwise silent, except for the sound of the water dripping from my jacket onto the checkered floor.

"How do you know that's the right one?" Sebastian asked, eying the doorman who hadn't bothered moving from his place behind the desk.

"Because I do."

413

"What about the doorman?"

I pulled the elevator's safety gate aside and stepped on. There was only one button labeled Garden. "He can't actually let you in anywhere. He's only there as a distraction to those who don't know better. If you try engaging with him, he'll talk you in circles until you give up, or at worst, he sends you the wrong way. Don't question it. Very little in this place makes any sense."

The ride to the roof was quick. The air of the atrium was sweet with the fragrance of roses, the rain pounded against the glass ceiling.

My sister was sitting on a lounger, sipping from a dainty teacup. The television in the corner cast a blue light over her.

"Hello, Mary."

She looked up, her expression turning bright. She wore pink heart glasses that matched her bright pink lips, beneath a large floppy hat like she was actually sunbathing and not sitting amid a thundering rainstorm.

"Gigi!"

I pulled out the garden chair and took a seat at the table.

"Goodness, look at your face ..." She leaned forward, looking at me over the rim of her glasses and brushed her fingers along my scars. The lace of her gloves was a soft brush against the still-sensitive wounds. "It's positively ghastly, even worse in person. How lovely."

I ground my teeth, tightening my fist hard enough that my nails cut into my palm. She leaned back and returned her attention to the television. "I was watching the most interesting news report."

It was only after she gestured to the screen that I realized what she was watching.

"I have a bit of the soup left from dinner if you and your little king are hungry." She twiddled her fingers at where Sebastian was hanging back by the elevator. "I should warn you, though, it's a bit bland. I keep telling the cook that she needs to add more pepper, but she never listens to me."

Pulling the soup carafe to me, I peered under the lid and scrunched my nose. I could smell the pepper from here.

"Mary, I came because I need help."

"I know! I've seen all about the insurgence. Just when I was thinking you'd finally claimed a throne of your own, too. It's a shame about that Ginger woman."

"I'm glad you think so because I need you to—"

There was a crack of lightning, the thunder booming loud enough to make me jump. The lights brightened with a surge of electricity.

"Oh, there she is."

Beside the news anchor, a small reel showed footage of Ginger being sworn in.

"Good evening, Emerald City. I'm Jellia Jamb. Today marks one month since the disappearance of Georgiana Grace, the recently crowned Queen of Ozmandria. Reports show that The Queen went missing after she and a small faction of Oz's military forces went into the wastes to address a group of insurgents known as The Farm.

The Farm was a known human trafficking ring led by the terrorist, Emily Rosen. Ms. Rosen has also gone missing in the aftermath. Following the disappearance of The Queen, the undersecretary to the former leader of the Southern Quadrant has assumed the role of maintaining state affairs. Ginger Revelton has been sworn in as acting Premier until an Ozmandria wide vote can be established."

"See, now that there is a smart political move," Mary said. "She's capitalizing on your propaganda while making her own actions appear to be in the sole interests of Oz. She'll probably win the Premiership in a landslide."

"That bitch led an entire army against a group that was only meant to handle Emily Rosen's people," I said through my clenched jaw. "If she had just come at me directly, she never would have won."

"I'd say that's why she did it, then. Seems to have worked out okay for her."

I hated my sister and her smug face. I hated that her friendliness was as fake as her tan. I hated that our mother loved her more and that she got Wonderland when I had to go to another country to carve out a slice of this world for myself. Mostly, I hated that I had to come to her for help at all.

Biting back my annoyance, I said, "We'll see how it works out for her when I put her head on a spike. The people still love me. They'll welcome me with open arms once I expose Ginger for the traitor she is."

"Following the disappearance of Sorren Singrala, Ms. Revelton has seen to the needs of the residents of the Southern Quadrant. You can see video of her helping to build new housing for those displaced by—"

The screen went white. It crackled with a haze of static. The Ozmandrian anthem played, while satellite footage of the battle in the desert faded in. The camera zoomed on my face, as I pulled the trigger killing the Kalidah whore.

The video feed stopped, merging into a disembodied head floating in the middle of the screen. The face twisted, the features melting to form and reform a face that was neither male nor female.

"I apologize for interrupting your regularly scheduled program. I have a message for Georgiana Grace, former tyrant of Ozmandria." The voice was heavily modulated, and a cold wash of

unease trickled down my spine. *"We've never met, but you know me as The Wizard. For today, I will be known as your reckoning."*

Mary sat forward, pulling her glasses from her face. "Ooo, plot twist."

"The people of Oz deserve to know the treachery of their leader."

A montage of grainy photographs and footage played across the screen. Some of them were decades old. Photos of me with the Premier and his family. In one photo I glared at Darren Gallant. In another, I shook hands with Eastin Witcher, handing her a large envelope of cash.

The woman you called Queen plotted for the day she would ascend. She, along with the Witchers and Emily Rosen, orchestrated the death of the Premier and his family. Twenty years later, she executed her conspirators assuming the role she'd groomed many years earlier.

The video footage switched to a much more modern resolution. I stood in the shadows of Eastin Witcher's corridor, pushing Dorothea Gallant onto an elevator, then returned to dispose of her body. Footage of me calling Emily Rosen and telling her of Dorothy's plans to contact the Wizard at the E.C. Central Bank, warning her that the money we stole from Darren would go dry if she managed to make contact with The Wizard.

"How did he manage to get video from inside my own damn apartment?" I cursed.

My apartment faded, the darkened interior of an old soda shop taking the place of my office. I sat beside Crowe on the counter casually talking about my plans.

"Why not? Right now their idiotic little brains do whatever the televisions tell them to. Why not me? Maybe if they follow what I say, then the world might improve."

"And if they refuse?"

"There's a hundred ways to thin a population."

He looked murderous, while I appeared indifferent to the concept of genocide.

Mary made an exaggerated exhale, "Ooo, that is not a good look. I like the body suit, though. It's very form-flattering."

"I could do without your sideline commentary," I snapped at my sister.

Mary mimed zipping her lips and throwing away the key.

The final footage was the nail in the coffin. It was from the interior of Head Shots. I pointed a gun at Dorothea and the men beside her. With a single gesture the members of the Northern Syndicate were slain. Then I shot Vincent. It was a brilliant plan, and the video showed just how complicated my manipulation of them had been. I looked every bit the villain as I stared the girl down. *"She's innocent,"* Dandelion proclaimed. I answered him, confirming that I'd known all along that Dorothea was never the villainous mastermind that I'd painted her as.

"Wow, sis, you really did a number on that poor girl," Mary said with a whistle. "It really was an impressive play. Check and mate all in one go. Too bad about that whole reputation thing. Don't know that anyone will believe you now."

She was right. My hard-won reputation was imploding with every second of the video reel.

> Ella Gallant came on camera, whispering, *"Thea baby, I'm recording this hoping one day you'll know the truth. I overheard my sister plotting with Gigi to murder your father. They plan to steal the Gallant fortune. We're getting in the car and driving north tonight. In case something happens to me, know I loved you more than anything. Your father's choices weren't always good ones, and many times, he had no option but to comply with wicked men. He didn't want to, and the guilt eats at him every night. Know every choice we've ever made was to give you a better life. If something should happen to us, I've put enough evidence with this recording to hopefully convict Emily and Georgiana Grace of treason. Never forget, baby, I love you. Momma loves you, Thea."*

I leaned back in my chair, blinking at the screen in astonishment.
I was done.
Everything I'd spent my life planning for crumbled in a single broadcast.

The footage changed back to Head Shots. Dandelion glared death at me, rising to his feet.

> *"This isn't over. Thea's a better person than anyone in this room. She deserves better than this."* I nodded, looking smug in my victory. *"This is Oz, Dandelion. People rarely get what they deserve. Haven't you learned? There are no happy endings here."*

The floating head returned, melting from face to face.

"It was a mistake coming for me, Your Majesty. Now, you will learn what it means when I come for you."

The television screen went white before returning to the news broadcast. Jellia Jamb watched her monitor with wide eyes, blinking slowly before someone in her earpiece made her aware that she was back on camera. *"Sorry, Emerald City. It would seem the National Emergency network was hacked by The Wizard. We'll be back after this brief commercial break."*

A toothpaste ad came on screen with an absurdly cheery jingle.

"Ooo, I love this song." Mary clapped her hands along with the dancing tooth.

I snatched the remote from her and muted the television. I needed two seconds of quiet to think.

"Hey. I was watching that."

My head fell into my hands, and I massaged my scalp, suppressing the urge to scream. After taking several calming breaths, I looked at my sister completely confounded as to what I would do now. My reputation. My crown. It was all done for. I thought of all the people I'd crossed. Of the people in those videos who would be aware of how I'd manipulated them. Decades of positioning the pawns on the board just to have the whole thing upended.

"What am I going to do?" I rubbed small circles into my temples.

"Well, Gi ..." Mary smiled, covering her face to hide her annoyingly bright giggle. "I think it's pretty obvious."

"How is anything about this obvious?" I shook my head.

"If The Wizard is coming for you, then you only have one option: Run."

The End.

The Wicked World continues in SAVAGE WONDERLAND, coming 2025.
Thank You for Reading

If you enjoyed this book I would be extremely grateful for a review.
You can leave one on Amazon and Goodreads.

To get all the sneak peeks and information on the next book, be sure to sign up for Geneva's newsletter.

You can also get in on the conversation at Geneva Monroe's Pretty St@bby Readers on Facebook.

Let's Be Friends:
Instagram: @geneva_monroe_author
TikTok: @genevamonroeauthor
Facebook: Geneva Monroe Author

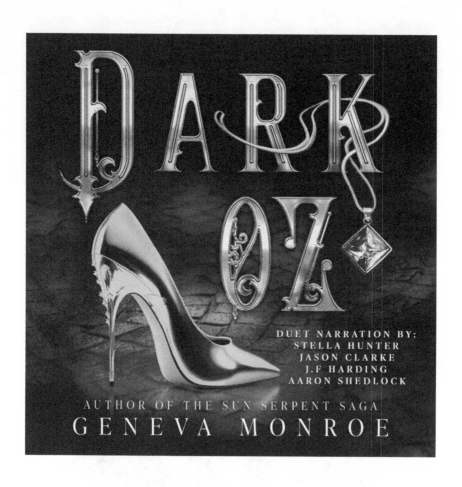

The dark world of Ozmandria is coming to audio.
Live the story again. Performed in DUET NARRATION by:
Stella Hunter as Thea Rosen
Jason Clarke as Nick Chopper
J.F. Harding as Vincent Crowe
Aaron Shedlock – Dandelion Kalidah
Coming Fall 2024

ALSO BY GENEVA MONROE

A cursed kingdom.
A Fire Singer seeking vengeance.
And a prince who is not what he seems...

Under the silks of her circus troupe's tent, Elyria Solaris dances with fire. She disguises her gift as showmanship, but longs for answers about why she has a power no one else possesses.

Somewhere in the city of never-ending night, Prince Cal is looking for the girl who burns the brightest. Only she can stop the horror inflicted on his kingdom by a sadistic lord who controls the minds of his victims.

When Cal spies Elyria, he knows without a doubt that she is the most beautifully dangerous thing he has ever seen. More importantly, she's the Fire Draken he's been waiting his whole life to find.

Moments after Cal serendipitously enters Elyria's life, a loved one's gruesome death sets her on the path of vengeance. Cal will do anything to protect his people, including lying to Elyria about who he really is and promising her the answers that she seeks.

But if Elyria trusts the undeniable spark between them, could it turn out to be the one fire she is unable to tame?

AUTHOR'S NOTE

D id you ever watch Wizard of Oz and think, "Glinda is one shady bitch?" Yeah, me too. If you didn't before, I bet you will now.

Here we are...the end. Part of me can't believe that I've typed those words. Writing a retelling has been a serious blast. I really love the challenge of finding an original element of a story and figuring out how to make it fit into this twisted world of my mine. Plus, I get pure joy out of dropping easter eggs. If you've been paying attention, you'll have picked up on several characters from other stories that I've woven into the past three books. The Wicked World has a lot in store for it.

The outpouring of support for this series has been amazing. Thank you for going on the ride with me. Now, who's ready to head on over to Wonderland?

ACKNOWLEDGMENTS

The past four months have been intense. They've been the hardest I've ever worked, and I can honestly say that the only reason I made it to the other side of this was because of the support of my husband. Thank you for giving me the time to explore this dream and for letting me ramble on about all things Wizard of Oz for the past two years.

To my editor Sierra Cassidy, thank you for being here with this series from inception. For the 2 am plotting days and the crazy messages at all hours of the night. Without our talks this plot would not be the wondrously twisty ball of chaos that it is.

To Reanna Breaux, One day I'll hand you a manuscript with more than 2 days to proof it. Thank you for always being there when I need you. Sorry for breaking your heart in the process. You only have yourself to blame. You just had to go and make me believe in myself enough to publish a book. Now look at us. 5 books later ... Who'da thought, right? Oh wait, you did.

To Jessica Jordan, I'm absurdly codependent on your feedback. Thank you for pushing me to make every scene hit its full potential. Not to mention the countless pep talks. I am truly honored to call you friend.

To my Beta Team, I said ASAP and you turned out edits in record time. You have no idea what it means to me, knowing I can count on you.

To the Crickets, I'm so glad that in writing these books, I've been able to bring us all together. You three are as close to sisters as I'll ever have. Thanks for letting me send you random AF videos and ideas. Thank you for always being the first people I can come to with anything. I love you guys and I'm already itching for our next weekend away.

To Erica Karwoski thank you for holding my shit together. Pretty sure I'd have lost it by now without being able to count on you.

To Dawn Darling and Fleur DeVillainy, thank you for being my writing back up. It helps so much to have you both in my corner. Going through this crazy process together has pushed me to be better and try harder. You pull my head above water daily. I love you both.

Lastly, Thank you to my readers. You all are seriously the tits, like glorious perky tits. I said what I said. I have gotten so many words of encouragement over these past few months. I screen shot every one. I have the letters in a holder on my desk and I literally look at them daily. Thank you for the love and support. Thank you for always coming out in force whenever I ask, and even when I don't. I tell everyone I meet that you're the best and I mean it every time. More than anyone, this book is for you. I hope that I made you feel something, mostly pride. Sorry if I also made you throw that kindle in the process.

XOXO,
Gen

Chapter 3

- *Ah aspetta* - Ah wait

- *Che cazzo è sta roba?* - What the fuck is this?

Chapter 6

- *Puttana di merda* - You fucking bitch.

- *Sei una donna morta, Gigi.* - You're a dead woman, Gigi.

- *Vostra Maestà. Siete una donna morta, Vostra Maestà.* - Your Majesty. You're a dead woman, Your Majesty.

Chapter 8

- *Da quella lurida zoccola degenerata e succhiasangue* - That degenerate and bloodsucking slut.

- *Leone - Lion*

- *Cazzo* - Fuck

- *Si, tranquillo. Sto bene* - Yeah, I'm good.

Chapter 9

Non farmi rivivere mai più una roba del genere. - Don't ever make me go through that again.

Chapter 10

Fogna - Sewer Shit

Chapter 11

- *Insieme.* - Together.

- *Sei la mia rovina.* - This will kill me

- *Bellissima.* - Beautiful.

- *Ti amo, Thea. Tu sei il mio cuore.* - I love you, Thea. You are my heart.

- *Senza di te c'è solo silenzio dentro di me. Non lasciarmi mai più.* - Without you, there's only silence within me. Never leave me again. "

Chapter 12

- *Sei un'idiota* - You're an idiot

- *Vai a fare in culo, Vin.* - Go fuck yourself, Vin.

Chapter 13

- *Vai a farti fottere* - Get fucked

- *Attento alle parole, Niccolino.* - Watch your temper, Niccolino.

Chapter 14

- *Ohhh fermi tutti* - Woah

Chapter 20

L'importante è che io possa godermi lo spettacolo in mezzo alle tue game a qualsiasi ora del giorno. - As long as I can enjoy that spectacle between your legs any time of day.

Chapter 22

Ma porca puttana. - For fuck's sake.

Chapter 24

- *Tutto okay?* - Are you okay?

- *In questo fottuto istante* - Right fucking now

- *le sue fottute rules?* - his fucking rules

Chapter 28

- *Che. Cazzo. Stai. Dicendo? -* What. The. Fuck?

- *No. Assolutamente no. -* No. Absolutely not.

Chapter 31

- *Presuntuoso di merda. -* Smug fucker.

- *Diamine -* Damn

Chapter 36

figlio di puttana - mother fucker

Chapter 37

Maledizione. - Fucking hell.

Chapter 40

Disgustoso. - Disgusting.

Chapter 42

Respira. - Breathe.

Chapter 43

- *É troppo presto. -* It's too early.

- *Smettila di preoccuparti.* - Stop worrying.

Chapter 44
la vecchia zarra. - Hag

Chapter 46
lenta e dolorosa - slow and painful

Chapter 50
"Brava, continua così dolcezza. - Good, keep going sweetheart.

Made in the USA
Las Vegas, NV
21 July 2024

92682569R00267